# FURIES
# "Thus Spoke"

## O'Brian Gunn

### *Praise for* FURIES "Thus Spoke":

*"Furies: Thus Spoke* starts like a rocket and never lets up. O'Brian Gunn gives us a wildly inventive vision of technology, the future—and what it means to be human. Don't miss it!"

- Nik Korpon, author of *The Soul Standard, Stay Gold,* and *The Rebellion's Last Traitor*

"*Furies: Thus Spoke* strikes familiar chords - people oppressed for their talents and distinctions. But, as you gaze into Gunn's tales of super-human characters, you may discover your own reflection looking back at you."

- R. Alan Brooks, writer and creator of *The Burning Metronome*

"With nerve, verve, and visceral thrills galore, O'Brian Gunn wields *Furies 'Thus Spoke'* like a weapon. His target: The superhero genre. The result: A punchy yet lyrical take on how power can both uplift and corrupt, scrawled on a fabulist scale."

- Jason Heller, Hugo Award-winning editor, pop culture contributor to *The New Yorker, Rolling Stone,* and more, and author of *Strange Stars.*

# FURIES

## "THUS SPOKE"

## O'BRIAN GUNN

SPACEBOY BOOKS

Denver, Colorado

Published in the United States by:
Spaceboy Books LLC
1627 Vine Street
Denver, CO 80206
www.readspaceboy.com

First printed March 2019

ISBN: 978-0-9997862-5-3

To Grandma Ruby

You've gone home, but your love and spirit remain forever in my heart.

# SOUNDTRACK

EPISODE ONE: CURTIS MAYFAIR "HERE BUT I'M GONE"

EPISODE TWO: DEFTONES "CHANGE"

EPISODE THREE: CHRIS CORNELL "CAN'T CHANGE ME"

EPISODE FOUR: JOHN COLTRANE "LUSH LIFE"

EPISODE FIVE: ZERO 7 "HAPPINESS"

EPISODE SIX: COCOROSIE "PROMISE ME"

EPISODE SEVEN: COLDPLAY "VIVA LA VIDA"

EPISODE EIGHT: REGINA SPEKTOR "US"

EPISODE NINE: DAVID BOWIE "HEROES"

EPISODE TEN: 311 "YOU WOULDN'T BELIEVE"

EPISODE ELEVEN: EMILIANA TORRINI "WEDNESDAY'S CHILD"

EPISODE TWELVE: ROGER MILLER "LITTLE GREEN APPLES"

# Dominion City – Century Heights

**THE** younger man sits leaning forward with his elbows on his knees. He starts to reach for the glass of water on the living room table, drops his hand and rubs it on his thigh. A palm rests on his shoulder.

He looks to his left at the older man who looks like him. "What is it, DJ?" Wrinkles deepen around the older man's eyes as he twitches his brows together. "It's just the two of us here, you can tell me."

DJ starts to speak, but rolls his lips under his teeth and bites down instead.

"Son, how long have I been telling you that you can tell me anything? Hmm?"

DJ blinks, lifts his chin.

"Are you...are you gay?"

Head shake.

"Is it, ah, is it related to sex?"

Head shake.

"Well, I can't sit here and guess all—"

"I'm an Alpha-Omega." The words tremble from DJ's mouth and his hands quiver.

DJ's father doesn't move for a moment. He slowly removes his hand from his son's shoulder and rubs it across his thigh as the muscles in his forehead twitch.

"I'm...I'm sorry, dad." The words are whispered.

His father's fingers curl into a loose fist as the weight of implication bows him forward over his knees. "Does your mother know?" He sees his son nod out the corner of his eye as he stares at the wall of family pictures behind the loveseat across from them. "What does your gene do to you?" He speaks from behind the wall of his hand.

The washer clicks to a stop in the laundry room down the hall, breaking the sudden layer of silence.

DJ swallows before he speaks. "I can see emotions. They're—"

1

He swallows the lump in his throat. "It's like seeing colored smoke around a person. I don't know how I know what the different colors mean." His shoulders slightly shake as he shrugs. "I just do."

His father grunts and scrapes fingertips across his forehead.

DJ looks over at his father, the motion made with utmost care as if the man will shatter if he turns too quickly or looks too hard. "I'm sorry."

"Okay." His father stands. "I need a second to process this." He stalks down the hallway deeper into the house.

DJ looks after his father as he leaves, resting his elbow on the armrest and flicking his thumb against his lips as he looks out of the window. He shakes his head and exhales a trembling breath. The truth released from his tongue feels like a fuse burning down to a domestic detonation. He wonders how bad the fallout will be. Or maybe it won't be as tragic as—

Footsteps sound from down the hall.

DJ lifts his head and sees his father coming toward him with a gun down at his thigh. He stops flicking his thumb against his lips, stops breathing, hears the distant hiss of the fuse. His father's mouth is twisted as it twitches to one side.

DJ starts to speak, but stops when his father glares at him and inhales deep through his nose. "Why me, hmm? Why are you targeting me and my family?" He stops on the other side of the table. "My life's not shot full of enough ragged holes, now I've got demons or aliens or whatever the hell you Alpha-Omegas are snatching my son up and replacing him with a clone." The gun lifts a few inches in his hand. He drops it when he realizes what he's doing.

"What are you—I didn't do this on purpose." DJ feels the hollow ache in his chest moments before the tears start to fall, mouth pinching to the side.

"What did you do with my son?"

DJ's expression shifts. "What?"

"What the hell did you do with my son, you alien freak?" He charges forward until the table no longer separates them. Fingers tighten around the gun. "Did you shapeshift into him after you kidnapped him? I know some of you have the ability to look like other people. Seen it on the news." The gun is lifted with conviction and pointed at the alien freak's head. "How long have you been impersonating him?"

"Dad, I'm—"

"DON'T CALL ME THAT! I AM NOT YOUR FATHER, YOU HEAR ME!" He presses the barrel of the gun to the alien freak's forehead hard enough to leave an imprint. Tears stream from the young man's eyes, eyes he inherited from his father.

"You are not my son." The words are pressed out between gnashed teeth. "My son is human. Even if he was one of you, he'd never tell me. He knows how I feel about this—this genetic reawakening bullshit. You messed up."

"I'm still human."

"This won't be the first time I've shot an intruder."

"Dad, please, I jus—"

The gun's pulled away for a snatch of a second only to blur towards him again. Pain and light and vertigo bombard DJ's senses and he is on the floor. A thin stream of blood drips warm and thick from his mouth.

Keys twist in a lock and the front door of the house is pushed open with a squeak. "Dwight Junior, I'm back. I hope all of your homework's done." The door closes. "Just bought that new martial arts flick you like." A plastic bag rustles and keys clatter on the counter. "I also picked up a little something for myself. I know we can just buy movies online and stream them, but I just don't trust..." Father and son look to the right and see a woman peep into the kitchen where Dwight Junior has left his backpack. "Baby boy?" They watch her walk down the hallway, not once glancing into the living room.

DJ looks at his father, at the granite hardness in his eyes, and keeps his mouth shut.

"DJ, I hope you're not—" The woman steps into the living room and her hands fly up to her mouth as she gasps. Blue eyes widen. "Dwight, what the hell are you doing? Put the gun down. Now."

The man sways where he stands and becomes a degree more docile. "Did you know our son's been replaced with one of those abominations, Annalise?" He nails his glare to the thing that looks

3

like his son and watches as the eyes they share are slowly blotted out to neon blue. "I knew it. Human eyes don't do that. Where's my son?"

"Your son is kneeling in front of you in tears because his father is pointing a gun at his head!" Annalise's hands clench into fists. "His eyes started doing that a few months ago. We talked about it, there's nothing wrong with him."

Dwight finally rips his glare away. "Are we both looking at the same thing? You did not give birth to *this!*" The gun barrel jabs accusingly. "You shouldn't have *talked* about it, you should've done what I'm doing now."

"Just give me the gun before you do something else you regret." Annalise swallows and steps forward with her quivering hand out. "We can go fill your prescriptions after this. You were like this the last time you stopped keeping up with your doses."

"Don't twist this on me, Annalise. I had to decide between buying my medication and taking care of my son." The father's eyes narrow on the bleeding boy. "This thing looks damn convincing, but it's not our DJ."

"Dwight, don't be foo—" She bites the word. "We can discuss this, all three of us, but first, you have to put the gun away." She takes two more steps forward. "Just give it to me."

"All I wanted was to rebuild our relationship, Dad."

Mother and father look down at their kneeling son.

"I've seen how unhappy and depressed you've been lately." DJ's voice trembles over the words. "Like a cave in your chest." Neon orbs stumble all over his father. "Now you're hurt and you feel betrayed...by me." He squeezes his eyes shut. "I didn't mean to do this to you, I swear. I just wanted for us to be closer."

"I'm coming for you, DJ." His father lifts the gun and squeezes the trigger at the same time that Annalise throws herself at her son.

*BLAM!*

For a few fragile moments, it's as if time stutters and gapes in naked disbelief at what it sees in itself. Then the mirror shatters and slices its way back on temporal track, bleeding truth as time hurtles forward to catch up with itself.

Annalise looks down at the hole in her chest, the blood soaking into her blouse. She looks over at her son, shoved out of the way. She eases down on her side as if preparing to take a nap, and her breath rattles as it wheezes out.

Both Dwights watch as Annalise Lucero dies.

DJ glances up, eyes still charged neon. He blinks. He opens his mouth. "You—"

*BLAM!*

Dwight watches as the thing impersonating his son dies.

Silence.

Mouth gaping open, the man eventually melts to his knees. Fingers twitch around the blood-warm contours of the gun. Anger dissolves to agony as the arm holding the gun flops limp. His moaning cries echo through the living room.

He turns to look at the bodies. He raises the gun to the picture of himself and Annalise holding their son just after he had been born. A sudden crack of anger seizes violently across his face. He fires shots into the wall of family photographs, bullet holes tearing through smiles, memories, laughs, and embraces.

He aims at the window pane Dwight Jr. painted when he was five and fires a bullet in it.

"A house full of lies." Tears roll down his face, drool stretching from the corner of his lips. "But I'm gonna find the truth, I'm gonna find you, son. The real you."

He walks out of the house. He stops when he remembers how DJ's mouth would always pinch to the side whenever he cried, the exact same way it had before he shot...him. He remembers because it was so rare that his son let anyone see him cry.

Thoughts ricochet in his skull, looking for a way out.

Minutes later, he goes back into the house full of lies, gun still in his hand.

# EPISODE ONE: *SHIFT*

"**WE** live in uncertain times, my friends."

Bishop Martin's eyes scan the congregation as he stands at the altar of the Dominion City Apostolic Faith Church. The pews are packed, leaving some members and visitors to either stand or sit in folding chairs in the back and along the aisles.

"We live in a most dangerous city, in a most dangerous world. But I've got good news." He smiles as he dabs at the sweat on his brow with a handkerchief. "God has sent his servants to us. Some people call them a scientific phenomenon, others a—a hiccup in evolution." He shakes his head. "But not me. No, I believe that these blessings, these Alpha-Omegas, have descended from heaven to show and remind us that God hasn't forgotten about us, that God is all around."

A clean-shaven man with brown-blonde hair and slightly parted lips nods from where he stands, blue gaze gripped by the bishop's words.

"Some of them have forgotten they're holy agents, vessels of the Almighty. Instead of guiding mankind from the clutches of Satan, they use their gifts, their blessing, for evil. They kill, steal, and destroy." He blinks and looks out at the crowd. "Just like Satan."

A ripple of agreement skips through the church.

"It's our job to bring them back to the light. Bring them back to God where they belong." His voice rises along with a few waving hands in the audience. "Back where we all belong!"

"*Amen!*"

"It is up to us, members of the Apostolic faith, to remind those who have been blessed by God but don't yet know him. We have to show them."

"*Yes!*"

"Touch their souls and show them the majesty of God!" He bounces on his heels and starts to stride back and forth across the pulpit in excited, jerky movements. "I refuse to allow them to wallow in sin, to drown in the black waters of evil and spiritual degradation."

His amplified voice grips his listeners by the bones and rattles them, jarring them from their seats into animated reply.

"*Preach!*"

"It is our job as Christians and disciples of God to gather His army, call His troops to the battlefield, raise the banner of war."

The interior of the church resounds with an effulgent chorus of, "*Yes!*"

"*Amen!*"

"*Hallelujah!*"

Bishop Martin walks down the aisle, pressing a hand to tilted heads and sending up supplications to God. He continues, offering a smile and a kind word to some and a stern stare and whispered advice to others. The blue-eyed man grips the pew as he looks up, parted lips working silently as he entreats the Lord to continue to give him the strength and wisdom needed to bring lost lambs back to the holy flock. The expression on the approaching bishop's face is one of bewildered wonder. He raises his arm almost absently, hand quivering at first and then stilling.

Bishop Martin spreads his fingers and touches the man's forehead, closing his eyes as he mutters an indecipherable word before gently shoving the man back.

A silver-white light that no one seems to notice glows where hand met flesh.

The blue-eyed man's spine goes rigid as he lifts his hands to the ceiling, to heaven, and begins to call out the Lord's name. Through half-lidded eyes he sees a silver glow cover his fingers, sparkling with warm radiance. The Lord's name catches in his throat and coils through his brain.

He opens his eyes wider and lowers his palms.

The silver-white glow wavers, wanes, and gradually fades.

The blue-eyed man clenches his hands into soft fists and lifts his eyes to the cross at the head of the church with the image of Jesus Christ draped across the wood and drenched in golden light. His Savior's eyes seem to focus on him. His Savior's eyes burn platinum.

The blue-eyed man drops to his knees as tears and prayers pour out of him. Members of the congregation gather around, laying hands on him and joining in prayer with clenched eyes and imploring tongues.

"Yes, that's right. Tell God what you need, tell Him what's on your heart. He already knows what's troubling us, but tell Him anyway." Bishop Martin returns to the pulpit and fans himself with his handkerchief. His eyes are glued to the man in the center of the mass of lifted hands. "Yes, Lord, yes."

The clean-shaven man with brown-blonde hair and blue eyes is named Adam Kensie.


Yellow-green eyes snap open as dry lips part and air rushes into deflated lungs.

Vision is a blurred and disorienting thing in the confines of the murk-smeared room.

A murk-smeared bedroom. The yellow-green orbs waver left and see the naked woman stretched out chest down next to him on the bed, red and gold locks spraying across her back.

She doesn't move.

A trembling hand rises into the frame of vision to touch her back. *Stillness.* Her cheek. *Cooling.* Her neck. *Nothing.*

The brain connects to the yellow-green eyes connect to the dry mouth that parts but emits no sound. The eyes register the body in which they reside sliding off the bed, emerald sheets slipping away. Balance is assaulted by disequilibrium. Ears are drowning in droning white noise.

The yellow-green eyes droop down and notice the slacks around feet and pallid ankles. *Confusion.* A flaccid penis rests between pale legs, the tip still a bit shiny and wet. *Embarrassment.* Hands draw up the pants and clutch them there with yellowing fingernails.

Feet shuffle forward.

The smell of perfume laces the air. A puddle of lingerie sits on the carpet. The air conditioner blows air over the small clumps of dirt on the floor.

Yellow-green eyes roll down to the lifted hand and notice the dirt streaking the palm. More smeared on the shirt. Fingers touch a face and find more dirt on a cheek.

"Where?" The word rolls foreign from wormy lips.

The yellow-green eyes sense the well-trimmed brows above them furrow together. The brain sluggishly trips backward in time.

"*Are you joking, my dear?*"

"*Oh—I—well. Sorry, Mr. Quintero, I thought that you would like this.*"

"*I would...if I were a brain dead retard.*"

Brain bumbles to the present.

"Saleswoman in Delgadar. Tried to sell me a...a tie?"

Brain shuffles through memory.

"*Excuse me, did you give a signal? No, Miss Chevrolet, I don't think you did. Get your ass back in your lane.*" He pressed his foot to the accelerator and the car obediently zipped forward to close the distance between him and the next car.

"*Idiot driving mother f—*"

He felt his heart trip-hammering before stammering in his chest. Felt his heart thump sluggish. Felt his heart stop working. Felt...nothing.

The present slips back.

"Driving ho—No, meeting Jessica for lunch when I—" Yellow-green eyes roll forth and back in a shaking head. "What happened?"

Feet seem to guide themselves to the blade of light stretching across the floor to the bathroom.

The past infects the brain.

*Darkness*

*Stale air*

*A void*

*A muffled crack*

*Oxygen*

*A flash of red and gold hair*

*A face*

The present returns with languid grace.

A doorknob is in a hand. The hand twists.

Blinding light filters the world down to smears, glares, and gleams.

Yellow-green eyes blink and focus.

The sunken eyes see their glowing reflection framed by red skeins of veins.

Sallow skin.

Handsome features.

Face of death.

The corpse with the yellow-green eyes is named Giorgio Quintero.

"Murder."

"What's that?" The officer behind the detective elbows into his mutterings.

The detective cants his head and looks into Dwight Jr.'s dead neon eyes.

"Ever notice how certain words sound like their meaning, Ehasz?" The detective straightens his head, stepping back to allow a member of the forensics team with a camera in his hand to step past.

"Not really, sir."

He mutters to himself: "No wonder you haven't made detective yet." He stretches up to his full height. "Take the word *clean*, for instance. *Clean*. Sounds pure and untainted, right? Now how about *dirty*? Sounds like sandpaper rubbin' against your tongue." He gestures at the two bodies in the living room. "*Murder*. Don't know about you, but even though I see and say it almost every day, that word still sends a little spasm up my spine." He glances over at Dwight where he sobs and stammers and sits in the kitchen, holding his head in his hands with occasional lifted glances at the bodies of his wife and son as he answers questions from the officer standing in front of him. "Glad he at least turned himself in."

Ehasz rolls his little gray eyes to the young corpse sprawled on the rug, blood soaked deep into the pattern. "Probably didn't know how to handle learning his son was a freak." He goes back to taking notes on a small pad of paper.

"What about that one?"

The officer's eyebrows have a meeting in the middle of his forehead. "Sir?"

"*Freak*. How does that word sound?"

The younger man considers it. "Odd. Like something alien."

"Exactly." A beat passes. "Hate how common cases like this are becoming, people actin' like they're in the presence of the culmination of their life's fears when they learn someone's an A-O."

"Anyone in your life genetically reawakened, sir?" Ehasz rubs behind his ear with his pen.

The detective scratches at his carefully unkempt dark brown hair. "Not that I know of." He shakes his head. "But I don't think it's all that different from someone with autism, dyslexia, or special needs." A puff of wry laughter. "Or being anything but heterosexual."

"Maybe we should have you take over sensitivity training, then." A tall, pudgy man in a suit and tie with a badge dangling around his neck walks into the room, clearing an easy path through the lively forensics team.

The detective turns to him, his slightly oversized nose wrinkling with contempt. "Get here when you can, McGarvey."

McGarvey steps heavily over Annalise's body. "Not too much to figure out here, gentleladies. Dwight was about to kill his son here when the woman jumped in front of the bullet." He makes a gun with his first two fingers and thumb. "Bang." He bends his thumb. "He offed the son next. Bang." Repeated motion. "Then, he's overcome with remorse for being a right bastard and calls us to take 'im in." He makes a book of his hands, shuts them as he looks over at Dwight being led out of the house full of lies in handcuffs. "Case closed. Let's wrap the scene up and call it in. My wife's expecting a package and the post office closes early today." He leaves.

"Heard they caught a perp over in Mercurmont boosting 8k TVs a few weeks back." Ehasz licks his lips as he stands. "Had no problem catching the guy, but they couldn't keep him." He releases a bitter chuckle. "Sonovabitch melted through a pair of handcuffs and did the same thing to the patrol car door."

The detective wrinkles his brow. "They stop him?"

Head shake. "Fired at him, but the bullets freaking melted before they hit him. Impact bruised him more than anything else."

The detective scoffs. "Don't teach you how to handle this kind o' shit at the police academy."

The detective's name is Perry West.


"Mail call."

11

The man in the lab coat looks up from the compound microscope as Paul walks into the laboratory.

Paul holds up the envelope in his hands, the Nightingale Industries logo tattooed in the upper left corner. "'nother job offer no doubt." He hands the other man the envelope. The man in the lab coat takes it...and tosses it on the table before going back to his microscope.

Seconds later he hears Paul ripping open the envelope.

The man in the lab coat tears his eyes away from the microscope once more. "The hell are you doing, Paul?"

"For someone so smart, you aren't very perceptive." Paul scans the single sheet of white paper. "Dear Mr. Kennington blah blah blah. Noticed your work with the yadda yadda yadda. We'd like to offer you...*Holy shit!*" His eyes grow two sizes larger as they zip down the page. "They want to offer you a position as senior chemist in their medical biochemistry division!"

"That's nice." The man adjusts the coarse focus, squints his eyes.

A beat.

"They're also guaranteeing a nice bag of steaming shit on your first day."

"They always do."

"This is the part of the movie where your character starts bouncing all over the lab, maybe run out into the hall shouting and dancing before you kiss the first attractive woman you see." His mouth tugs to the side. "Vanessa's in the computer lab down the hall."

"Yeah, Paul, and Francie would slap the taste outta my mouth if she found out I even—" The man in the lab coat presses his thumb and middle finger to his temples, eyes slipping shut. "Could you give me a few minutes, please?"

"Sure. I'll let you celebrate in private." Paul smiles a bit, but it doesn't reach his eyes. He whispers out of the laboratory.

The man in the lab coat stands and moves to pick up the letter where Paul left it and reads over it for himself, lingering over the offered salary.

Crumpling the letter in his gloved hands, he sucks air through his nose and feels the hot threads of anger tighten his muscles. He stops himself before he can throw the letter in the trash.

He goes back to the microscope and takes another look at the stained cluster of chromosomes. His stained cluster of chromosomes.

"Damn."

He studies the faint blue speck of a gnarled chromosome that should not be there, unchanged from when he first noticed it three weeks ago. The organized structure glows and pulses and fades like a submicroscopic heartbeat. His hand clenches, and for a minute, it is almost as if he can feel his blood changing, stretching, pulling at the presence of this new...anomaly.

He brings his head back and his eyes slide to the newspaper draped across his desk.

**"GENETICISTS ATTEMPT TO DISCOVER THE ORIGINS OF ALPHA-OMEGAS"**

He looks at the crumpled job offer from Nightingale Industries on top of the job offer from the tech division at StarPharm Medical, next to the offer for head of the science division at ChemBio International, underneath the letter from the biochemistry branch of the U.S. military.

He looks at his chromosomes, at the work of his active Alpha-Omega gene.

The man in the lab coat studies his reflection in the stainless steel freezer next to him. He steps closer to himself, running fingers through black hair cut close to his scalp, dragging a gloved finger down his widow's peak. He eyes the small mole on the left side of his face, studies his lightly tanned skin, stares into light gray eyes with a slight brown sheen around the pupil. "Poisoned eyes and poisoned skin to go along with your poisoned blood." He shakes his head at his reflection. "Everything about you is a damn swirl, a tainted swirl."

The alien sensation uncoils inside the man in the lab coat once more. "No." He feels his entire body *pulse*, a thin screen of light coming from his core. The world goes silent and he can hear...feel...sense something turn on in his veins.

His phone vibrates.

FRANCIE

As he reaches forward, his skin tingles tight. A dense and near invisible force wraps around his hand, shoving the phone inches away from his fingers like a magnet, just like it shoved away the microscope earlier that day and sent it clattering to the floor in expensive pieces, just like it knocked over a conical flask last week and ruined an experiment, along with a week's worth of medical research.

Frustration rips through his nostrils in a hot breath.

He reaches again.

The phone is pushed back by the faint silver-blue haze enveloping his fingers.

He clenches his fist closed, clenches his eyes shut, and drags the vexation into a mental closet using one of the breathing techniques he'd learned recently.

The near tangible force diffuses. He wraps his fingers around the phone and accepts the call.

"Hey, Francie." His voice is forced calm.

"Hey, baby, thought I was going to get your voicemail for a second. How's work?"

The man in the lab coat glances at the microscope. His sigh rattles through the phone. "Turning out to be one hell of a day, beautiful."

The man in the lab coat is named Leo Kennington.


The cross swings back and forth along with Adam's eyes.

He stares. He waits.

Five minutes pass before he puts the necklace down and takes up the Bible on the coffee table. He opens it to the book of Galatians. His eyes rove, but they do not read.

Ten minutes pass before he closes the book.

He wipes his hands down his face and breathes deep. "What in the world am I doing? Probably just a short in the lights or something that made me think my hands were..." Adam looks at his palms, looking from one...to the other...and back.

He studies his long, lined fingers and the slight quiver running through them.

But they do not glow.

He searches around the house for something he cannot find before he flips on the TV.

"—*will love the new cleaning power of orange fresh—*"

"—*never told him that I would go to—*"

"—*that slam dunk from Chase! I tell ya, this season he's—*"

"—*only in theatres June 11th—*"

"—*has to be God. And the nations of the world will be shaken by the Hand of God. It's a scary time to be alive, but it's also an absolutely thrilling time to be alive. God wants to demonstrate His power not only to little Israel, but to all of the world. You see, in chapter forty-nine it says 'all of my people will know me.' Folks, I encourage you to pray for Israel, God wants you and everyone else to pray for Israel. You can join us on our website at—*"

Nothing.

Adam turns the television off and looks up. He gets down on his knees and folds his hands together.

"Are you trying to send me a sign, God? Is Bishop Martin right, are these Alpha-Omegas your heralds? Is it our duty, my duty, to bring them back to the light? Why did you lead them astray, God? Away from the flock?" He shakes his head. "I don't understand what it is that you want me to do. Since I was quickening in my mother's womb I was taught that You are the word, that You are the way...the only way." He pauses. "Tell me where to go, God, order my steps." He touches his forehead to his interlaced knuckles. "Speak through me, dear Lord, please speak through me."

His next breath comes in a hitch. He shudders. He opens his eyes and hauls in a lungful of air.

LIGHT

The room is pulsing with pure platinum light.

Adam is held in awe as shafts of ivory brilliance cascade around the walls.

He looks down and sees that the light comes from him.

Joy


Giorgio stumbles back from himself, breathing heavily.

Breathing heavily.

Breathing.

He stops breathing. His head does not throb and thump with a buildup of blood. His chest does not ache. The world isn't spotted and dotted with gray motes of approaching unconsciousness.

"Because I'm not alive."

He lifts up his hand and sees that although it is just as smooth as it was in life, the color is now wan and weak. He touches his cheeks and finds them smooth and cold, the prominent bones now even more so beneath his dead skin. He forces himself to look at himself. "How am I still...alive...undead...reanimated..." He pauses. "How am I still here?"

Giorgio walks back into the bedroom and finds the dead woman as he left her. There are only discarded wisps of garments on the floor, wrinkles in the bedsheets, and dirt on the pillows.

Graveyard dirt.

Giorgio steps toward the woman, grabs her shoulder to turn her over, and remembers it all in a flash.

*His heart stopped on his way to meet Jessica just as he entered Cade District.*

*Death.*

*Darkness.*

*A sense of no sense of time.*

*Sleep paralysis draped lackadaisical over rigid limbs.*

*The top of his coffin splintered and cracked.*

*He saw her blurred face wreathed by a mass of red and golden curls.*

*Too dead to be conscious and too comatose to be cognizant, but still his dead eyes saw everything through the slight crack in his eyelids.*

*She removed his body from his coffin and pulled him gently from his final resting place, kissing him on the forehead. "Poor, Giorgi. Kimmy's gonna take you home and take good care of you, okay? Good care of her man."*

*Time stuttered forward in drunken minutes and wobbling hours.*

*He was in the bed, this bed, and she stood before him in silk lingerie. "You didn't want anything to do with me when you were alive; you were too much of a pretty boy. Thought I was too basic for you, didn't you?" She slipped out of her bra. "My breasts were too big for your dainty fancyman hands." She hopped onto the bed and straddled his corpse, hands wandering. "My mouth was too small." She unzipped his pants and dragged them down to his ankles. "Is it too small to do this?" Her lips wrapped around* his unresponsive penis and worked eagerly. She looked up after a while. "Still too small for you, Giorgi?" She slipped out of her panties and tossed them to the floor. "Kimmy's too much for a hot-blooded man, only the dead make her feel alive." Her palms ran over his cheeks, through his limp brown curls, fingertips tickling over his nose. She lowered her warm mouth over his cold mouth.

A kiss.

A jolt.

A death.

A rebirth.

Yellow-green eyes SNAP open as dry lips part and air rushes into deflated lungs.

Kimmy had been killed by his kiss, and he had been revived by hers.

Giorgio glances down and sees the flesh of her corpse has now gone gangrenous, paper-thin, and brittle. He reaches out to touch her hair when he feels an electric rush jolting into his fingers.

His pink fingers.

His alive fingers.

He goes back to the mirror.

Giorgio Quintero is alive again.

To all appearances.


Commissioner Willard Moskovitz.

Moskovitz adjusts the nameplate as he sits behind his desk, crossing his legs and bobbing his foot as he offers West a professional smile.

"So, Detective West, what can I do for you?"

Perry leans forward on a chair back, drumming his fingers on the fabric. "You hear anything about the murder that took place in Century Heights last night?"

The commissioner puffs out a laugh. "I've been in meetings with city officials all day trying to convince them the precinct needs more funding. I'm up to my considerably tight ass in paperwork and forms, so forgive me for not having been updated on the latest rash of felonies that have taken place." He pauses a beat. "And I mean that sincerely."

Perry nods. "I understand." He rolls his shirt sleeves up over his forearms with quick, efficient movements. "At approximately six o'clock last night, a father accidentally shot his son's mother before murderin' his son and voluntarily turnin' himself in. He thought an Alpha-Omega was impersonatin' his boy, makin' him believe his son had been genetically reawakened. Unfortunately, forensics determined that the corpse was in fact his son...and an A-O."

The commissioner rolls his tongue over his teeth. "Bottom line?"

Perry drapes a forearm over the chair back, straightening his tie. "Bottom line is that this is only one in a quickly growin' number of crimes committed because of or by Alpha-Omegas. The things these people can do aren't somethin' that can be overpowered by pepper spray, a Taser, or even a bullet. They operate outside the limits of non-powered human law. What I want to know is, are there any laws being created specifically for A-O criminals?"

"Laws like what?" The commissioner swivels and squeaks in his chair.

"Will they receive harsher punishment than non-powered perps if they commit a crime usin' their powers? I know there are special cases, but a lot o' these people are aware of what they are and what they can do. Chances are, some o' 'em can even control their abilities. Court can't allot special circumstances for 'em, neither can we."

Moskovitz rubs at his incisors with his tongue. "Legally, we can't create laws against Alpha-Omegas since that would be considered discrimination. It would be no different from me discriminating against a handicapped person...or you because you're gay."

The detective glowers. "You're talkin' 'bout the same system that hogties and hobbles the rights of gay men and women, and I've yet to see a report that either proves or disproves without exception that homosexuality is biological."

The other man exhales. "Please don't turn this into—"

"I'm not, just makin' a point."

"The point you're trying to make is unethical and will be met with a great gnashing of teeth, detective. Singling out a group of people does nothing but result in blowback, a blowback I will have to respond to with equal force by sending out women and men, husbands and wives, daughters and sons to counter. Do you want to be the one to call someone's parents and tell them their child was killed in a revolt led by a group of pissed off super-beings? You want to be responsible for taking a person's life because he or she wanted to take away your basic human rights?"

Perry quirks an eyebrow. "Never figured you for an activist."

"I'm not, I'm a commissioner. Anything any of you do in the streets is on me." He leans forward and points at the detective. "Not on you." He points at himself. "On me. I'm the one the press and the public are going to maul." He offers a feeble smile. "Not a huge fan of standing in the path of a loaded chain gun."

Perry keeps his mouth shut.

Moskovitz leans back. "Besides, I would think you'd be all up in arms about protecting a minority group, not the first to drag out the noose."

"You think every gay person gives a good damn about gay rights? That every person with a disability speaks out against ableism?"

Commissioner Moskovitz folds his hands behind his head, exposing the generous sweat stains soaked into the armpits of his shirt. He nods at the other man's point. "So, what are you gonna do, West?"

Detective West pushes away from the chair and stalks toward the door. "My job, commissioner, gonna do my damn job."


*"Dammit!"*

Leo lifts his head and sees his coworkers stopping to stare at his hissed outburst. He ignores them, going back to his notes and furious scribblings.

"Isolate this..." *Scratch.* "...base pair..." *Scribble.* "...protein barrier around..." *Circle.* "....next, and that will..." He looks over the equation. "Likely put me in a coma the next time I go to sleep." He scratches at his head in agitation. "*Shit!*"

"Kennington?"

Leo looks up. "Yes, Mrs. Acker?"

The older woman sidles over to him, stuffing her hands in her lab coat pockets as she throws a disarming glance and a smirk at the curious employees. He skips his eyes to the blood sample under the microscope. "I know our current project may be a bit...tedious for someone of your aptitude, but I don't think that now is the time for you to divert your attention to personal projects." She takes in the crumpled papers, equations, and diagrams eating up table space. She frowns. "Just what is it that you're doing?"

Leo blinks.

"My A-O gene activated a few weeks ago and the force it's projecting from my body is keeping me from working. Devin was laid off when he told HR he's an A-O, so I'm trying to figure out a way to either suppress or, preferably, destroy my gene so I can keep my debilitating depression and anxiety in check by burying myself in one of the few things in my life that brings me true joy. Is that okay?"

Leo blinks. Just a fantasy.

"Just trying to help out Joiner with his—" Leo begins.

"Joiner?" Acker's mouth wrinkles. "The intern? How is he supposed to learn anything if you're doing all of his work for him?" She puts a hand on the table, leans closer to him, and whispers. "Is this a race thing? Trying to help a...a *brother* out?" Her hand flutters in a circle at the word.

Leo's jaw muscles tense. "No, ma'am. And I don't appreciate comments like that." He watches as she focuses on his poisoned gray and brown eyes, then drops her gaze to the poisoned light brown skin of his hand.

"Well, in any case, you should get back work, I don't pay you to do another person's job." Acker reaches for the papers.

Leo snatches them out of her reach.

Shock jolts through her expression. "Give me the papers, Kennington." Acker holds a hand out.

"I'm sorry, but I can't."

"I won't ask again."

"You don't understand."

"I think I do. Give me those papers, Mr. Kennington."

Anger crinkles his brow. "You need me here."

"One."

"If you would just listen—"

"Two."

"Mrs. Acker, please. These papers—"

*Flare.* The next pulse in his body feels wrong. His skin tingles tight and he knows it's happening again. "Not now." He clenches his hand and tries to pull the force back, tries to force the force. He feels it shivering along his fingertips like silver-blue sparks. The air pulses. He grits his teeth.

"Thr—"

Mrs. Acker cuts herself off as Leo suddenly releases the papers and snatches up the pair of scissors at the edge of the table.

And stabs them into his palm.

She gasps.

Leo grits his teeth together as he jerks the scissors from his palm with a squelch. He almost places the scissors back on the table but sees the blood coating them.

Tainted blood.

He holds the scissors in one hand, clutches the papers between his arm and body while cradling his bleeding palm close to his chest, and walks out of the laboratory.


Mercurmont breathes and seethes around Adam as he sits on the stoop next to the young man in the red beanie. It's nighttime and downtown Dominion City lingers in the background, watching as the young man fights to keep the tension slithering over his body from settling in once place, hunching his shoulders, wringing his hands, twisting his neck.

"The first few days out of prison are the best, but they're also the worst." Adam looks out at the other houses lining the street as he talks. "You're finally experiencing the freedom you've been waiting for, but it's almost like slipping into old clothes that don't fit anymore."

The young man bobs his head, sniffs. "I've been praying, Mr. Kensie." Foot bobs. "I've been praying a lot."

"That's good, Robbie. Remember that just because you're out of prison doesn't mean you're free." Adam pulls a small Bible from the messenger bag at his feet. "I'd like to give this to you."

Robbie accepts the book with care and reverence. "Thank you."

"My parents blessed that before they gave it to me, and I blessed it before giving it to you." He taps a finger on the cover. "Hope it helps you in the transition."

Robbie thumbs through the book. "Do all parole officers give Bibles to their parolees?"

Adam grins. "They do when they specialize in people being released from both their spiritual and physical prisons." He watches as a man makes his way down the cracked sidewalk toward them, edges of his flannel shirt flapping around his broad form as he walks in and out of the pooled shadows untouched by the half-hearted glow of the streetlights.

"Mind if I ask you something?" Robbie keeps his eyes on the step below him as he speaks.

"As long as you don't mind me answering."

The man in the flannel shirt is two houses away. He walks with his hands in his pockets.

Robbie's smile is weighed down by his thoughts. "How do you have such strong faith after what you see, and the people you interact with?"

Adam leans back and props himself up by his elbows on the step behind him. The man is one house away when he starts to answer. Then he sees the man is not a man but a woman, a woman pulling what he knows to be a gun from her waistband.

"Snitchin' muthafucka!" Words shoot out from her mouth. Bullets shoot out from the gun.

Adam shoves himself off the steps and bends his body in front of Robbie. Air rushing past his ears suddenly thickens to syrup, golden-infused clouds whispering over goosebump-speckled flesh. Sound spirals distant and sensation is heightened as it's lowered, his shirt rippling slowly across his body.

The bullets feel like knots of heated rubber smacking into his back. They *ting* onto the steps like loose change, instead of deadly projectiles.

Adam pushes away from the stoop, bumbling down the last three steps with the force of his hurried momentum. He grabs the woman by the wrist as she looks at his unmarked body with a bewildered expression. The gun is wrestled away with ease. He shoves her, a flurry of power igniting through his muscles and skin as she's knocked back into the empty street with more force than he intended. His hand flashes silver-white for a full second before snuffing out.

There's a muffled snap as she throws her arms behind her to catch her fall. She howls out in pain, curses a violent streak, and calls Adam everything but a child of God.

He turns back to Robbie, who's breathing heavily with the Bible clutched to his pumping chest. "She—she shot—" He shares the howling woman's bewildered expression as he notices Adam's lack of gunshot wounds. "She shot you...didn't she?"

Adam presses a hand to his sternum. He can feel the flow of the platinum light simmering just underneath his flesh. "No weapon formed against me." It's like glory flows through his very bones.

Later finds Adam standing in front of his bathroom mirror toweling himself off as threads of steam curl and unfurl around him.

He is rubbing his hair dry when he looks at his reflection, turning to look at the developing gunshot bruises on his back. He stops. He lifts an arm and spreads his fingers.

Nothing.

He does the same with the other hand.

Nothing.

He focuses on his chest and waits and waits and nothing.

He slows his breathing and focuses on his entire body, sipping each breath in and easing it out as if it's his last.

More nothing.

He squints his eyes in frustration before shutting the light off.

He shuffles into the bedroom and slips into a pair of pajama bottoms and a tank top before sliding into bed. He reaches over and taps the lamp out.

Seconds later, he pulls the covers aside, slides out of bed, and gets down on his knees.

He whispers an unheard prayer before getting back into bed.

He dreams.

The next day at church:

Adam stands up and the world clicks off mute. Voices, handclaps, broken bits of hymns, and shouts of praise engulf him. He collects the length of the chain in his hand and makes a fist, feeling the cross attached to the necklace bump softly against the side of his palm. He banishes fear from his heart and walks toward the altar.

"Brother Adam has come to testify!" Bishop Martin roars into the microphone. "Come on up, son; share what the Lord has done for you." He gives Adam a reassuring smile and perches a hand on his shoulder as Adam stands next to the pulpit.

He clears his throat and speaks.

"This is my first time giving a testimony, so bear with me.

"None—none of us know the reasoning behind God's work, why he gives to some and takes away from others. But we know that His will, His works, are all for the best...whether we're aware of it or not." A hush descends. "For some reason, God has given me a gift, a most precious gift. It's something that I can't even begin to try to comprehend, but maybe I'm not supposed to. It finally came to me in a dream last night." He swallows. "At least I think it was a dream. I was surrounded by golden light in a sea of ivory when a voice said unto me, 'Go now, my child, go forth and do my work with my blessing. My strength is yours, my speed is yours, the wings of my angels are yours. Let my will be done.' " People stop fanning themselves. "When I awoke, I felt different, I knew I had been graced with God's touch. A word was on my lips, buzzing and beating against my tongue. I spoke it, and was changed." His voice is an amplified whisper.

"What was the word?"

He looks in the direction of the voice. Then he utters *the word.*

"*Ascension!*"

A golden star is born beneath his flesh, showering him in a golden-silver light and ruffling his suit. The microphone gives an electric squeal and the speakers pop with snaps of electricity before dying. Adam's skin ripples with shafts of platinum-ivory outlined in metallic gold, his eyes are doused in neon white.

The brilliant being speaks. "God has remade me into His Sovereign. I am His agent on Earth, paving the road to Paradise and cleansing the world of all evil. Let His divine will be done."

The congregation collapses down on their knees. All but one woman who stares at Sovereign with wide eyes and mouth agape.

Her name is Maggie, Adam's wife.


The murk sifts through the air intertwined with silence.

Giorgio hauls himself up from the couch, goes into the bedroom, snatches up his clothes, and follows the lingering, artificial scent of a mountain breeze to the laundry room.

Seconds later, his clothes are being battered by water and suds as his new old body is being battered by the individual streams of water spouting from the showerhead.

An hour passes and he's standing in front of Kimmy's mirror slipping into his shirt, taking note of how the freshly laundered cloth feels as it slides across his skin. He pulls the shirt on slowly, experiencing it.

As he buttons up, he looks in the mirror and sees Kimmy's remains staring at him with her mouth agape. His yellow-green eyes dance away from the body as his hands lift to arrange his thick brown curls.

He stops.

He blinks.

He stares.

Giorgio slowly lifts his hand and presses it to the mirror. *Cold.* He puts his hands to his face and smooths them down his jawline. *Inert.* He licks his lips. *Barren.* He lightly traces the tips of his fingers across his collarbone. *Insensate.* He looks slowly from left to right as if seeing the world for the first time. *Dead.*

"Just what are you now...Giorgio Quintero?"

He leaves.

He finds himself in Oswyn hours later, a neighborhood he had never visited in life. He gazes around with a sense of alien familiarity.

Somehow, the feeling, the sensation, the *experience*, is numb.

There is a void where emotion once existed.

As he walks past the Dominion City Post building, he's momentarily distracted by the news report playing on the massive screen on the side of the building. *"...family of A-Os that shares the ability to make people happy. They've actually set up a special practice in Dominion City devoted to not only freeing people of the emotional weight dragging them down in life, but also helping people realize what truly makes them happy, fills them with joy, and does more than make them merely content.*

*"Since setting up their practice, the Johnson family has treated suicidal patients, guided some to true love, and have even helped improve the physical health of some of their patients. If you're interested in receiving a bit of happiness while finding out for yourself how effective their ability is, you can—"*

"Remember where you left your ability to feel before you died and were brought back to life." He turns away from the screen, away from the possibilities.

Various scents scatter through his nose, but neither repulse nor sway him to hunger.

Sight is both old and new, but what was once color is now muted and flat.

"'Scuse me."

He turns to a short redhead with glasses.

"My phone just died on me and I don't wear a watch." Her nose crinkles. "Do you have the time?"

Giorgio stares blankly. "Does anyone?"

She cracks her mouth and dances her eyes around in search of distraction before walking away. The response feels familiar to him.

*Feels.* Funny.

He stuffs his hands in his pockets and saunters toward a closed auto shop, shoulders hunched.

He speaks to himself. "Have to be the first living undead ghost in history."

He responds to himself. "As in life, so in death."

"Ghosts only exist because they have unfinished business,

attachments. What is there left for me to be attached to?"

"Nothing."

"Exactly. You can't form an attachment with a void, there's nothing there to grasp."

"Then why do you still cling to it?"

"I'm not!" He whirls on empty air and sees nothing.

That word again: nothing.

Giorgio clutches a hand to his chest, grips the fabric of his shirt as if it is a tether. He swallows, air slithering thick and tasting of leftover bile. He claws a hand through his curls as oxygen inflates and deflates in his lungs.

"Can't—no, no, I—" He swallows. "—I can't, mm-mm, can't do this, can't do this."

The mobile cadaver crushes his eyes shut. He stumbles back into the wall of the auto shop, withers down to the ground, rips at the buttons on his silk shirt, and takes a deep breath.

"There, that's—" Another breath. "—that's better. Just need to breathe."

He puts his hand to his heart...and feels it doing absolutely nothing.

Giorgio Quintero stops. Giorgio Quintero blinks. Giorgio Quintero laughs.

"Even in death we're creatures of habit." He smiles as he lifts a hand to his face and studies it. He makes a fist, uncurls his fingers, turns his palm over and back before looking at the lines and veins. He traces them with a finger.

"All of these little lines. Where do they lead? What do they mean? Are you coming or are you going...little line? Did you lead me here?"

He drops his hand and leans his head back against the chilled bricks as he looks up at the great empty sky.

"Someone up there is mocking me, pointing a great universal finger and clutching at their gaping black hole of a stomach. Why, hmm? Why me?" He laughs at his own question. "I wager you hear that a lot, don't you?"

He climbs to his feet, opens his arms.

"Well?" Headlights splash over him. "Why am I back?"

A beat.

"TELL ME, DAMNIT! TELL ME WHY I'M BACK!"

Wind blows.

He drops his arms.

His mouths something, but his next words are lost in the breeze.


Dwight Senior stares with vacant eyes at the fresh pair of handcuffs shackling him to the table, keeping him fettered to reality and preventing him from killing someone else he claims to love. His gaze is fractured when Detective West steps through the door held open by a uniformed correctional officer. "Be right outside if you need anything." The woman slices a glance at the man in the prison jumpsuit chained to the table, eases out of the room.

Perry pulls the remaining chair out from the table, eases down into it. "How ya doin', Mr. Wheatley? They give you your medication?"

Dwight nods. "Yes, thank you." He tries to sit up straighter in his chair, instantly slumps forward again.

West leans forward on his elbows, waits until the other man meets his eyes before speaking. "Didn't come here to churn up any more guilt or point any accusatory fingers. Just wanted to let you know I think I understand why you, uh..." He scratches at his cheek. "Why you did what you did." Eyebrows quirk. "You were protectin' your family."

The handcuffed man scrunches his eyes shut, but it's not enough to hold back the fresh roll of tears, face red as he struggles to fight back the tide. His mouth cracks and a sob rattles through. "Since when is murdering your family the same as protecting them?"

"Growin' up, I had a father who never learned how to communicate or work through his emotions in a way that was healthy. He smacked my mother, sister, and me around. It was only sometimes, but..." He flicks fingers and squints his eyes as he's submerged in remembrance. "He always apologized afterward, said that he loved us no matter what, just that we made him angry sometimes. He had a trigger temper, ya know, everything bottled up came smashing out. An' I believed 'im because I thoug—no, I *knew* he loved me." The detective rolls his sleeves over his forearms, focuses on Dwight. "At that age, it's your parents who help you lay the foundation for your definition of love, and that was mine. But then it was like he actually managed to smack some sense into me, hit me like thunder 'n' lightnin' covered in flesh and rage. Love shouldn't make you seize up every time it steps into the room. Love shouldn't make you feel like no matter how many times you course correct, you're still doin' somethin' wrong, like you were born guilty." A smile wrings its way across his mouth. "I realized my dad didn't love me, not in the right way, at least." He sniffs. "So I blew a hole in his chest with a gun I stole from our next door neighbor the next time he raised his hand at my sister."

The words temporarily sever Dwight from his remorse.

"Not comparin' us or anythin', just sayin' that sometimes we go to the extreme when it comes to protectin' the people we love, keep 'em from becomin' victims, and we don't always make the best decisions. You sacrificed your mental health to take care o' your son."

Dwight shakes his head. "But still the fact remains that I shot my son." He pauses. "I s-s-shot my son." The tears come on anew. "And I wish I could bring him and his mother back."

"You might very well soon have that ability, Mr. Wheatley. You, or someone else."

The sound of Curtis Mayfair's "Here But I'm Gone" fills Leo's ears.

He looks out of the window of the bus, watching as Phosphorus Park rolls by. He adjusts his headphones, looking down at the bandage wrapped around his hand. He runs the tips of his fingers over the tan material. If only he could rub *it* out. His hand flexes open and closed.

He reaches for the scissors stashed in his messenger bag and pulls them out, watching the way the dried blood seems to swallow the light. He pulls the scissors open. Snaps them shut. Pulls them open. Snaps them shut.

*Snicker Snak Snicker Snak*

He slaps them across the vein on his wrist.

Lyrics unwind in his ears. How *did* he get so far gone?

Leo's hip buzzes. He slides his free hand into his pocket and pulls out his phone.

FRANCIE

He hovers his thumb over the accept button. He grits his teeth, looks out of the window, and allows the small tremors of the phone to jar him to his bones.

A minute later his phone loosens a final pulse.

1 NEW VOICEMAIL.

He pulls out one earbud and brings the phone to his ear.

*"Hey, baby, I was just calling to ask if you still wanted to go see the new Afrofutara movie tonight, know how caught up you get in your work sometimes. And, I was thinking that we should do something about the tile in the bathroom. I have to shower with my eyes closed it's so nauseating. Good thing there's already a toilet in there."*

Francie's laugh rolls heavy through the speaker and makes him smile.

A beat passes.

*"Let me get off here and get some of this work done, papers are starting to look like a column. Your pretty butt is cooking dinner tonight, hope you didn't forget. Bye, brown beau. Love you."*

Leo's hand is halfway to his mouth before he realizes that the strange sensation he feels is a smile leaking across his face. He slips the scissors back in his bag, rests his elbow on the edge of the window and tries his best to hide the single tear that blurs his vision before rolling softly down his cheek.

"I love you, too, baby. Thank you."

The bus rolls to a stop at the corner of Cherry and 8th. Leo Kennington steps out and breathes deep. He adjusts his shoulder strap as he walks down the sidewalk, mumbling the words of the next verse.

Across the street he pauses to watch a woman burst into ecstatic acceptance at the man on bended knee. She beams. He beams. The ring beams. They hug and kiss as the small gathered audience applauds.

"Thank you, ladies and gentlemen. We'll be here all week." Leo puffs out a bitter laugh. He moves on.

Ten paces away he pauses.

Their happiness is almost blinding, enough love to rival the brilliance of a hundred suns.

Leo looks over his shoulder at the couple, chewing on the inside of his cheek and wishing he could burn out his mind with all that blinding happiness.

## EXCERPT FROM LAMAR KOEHLER LIVE:

"Welcome back. I'm sitting here with someone whom some are already calling the singularly most remarkable woman in history, Nikki Mullen. Again, thanks for joining me, Nikki."

"It's my pleasure Lamar. Thanks for having me."

"Now, I know you've created quite a name for yourself in the past couple of years, but could you explain to the viewers who have just tuned in and for those of us who have been living under a very large rock for the past few months what makes you so remarkable?"

"Sure. I'm an Alpha-Omega with the ability to retain and recall any information that I receive through my five senses."

"Anything that you read or hear, see or smell?"

"Yes."

"So you remember where you were, who you were with and what you were doing a year ago today at this exact time?"

"Correct. I remember that I had just finished reading page one-hundred and nine of Amel Braxton's novel, *Kettleblack*. My cat was napping at my feet and the 312 bus was rumbling past my window."

"What was the weather like?"

"Spring had come early to Fossoway, and in two minutes and fourteen seconds I'm about to open the window."

"Remarkable. Before the break, we were talking about how your abilities made it possible for you to become not only an author, but an actress, doctor, guidance counselor, and a psychologist as well. You don't like to sit still, do you?"

"No, I don't, Lamar. I don't think my A-O gene will let me."

31

"Now, despite all of the marvelous things that you have done in the past two years and the things that you have yet to do, there are still some out there who, quite frankly, despise you simply because of who you are, an Alpha-Omega. How do you deal with that?"

"I don't, to be honest. I think that if I stop and dwell on how many people there are out there who despise me, I won't be able to keep doing what I'm doing. And unfortunately for me, I can't forget or block out a hateful comment or incident; it's crystal clear and right there in front of me."

"So you have no choice but to remember the good times as well as the bad?"

"Right. And some people might view that as a bad thing, but sometimes it's nice to remember what triggers an especially bad day. Sometimes, ah, it's something that's completely out of my hands and I have to handle it the best I can, but other times, it's something that I can stop, look at, and say to myself, 'you remember what happened the last time this happened.'"

"Now, Nikki, I have to ask you: How do you feel about the existence of people like yourself? Do you think that you're all stars burning brightly and briefly, or do you think that Alpha-Omegas are simply a new minority?"

"I've given that question a lot of thought, Lamar. Um, I certainly don't believe we're all devils just as I don't believe we're all angels. And I'm not saying that to simply be neutral or politically correct, but what I am saying is that our planet has been host to some of the most wonderful things just as it's been the stage for horror and atrocity. I'm not sure which A-Os are, a wonder or a tragedy. But I do think that each of us, each individual with an active A-O gene, has a decision to make, be it right or wrong. We're here, we exist, and just as a mother can't push her child back into the womb, neither can we take back who we are."

"What's done is done and can't be undone."

"Exactly. And I just want to wrap up my answer by saying this to any other A-Os who may be watching: We have to remember that we are human first and Alpha-Omegas second."

"Well said, very well said. Moving on. Uh, we talked about this briefly during the break, but would you care to share with the audience what you're doing right now with your skills as a scientist?"

"Absolutely. Currently, I'm trying to discover why the A-O gene is activated in some individuals, but not in others. Ah, are there certain groups of people who will never bear an A-O gene much less an active one? Are there family lines that will have an active A-O gene in each generation? Why have gene activation and A-O power levels ramped up so much in the past several years? These are the types of questions I want to answer."

"And what have you found so far?"

"You'll just have to wait and see like everyone else."

"You heard it here first, ladies and gentlemen, we'll just have to see for ourselves.

"Now, let's talk about your acting career. When can we expect the release of *Blue Man's Comet*?"

## FADE OUT

## DOMINION CITY – OSWYN

"PLEASE." She takes his hand in hers. "Do it for me."

He presses his chapped lips together. His black eyes look down at the hand enfolding his, eyelids slowly close. "I can't."

"Yes, you can, Brad, you can." Mucus clogs her nostrils and she sniffs it away. "I know that you don't think you're strong enough, but I can be strong enough for the both of us."

He drops her hand. Slowly.

"It's not enough, Terry." The heels of his palms are pressed to his forehead. "You're the strong one, you've always been the strong one. I'm weak. That's why I started, because I'm weak." He shakes his head. "I don't know how to quit. To be honest, I...I really don't want to."

"Brad, if you—"

He takes her hand. Quickly. "Have you ever felt a color, Terry? Have you ever felt a—a cool blue, or a burning red, or a sparkling green? Have you ever felt anything like that?"

She shakes her head.

He drops his voice. "That's how it is. You feel things you didn't even know you could. It's like waking up a totally different part of your brain and just...just swimming, *drowning*, yourself in...something new, something better."

Her face hardens. "That shit is killing you, Brad."

He pauses when he sees her expression. "Then it's the sweetest death I know."

She regards him, studies the light in his sunken eyes, watches as it almost illuminates the bags under his eyes. "Nothing I say can—"

"No." His head bobbles and shakes. "Nothing."

She leaves.


"It has to be voluntary, Ter."

"Fuck voluntary!" She slams her hand down on the steering wheel. "Brad doesn't have enough sense to fill a disposable paper cup; how is he supposed to help himself when he doesn't think he's in trouble?"

The voice on the other end of the phone drops a bit. "Terry, you cannot force an addict into rehab. If you do, they're only going to stay long enough to please you, and the minute they're out, they're going to be looking for their next fix."

Her fingernail is between her teeth as she starts to cry while stopped at at red light. "But I love him, James." The words are hoarse.

"Sometimes love isn't enough, lil' sis."

"You never were good at telling a comforting lie."

He can hear a thin smile mixed into her words. "I know, I'm sorry."

"No you're not."

"You're right, I'm not."

Terry presses her foot against the brake pedal a bit harder and looks out of the window.

"I could make him go into rehab."

"Terry, no. You know that's not right."

"I can turn his addiction towards something else, something healthier. I've been practicing and I think I can do it."

"Who have you been—Never mind. His mind is already messed up enough as it is without you screwing with it."

"But he would be off of the drugs."

"And you could put him in the hospital, or you might kill him. I understand your need to help your best friend, but this isn't the way. If you want Brad back, he has to come back on his own. Okay?"

She pauses.

"'Kay."

The light turns green.


Terry stares at Brad as he slides into the car. Her eyes drift past him to the apartment building and back to him. "Who lives here?" She shifts into D.

"Just a friend." He sniffs, twitching one side of his nose up.

The interior of the car suffocates on silence.

"Are you fucked up right now, Brad?"

She feels his eyes on her as she makes a left turn. "Wh—what?"

"Are. You. Fucked. Up. Brad?"

"Wha—No, I'm...I'm not fucked up. Damn, Terry."

"Give me your hand." She takes a palm from the wheel and holds it out.

"Terry, why—"

"Please, Brad." She spreads her fingers.

He slides his hand from his jacket pocket and places it in hers. His palm is damp.

She squeezes his hand, pauses for a moment, and her eyes go distant.

The car rumbles along.

When she speaks next, her voice is compelling, intoxicating.

Addictive.

"Brad, I want you to do something for me."

His eyelids droop lazily.

"I want you to check yourself into rehab, and then I want you to turn all of that time, all of that attention, and all of that passion you had for purple meth and focus it on becoming the absolute best financial advisor you can possibly be. I don't want you to ever even think about purple meth or any other kind of meth. You'll do that for me, won't you, Brad?"

His pupils spiral distantly and his forehead twitches.

"I'll do that for you. Anything for you, Terry."

# EPISODE TWO: STRUCK IN CHAINS

The vigilante watches Theodore Gordon step out to greet the day with a smile plastered on his face. Theodore waves congenially to his neighbors, drops an envelope into the mailbox, and slides the red flag up before ambling down the sidewalk, zipping his jacket against the chill air.

The vigilante follows with a smirk.

He shoves his hands in his pockets and tries his best to ignore the cool-kissed air slithering over his shaved head. He trails Theodore to the market and watches as he buys a shiny red apple and newspaper, telling the cashier to keep the change. He watches as Theodore munches on his apple and flips through the paper while riding the metro to Greenbriar and Bujore. Had Theodore's eyes not been glued to the sliver of exposed skin beneath the short sweater of the woman across from him, he might have noticed the vigilante shadowing him across the platform.

He might have.

But instead, the tip of Theodore's tongue slithers across his thin lips and tastes the air, tastes at the woman's exposed belly. Golden. Soft. Toned. He snatches his gaze away and something seems to crack in his ravenous eyes. They droop with sudden guilt. He exits the train, across the platform, and up the steps to the streets above.

The vigilante follows.

He can almost feel Theodore's hunger as the man meanders down the sidewalk. A woman raises an arm to hail a cab, causing her jacket to lift and expose a small roll of plumpness around her thick middle. Theodore's fingers curl at his side.

He slides up next to Theodore.

"'Ey there, Teddy. How are ya this mornin'?" His Puerto Rican accent rolls thick from his tongue.

Theodore glances over at him, glances behind him, glances back. "I'm sorry, do I know you?"

"Nah. I'm sure if you did, you'd be runnin' right now." A

smirk blossoms on his face.

"Should I be...running?" Theodore calmly slides his hand in his pocket, newspaper smashed underneath his arm.

"Take your hand out of your pocket, Teddy."

"Stop calling me Teddy and back the hell up, spic. I've got—"

"A small blade in your right pocket, a dagger at your left hip, and a scalpel taped to your left wrist."

Theodore stumbles.

"Keep walkin'." The vigilante doesn't bother to look at him as pedestrians stream oblivious around them.

Theodore keeps walking.

"Who the fuck are you?"

"*Mmph.*" The man winces. "Better not let your neighbors hear you spoutin' off words like that, may not invite you to their cookouts anymore. Tell me, how do they feel about having a recently released felon holed up next door?"

Theodore's expression dissolves. "How do you know that?"

"Can find out all kinds o' interestin' things with a blazin' fast Internet connection." The vigilante leans closer. "You still have the urge? The urge to slice into a woman's stomach as she screams? I can see it crawlin' around in your eyes, gnawin' at your fingers. 'S like an addiction."

"I got help for it in prison."

The vigilante scoffs. "'Parently, not enough." His eyes flick across the passing people. "Think all o' your counselin' would do you good if these streets were empty, if the sun wasn't up to shine light on what you're itchin' to do?"

"What do you want?"

"I just want to talk is all." The vigilante shrugs. "People think that when you do bad things, spend a few years in the pen with therapy and all that you come back a better person."

"Some people do."

Shrug. "And some people don't. Which are you?"

Theodore pauses on the sidewalk and is silent. Dominion City breathes, lives, and pulses around them.

"You'll never be healed. Don't care what those optimistic counselors told you. Truth is, you're tainted and you'll always be tainted no matter how many steps you take; twelve, twenty, a hundred."

Theodore starts to makes a move.

The vigilante grips the man's shoulder, leans close as if to whisper sweet everythings in his ear, and eases a hidden needle right into Theodore's throbbing jugular. "This is Tina, Teddy. Don't worry, she'll make it all go down easy, you might even enjoy this part."

Theodore's spike of shock is blown away by a euphoric rush as his eyes slither shut. Head tilts as spine seems to soften to jelly, muscles uncoil with langor, and a pleased little moan puffs out.

"Just remember, I'm doing you a favor." The vigilante slaps him on the shoulder and jogs away.

*Squeeeeeeel*

A snort of exhaust stains the air as a bus skids to a stop, brakes smoking.

The vigilante turns back and stares at the vicious red smear formerly known as Theodore Gordon.

The blood-spattered newspaper that was tucked underneath Theodore's arm flutters on the breeze,.

The vigilante snatches a page from the air.

**"GENETICISTS ATTEMPT TO DISCOVER THE ORIGINS OF ALPHA-OMEGAS"**

The vigilante looks again at the bloody remains of Theodore. Bloody. Blood.

Blood.

It seems to sing.

The vigilante is known as Noir.


"You think you're an angel."

The patient opens her mouth and instantly deletes the response about to come flying from it. "That's not what I'm saying."

"That's what it sounds like to me." The therapist waits for her patient to respond, studying her and watching the collage of emotions smear across her face.

"I'm just saying that..." She exhales, composing herself before continuing. "There are two—" She averts her eyes "—entities trying to take over my body."

"An angel and a demon?"

"Yes." She drops the word on the air with the weight of a feather. "They whisper things in my, my mind. Horrible things. Wonderful things."

The therapist folds her hands on her lap. "I believe this may very well be an extreme manifestation of your super-ego and your id, although I don't know why at your age you would have an incident like this."

The patient shakes her head. "No, no, it's...it's more than that."

"Please, explain."

The patient frowns. "I tell you and I'll wind up in a straightjacket and a room with foam walls."

"I'm here to help you. Let me do that."

The patient looks in her therapist's eyes, looks at the faint images of falling feathers swaying lazily back and forth in her vision. "The angel calls herself Seraph; she only comes out in the day. She tells me that I can heal the sick, that I need to protect those who can't protect themselves...that I'm a guardian or something." Her eyes go distant, and a lazy smile curls her mouth. "She makes me feel as if she's who I was meant to be."

"And the other personality? The demon?"

The patient's eyes go hollow along with her face. "The Dragoness...she comes out at night. When she does, I want to do things. Things like...tear someone's throat out with my bare hands." Her fingers curl. "I can—I can feel her underneath my skin like a snake pushing its way out. She stands in a field of blood, skulls, and snakes, beckoning me."

*Tick-tock*

*Tick-tock*

"Do you ever have any time to yourself? Are these voices, these entities, ever silent?"

"It's silent only in the moments after the last ray of the sun drops over the horizon and again right before the sun breaks across the sky. The night comes and sometimes I..." She lifts her head and her brow is creased. "I think my nails are longer, sharper. I'm stronger at night."

The therapist's eyes flicker to her patient's clenched hands.

"Do you think there's a reason you should be hearing these voices? Is there a monumental decision you're having trouble with? Anything that's plaguing your thoughts?"

The patient shakes her head. "I don't know what's going on in my head. I'm afraid that I might hurt someone."

"You have to remember that no matter what you think, you are in absolute complete control of yourself."

"Have you ever heard of anything like this? Anything this extreme, I mean?"

The therapist's pen scribbles. "Not quite like this, no. But everyone's mind works differently." She looks up. "Is Seraph saying anything right now?"

The patient's mouth is slightly agape as she looks away, listening. She looks back at her therapist. "She's telling me that your baby boy is hungry. You should eat some more peanut butter, he seems to like that." Her smile hangs crooked now.

The therapist's eyes widen before she schools her face, smoothing a palm over her nearly flat stomach. She looks down at her pad and scribbles a few needless notes. "How do you feel about going on medication?"

The patient's name is Bisset Torres.


*The activation of a person's Alpha-Omega gene seems to occur under irregular circumstances. Research shows that activation can happen at birth, during puberty, and, at times, even upon a person's death.*

*So far, scientists have not been able to decipher just what triggers the activation of an A-O gene, nor have they been able to determine how to deactivate it, essentially blocking an A-O from utilizing his or her abilities.*

Noir glances up from the computer screen, curls a finger over his lip, and roves his eyes around the computer lab.

The woman at the printer.

The man with glasses staring at the computer screen.

The little girl clutching the hand of the woman at the front desk.

The older man with a backpack tucking a book onto the shelf and ambling his way toward that bathroom moments before a teenaged boy slides the exact same book out, flipping to the middle and reading the note between the pages. He crumples the note and heads to the bathroom with anxious movements.

Noir's eyebrows twitch.

He clicks a series of **Xs** and collapses the overlapping windows, waiting a handful of beats before walking to the restroom. The cobalt blue tiles stare back as yellow liquid splashes against white porcelain. He shakes, stuffs, zips, and flushes before washing his hands. The ever-so-delicate sound of a zipper after he shuts off the faucet.

In two blinks he is in front of the handicapped stall with two clumped shadows stretching together across the floor, his foot lashes out at the door. Metal protests, but breaks and the door bangs open on the teenaged boy with money in his hand and the man with the backpack who quickly stuffs the gun he's holding back into the depths of the pack. "The fuck, man! What you doing?"

Noir grabs the man by the shirt and hauls him out of the stall, backhanding him across the mouth. "Gettin' here just in time, by the looks of it." He shoves him back against the row of urinals.

"The hell is wrong with y—"

Noir responds with another blow to the jaw. It spins the man around and slams his cheek against the hard metal handle of a urinal. Water cascades down, the activated drain gobbles it up. Noir slams a kick into his stomach and a gout of blood spews from the man's mouth.

He pummels poetry across the man's body, hammering staggered lines of frustration and fury into flesh, bone, and muscle.

Noir stands over him, one boot in a spatter of blood, hands seized into fists covered in crimson and cuts. The man glances past his assailant. Noir follows his eyes.

The teenaged boy looks out from the stall.

"He was helping me out, dude. I need a gun to protect myself."

"I'mma need you to bounce, lil' man." Noir glances down and to the right.

The uncertain shuffle of sneakers. "If I leave here without that g—"

"BOUNCE!

The boy complies with haste.

Noir turns just as the bleeding man on the floor swings the backpack at his head. The world shatters in shards of light and rushing gyrations as the bulky contents spark stars and agony in his skull. He sways to the side, muffled mind briefly contemplating the arms of unconscious oblivion to escape the pain. A wavering eternity passes before Noir is able to peels his eyes open.

And sees that the man has fled.

He leans against the sink, breathes and stares at his bruised and beaten reflection. Fingers curl into a bloody fist, but they do not career into the mirror like he wants them to.

More blood. But no song this time.

Not this time.


Maggie lifts her glass and smiles as Adam watches her across the table.

"What're you grinning about over there?"

He leans forward in response to his wife's question and wipes a drop of water from her mouth with the pad of his thumb, the movement sensuous and slow. "The beautiful woman on the other side of the table, of course." He rubs a finger over his thumb.

"Of course."

"This is quite an elegant restaurant." He surveys the room, golden candlelight dappling his face.

"I hadn't noticed. The way you look in that suit..." She breathes deep.

He chuckles softly and reaches across the table to take her hand. "Whatever it takes to please you."

She rolls her lips over her teeth and bites on them gently, right dimple crinkling her cheek. "So, what'd you do last night? Save any lives, or did you spend it giving directions to tourists?"

He leans back a bit, fingers still curled around hers. "I spent some time learning how to fly, which isn't very subtle when you're burning with silver flames. I did more bobbing in the air than I did soaring." He chuckles. "After that, I ministered to a man who was about to take his life; he's actually coming to church on Sunday. Then I headed over to Mercurmont and helped the police out with a nasty drug raid. They wanted me to stay and answer some questions, but..." He pinches his eyebrows up and gives a small shake of his head.

"Not sure if you're ready to go fully public?"

"I really don't. I've asked God about it, but I feel like He's telling me that I have to decide on my own. With a neighborhood as bad as Mercurmont, I think it would do both the police and the citizens good to know someone like me is out there."

His wife cradles her chin in her palm. "Did you pray to God about revealing to the church your...your transformation?"

It grabs his attention. "I didn't really have to. I felt so moved to share it that—"

She slowly takes her hand from his. "You didn't feel moved to tell me first?" The mirth evaporates from her face. "Your wife."

"Maggie, I—"

"Brother Kensie?"

Their bubble falls around their ears as a young man walks up to the table with a wide smile. "Thought that was you." He holds his hand out.

Adam stands and shakes with an immediate pleasant smile. "Brother Harold, wonderful to see you. How are you?"

"Good, good." He clasps his hands behind him as he turns to Maggie. "A blessing to see you, Sister Kensie."

She beams warmly. "Likewise."

The two men begin to chat and five minutes pass before Brother Harold bids them good night.

Adam slides down into his seat with the remnants of a shared laugh on his face. "Brother Harold should take his act on stage. Just the idea of a Christian comedian is funny enough."

Maggie sits with her legs crossed and her index fingernail rubbing at her lower lip. She looks away and sighs.

Adam sobers. "Sorry, angel, you were saying something?"

She turns her head and glares at him with glaciers glittering in her gaze.

"Nothing, Adam."

The sun sits solemn between the IBEE Bank Building and the Crown Tower, showering downtown Dominion City in shine and shadows.

Bisset steps into both as she exists in neither.

She shakes her head in an attempt to rattle the twirling ivory feathers from her vision. "Please, leave me alone." She grits her teeth. "Why won't you leave me in peace?"

"I can't, Bisset." The voice is like honey, heavy with compulsion.

"Why not?" She looks away as the man walking towards her glances at her.

"I can't leave until your quickening is complete, until your spiritual development has reached its coda." The voice pulses through her mind. "You don't know what you're capable of, Bisset Torres. I do. The power to heal, mend, and restore sparks at the tips of your fingers. All you have to do is shatter the barrier and use it."

She runs a hand through her thick brown curls. "Going to go home and swallow half the bottle of whatever Dr. Garret prescribed me. This is getting out of—"

A woman's hand pulses dark purple as she walks by. She grimaces, clutches her palm, and begins to massage it.

"—hand." Bisset pauses and watches her. An old man passes by with a slight hobble. His spine glows purple, his left leg throbbing with a sick mauve. A girl sweeps by with a rotted black core, her face pinched and her eyes distant. A Welsh Corgi trots by with a matrix of violet motes eating at his stomach.

Bisset sees them all, *feels* them all. "Why are—What is this, why are you showing me this?"

"I reveal nothing. What you see is what you allow yourself to see. The suffering, the decay. It resonates down to your marrow as if the afflictions were your own." The voice pauses. "You can heal them, Bisset. But only if you allow yourself."

She shakes her head and resumes her walk. "I don't know any of these people, so—"

"You don't have to. You're all siblings in this existence, as you are in every existence, visible and invisible."

"—why would I take them into my arms, my crazy, deluded arms, and heal them? For all I know, they don't want to be healed. Maybe they enjoy being in pain, makes them feel alive. You ever stop long enough in your divine meditations to think about that?"

Silence.

"I don't hear you responding."

The retort is gentle. "You've lost your way, you all have. Suffering is a part of the human experience, true, but unending suffering was not meant to be woven into the pattern. Your physical suffering shifts to spiritual suffering just as your spiritual suffering gnaws at your physical body. You and others like you can ease the agony."

Bisset swallows. "What are you?"

She feels the entity falter. "I...I can't remember."

Bisset snorts. "Just what I need, a malfunctioning psychosis ."

"But I do know you're not suffering from a mental disorder. People who have been set aside to do great things in the world often confuse their charge with insanity because it makes it easier to deal with. But in reality, it only corrodes the path you've been chosen to walk, causes you to hesitate and your steps to tremble."

"Causes me to slam my palms on the sides of my head to try to knock the jabbering voices out."

She accidentally bumps against someone.

"Excuse me, I'm sorry." Her forearm tingles where they touched.

The man looks at her. "It's fine." His brow furrows as he rolls his shoulder. He shows a flash of a grin. "Have a good day." He walks on.

As Bisset watches, she notices the angry purple stream flowing down his arm wash into a gentle ribbon of gold. Her arm alights with a sharp pain that melts away into her bones.

She shakes her head. "Go home, Bisset."


The air is thick with the stench of marijuana, uncurling lackadaisical fingers through his body and massaging his mind into a mellow mass.

Noir brings the joint to his lips and tokes. The tip of the roll burns like a spot of lava. He holds it. Holds it. Holds it. And—

"Mmmmmmmm." He grins as smoke tumbles from between his lips, brings his head back on the couch and watches as the TV screen explodes in a mutiny of color and sound. "Grade A dank, baby."

His apartment living room is lightly littered with the remnants of take-out, strewn jackets, fully- and half-empty beer bottles, and cigarette butts smashed out and wrinkled in the ashtray. The cramped space is sparsely decorated and somewhat well-kept. A small collection of knives sits displayed in a case in the corner.

"The fuck are you doin', you dumbass bitch?" He spreads the fingers of his upturned palm at the TV screen. "You know damn well he's in the next room." He takes another puff and watches as the man turns the corner and screams as a jagged butcher knife is stabbed into his neck. "Ooooooo." Noir cringes and smiles as an exaggerated torrent of blood gushes from the man's wound. "Toldja."

Something outside the window tears his half-lidded eyes from the screen.

On the sixth floor of the building next from him, two men are in a heated argument in a low-lit room. One is shirtless with his arms stretched out at his sides as his mouth works furiously, his face knotted with anger. The other stumbles back a step, hands clenched into fists that look as if they are aching to lash out. Noir watches them for a moment before sliding his eyes back to the screen.

"Gahdamn." He brings the joint to his face. "Just suck each other's dicks and get it over with. Shit." He winces and coughs around the next exhale.

A lit lamp slashes across the room, a comet from this distance.

Noir gets up from the couch and pads over to the window to draw the curtains closed. "Fuckin' up my high."

He pauses.

The shirtless man stalks toward the cowering man stooping to pick up the pieces of the broken lamp. His hands are at his sides and Noir can just make out the muscles in his forearm bunching. The shirtless man flexes his hand...

...and several inches long claws grow from the beds of his nails.

The burning joint almost tumbles from Noir's fingers as his mouth unhinges.

The shirtless man lifts a clawed hand in the other man's face, snarling. With his other hand, he yanks the curtains closed.

Noir's eyes dart to the newspaper on the table.

**"GENETICISTS ATTEMPT TO DISCOVER THE ORIGINS OF ALPHA-OMEGAS"**

He smirks and snatches up his boots and three blades.


Leo worms his index finger beneath the bandages to scratch at his itching hand, thinks better of it and scratches lightly at the wrapping instead. He looks around the office as his fingers work, remembering the first time he was here, when he was hired. Then again when he was promoted. And once more when he was named Employee of the Year. And—

"*Ouch.*" He looks down and sees a spot of blood. He grimaces and stops scratching.

The door opens.

"Mr. Kennington." Mrs. Acker steps in. "Good to see you." She sits down behind her desk, folds her hands, and spreads a smile across her face. "How is your, uh..." She flutters fingers at his hand.

"It's fine...fine." He clears his throat and flexes his fingers.

"Good. Well, I think you'll agree that we last parted ways on a not-so-good note, but I'm willing to overlook your little *outburst*—" Her eyebrows jump. "—and allow the past to remain where it is. I understand how difficult it must be for someone like you to—"

"Mrs. Acker, I just need to take a leave of absence, get my head and everything in it in order."

Her eyelashes flutter. "I'm glad to hear it. I'd hate to lose you and your prodigious intellect and grasp of medical biochemistry. Just know that the shorter the absence, the better." She holds her palms up. "Not to rush you or anything. You're without a dissected doubt one of our best and most valuable employees, but we've received a few solid candidate applications recently, some who have Alpha-

Omega abilities that make them exceedingly qualified for—"

"Do you care, Mrs. Acker?"

She sobers. "I'm sorry?"

"Do you care? Do you even care that one of your employees willingly stabbed himself with a pair of scissors? Do you even give a damn?" His brow wrinkles.

Her mouth works, hands fumble, eyes dart. "Mr. Kennington, I'm terrible with emotions and emotional responses, and I'm even worse with my own. I apologize if I seem callous, I'm not." She gives him a level stare. "I'd like to remind you that we have a professional psychologist on staff if you need someone to talk to, if there are problems in your life you'd like to discuss."

"I'm fine." He looks out of the window. "And what did you mean by your comment earlier? That you understand how difficult it must be for someone like me. What about me?"

The water cooler burbles gently down the hall.

"I don't know many mix—biraci—" She stretches her fingers out on the table and tries again. "I don't know of many people with your particular racial background, but as a white woman, I do know what it's like to be a minority within a majority. It's like two separate people shoved into a single body, or having to pick one label for yourself and sticking to it for the rest of your life. I realize that by saying this I may be grasping at straws in an attempt to make a connection with you. You don't have to prove anything to anyone at this comp—"

He holds up his uninjured hand. "Let me stop you before you puff yourself up too much. I know who I am and I know what I am. I'm Lebanese, I'm European, I'm Jamaican, I'm Native American, and several other races. I may be able to—to *pass* for white most of the time, but when I close my eyes at night, I know the man I am, okay? I *know* who I am. I'm a human being." He regards her. "Now, can we stop making an issue of my race so I can get my paycheck and fill out all the necessary paperwork for a leave of absence, please?"

She pushes away from the desk and walks for the glass door. Her fingers are around the handle when she pauses. "The only person making an *issue* here is you, Mr. Kennington. I'll talk to HR to see what I can do about improving the chances of them accepting your request."


Bisset nearly sucks her lungs up her throat when she flicks the light on in the darkness of her apartment. The plastic grocery sack hooked on her index finger slips off and the sound of egg shells cracking is a wet, muffled one.

Her reflection sits in the easy chair, legs crossed with an expanse of brown thigh glowing in the light beneath the jade dress. Her hair is a glossy smooth swath arranged in a tail coiled over one shoulder. Her eyes smolder golden with verdant swirls.

She gives a tug of lips. "Hello, Bisset."

"Dragoness…"

Her reflection lifts a slender finger. "*The* Dragoness. In the subliminal flesh." She slides from the chair and stalks across the room. "I hear the angel has been flapping her wings in your ear, drowning out the voice of reason." She leans against a wall with her hands behind her back. "My voice."

Bisset glances down at the smashed eggs and places the rest of the groceries on the counter before retrieving the dented carton. "You're not real."

"And neither are you."

She stuffs the bag and all in the garbage, looks at her yolk-stained fingers. "I'm about to make myself something to eat, can't take my medicine on an empty stomach." She walks to the sink and washes her hands, rubbing at them with hand soap a bit too roughly. "Will you be staying for dinner?" She goes about putting the rest of the groceries away.

"That medicine isn't going to help you, Bisset."

"It better, cost enough."

The Dragoness pushes away from the wall and glides toward her, speaking in soothing tones. "Pharmaceuticals are for the body and the mind; what you're dealing with is spiritual. You think it's an affliction, but it's not."

Bisset whirls on her, jabbing with a loaf of bread. "THEN WHAT IS IT? Please. Explain to me why you're in my head."

The Dragoness pauses. "I'm choking on the words as I say this, but Seraph is right. You've been blessed. The only problem is that she thinks you've been blessed to end all human suffering."

"And what do you think?"

The smirk is poison slicked over her mouth. "That you've been blessed to cause it."

Bisset growls and throws up her hands. She feels The Dragoness step behind her.

"It's not as nonsensical as you think. Humanity has benefited more from suffering than it cares to admit. Where do you think the expression 'that which does not kill us makes us stronger' comes from?" Her words slither sweetly. "Suffering forces you to reach deep inside of yourself for strength you didn't even know you possessed." Her voice pitches an octave lower. "Think about it. Infectious disease outbreaks, social unrest, wars, financial crises. All have forced humans to step out from their boundaries and look elsewhere for solutions, to make a connection. A human connection."

"That's insane."

Her voice scorches. "What did I just say? How many groups of people, nations, and communities have come together because of the AIDS pandemic, hm?"

Bisset listens silently, swallowing.

"Suffering is necessary. It balances the universal scales. The one thing that righteous angel neglected to share with you is that which sparkles often blinds you...to the truth."

"And what's that?"

The Dragoness cuts her eyes to the left. "The truth is that a divorce is about to take place next door."

Bisset stitches her eyebrows together as she turns around. "What?"

"Michelle and Ben have grown tired of each other; one no longer appreciates the other." She plucks an apple from the fruit bowl, examining it. "The divorce rate in America is abysmally high." Her golden-green eyes flash up at her reflection. "Maybe you should make them realize just how blessed they are to have each other." She puts down the apple, takes up an orange and tosses it at Bisset, who fumbles to catch it. "I hate apples."

Gone.

The door peels open with the same weary creak. Footsteps. Labored breathing.

Light

Noir grits his teeth and glances down at the slash marks on his stomach underneath his jacket. He limps and winces to the bathroom, flicks on the light. Carefully, he peels off the shredded t-shirt and examines the injury, studying the throbbing red lines on his face.

He turns on the faucet, releasing water and memory.

*Noir scoffed as The Shirtless Man tried to hit him for the fifth time.*

*Mouths were opened, insults and threats threaded the air. Then The Shirtless Man picked up a baseball bat.*

*Noir ducked. Another lamp was smashed.*

*He jerked back and the bat hit the wall, showering them both with flecks of plaster.*

*The Cowering Man stood shuddering near the hallway, wringing a phone in his trembling hands.*

Noir sucks in air between his teeth as alcohol trickles and stings over ripped skin.

*The Shirtless Man swung left. Missed. Right. Noir ducked and rolled left before popping back up again with a twisted smile on his face, gloved fingers twitching with sparks of anticipation.*

*He bounced his eyebrows as The Shirtless Man's face contorted in fury. He flexed fingers that seemed to harden and lengthen for a moment.*

*Noir stepped into the man's next swing, grabbed him by the wrist with one hand, and jabbed the ramrod fingertips of the other into the man's throat. The Shirtless Man's eyes went wide as his throat clogged, the bat falling from his limp hands to clatter to the floor. Wrist still in his grip, Noir wrenched it behind the man's back at a painful angle as he slinked behind him.*

Noir quivers his fingers, shaking off the wrapper and stretching a Band-Aid over a cut. Tigger's image bounces with joy on the bandage.

*The Shirtless Man rammed the back of his head into Noir's nose, slithering out of his grasp.*

Noir mumbled a retort and pressed a hand to his bleeding nose.

The Shirtless Man's hand flexed and relaxed as his mouth worked, throwing words.

Noir rubbed his bloodied fingertips together down at his side. He smiled. Then he yanked a blade from behind his back and rushed him.

Claws sprouted.

Blows were traded.

Noir carefully wraps his torso with an elastic bandage, trying his best to keep still.

Claws ripped across his arm. He blocked the next slash, but not the next or the one after.

Noir spilled the man on his ass with a leg sweep. Then he slammed the knife into a wrist, the pain cracking his opponent's mouth open, stitching his eyes shut, and shocking his body into rigid stillness for a moment.

The Shirtless Man started to struggle, but Noir yanked out another knife and buried it in the other wrist. The Shirtless Man stopped struggling and started groaning deep in the back of his throat.

The Cowering Man wailed, shuffling back in fear and stutter-stepping forward in devotion.

Noir looked up at The Cowering Man and spoke.

Noir looks at the blood spatters in the sink. Looks at the blood soaked through his t-shirt.

The Cowering Man lifted a hand to the stitches on his forehead, fingers grazing the bruise around his eye and the slight red bump on his jaw. He shook his head as his mouth worked "no."

Noir straddled The Shirtless Man's waist. He wrapped his dirty fingers around the man's throat and squeezed, wringing his hands around the other man's skin as if he wanted to sear his fingerprints into the flesh. Noir's mouth shaped the question "What are you?" He bashed the man's head into the floor with each word, fingers still clenched over his windpipe. Spittle mixed with blood flecked the air like confetti.

Noir released him and The Shirtless Man replied.

Squelch

The man's eyes flew wide. On the next exhale his heart stopped beating.

Noir yanked out the knife he had just buried in The Shirtless Man's chest and cleaned it on the corpse's pants. He looked at The Cowering Man.

*"Did you a favor."*

*He got up and looked down at The Shirtless Man's still-warm body before his own injures flared to life. He pressed his hands at the wounds scrawled on his stomach and hobbled toward the door.*

*The Cowering Man watched him go. Then he scrolled his gaze down to the dead eyes staring up at him from the floor. He looked at the yawning door as he spoke. "Thank you." He grabbed his jacket and left.*

Noir stares at his bloody palm. He raises a finger to the mirror and smears a long line of red down the surface.

*Jolting image of:* Theodore Gordon exploding in a red eruption against the bus.

*Quick flash of:* The man in the bathroom spewing blood from his mouth.

*Twitching splash of:* The Shirtless Man's gleaming claws slitting tender flesh and spilling blood.

The song returns.

**B L O O D**

Noir raises his sticky red fingers to his face, parting his spasming lips. "Blood." His tongue eases out to taste. "Blood." He looks at himself. "Blood."

He opens the medicine cabinet again, snatches a fresh insulin syringe, and quickly returns to the scene of the crime.

The body of The Shirtless Man lies cooling with his vacant eyes glassy and mouth gaping. His hands end, once more, in normal fingers.

Noir's own fingers spasm slightly as he looks down at the man he murdered. He looks over his shoulder at the gleam of light seeping through the cracked door. He swallows and turns back to the corpse.

Cooling body. Glassy eyes. Gaping mouth.

"Fuck it." He kneels down with a suppressed grimace before jabbing the needle into the jugular vein and pulling the plunger.

**B L O O D**

It fills the syringe, stuffs his head with a sanguine symphony. His tongue darts out of his mouth and he pulls the needle out of the vein.

A noise.

Someone barges into the apartment with a gun drawn,

sweeping the darkened living room.

Nothing.

Eyes settle on the corpse illuminated by the light of the full moon.

A curse slices through the air.

Like claws.


The light from inside gilds her exposed back, accentuating curves, lustrous skin, and the blood red silk of her gown. She smiles and a star is set aglow beneath her cheeks. The champagne flute softly meets her lips, and she sips. She touches elegant fingers to the gentleman's forearm. He looks at her and seems to float on air.

Giorgio watches his mother toss her head back and laugh. She'd always had a wonderful laugh. It makes him sm—No. It makes him remember that she isn't mourning her son's death. In fact, she looks to be celebrating.

"You always were full of crocodile tears, mother."

He stands in the shadows of the pine trees lining the perimeter of the mansion. His home. His childhood.

"What would you say if I walked up to you right now and embraced you? Or if I just stood there and waited for you to let me know that you missed me, that there's a gaping chasm in your heart where I used to be?" He scoffs. "Or at least a pinhole."

He watches the guests sitting out on the veranda playing cards, dancing, smoking, talking. Some linger in the shadows in hushed voices. Others stumble into the house with shimmering wine sloshing over the rims of their glasses.

Life goes on before his eyes.

"It's like a dream. Something that never happened...to me at least." His jaw clenches. "Only it did, and now I'm awake." His eyes rove left to right. "So why am I still dreaming?"

His mother finishes her drink. Her companion takes her flute, mumbles something, and breezes back inside. She stands alone in the wind, wrapping her arms around herself as her delight slowly curdles and wilts. She picks up her phone from the table next to her, glancing over her shoulder, and dials.

Giorgio silently glides closer.

The dead make no noise.

"Hi, did I...did I wake you?"

She listens.

"No, everything's fine, I was just calling to see how you were doing."

She listens. She nods.

"No, I—I haven't cried. Not one tear. Giorgio was my son, your brother, and I can't even force myself to feel grief for his passing." A beat passes. "Did I love him, Gwen? Did I love my own son? I gave birth to him, protected him, fed him...but did I forget to love him?"

She listens.

"I know, I know. It's like he wasn't even here, like I've been dreaming for almost three decades." She looks over her shoulder. "He brought this family nothing but grief, embarrassment, and shame." Her brow crinkles. "And he was still my son. Wasn't he?"

The gentleman returns with her drink.

"I've got to go, love." She tucks a curl of brown hair behind her ear. "Yes, we're still on for the spa tomorrow. Pick you up at two. Bye."

"You never called me 'love.'" His lips barely move and his expression is blank. "I hope you die next." He pushes away from the wall and stalks off. "Unerring bitch."

His mother looks at his retreating back, but doesn't seem to recognize her own son.

"West."

"Detective West?" The voice on the other end is strangled with panic. Another voice booms violently in the background.

"Yes?" West frowns and puts a hand to his opposite ear. "I can barely hear you, you're gonna have to speak up."

"This is Walter Hornst. I really hate to bother you like this, but I need your help."

Confusion. "Walter Hornst?" Recognition. "Oh, Walter Hor— What's the matter?"

"He—" *C R A S H !* "He's doing it again."

"Matthew?"

"Yes. He's throwing shit around and threatening to kill me. It's never been this bad." He sniffs. "All I did was ask him how his day was. That's all I did. I swear."

Something shatters in the background. West can hear another voice. An accent.

"Holy f—OhmyGod, someone just—Matthew. MATTHEW, NO!"

The line goes dead.

"Walter? WALTER!" West shoves the phone in his pocket and snatches up his jacket. A minute later, he is in his car.

Nine minutes later, he is pulling into The Lakes in Mercurmont.

Ten and a half minutes later, he explodes into unit F-2, his gun drawn.

Darkness.

He surveys the room...and finds Matthew's corpse on the floor in a pool of moonlight with two knives pinning his wrists to the ground and a red ruin where his heart once was.

"Shit." The curse seems to slice through the air.

Like claws.

"Walter?" He searches the apartment and finds nothing. Before he leaves, he takes a final look at the corpse. He kneels down and notices a small red mark on the man's neck. A needle's kiss.

He returns to his car to call-in the scene..

"Detective West?"

He whirls around. It's Walter.

"T-thank you for coming."

"Walter. Did you..." Eyes trail up the apartment building. "Did you do that?"

Walter shakes his head. "No. No! I didn't. I know it looks like I did, but I...There was this crazy Hispanic guy who barged in and—and started pummeling Matthew." His eyelids flutter rapidly. "Just started beating him." He looks at West. "He was so fast and...and then he...he had all of these knives and he asked Matthew what he was before he..." He glances down, then up, swallowing, trembling. "Matthew...He wasn't human."

Perry pulls out his phone. "I know, your boyfriend was an

abusive bastard." He presses 2 and then the green phone icon.

"No, that's not what I mean. He was an abusive bastard, yes, but he wasn't human."

"Dominion City Precinct, Bishop."

"He was an Alpha-Omega."

"Hello? Anyon—"

The detective gazes at Walter, thumbs the red phone icon.

"He had these claws. At first I thought they were kind of...you know, kinky. He would drag them down my back whenever we—" His mouth becomes a hard line. "Then it all got a bit too rough. Then he got changed. He got rough. And I got scared."

Perry stands in the streetlight staring at him for a second. He finally speaks. "Do you have anyone to call?"

Walter thinks a moment before shaking his head. "No one I can really depend on."

Perry looks away and sighs. "Get in the car."


Bisset rifles through her mail as she walks back to her apartment.

Bill.

An invitation to reclaim her happiness at the Johnson Family Boundless Joy Clinic.

Junk mail.

A postcard from a friend vacationing in Sao Paulo.

A crying neighbor coming down the stairs and blocking her path.

"Michelle, hi." She notices her expression. "What's wrong?"

"Oh, it's Sophie. We couldn't find her this morning. I looked all over the apartment in her favorite hiding spots. She's such a little dog, you know?" The woman inhales deeply through her mouth. "I had to go to work and...and Ben had the day off. He said that he was going to keep looking for her. Anyway, I was walking under our balcony...and...and..." Her eyes overflow with tears. "And there she was in the street." She squeezes her eyes shut. "Her neck was—and her little paws...and her eyes were just—Oh, God, Bisset." She fills the other woman's arms.

Bisset holds her awkwardly. "I'm sorry, Michelle, I know how much you loved Sophie."

"She's been my little baby ever since I found out I can't have children." She takes her head from Bisset's shoulders. "Next week would have been her birthday, you know?" She heaves a deep sigh. "I just can't figure out how she got out onto the balcony. Or how she..." She flicks fingers.

Bisset nods.

Michelle blinks tears from her eyes. "But, you know, it's a little odd. When we found out, Ben was so supportive." Her eyebrows bounce and she shrugs. "It's been just like it was when we first got married. He's attentive, he listens, comforts me." She sniffs. "He even ripped up the divorce papers. I just hate it that it took something like this for me to realize that I still love him." She looks at Bisset. "God works in some pretty strange ways, you know? I couldn't imagine going through this without him."

Bisset smiles slightly. "He does, he does." She rubs her shoulder.

Michelle waves a hand at her. "I shouldn't be bothering you with all of this. I'm sure a pretty young woman like you has better things to do than listen to some old broad mope about her pet."

"Oh, no, no, it's fine. What are neighbors for?"

The older woman grins at her as she wipes away a lingering tear. "You're a sweet one, Bisset."

"I'm glad to hear that you and Ben are working out your differences."

"A good thing, too. One more minute of his asshole routine and it would have been him that went over that balcony, you know?" She reveals a small smile and a brief laugh around the lingering tears.

Bisset watches her walk away for a moment before heading into her apartment.

The last ray of the sunlight sloughs down over the horizon.

The Dragoness manifests across from her.

Bisset's eyes roll to the ragged chew toy on the floor.

The Dragoness gives a wicked smile, one at odds with Bisset's uncertain expression.

Noir waggles the syringe in his face.

He lays stretched out on the couch with one hand behind his head. He sets the syringe on the table and takes up the carton of cigarettes, tapping one out. He reaches for the lighter and flicks it before touching eager flame to the tip of the cylinder.

He inhales.

He exhales.

Smoke syrups thick through the air along with the hoarse opening verse of Deftones' "Change" playing on the stereo.

He eyes the syringe and moves the cig to one side of his mouth as smoke dribbles from his lips, fluttering on the air like the wings of a nicotine butterfly.

He takes up the lighter.

*Flick*

Flame.

*Flick*

Flame.

*Flick*

Life.

*Flick*

Life.

*Flick*

Blood.

Noir tosses the lighter on the table and picks up the syringe. Gently. He runs the cold needle down his bare chest, taps it against his sternum. He touches the tip of the needle to his index finger, presses and stops.

He takes a drag.

He gets up and goes to the window to pull the curtain back. The scene of the crime is dark and docile. The needle taps against the window.

*Jolting image of:* Theodore Gordon exploding in a red eruption against the bus.

*Quick flash of:* The man in the bathroom spewing blood from his mouth.

*Twitching splash of:* Matthew's gleaming claws slitting tender flesh and spilling blood.

Two songs roll through his ears. One slides through his veins and the other resounds in his skull. He becomes enthralled.

Noir looks down and finds the needle gnawing into a vein in the crook of his arm. He presses the plunger. The borrowed blood dances, unravels, and vibrates in his veins.

His head is knocked back and his eyes peel wide.

Then the blood burns. And burns and burns and burns.

There is acid in his veins. Hot, biting, freezing, gnashing, poisonous acid.

His body seizes with near lethal ecstasy. As he tumbles from the couch, he notices the curtains billowing outward, the smoke from his cigarette forming constellations in the air, his vision gravitating to a black void.

His body hits the floor and does not move. The cigarette rolls from his lips, still smoldering.

Changed.

# Excerpt from Lamar Koehler Live:

"Good evening. I hope you're all doing well tonight. Thank you for joining me on another episode of Lamar Koehler Live. I'm your host, Lamar Koehler.

"I'm joined tonight by a very brave man whose name many of you may recognize from the tabloids, the press, and television. He's a man who has received death threats, attempts on his life, public ridicule, and scorn wherever he goes, and yet he's also a man who is deeply apologetic for what he's done. Ladies and gentleman, I'm joined tonight by Sean Pierce. Thank you very much for joining me, Sean."

"Thank you for having me, Lamar. Not many TV personalities would."

"I'm sure I don't have to tell you that I'm not most TV personalities. Now, I was going to inform our viewers of who you are, but you've just decided to do that for yourself, instead."

"Yes, I thought it would be better if it came from me."

"So tell us who you are."

"I'm Sean Pierce, I'm thirty-eight...and...I...I'm, uh...I'm responsible for hospitalizing thirty-two people and taking the lives of twenty-three. I'm also an Alpha-Omega."

"How did all of this happen, Sean?"

"Well, I was at my high school reunion when my A-O gene activated. I was feeling fine beforehand, had a few drinks in me and was catching up with my classmates. Uh, the next thing I knew it felt like a star had exploded in my head. At first, I thought Brian Massey, our class clown, had spiked the punch, but it...it didn't feel right. I started getting dizzy and felt as if every inch of my skin had suddenly gone numb. It was like I was on fire while freezing; strangest sensation in the world. I must have blacked out, because the next thing I knew I was waking up in the hospital with my best friend beside me with this odd expression on his face. It was a mix of relief, fear, grief, and—and something else. And, ah, then he told me."

"What did he tell you?"

"He told me that twenty-three of my classmates were dead and that thirty-two were in the same hospital as me. Then he told me that doctors thought I was the cause, and that...that my wife had been one of the casualties. He told me that I had killed the love of my life."

"How were you responsible for all of that?"

"With the strange circumstances of my case, the hospital's A-O specialist took a look at me. Every state is now required to have at least three A-O specialists scattered throughout. Ah, they were able to determine that the punch I drank had been spiked and that the drug caused an allergic reaction that caused my A-O gene to activate. They told me I released a violent bio-electric pulse that essentially shut down the bodies of those closest to me and put anyone else in a fifteen-foot radius into a coma."

"How did you feel when you heard this?"

"I thought it was a prank at first, but then I looked in the doctor's eyes, looked at my friend's expression, and saw that they weren't joking...I had killed all of those people."

"What happened next?"

"I felt like someone had yanked out my stomach. I mean, I didn't feel any different, I still felt like me. The doctor told me that as long as I stayed away from certain medications, there's a good chance my powers won't flare up again. After that, a woman came by and introduced herself as Shelly Pirkle...Then she told me that I had killed her sister."

"Awful."

"You can't imagine. She looked at me with so much hatred in her eyes, called me names, threw her sister's picture at me, screamed. She flung herself at me before she was restrained, but I didn't want them to restrain her. I wanted her to hit me, slap me, spit on me, anything to...to replace the dead feeling I had."

"Did anyone press charges?"

"Most of the families of the deceased did, but the courts said that legally there was nothing they could do. I had murdered people, it was involuntary manslaughter, but it was something beyond my control, there was no precedent."

"Did anyone try to make a precedent?"

"Plenty of people tried, but nothing held up. Alpha-Omegas have been around for a while, but legislators are just now starting to devise laws specifically for us. The problem is, all the proposals restrict our liberties as humans in some way. The laws they are trying to pass basically state that every single Alpha-Omega man, woman, and child with a harmful and uncontrollable ability should be rounded up and kept away from non-powered humans."

"And what do you think of that?"

"I think that there should most definitely be, if not laws, than at least some type of regulations, uh, boundaries or something applied to A-Os like me with fatal powers, there're going to have to be. There should also be early signs of detection for children to determine if there's an increased chance of their A-O gene activating and when."

"I hear they're already working on that."

"They are, but many of the procedures are expensive, and none of them are harmless. They're trying to make it so that each and every child born in the U.S., and eventually the world, will be tested to see how strong their A-O gene could be if it were to ever activate."

"Our world has changed so much in the last few decades, and I have a feeling it's going to change a lot more in the years to come. Now, Sean, I don't want to demean what you've done, but I also don't want to shovel a pile of guilt on you that I already see on your face. How are you making amends with what you've done?"

"...I, uh, I've gone to the families of those affected by my genetic outburst and apologized. Some of them have been understanding, but more than most of them have threatened to kill me, and I'm sure those threats would turn into more if they weren't afraid that what happened at my reunion would happen again. I've made several trips to the doctor to ensure myself that my, uh, my ability remains dormant, and I've even tried to see if there was any way that they could...get it out of me.

"There's so much speculation, ignorance, and...and hype surrounding Alpha-Omegas, and the truth is that all of us are scared. We're scared **BLEEP**. And I'm sure some of the people watching this program are scared, too. In the past, we mostly knew where we stood as human beings, as children, as adults, as the middle class, the homeless, whatever. We knew who and what we were, we had agency. But nowadays, there's even more to consider when it comes to our individual identity, and not all of it is under our control or within the parameters of our desires, our will. We don't know if we're going to wake up tomorrow on fire and not burning, if one day while in the shower we notice our body hair is razor sharp. We don't know. It's scary, Lamar."

"I could wake up tomorrow as an Alpha-Omega."

"Exactly. There isn't a day that goes by that I'm not reminded that not only did I kill the woman who shares my soul, I killed twenty-two other people, I ended twenty-two relationships, ended twenty-two lives. That's on me. I didn't mean to do it, but that doesn't change a damn thing. I've actually even tried to get them to throw me in prison, to put me on death row. My friend told me that that was the coward's way out. He said that if I died, then I wouldn't have to feel grief anymore, that if I were in jail, I wouldn't have to see the lives I had destroyed, the lines I had erased. Being free should be punishment enough, he said."

"And do you agree?"

"I do now...I do now. It's astounding that he's stood by me this long, and I'm very, very thankful that he has. It reminds me that there's still...something in this world. Compassion, kindness, understanding. Whatever it is, it still exists."

"I'm very glad you've found a degree of solace, Sean. I honestly don't know what I would say to you if one of my loved ones had been killed during that incident."

"I think you do, Lamar, I think you do. It's okay to want to see me dead. It's a human reaction, it's natural. Just because you have millions of viewers doesn't make you any less human than they are...doesn't make you *any less human than I am."*

"That interview took place earlier this year on the fifteenth of March. After Sean left, I asked myself if what he had said was true, that it was okay if I wanted to see him dead. Truthfully, I still haven't come up with a sensible answer.

"Sean Pierce, unfortunately, took his own life early this morning. He was found in his home in Portland with a self-inflicted gunshot wound to the head and twenty-three letters of apology, including one to his wife, Emma.

"I'm Lamar Koehler, and I hope you'll join me next week when I sit down with the First Lady, Janelle Dial. Good night, America."

## FADE OUT

# EPISODE THREE: *VICTIMS OF THE EUREKA TIMEBOMB*

*LEO*

**HE** opens his eyes and squints at the clock.

7 AM. He should be up and getting ready for work right now.

He rolls his eyes to the sun swelling behind the curtains, listens to the sounds of traffic rolling past his window. A horn honks, tires squeal, brakes protest, and someone shuffles by on the sidewalk outside, dragging feet.

He rolls his eyes back at the clock.

7:01 AM. He should be in the shower with Francie right now.

His eyes drift closed and the world goes black for a single moment. He opens his eyes again and sees that twenty more minutes have passed. The steady stream of water is suddenly shut off and he hears the bathroom door open. Feet pad across the carpet and he feels the bed dip on the other side.

He breathes in Francie's smell and listens to her towel her hair dry.

Motionless.

The mattress shifts.

"Leo." She waits. "Leo, I know you're awake."

"Morning." He scratches his arm.

She looks over a bare shoulder at him. "You going to tell me why you suddenly quit your second love, or am I going to have to wait two more days?" She goes back to drying her kinky locks.

"I didn't quit, Francie, I'm on a leave of absence."

A dresser drawer opens. "I'm really trying to be understanding right now, give you your space." The drawer slides shut. "But this left in the dark thing is testing my patience, Leo. You come in and tell me that you quit without any explanation whatsoever and I'm supposed to just sit here and accept it. You know I trust you, baby, but you've got to give me something to work with." The scent of shea butter clings to the air. "You aren't—" She cuts herself off, steels herself before continuing. "Are you having suicidal thoughts again?"

Leo remains silent on the other side of the bed. He sniffs and shifts his legs beneath the sheets, motions fused with an undercurrent of tension. "Trying my best to keep the dark thoughts at bay." The words are barely audible.

The warmth of Francie's hand on his back is like a kiss of sunshine. "Leo, I know I've said it before, and I'll keep saying it until the day I die, but I want you to come talk to me if it ever gets to be too much. Please." She wraps her arms around him, squeezes. "Or at least talk to someone else, if not me. I don't want to lose my king or have him drowning in sorrow."

He turns his head to look her in the eye. "I promise." He kisses her. "My queen."

Ten minutes later after Francie finishes getting dressed, she kneels down in front of him with her generous afro swaying and parted on either side.

He stares at her.

She takes his hand, kisses it. "Do not sit in this apartment all day, Leo. Your brooding, your pondering, your soul searching, your whatever-it-is-that-you-do-to cope, do it outside in the fresh air, clear your head. You sit in this apartment for one more day and I'll burn it down with you in it, I swear I will. We haven't filed a claim on our renters insurance yet."

It makes him grin.

"There's my shining star." She kisses him on the mouth. "We can cook dinner together when I get home."

Francie stands up and washes the air in her sweet perfume. She slips out of his sight and he listens as she grabs her keys and bag before shutting the door behind her.

Leo looks around the room as if noticing it for the first time. He sits up, brown sheets sliding down his naked chest, and braces his elbows on the mattress. He yawns and stretches.

Then he plops his head back down on the pillow and sleeps until noon.

The keys slide from Leo's hand onto the table by the door. He pushes the door shut and slips out of his jacket. He checks the phone. No messages. He flips through the mail. Nothing new.

"Want one?"

He jerks so hard he nearly dislocates his shoulder. "Motherf—" He lets out a panicked breath and takes a calming one as his heart chisels Morse code into his sternum. He turns and finds his beloved on a stool with a bottle of beer in hand. "Francie, what are you doing home?"

She laughs and brings the beer bottle to her lips. "Well, welcome home to you, too. Boss lady had her baby shower today. Told them I was going down to my car for the Diaper Genie." A shrug. "Didn't go back up. Hope someone else got her one."

"The way you scared me I'm gonna need a Diaper Genie for

myself." He hands over her mail. "I'll get started on dinner."

She hops off of the stool. "I'll help."

"Baby, I can do it." He cracks open the refrigerator.

She arches a brow and puts a hand on a well-rounded hip. "I know you can do it, Leo. Just let me help." They stare at each other for a while.

Leo finally steps away from the fridge, leaving the door open, and goes to the cabinets to retrieve two pots and a pan. "There're chicken breasts defrosting in the sink; you're better at seasoning than I am."

"Damn right I am." She shuts the door with her hip and a laugh. "Last time I let you season the vegetables I thought I was going to—"

"I'll tell you what happened."

She stands with an onion in a plastic bag and a Styrofoam carton of mushrooms in hand. She puts them on the counter and unwraps the mushrooms. "I'm listening."

He sighs. "I don't know how to say this, Francie."

"Then just say it." She glances at his bandaged hand as she grabs a knife and cutting board and starts slicing mushrooms.

"A few weeks ago I was looking at a sample of my blood. I've been feeling sick lately, but not in my...not in my body." He pauses before running water in the pot. "But I found something that didn't...*doesn't* belong there." Leo looks in Francie's eyes. Thoughts eddy across their surface.

"Leo, do you—" She breathes for a moment. "Do you have can—?"

"Nonono, it's not that." He looks away. "Or maybe it is. I don't know." A scoff. "I'm a biochemist and I have no idea of what this is in my blood. But I do know what others think it is."

He grabs his phone, unlocks, swipes, taps, and hands it to her.

**"GENETICISTS ATTEMPT TO DISCOVER THE ORIGINS OF ALPHA-OMEGAS"**

Francie shakes her head, brow frowning. Then her lips part a bit as it becomes clear. She looks at him. "You're telling me you think you're an Alpha-Omega?"

In response, he sets the pot on the stove and fans his fingers open, skin stretching tight. A small globe of silver-blue force flashes for a full three seconds over his palm before dissipating.

Francie's mouth falls open.

"I can't control it yet. From what I can tell, it's fundamentally a solid force that I can emit from any part of my body."

"Like a force field?"

"Yeah." A smile twitches at the edge of his mouth. "Like a force field. I was afraid to tell you because I...thought that you would—"

His next words are smashed between a kiss that washes away the slight trembling in his body.

"If you think something like this is going to make me reject you, Leo Kennington, then maybe you don't know the woman you fell in love with." The raw relief she sees in his expression makes her reach up to touch his face.

He kisses her palm, hands around her waist. "Thank you, baby." He enfolds himself in her arms, chin resting on her shoulder for a moment before slowly pulling away from her.

"But I still don't understand why you're taking time off." She watches him lean against the counter watching the water begin to boil.

"I can't control this...this *burden* yet. Flare ups at—" He feels the flesh of his right hand shivering smaller. A globulous glaze of energy coats his hand down to his forearm before sizzling out into the air and evaporating like steam inches from his skin. Leo shakes his hand out, massaging his palm. "*That* keeps me from doing my job, makes it dangerous for me to be in the lab. Might as well come to work sick." He studies the slow-boiling excitement of the water in the pot. "It was either take some time off and try to learn to control this or put myself, other people, and our medical research at risk. But..." He makes a fist, kneads it against the counter. "But working in the lab was my anchor, kept me rooted. Since I saw my active A-O gene, I can feel my old demons breaking through the walls I put up around them." He squeezes his eyes shut for a moment. "The joy and excitement of work gave me something to focus on, kept the lights on up here." He taps a finger at his temple.

"Leo." Francie rubs his arms, her face drawn.

"Francie, I don't know where I am. I've been lost for twenty-eight years and I didn't even know it." He tilts his head back and squeezes his eyes shut. "I...I can't control my emotions, my reactions, and now I can't even control my body." He holds his arms out. "It feels like someone's run off with me."

Francie frames his face in her hands. "You are magnificently blessed, Leo. You're not lost, you're just turned around. I'll be your map." She takes his hands in hers. "I'll guide you back to yourself." She puts her head on his shoulder. "I've heard of a place in Mercurmont you can go where there are others like you, a kind of support group. It's called—"


Light of the Sun & the Moon. *An outreach for the genetically reawakened and those touched by their light. Be welcome.* Leo shakes his head as he reads the sign and walks into the gymnasium. "Francie, where the hell did you send me?" He mumbles the words to no one.

Minutes later he is in a circle created by smiling/ unsure/ worried/ grim/ open/ empty/ uncomfortable faces. A short man stands up and walks to the middle of the gathering, pushing up his glasses with an index finger before speaking. "Hope everyone's doin' all right today. For those of you that are joinin' us for the first time, welcome to Light of the Sun & the Moon. This is a safe place where Alpha-Omegas can come when they're feelin' afraid, confused, or just unsure about who and what they are. But this isn't a group exclusive to A-Os, it's also for the family and friends of A-Os and for anyone who just wants to be educated about people like us." A pause and a good-natured smile. "Yes, I know it may come as a shock to some, but we are still people. Hell, some days I ask that same question about you non-powered folks."

A wave of laughter.

"Now, let's get started, I'll go first. My name is Marlon, and I'm an Alpha-Omega."

Leo sits back and listens. Forty minutes later, a woman named Vanessa finishes speaking and takes her seat, and Leo feels the weight of Marlon's eyes on him. "See some new faces joinin' us today." He offers Leo a friendly pull of lips. "Care to say anything?"

Leo stands, hesitation making his motions jerky. "Hi," he clears his throat, "my name's Leo." He gives them a smile that he doesn't feel. "I found out a few weeks ago that I'm different. I was— *am* a biochemist." A nostalgic smirk splits his face. "I had big plans for myself, big plans for my future." He looks down at the tiled floor, eyes slowly tracing the cracks in the pattern. "But all of that started to change before I realized it when I studied a sample of my blood and found this...this anomaly in my genes. Felt like it was looking up at me and laughing because it knew that all of my carefully laid out plans had just been shot to hell." He looks at the circle of faces with a numb expression. "It's just—" He takes a deep breath and starts again. "It's the idea that a single gene, something that can't even be seen with the naked eye, is keeping me from being who and what I want to be. It's confused me about...about *what* I am. Our genes are what make us who we are physically, and, in some cases, they're who we are mentally. I feel like I've been betrayed by myself, my own body, and that's hard to convey even to my girlfriend." He finally lifts his head. "I hate myself for being an Alpha-Omega."

His words resound. Silence reigns.

Some look away, others stare at him while a few shake their heads in shame.

Leo takes his seat and listens to more stories of people like him, people whose abilities have made their lives better, made them outcasts to their friends and family, made them subjects of public ridicule, or haven't changed their lives at all.

When everyone has said their piece, Marlon speaks up. "I just wanna say somethin' to Leo." Leo looks up. "Ain't nobody here who can argue that havin' an active A-O gene is easy, a'ight? It can fuck up our lives as easily as the wind blows. But you gotta remember that this is your gene, your body. It's like your arms, legs, or feet. They're yours, what you were born wit. Now you can sit ova there and wallow in self-pity and self-hate, or you can pick yourself up and overcome what you see as a curse and make it into a blessin'.

"My gene allows me to make sparks, something about ampin' up the natural electric current in my body. I can't do anythin' cool like conduct electricity just—" He lifts his hand and several sparks snap in the air above his open palm. "—that. It's pretty useless as far as powers go; I'm always blowin' out light bulbs. Don't expect me to be kickin' bad guy ass anytime soon. But being an Alpha-Omega ain't no different from bein' black, Jewish, gay, mentally disabled, or, hell, poor. There's always someone else like you in the world, you just gotta look hard enough." He pauses. "We'd love for you to come back again, Leo, we wanna support you. But we also can't have you here if you've already decided yourself a quitter." Another pull of lips that loosely resembles a smile.

Leo nods.

After the meeting is over, he hurries for the door, taking a deep breath once he's outside. He's down the stairs and walking down Sherman Street when he notices the person next to him.

"Pretty intense group, huh?" The woman says to him. She pulls her black hair back into a ponytail.

"'S all right I guess."

She stops and holds out a hand, beaming. "My name's Emma."

"Leo." They shake.

"Yeah, I remember." She tilts her head back at the gym.

He slides his hands in his pockets. "I'm sure everyone remembers me." He looks out at the boarded up storefronts across the street. "Narcissus' wayward brother."

Her eyes narrow a bit. "I don't think any of them expected someone like you to show up. I've been coming for about a month, my sister's an A-O, and so far, everyone in that room is either proud, unsure of what they're becoming, or driving themselves crazy worrying about what's going on inside of their bodies." She shakes her head. "They think they've got it so hard, they should try being a woman on her period and *then* come back to a meeting."

Leo smiles.

"She wouldn't tell me, but when my sister first found out, I think she felt the same as you."

"She ever get over it?"

Emma juts out her bottom lip a bit. "I believe that she has. She just...she glows now, and not because of her ability. So I understand how you feel, Leo, but at the same time I have to agree with Marlon. People come to these meetings for support. They want to be helped and they want the truth, but they want it on their terms.

Not saying this to make you feel bad." She lifts a shoulder. "I just think it's better this way."

He nods.

"Take care of yourself." Emma pats his arm before walking in the opposite direction.

He watches her for a moment, contemplating. Then he turns and walks away, crossing Belaire and Chambers when he notices the small crowd gathered in the parking lot of The Lakes. Police cars are scattered behind the gates as officers cordon off the area and CSI units enter and exit the building with cameras, satchels, and small forensics kits.

A news reporter stands just in front of the gate.

"—was reported a few hours ago. Authorities have yet to render a statement, but what we do know is that the victim was found with knives embedded through both wrists and a single stab wound to the heart.

"Neighbors report that they heard arguing from unit F-2 a couple of nights ago around nine and sounds of violent fighting soon after. We'll keep you updated as information becomes available. I'm Carmen Alexander with DCBN News. Back to you, Sam."

It all looks small and insignificant and foolish from up here.

Nothing is real.

Leo sits with his thighs to his chest and his arms wrapped around his knees as a chilled bottle of beer dangles between his index finger and thumb. The sun is setting to his right and from here, downtown Dominion City looks like nothing more than steel and glass and concrete gilded in sunlight. Evening traffic trickles down Lynord Street. Bone-rattling *thumpa-thumpa* bass from a white Humvee blasts down the avenues of Cade District, booming up from below as the local glitterati walk down the pristine streets. He looks to the east towards Oswyn, home of Dominion University and Sankosha Stadium.

"Tell me why I've never come up here before." Leo turns and looks at the man beside him reclining in the small hammock set up on the large patio.

"You mean Cade District?" The bottle finds its way to the man's lips.

"No, I mean your apartment. This view is spectacular."

"Come out here almost every day and sometimes my mind still doesn't believe my eyes. Don't think it ever really will." A pause. "Just like I don't think I'll ever get used to you not coming into the lab every day."

"Paul, I told you—"

"I know, I know. You had your reasons, reasons that you think you can't tell me...your friend."

"Everything's gotten complicated." Leo sighs. "All this mess just hit me like a bolt of lightning from a blue sky." He swigs beer. "Funny thing is, I actually miss that place. Walked into that lab almost every day for the past three years and didn't think squat of it. Been gone for only two days and it's the only thing on my mind."

"If I believed in that sort of thing, I would call that a sign." Paul tips his bottle at him. "And if I wasn't your friend, I'd let that flowing stream of bullshit you fed me just trickle on by."

Leo gives him a look. "What? You think I got fired or—"

"Oh, I know you didn't get fired. Not only would Acker have to be a bitch, she'd have to be a crazy-ass bitch to let someone like you go without a fight." A smirk. "I *still* don't know how you developed the Triple A-13 formula last year."

The muscles in Leo's jaw pulse as he takes a final swig of his beer, casting his gaze towards the sunset.

Setting sunlight glares off glass.

"You still getting depressed like you used to?" The bottle cap makes a sharp *sschik* as Paul pops it off. "Might wanna think about getting some help if you are." The wind launches over the patio. "Maybe a prescription, one you helped create."

"Not really the kind of help I need right now." Leo swallows and glances at his friend.

"How's Francie feel about all of this? Sure your mahogany queen can't be too happy about having to support both of you until you're back in the centrifuge saddle. But she's been with her company for what, one and a half years? Sure she should be up for a raise some—"

"Francie and I will be fine." The words are low and loaded. "I've got plenty of money in the bank. I wouldn't put her in that position."

Paul sips and stares and sits quietly. He clears his throat, scratches at his head, but keeps silent. A full minute passes before he speaks. "I wasn't suggesting that you can't take care of her, or that you can't take care of you; was just asking a question. You don't have to blow things up and make an issue out of nothing." He gets up and goes inside. "Gotta break the seal."

It triggers a memory: *The only person making an issue here is you, Mr. Kennington.*


That night, Leo has a surprise dinner with his parents at The LiveWell Bistro.

"How long are you in town for?"

His mother swallows a sip of water and sets the glass on the table. "Oh, just for a few days. Couldn't go flying off to Tahiti without checking in on our baby." She reaches over and pats her son's hand.

"Come on now, Grace, he's twenty-eight years old, he's not a baby." His father gives her a weak scowl. He looks at his son. "Do you think you can do some kind of experiment to see why mothers insist on referring to their children as babies even when they've been out of diapers for years?"

"That's the way of a mother's heart, Robert." She rolls her eyes good-naturedly. "Where's Francie?"

"She's working late tonight; she sends her love." Leo looks down at the tablecloth, partially concealing his expression.

His mother waves a dismissive hand through the air. "My Lord, you young people work too hard. No wonder you're starting to go gray so early. Francie is gorgeous enough as is without having unsightly wrinkles on her face."

They pause as the waiter comes by to take their orders.

"So how is work...*baby*?" His mother's face brightens at her quip.

Leo runs the tip of his finger across the tongs of his fork. "I, uh…" He scratches above his upper lip. "I decided to take some time off."

The forkful of salad wavers at his father's mouth. "Son, is everything okay?"

"Yeah, dad, I'm just—just figuring some things out."

He instantly recognizes the expression on his son's face, the one that says he'll say more when he's done solving the mental equation scrawled on the whiteboard of his brain, the one he wore often when he was younger. "Oh, well…Your finances okay while you're figuring things out?" Another thought bolts across his face. "Are they going to save your position while you're—"

"Robert, please. You can see he's distraught enough as is. No need to overwhelm him." His mother places a hand on his wrist. "Don't hesitate to let me know if you need anything. Anything at all." She gives him a reassuring nod. "And that includes a financial boost. Our investments have been doing better than we expected."

Their son's smile is wan at the edges. "I'll let you know, mom. But thank you."

The waiter breezes by to refill their water and wine glasses.

"Good to see we didn't raise a son who lets his pride get him in over his head." Robert winks at Leo.

Leo looks at the two of them on the other side of the table. His brown-skinned mother and his fair-skinned father. His parents. His creators. His blood.

"Yeah, you raised me well." He hesitates with parted lips. "You also raised me to be weak."

His father's mouth wrinkles. "What?"

"I'm probably about to say something that I'll hate myself for later, or maybe I won't. Maybe it's just the thing to make me feel better. Either way, I'm saying it: your son is weak, and it's your fault." He rests a forearm on the table.

"Leo, why—"

"You put me in a box when I was growing up. I didn't live a real life, I lived in a—in a fantasy. I was some sheltered child actor in a play. You told me who I was, where I came from, but you didn't let me hear who or what everyone else thought I was. You didn't show your child the real world even though you knew, you *knew*, that I would have to step out into it."

"Son, you don't need anyone to tell you who you are. Your heritage, your family, your color..." His father cuts a hand through the air. "That definitely molds you into who you're going to be, but it doesn't lock you into who you're going to be." He jabs a finger at his son. "You write your own damn story. You're our son, we love you." His father shakes his head. "We never lied or hid the truth from you."

"But you never exposed me to it either! Heritage, family, color—" He slaps at his chest twice. "All of that is in my genes...along with something else that doesn't belong there. I—I—I don't know what I'm supposed to say or what I'm supposed to do when someone makes a wayward comment when I tell them I'm bi-racial. I blow up every time someone make a harmless joke because I think that's what I'm supposed to do, get defensive, stand strong for myself. And the reason for that is because I spent my childhood looking through a pretty window. I wasn't part of the real world."

His mother's confusion leaks through the pain on her face. "Why would you want to be?"

"BECAUSE IT WOULD HAVE GIVEN ME CONTROL!" He slams a fist on the table, toppling glasses of water and wine as he stands, skin humming and itching with the awakening power of his A-O gene swelling just underneath. "Because it would have made me strong! I feel like a damn idiot yanking out my guts in front of a circle of strangers, telling them how much I hate myself, hate what's inside of me. If I had learned how to process all this as a child, maybe I wouldn't be feeling so *fucked up* right now!"

His mother looks up at him, ignoring the restaurant of stillness and stares. "Sit down, Leo." He remains standing. "Leo, please sit down." He slowly sits. She looks at him. "You are casting stones at the wrong people. Everything your father and I did in raising you we did because we love you. Is that wrong?"

"Yes."

"Every parent does the best they can when raising a child. You can read every book, every pamphlet, every manual there is on parenting and you still won't be prepared for the life you bring into this world. Every word you read is obsolete the moment that child is born. We didn't raise you around the ugliness out there—" She jabs a finger at a near window "—because we didn't want it to poison you." She blinks. "But somehow, it has."

Someone slurps their water.

A muscle in Leo's cheek twitches along with a corner of his lip. A tear glimmers in his eye. He stands up. "It's not the ugliness that's poisoning me." He walks out of the restaurant.

Outside he stalks down the nearest alley, ignoring the stench of rotting garbage as he rakes his fingers over his scalp, trying to scratch away his frustration. He mutters incoherently to himself as he paces back and forth. He crosses his arms over his chest, spinning right on his heel. He uncrosses his arms, spinning left on his heel.

His blood thrums, flares, rushes, and blazes in his veins.

Along with his A-O gene.

His skin tightens and he welcomes it. The world goes silent and he welcomes it. A dome of silver-blue wavers into the air and solidifies around him. And he welcomes it.

He opens his mouth and releases a savage scream that scours his throat raw.

*His mother teaching him about Dr. Martin Luther King and his message. Reciting to him the poetry of Claude McKay and Nikki Giovanni.*

*His parents interlacing their fingers, showing Leo that his skin is their skin and their skin is his skin.*

*Leo looking out at the playground for classmates who look like him and finding none.*

*Leo playing with his classmates with a child's joy, a child's purity, a child's benign ignorance.*

*Leo crying in his mother's arms after Harold Gunter pushed him off of the monkey bars and fractured his wrist after calling him a nigger cracker.*

*Leo studying his reflection.*

*A portrait of Leo beaming and sitting between his parents, looking like both of them and neither of them.*

The furious force field explodes omnidirectional with his voice, shattering the window pane behind him and slamming into the solid wall in front of him, smashing several bricks in a jagged imprint as a backwash of wind tears at the air.

Leo studies the destruction he has wrought, chest heaving.

His tongue darts out to lick his lips and his breathing returns to normal. He looks to either end of the alley and sees no one. He deflates down to his knees and rests his palms on his thighs, utterly empty. And he welcomes it.

## PERRY

"So you know exactly who killed Matthew Maddrox McCain?" The blonde woman across from Perry looks up from where she sits with her elbow braced on the desk, fingertips pressed to her temple holding back her disbelief. "And the boyfriend, who sounds more like another victim in all this, is staying with you?"

Perry rocks forth and back in his chair. "I know *inexactly* who killed McCain, Jill. All Walter said is that it's a Hispanic male."

Detective Jill Torv rifles through the stack of papers neatly stacked on her desk. "Well, whoever he is, it might not be the first time he killed someone." She consults a sheet, eyes roving. "We weren't able to lift any prints from the knives in McCain's wrists or heart. And while forensics was able to find a blood sample other than McCain's, it's...wrong."

Perry stops rocking. "What do they mean wrong?"

Jill eyes resume roving. "There's no specific blood type, it's continuously shifting. According to the analysis, it may have to do with some type of enzyme." She looks up at him. "Might be an A-O."

"A-O on A-O violence?"

She opens an empty hand. "Very well might be."

Perry rubs at his bottom lip with his index finger. "Gahdammit. Somethin' else to add to the pile."

The other detective interlaces her fingers and rests them on her stomach as he leans back in her manager chair. "You know, honestly, I'm almost tempted to throw this case to the bottom rung. I mean, from what you tell me about about Matthew and Walter, it almost, *almost*, seems as though Matthew got what he deserved for being an abusive asshole."

Perry starts to spark off a retort. Jill holds up a hand to fizzle his words.

"But he was murdered in his own home when he only deserved to have his ass handed to him on several different platters." She leans forward. "Which means we need to catch a potential vigilante with an ever shifting blood type and hope that we don't get our asses handed to us in several different caskets."

They get to work.


Perry stops in the doorway. He's come home to find his apartment clean and pristine and smelling of sage and citrus. The setting sun slices through the open window in warm shafts that seem to make the place glow.

He set his keys on the dust-free table next to the door and goes to the closet to put his jacket away, noting the vacuum tracks along the carpet and the fading scent of jasmine. The kitchen counters nearly blind him with their sparkle, and he finds that the colors of his dish rag, towel, and pot holders now match.

"What do you think?"

He turns to see Walter folding a bath towel with a pleased little smile on his face, brown eyes aglitter behind his lenses.

"This isn't my apartment."

"Hope you don't mind." Walter puts the towel in the hall closet. "I made a list of how and where everything was if you don't like it."

Perry runs his fingers against the marble countertop. "It's fine. Nice, in fact." He looks at Walter. "'Preciate it."

"Just wanted to show my thanks." Walter disappears down the hall.

Perry takes the teakettle from the counter, fills it with water, and sets it on the stove. "You know, Walter, there are easier ways of saying thank you." He takes down a box of assorted teas from the shelf over the oven, flips through it.

"Like what?"

Perry decides on a bag: mint green. "Like verbally saying thank you." He shuts the cabinet door.

Walter returns with a towel folded over his arm. "Dinner's in the oven...if you're hungry; should still be warm."

The other man looks at him. "You cooked?"

A nod.

Perry bends down, opens the door, and sees a plate of green beans, steamed broccoli and a large hamburger steak smothered in mushrooms and shredded cheese and topped with tiger dill. His head pops up, everything below the top of his nose hidden behind the oven top. "What'd you do?"

Walter stops folding the towel. "What did I--Nothing, I just wanted to fix you dinner. Something wrong with that?"

Perry takes the still-warm plate from the oven, grabs a knife and fork and sits down at the table. "Where's yours?" He slices into the hamburger steak.

"I already ate, didn't know what time you'd be back and I was starving." Walter's voice calls distant from down the hall.

Perry chews...and stops. He swallows. "What'd you season the meat with?"

Walter pops his head around the corner. "You like it?"

"Yeah." He takes another bite. "Texture's a little funny."

"It's seitan."

A bite of green beans. "Satan?"

"Sei-tan." He pops around again with a bedspread tucked beneath his chin as he folds it. "It's a meat substitute, healthier for you."

Perry loosens his tie as he looks over his shoulder. "Will you stop folding and come sit down?"

Walter finishes folding the bedspread and lays it on the table. He watches Perry. "How'd your day go, get in some good detecting?"

The detective eats a mushroom. "Investigated a crime scene."

The other man squirms in his seat. "Where was it?"

He looks at him for a second. "Guess." Chews. Swallows. Slices.

Walter's expression collapses. "You saw—" He swallows. His lips part and he looks away as sweat stains his forehead.

Perry nods. "Mind if I ask you a few questions about that? If you think you're okay to talk about it, that is."

Walter visibly struggles to get his breath under control, bobbing his head in a nod. "G—go ahead."

"You said the Hispanic man let you leave before he killed Matthew. Mind giving me more details on what he looked like?"

Walter looks down at Perry's plate, watches as he eats. "To help you build a case so you can arrest him?" He scrolls his eyes up to the other man's face.

"'S the idea."

Walter grazes his fingertips across the freshly washed tablecloth. "What if...What if I don't want him to be caught? I never would've left Matthew on my own, didn't have it in me. That guy made it so I didn't have a choice but to leave him. Did me a favor."

The fork wavers near Perry's mouth as he stares across the table at the stinging sorrow seeping from the other man. "Walter—"

"I get the distinct impression that you're all about doing things by the book, Detect—Perry. That you might even write and update the book yourself when need be. But I'm starting to feel like I've been given another chance here, a chance to do things right. For myself this time." The smile on his face is cracked and wavering.

Perry lowers his fork.

"I'm sorry, but..." He swallows the anxiety welling up in his throat. "I don't think I can help you, detective."


While Perry should be building a case to track down and capture Noir, he is instead researching SWAT teams and techniques used specifically to capture or take down A-Os with dangerous abilities. A special U.S. government-sanctioned operation known as Gladius is in development to address Alpha-Omega threats across the country using a combination of soldiers and specially-trained Alp—

"Thinking about joining the army?"

Perry jerks at Walter's sudden voice behind him. "Shit!" Shoulders are hijacked up to his ears. Adrenaline-spiked muscles seize between flight and locomotoring his fist into the other man's face. "Need to get you a damn gong to wear while you're here."

Walter laughs as he sits beside Perry, grazing a palm across his shoulders as he passes behind him. "Sorry."

The detective feels the combustive shock drain out of him. "Was just preparing for the possibility that our guy might have abilities of his own." He eases his reading glasses from his nose. "And know that I understand your reasons for not wanting to help me with this case."

Walter nods. "You're not going to force me to tell you what I know? Use the law?"

"I could, but I..." Single-shoulder shrug. "I don't wanna violate the trust you have in me."

Single-sided smile. "Who says I trust you?"

"The fact that you called me when the shit shredded its way through the fan."

"Fair enough. I guess." He points at the open laptop. "Now you're starting to get an idea of how I feel."

Perry's eyebrow raises a question.

"Like a victim."

The word hits the detective like the blow he almost sent careening at Walter. "I'm not a victim here."

"You feel powerless don't you? A lack of control. Vulnerable. Like you're experiencing a new kind of fear tailored specifically for you?"

"Don't know if I'd go so far as to use the word *victim*."

Walter angles his upper body forward. "Why?"

The detective keeps his response clenched behind his jaws, bolted up tight inside his mental fortress. He sidesteps the question instead. "I'm just tryin' to keep you and everyone else in the city safe."

Eyes meet.

The detective feels another combustive shock run through him. One that goads him to neither flight nor fight.

He tries to smother it just the same.


"Think it might all be, I don't know, like, mind control or something?" Ehasz picks up the evidence bag containing a blood-streaked knife found in McCain's wrist.

Perry and Jill look at each other before entertaining the officer's ramblings. "What's firing through your brain this time, E?" Jill tunes her attention back to the reporting officer's narrative on the incident report. Perry doesn't bother looking up from the folder in his hand.

"Just that this is the third murder of an Alpha-Omega that's occurred in, like, a week." His head rattles back and forth between the two detectives. "Under any other circumstances, what I'm bringing to the table would sound like I needed to visit Dr. Chiavarini for a psychological screening, but we've got victims with claws, neon eyes, and two sets of vocal cords." He jots down a quick note on a reporter's notebook. "It's all kinds of possible Dwight Senior and our other murderers were being controlled by a telepath."

Perry blinks several times before lifting his eyes to the other man. "Dwight was off his meds. And McCain wasn't exactly the neighborhood sweetheart."

Ehasz stabs a vigorous hand at the detective. "Making them perfect targets if you're looking to mind control someone into becoming a murderer without making it look like mind control." Excitement grabs hold of him, possessing him mind, body, and soul...controlling him.

Jill curls a finger over her lip. Her gaze unravels into something ill-defined. "You might actually have something there."

It's Jill's turn to be on the receiving end of a gesture gyrating with vigor. "Thank you!"

Perry lifts empty palms. "Hold on, guys. How the hell are we supposed to gather evidence that there's a telepath causing these murders?"

"Catch whoever killed McCain, ask him and Dwight if they were acting out of the ordinary, felt compelled or controlled before they scratched the itch."

"And what makes you think the psychic will let them tell the truth?"

The question is a brick wall, a sudden deer in the headlights that makes Ehasz veer off the street of speculation he was once coasting down. He deflates. "Well...I mean..."

The expression reminds Perry of Walter. He sighs. "Sorry, Ehasz. There's a possibility that a telepath, or something very similar, is behind this, and you can most certainly continue to look in to that, I'm not stoppin' ya. But I am gonna do what I can to find the puppet that I know exists rather than a puppeteer that just might be a trick of light and shadow."

He goes back to work, but misgiving has already started to seep into his mind, spreading across its hemispheres with irrefutable temptations.


Perry leans over the balcony railing, unlit cigarette pinched between two fingers as he watches the setting sun drape itself heavy and heavenly across Dominion City, dredging shadows up from the ground and adorning the De France Pedestrian Bridge in thick beams of tangerine.

The door slides open behind him. "Didn't know you smoked." Walter leans next to him.

"Quittin'." Perry looks at the white cylinder. "Tryin' to, at least. Just the ritual of it helps me think."

"Lightning strike yet?"

Slow head shake. "Guess both me and Eureka are on smoke break; 'cept she's not just goin' through the motions."

"Why—" Walter measures the words in his head before breathing them into existence. "You should arrest me." He looks over at him. "I'm obstructing justice."

Perry brings the cigarette to his lips, takes a not-drag, lowers it. "Maybe. But you got your justice." Deep exhale of carbon monoxide free of nicotine.

"Sooo...you aren't doing everything you can to find this guy because you aren't fully convinced he's a criminal?"

Pinched brows. "Definitely wouldn't go that far. We can pin at least one murder on 'im, and there might be more we can't connect yet." He turns to Walter. "We'll find this guy. Right now, I just want you to enjoy your freedom, lemme do the worryin'." Eyes linger.

Walter rubs a fine-boned knuckle against the back of Perry's hand. "Thanks."

Perry's hand twitches, but doesn't open. He raises the cigarette to his lips again instead. "Ready to go back in? I'll make us a late dinner."

# GIORGIO

B.D - Before Death

*An ecstatic explosion of euphoria!*

*Their shared exhale twined together like limbs as Giorgio collapsed on her sweaty breasts, his ear to her thundering heart.*

*"Oh my God!" The woman pressed the heel of her hand to her brow.*

*"Mmm-hmm." He licked at her sweaty skin.*

*"We've been having sex two months now, and you've never done that before."*

*"Making love is about more than two bodies bumping and thrusting together in various positions." His finger twirled around her nipple. "It's about exploration, mutual pleasure, and reaching the magnificent pinnacle of a shared experience."*

*Her chest rumbled as she purred. "I sure reached my pinnacle. More than once." She slicked a hand through his hair. "I love you, Giorgio." Her heart thumped.*

*His heart stuttered and he cringed.*

*"Giorgio?"*

*"Mmm?"*

*"I said I love you."*

*His finger twirled with insistence around her nipple. She covered his hand with hers, placing her fingertips under his clefted chin and forcing his head up.*

*"I don't expect you to automatically tell me you love me, but I would like some kind of response. Don't lay there and ignore me."*

*"How could I ignore you, Patricia? You're absolutely magnificent." He kissed her knuckles, rolled off her, covered her breasts with a sheet, and reached over to the cluttered nightstand for a cigarette. "I only smoke during afterglow." He grinned devilishly and lit up.*

*"I did this for you."*

*He exhaled. "Did what?"*

*"Don't do that. Don't act like you can't tell the difference. I saw it on your face while you were working your golden tongue in my—"*

*"Patricia." The word held gravity.*

"Four thousand dollars for my breasts, twelve thousand to lift my buttocks, twelve thousand for my legs and stomach, and three thousand for my cheekbones. All of that for you."

His lip curled as he looked at her, blinking and blowing smoke. "You didn't go to Dr. Garret at Zenith did you?"

Her eyes darted. "He's the best."

"For the poverty-stricken and deprived perhaps." He ran a finger down her thigh. "That quack with a forehead doesn't give a damn about good results or satisfied patients. He only cares about putting fat in his bank accounts as he sucks it out of yours. A proper surgeon would have addressed the individual needs of your musculature. You now have the thighs of an Auschwitz survivor tapering down to the legs of a dancer attached to a pair of ankles that belong on a Sumo wrestler."

Vision blurred, his cheek flesh burned, and the air was bitten by a sharp sound.

He rubbed at his face.

"You motherfucking asshole. You and your fake-ass British speech patterns."

"No, my dear, my name is Giorgio. And you can blame my glorious speech pattern on the best overseas schooling desperate parents and old family money can buy." He brought the cigarette to his lips and put his arms behind his head.

"I hope you fuck some disease-ridden whore and die of AIDS." She slapped him again, knocking the cigarette from his mouth. And again. And ag—

He grabbed her wrist and she struggled against him, flinging out an abrasive string of curses. Sheets fell to the floor and the bed squeaked, sparking memories of the sound that occurred just moments before. Same sound, different sensation.

"You're not good enough, Patty, you never will be! Go back to Dr. Garret; tell him to take all of that silicone and plastic out of you; and go get yourself a mild-mannered, bland, pencil-dicked husband who plays fantasy football and never learned how to properly do laundry." He shoved her out of the bed.

She covered her naked body as best she could, the same naked body that she was so willing to reveal and share hours before. "You're a corpse. There's nothing inside of you but shit and maggots."

"Get out!" He stood on the other side of the bed in all his naked glory, picking up the cigarette on the floor and relighting it.

Patricia snatched up her clothes and left, bare feet stomping across the floor.

Giorgio put a hand on his waist, took the cig from his mouth, and scratched at his forehead with his thumbnail. For a half-hearted moment, he looked bothered by her words.

He shook his head and puffed out a brief laugh. "Knew I should've had her keep the gag in."


"No."

The sewn abomination disguised as a slim fit blazer was hideous, something not even a blind man who had never heard of haute couture would wear.

He looked at the beaming saleswoman, the name TRISH inscribed on her nametag.

"Are you joking, my dear?" He lifted a perfectly sculpted brow .

Her beam was bashed. "Oh—I—Sorry, Mr. Quintero, I thought that you would like this."

He jutted out his lower lip and blinked several times. "I would...if I were a brain-dead retard." He flapped his hand in her face and turned away from her. "Away. Send Justine, she always knows what I like. And see if you have this shirt in a smaller size. I've been working on my abs and don't want to deprive anyone of a view of perfection."

"Yes, Giorgi—Mr. Quintero." She stalked off.

Giorgio studied his reflection in the mirror, frowning as he eyed the small pinch of fat caressing his lower buttocks, practically stretching the designer pants out of shape. "Delgadar would murder me herself if she saw how I was brutalizing her spring collection."

He reached for his calfskin jacket draped over the chair and pulled out the slim little phone. His thumb danced over the screen until he reached the memo option. Extra hour of explosive lunges. Cut back to two small meals a day. He tucked the phone back in his jacket and turned back to the mirror, sighing.

Thirty minutes later, he left Delgadar's empty-handed, staring straight ahead as Trish shot a look at his green mesh-clad back. Giorgio looked over his shoulder, profile perfect. "Call me the second the fall line arrives. I abhor it when you put clothes back on display after other people, poor people, have tried them on. They should be burned...and the clothes donated to Goodwill."

He sauntered out the door and walked down Fashionado Avenue, ignoring the appreciative glances he received from both men and women. He slid his wraparound designer sunglasses over his yellow-green eyes.

He was walking across the crosswalk when a man stumbled and stepped on his loafers, leaving a slight smudge behind.

"Oh, I'm sorry, bud, excuse me." The shorter man smiled an apology before walking on.

Giorgio stopped, inspected the offense and called out to him. "I beg your pardon."

The man looked over his shoulder, stopped, and turned around. "You okay?"

"There is dirt on my shoe."

The other man narrowed his eyes. "I said I was sorry."

"Sorry doesn't remove this stain. Sorry doesn't excuse the fact that you could have broken a toe with those offensive, chicken-chasing leather boots of yours." He snatched off his glasses and stepped to the middle of the crosswalk, mindless of the cars braked behind the white line, mindless of the flashing red-orange hand.

"That's all I got, pretty boy." The other man held up his hands as he stepped back onto the sidewalk.

"Apparently—"

A car honked as the light turned green.

"EXCUSE ME!" Giorgio's throat muscles bulged as he unleashed his agitation at the driver. He turned back to the man. "Do you have any idea how much these cost me? How high can you count?"

"You're holding up traffic, buddy."

"I always hold up traffic. My very presence is distraction enough." He scoffed and looked the man up and down. "I shouldn't even bother addressing motes like you." He took a last look at his loafers, slipped his shades back on, and walked to his gleaming navy blue Lamborghini Huracán parked in front of a fire hydrant. He snatched the parking ticket from the windshield and flung it into the breeze.

He slid into the car, molded carbon fiber interior welcoming him with luxurious languor, and pulled out his phone as he started the engine, dialing as he darted out into traffic with a split-second glance in the mirror.

HONK! HONK!

"Love you, too, asshole! Hello, Jessica, my radiant beauty. How are you?" The wind whipped through his loose brown curls, shafts of sunlight catching the honey-gold highlights. "Yes, yes, I'm up for lunch...Ah, no, can't go there...Because their wine selection is abysmal, that's why. What about Impeddo's?...Fantastic. I'm on West Ivory Avenue, pick you up in twenty minutes. Adore you, too, beauty."

He tossed the phone in the passenger seat as the upper east side loomed ahead, sparkling pristine with an alabaster sheen.

"Excuse me, did you give a signal? No, Miss Chevrolet, I don't think you did. Get your soccer mom ass back in your lane." He pressed his foot to the accelerator and the car obediently zipped forward to close the distance between him and the car in front of him.

"Idiot driving motherf—"

He felt his heart trip-hammering before stammering in his chest. Felt his heart thump sluggish. Felt his heart stop working. Felt...nothing.


Now.

Giorgio watches as the dry leaf breaks off from the plant and flutters down to the yellow-tinged grass. He takes his finger away and looks at his hand, noting that some of the sallow tinge to his skin has blended away to flawless flushed flesh.

He touches the tip of a finger to another flower and watches as the rich green bleeds away to sickly green, petals drooping and drawing up before falling away.

"I am become death. Everything I touch turns to dust and memory."

He leans back against the tree, not noticing how the bark gradually fades from vibrancy to corroded brown. Leaves crinkle and curl on the branches before falling in a wash of tarnished gold.

The man who steps into his vision has eyes of green-gold, tight bronze curls that droop over his forehead, and handsome features. A familiar smile wrinkles the sides of his mouth, punctuating his cheekbones.

"You."

"Me."

"Who are you?" Undead Giorgio watches himself.

His double sits down next to his living corpse. "I'm God." He rolls his eyes to himself as he rests a forearm across a bent knee.

"You're God?"

God nods slowly.

"Then why do you look like me?"

"Fantasy-land. You create this world as you see fit from your memories and information shrapnel embedded in your subconscious. So in a way, you are God. Besides, even if you are dead, I'm sure you still remember what a self-absorbed ass you were...are...whatever." He picks up a dried leaf and rolls the stem between his fingers.

"I'm undead."

"Yes, and as a shambling corpse, you're still one narcissistic SOB. *Why am I still here? Does anyone miss poor Giorgio? Did anyone ever love me when I was alive? Are all of my designer clothes still in my closet?*" The leaf dissolves beneath the clenched fist. "Selfish prick."

"So what should I be asking myself?"

"Why you're still here." He pulls a deck of cards from the inside pocket of his silk suit jacket and shuffles them.

"But you just said—"

"It's not what you ask, it's how you ask it." He begins a game of solitaire. "Not like you're the only person shitting your life away."

"For God, you're hardly eloquent."

"Eh." He places a red seven over a black eight. "All of my eloquence went into the Bible." His next card hovers as he frowns. "Not that I personally wrote the Bible, per se, but that's a yarn for another delusion." An ace to the top row. "My children spend their lives inquiring and fretting about the unknown while you should be enjoying the gift I've given you." He takes a card from the deck. "You spent your life worrying about how you looked, how everyone saw you, how hard you could grind the hearts of countless faceless women and more than a couple of men under your expensive and well-polished heels." He places the overturned card beside the deck and flips over another. "Now you spend your second life, because no matter what you think, that's what this is, worrying about the bigger questions that most humans do during their time on my earth." God scoffs. "Can't do anything right, can you?"

"I didn't put much stock in you when I was alive, and now that I've met you, I can see why."

God pauses in his game to stare at him. "Are you...are you trying to hurt my *feelings*?" Heavenly chuckle. "I created emotions. Blew them right into you when I breathed life into Adam. Now look how the both of you repay me." He turns back to his game. "The things children do to their fathers. Ungrateful upstarts. And now you start to ask yourself if I'm exacting my revenge on you through all the world's turmoil. Take a good long look at what you've done to me, done to each other in my name, and ask that question again."

"So did you do it?"

God scans the cards and places a king on top of a queen. "Do what?"

"Bring me back."

A divine shrug. "Right now I'm keeping the world in motion, planting a seed in a woman's womb, and giving a little girl the ability to walk again...among other things. So many cards in play." He tilts his head at Giorgio and winks.

"You have a reputation for being all-knowing, wise. Why did you allow me to live my life as I did? My existence was a waste of breath."

"Looks like someone had an epiphany." He taps a card against his lip in concentration. "I hate the way that word is tossed around these days. Epiphany. Take a word that's supposed to be about my only begotten son and make it about yourselves." He looks up. "Oh, me, now I'm doing it. Perhaps it's no coincidence that we look alike." He takes a card from the deck, plants it on a pile and takes another. "Maybe you squandered your first life so you wouldn't mess up this one."

"You say that like I knew I was going to suddenly die in traffic, wake up in a necrophiliac's bed, and kill her as she revived me with a kiss."

God flicks chartreuse eyes at him and hints at a smile before going back to his game.

Giorgio stops.

"Are you trying to tell me that on some level I knew what I was doing, that I knew what was going on in my life and didn't do anything to stop it because if I had I wouldn't be here as a living corpse having this conversation with you?"

"No, Giorgio, that's not what I'm telling you."

"Then, what is it that you *are* telling me?"

"Simple, nothing." He finishes the game, smiles, and gathers the cards. "You, and by *you* I mean your kind, give me too much credit. I know I'm omnipotent, glorious, astounding, all-giving, wonderful, the Prince of Peace and Lord of Lords, but at the end of eternity, I'm just a divine force, the oil that greases the cogs of the universe. I gave you a brain because I knew I'd be sick unto death of thinking for you." The cards dance and shuffle between his hands in a blur. "Now, what do you think?"

Giorgio looks out at the field of dead flowers. "I think that I was brought back to get a second chance at life, to take the experiences of the first go-round and use them in this life...death...existence."

"Go on."

"I did waste my first life, and so do plenty of other people."

"And?"

"And why were people like me born in the first place? Why did you, someone who knows the entirety of our life before we take our first breath, give someone like me the chance to be part of this world? Why put someone like me on the Earth in the first place if you knew who I would be, who I would always be?"

God raises an eyebrow.

A leaf twirls down to the grass.

"You didn't bring me back to life, did you?"

God shakes his head.

"Then who or what did?"

Music plays in the background Giorgio's divine manifestation: Chris Cornell's "Can't Change Me."

God suddenly starts flinging cards away, watching them spin and spiral out. "None of you know what it is just yet. It could be a curse, could be a blessing. Might be a cure, or it might be a disease. Or maybe it's the next step...could be the last step. Some call it a mistake while others say it's My will. The curious want to study it and the greedy simply covet it."

"So what is it?"

God stops flicking cards. "I just told you."

"You told me nothing!"

"And nothing must come before something." God leans his head back against the tree. "But I'll give you a hint: what you're looking for isn't a thing, it's an entity, one that's existed even longer than I have."

Giorgio waits just one minute here.

"Many of you don't realize this, but I have a wife, and it's she who brought you back. Why, I don't know. She's been quite wroth with me these past few eons and refuses to converse with me. But I can still feel her, just as she can still feel me. One phrase keeps bubbling up when she's near: Alpha-Omega."

"I think I've heard of that."

"You should, it was born in the city in which you died."

"Alpha-Omega."

"The beginning and the end intertwined as one." God shudders.

"Am I ever going to see you again?"

God holds his hands up. "That's entirely up to you. For all either of us know, you may live forever, or you may fade tomorrow. But I can tell you that I won't be visiting your unconsciousness again. Touching a living mind with the barest inch of my essence is enough to drive a person deliciously insane. But you're different." He drops a card on Giorgio's lap as he stands, walking away on a field of dead leaves.

"Wait."

God stops, but doesn't look back.

"Who's your wife?"

God chuckles. "Nature, of course." He pats a tree trunk as he continues on, placing a gentle kiss on a bent branch. "She's going to change the world."

Giorgio looks down at the card as God vanishes.

There's nothing on it.

He returns to undead consciousness in a park and finds that

the night is almost over. A leaf flutters to the grass. He looks down and sees that the leaf is brown and thin with cracked veins. He sees that the grass around him is dead as well, as is the nearby bed of flowers. Giorgio lurches to his feet and sees that the trunk of the tree is wan gray and brittle. Lifeless.

Giorgio looks down at his hands.

They couldn't be more alive.

Giorgio looks up at the sky.

"I don't know what to make of you. You sit up there and unravel my sanity as I wallow down here having conversations with myself, questioning my behavior, my reason." He takes up a brittle leaf. "This leaf is dead, and yet it brings life with its death, returning to the earth, enriching it as it takes place in the cycle of nature." A puff of laughter. "Your wife." The leaf twists. "Even though she doesn't say a word, she speaks." He brings the leaf closer to his ear. "Alpha-Omega, you say? The beginning and the end intertwined as one."

He stands to his feet and the leaf flutters from his fingers as he walks. "Where there's one leaf, several more are sure to be found close by. And when you find the leaves, the tree is sure to follow."

Giorgio passes a sign.

*Welcome to Dominion City*

## FADE OUT

## DOMINION CITY – PHOSPHORUS PARK

SHE ruffles her hand through his hair as colors from the screen flash across his face. She traces her finger down the line of his nose and over the smooth circumference of the silver ring protruding from the corner of his bottom lip.

He looks up from her lap. "What?"

The sides of her generous mouth raise. "Nothing."

"Thought Tuesdays were your nights with Rod." He rubs her arm.

"He thinks the two of us may be spending too much time together, said it was okay if you and I saw each other more."

He shifts on the couch. "He starting to warm up to the idea of being in a polyamorous relationship?"

"...I think so."

He tenses. "The two of you haven't talked about it?"

"No, we have. He just doesn't like to go into detail."

"Well, it's the details that make this kinda thing work."

A commercial blares noisily across the screen.

"Did you ask him?"

She picks up the remote and flips channels. "About what?"

He gently squeezes her wrist. "Jo."

"Thomas, it was hard enough for Rod to adjust to you and I dating, now you want me to ask how he feels about being in a threesome with boyfriend number one?" A sigh barrels from her nostrils as she glances at the DVD player, noticing the time. "I've got to go." She kisses him on the mouth. "Love you."

"Love you, too."


Jo stands in the doorway as the door swings open, keys jingling softly where they hang out of the lock.

"Going somewhere?"

Rod spins at her voice, the folded shirt in his hands forgotten. He notices her noticing the half-packed suitcase. "Jo, you're um..." He casts his eyes down as he wads the shirt in his hands. "I thought you would be with Thomas all night."

Jo steps into the house and repeats herself. "Are you going somewhere?"

Rod glances down the hall before looking back. "Jo, I can't do this. I thought I was open-minded enough about the idea of being in a relationship with a woman that has two boyfriends, but I'm not."

**96**

"So just say that! It's okay. You don't have to leave without saying a goddamn word!" She shrugs her purse off her shoulder. "You were just going to pack your shit up, drop some half-assed note, and leave?"

His jaw goes slack and words fail him. He looks at her feet. "I'm sorry."

Her hands ball into fists. "Sorry does not—"

A door opens at the far end of the hall. "Rod, did you want me to pack your—" The brunette woman looks up from the suit in her arms and stumbles to a stop when she sees Jo glaring at her. Her eyes snap to Rod.

Jo lowers her voice. "Tell me what the hell this bitch is doing in my house."

The bitch draws her thin brows together. "This was my house first."

"Which you lost when the two of you got divorced, dumbass!" Jo turns her fury to her boyfriend. "Rod, please tell me you didn't get back with her."

His eyes flutter as he blinks. "No one else would help me pack on such short notice."

Jo advances a step. "So you call the cunt who you said ate your heart and shat it out?" A palm slaps her chest. "Explain this to me!"

The cunt disappears down the hall.

"Why didn't you talk to me about this?" Jo braces an arm on the wall. "I told you that it was okay if you didn't want to do this, that it was fine if you wanted me to spend more time with you. I love you, Rod, I honestly do. I want you to—"

The brunette walks into the living room with a cooing baby in her arms. "I'll put Curtis in his car seat."

Jo explodes toward the door. "NO!" Her body is a barrier. "You are not taking my son out of this house."

"He's *my son*, Josephine. *My son*." She moves Curtis to her right shoulder. "Move out of my way."

"I move when you put him back in his crib."

The woman holding the baby looks over her shoulder. "Rod, call them."

"Penny, if you just—"

"Do you want to leave or not?" Penny eyes him.

Rod reaches for his phone.

Jo doesn't move from the doorway. "You're calling the police? You think they can get here before I beat her skinny ass?"

"We took the precaution of calling a couple of friends in case you did exactly what you're doing now. They're parked down the block."

Jo darts for the baby. Penny wrenches him away. "Get away from my son!"

"You don't know how to take care of your son! I am more of a provider for him than either of you ever were!"

Two men walk in through the front door. The one with red hair holds his hands up. "Jo, you need to let Penny through. You don't want to accidentally hurt Curtis."

Jo grabs for the baby. "Don't let her take Curtis! Please!" Vices masquerading as hands grip her by either arm. She kicks out, struggling to break free, thrashing madly as Penny glides out the door.

"Jo, stop it!"

Jo continues to struggle.

They shove her down to her knees.

Jo continues to struggle.

Hands on the back of her neck.

Jo contin—A peculiar sensation boils through her skull. Heat collects around eyes clenched in fury and threatens to liquefy the gelatinous orbs. She obeys the instinct that commands her to open her eyes. The world blazes neon indigo. Lasers erupt from her eyes and sizzle right through the window.

"The fuck?" One of the men loosens his hold.

Curtis wails outside.

Jo turns her head as the overbearing heat gathers again and is released as her eyes rest at the man on her left.

Curtis's wails mix with the jagged scream pouring from the man's throat as twin lasers lobotomize him.

The man on her right yells, releases Jo, and flees the house.

"What the fuck was that?"

Jo squeezes her eyes shut at Rod's voice. "Shut up, Rod."

"But what you just—What was that that came out of your eyes?"

Her fingers curl into fists. "Rod!"

"One of those things went right through the window. What if—what—what if you hit—"

"ROD. SHUT. UP!" Her eyes peel open. Heat spews at Rod.

Words are jammed in Rod's throat. He looks down at the hole eaten through his chest. He expected to see more blood and less charred flesh. The crumpled shirt falls from hands he can no longer feel. His knees hit the hardwood. His face is next.

Jo whimpers with tears rolling from beneath shut lids. "Rod?"

Silence.

"Rod!"

Curtis cries.

Jo stumbles outside, catching herself on the doorframe, slamming her legs into the porch swing. She stops.

"Where are you?"

A fly flicks past her ear.

The heat presses against her eyes, throbbing at her temples and aching to be released. The wind blows and carries the slight smell of blood twined with baby powder.

Curtis hiccups and Jo spins her head at the sound, adjusts her aim, and opens her eyes.

*SSSSHHHHHRRRR!*

Penny screams and falls back.

Jo instantly smashes her eyes shut.

"Curtis?"

Nothing.

"Curtis?"

More nothing.

Jo doesn't dare to open her eyes as she goes down to her knees and searches for the child.

Her child.

# EPISODE FOUR: *In Glass Boxes*

**"WHAT'S WRONG?"**

"Nothing."

"Are you okay? I'm not hurting you, am I?"

"No, Adam, it feels fine."

"Then what is it?"

"Nothing, it...it's just that we've been trying to make a baby for a year. And we've been in this bed for...three hours now."

"It didn't sound like you weren't enjoying those three hours."

"...I've wanted a child of my own to care for ever since I was little. The day I met you, I knew that it was your child I was meant to carry."

"So why are we stopping?"

"I've talked about this with an obstetrician. She told me that I'm perfectly healthy, that there's no reason I shouldn't be pregnant...especially as much as we've been trying lately."

"Maggie, what are you telling me?"

"I'm telling you that there's nothing wrong with my body, Adam."

"But you do think there's something wrong with mine?"

"I..."

"You can say it if you think so."

"When was the last time you had a physical?"

"I'm in perfectly good health. If we keep trying, we'll make a baby."

"Adam, we—

"No, Maggie! We *are* going to have children. Look at us; Heaven holds us in the palm of its hand. It won't forsake us now and we won't forsake it, we can't. We were meant for each other, we were created for each other."

"I'm not saying that's not true, I'm not. But there are some things you and I can't control no matter how hard we try. I called Dr. Hannigan and he has an opening on Tuesday."

"You what?!"

"Adam—"

"I can't believe that you would—"

"That I would what, care about you and your health?"

"Honey, I'm telling you that—"

"Let the doctor tell you. Let him tell us...together."

"...All right. What time?"


A house of life and death intertwined, where one held the hand of the other, forever swaying, forever joined.

Bisset grimaces at the paradox as she walks the halls of the Dominion Medical Center, stepping past birth, life, recovery, death, and those leaning in the limbo between. She feels the joy, the pain, the relief, the emptiness, and the despair. She sees the sickness, the cancer, the disease, the anguish, and the decay. She leans against a wall with a hand clutching at her heart.

"Turn it off."

Seraph steps out of the room across from her. "I'm sorry, I can't."

"The hell you can't." Her lungs are lazy. "You gave me this...condition, now turn it off."

"It wasn't mine to give, Bisset, only to guide. And it's not a condition, it's a blessing."

She sucks air through her teeth. "I thought The Dragoness was the one who believed blessings came in the form of suffering, of feeling the woman down the hall take her last breath."

The angel in ivory steps forward and takes Bisset's hand. "Control it, step away from it. Look at me...Bisset, *look at me*."

Her eyes roll up and collide with golden globes.

"Yes, drown yourself in me." She clutches Bisset's hand and watches as her breathing returns to normal. "It's hard isn't it? To be the vessel for suffering as well as salvation."

"I healed that man on the street the other day, didn't I? The one I bumped into."

Seraph nods.

Bisset looks around the corner into the nearest room and sees a man in bed with a tube shoved down his throat. His life is measured in beeps. Seraph peers over her shoulder.

"Some of the people in here are victims of their own suffering, suffering The Dragoness wants you to multiply." She steps softly into the room, tugging Bisset behind her. "Suffering can't always be used as a catalyst for strength. At times, it simply is what it is: ugly and painful."

The man in the bed peels opens his eyes and stares weakly at her. He blinks.

"Talk to him." Seraph puts a hand on her shoulder.

"Wha—What do I say?"

"Just talk to him." She guides Bisset's hand to the patient.

"Hi, my name's—my name's Bisset." She sees the burning black hole through his disfigured lips, the slow churn of murk drizzling down his throat and over his sternum. Something throbs inside her and golden threads of light shoot down her arm into his, ripping through the darkness, but not destroying it. "How are you?"

He nods pitifully, a bit of relief unraveling through him at her touch.

"You can't fully heal him yet, only take away some of his pain." Seraph stands on the other side of the bed, her hand grasping the patient's.

"What's wrong with him?"

"May I borrow your vision?"

It makes her look up. "What?"

"I need to see with your eyes. To do that, I need to take temporary control of them, and to do that, I have to have your permission."

Bisset nods and swallows. "Alright."

Seraph's golden eyes go distant and Bisset feels something

stirring gently in the air. Her eyes move by themselves. They study the darkness lacing the patient's mouth and throat. The air stirs again and Seraph blinks rapidly. "His tongue is missing. It looks as though it was burned out." She shakes her head. "You're not yet strong enough to even begin to heal that kind of damage."

Bisset looks back at the man on the bed. "I'm sorry you're in so much pain. I know that doesn't sound very comforting, but—" He squeezes her hand, gives her a single nod.

"I wasn't aware that Yonnie had a visitor."

Bisset turns to see a middle-aged man in scrubs walk into the room. His black hair shines in the light, quick grin flashing across his pale visage.

"Family?"

Bisset looks at Yonnie. He gives a barely perceptible dip of his chin. "I'm his cousin."

"He's been here for four days. I was starting to wonder if he had any family or friends at all." He stands next to Seraph, looking down at Yonnie. "My heart goes out to him after what he's been through."

"All I heard was that he was here in the hospital."

The man in scrubs looks up at her. He opens his mouth, inhales, closes it, and breathes out, collecting his thoughts before trying again. "We had to get him to write out what happened once he was stable. Seems that Yonnie and his girlfriend were...in the throes of passion when her A-O gene manifested. From what we can tell, her saliva became acid while they were kissing. Ate away his tongue and a majority of his esophagus. It's a miracle he's still alive." He smiles down at Yonnie. "But you're a fighter, aren't you Yonnie?"

Yonnie rolls his eyes to him, curling his hand into a thumbs-up.

The doctor's smile curdles around the edges. "We're getting more and more cases of Alpha-Omega-related injuries every day. I think we're going to have to build a new ward specifically for them."

"What's an Alpha-Omega?"

The man in scrubs and Seraph look up at her at the same time, both of them wearing the same expression.

Eyes flutter open. Fingers twitch. Breaths rattle. Mind stumbles back into bleary consciousness. Noir takes a moment and waits for the pieces to slide back into place.

**BLOOD**

It thumps and pumps through arteries and veins. And just like that, he remembers. He looks down, vision smearing to and fro, and sees the burning red dot at the crook of his elbow. The needle sits innocently next to him, plunger depressed. He sits up on his elbows, hand going to his throbbing head.

"Mother... *fuck!*" The words are crushed out through clenched teeth. "The hell was in that shit?" He squeezes his eyes shut as he gets to his feet, wobbling precariously. He swallows and blinks several times, thankful that all the lights are off. He turns and sees that the sky is painted in sunset hues beyond the parted curtains. He walks closer to the window and sees that the world has been burned down to nothing but golds, yellows, reds, and oranges.

Dominion City is no more.

"The hell?" Noir shuffles backward, stumbles over something, and falls. He cracks his head on the edge of the table and winces as he rises up enough to see what he tripped over.

His body lies unconscious on the floor.

Words, thoughts, curses, and confusion wrestle with his tongue, but none of them are given voice.

"You're awake." A unison of voices.

Noir looks in his kitchen and sees three Noirs and a child Noir, all of them with varying expressions on their shared faces.

"Madre de Dios."


"Love.

"God wants us to love, needs for us to love. We have to love ourselves as well as each other if we expect to have any hope of taking a closer walk with God.

"I know some of you may think that the world is full to bursting with love, and it is. But that love is corrupted. Vile. Evil. It's evil because it's the love of the wrong things. Love of money, cars, power, fame, physical sensation, and pleasure. That's the kind of love that can kill.

"The kind of love I'm talking about is pure, blind, all-encompassing love. You don't consume love, love consumes you. When you're inside of that love, you are inside of God, just as God is inside of you. Think of it as a circle. It has no beginning, and it has no end.

"I know how difficult it is to love your fellow man in this day and age. How is it possible, how is it logical, to love someone who looks right through you? To love a liar, a cheat, a pederast, a sexual deviant? As humans, we can't, but as Christians, we must. We must love our brothers and sisters no matter what they have, are, or are going to do. Thank you."

Adam steps off of the pulpit.

Later, he's approached by one of his probationers: "I just wanted to tell you how much your testimony touched me."

Adam finishes zipping up his jacket and turns to the older man walking down the steps of the church behind him. "I appreciate your kind words, Brother Rhodes."

The other man lifts his hands, keeping the comment at bay. "Call me Alan. I got used to a lot in prison, but it's gonna take me awhile to think of myself as a brother in Christ."

Adam pauses at the bottom of the steps, puts his hands in his jacket pockets. "You're making an honest attempt to change your life for the better; you're more than deserving of the title just as you're more than deserving of God's love." Shrug. "We all are."

The gravity of the implications weighs Alan's eyes down as he considers. "There's a lot to get used to now that I'm...now that I'm out." He exhales. "But I'm working on my faith. Day by day." He meets Adam's gaze and gives him a firm nod.

The man's resolve brings a smile to Adam's face. "Day by day is the only way to take this life. Keep the faith and the faith will keep you."

Alan's lips part, gape for a moment, and seal shut.

"Say it." Adam eases himself down on a step, gestures for Alan to do the same.

The other man sits and rubs his palms on the knees of his

khakis. He tries speaking again, successfully getting his words out this time. "How do I learn to love myself again after what I've done? Is that even possible?"

Adam's expression loses a shade of its brilliance. "It's entirely possible, yes, but it's also up to you. God's already forgiven you, already loves you despite any crimes you've committed, any wrong you've done."

Alan stares at Adam. "I'm sorry, Adam, but I don't..." He pauses a beat. "I'm new to this religion thing, and I don't know if I believe that."

Adam's shine returns, a bit of it manifesting in a subtle platinum glow around his head. "The great thing about religion is that concepts like divine forgiveness work even without your belief, but they're stronger with it. I won't sit here and tell you what I think you want to hear, but I will tell you that it's likely going to take a while before you're able to even start to forgive yourself, and that's perfectly okay. It's what else you're doing in the meantime that helps you to get to that space."

The other man mulls over the words for a moment, gaze unfocusing a bit. "Think I'm starting to understand."

"Good. So what are you going to do in the meantime?"

Alan snaps his focus on Adam. "Learn how to love other people and hope that a bit of that reflects back on me, keep coming to these meetings, keep reading my Bible."

Adam nods. "Sounds like a solid foundation. Just take it one day at a time...Brother Rhodes."


"You're joking, right?" The man in scrubs creases his brow, corners of his lips prepared to lift in amusement.

Bisset blinks blankly.

"You're not joking." The man shakes his head slightly and studies her expression. He gestures at the table and chairs next to Yonnie's bed. Bisset gives the patient a little smile and his hand a pat before joining the doctor.

"While there was minor evidence of Alpha-Omegas as far back as two centuries ago, science has advanced enough that we're now able to better understand just what's going on with the A-O gene. That, and A-O abilities are now more apparent, more undeniable than they were two-hundred years ago. Alpha-Omegas now have more abnormal abilities; telepathy, healing hands, injury resistance..." He shoots a look at Yonnie whose eyes have drifted shut. "...Acid saliva."

"So Alpha-Omegas are superhumans?"

The question makes him wince and roll his eyes to the side. "Yes and no. Some A-O's powers are so mundane they have no impact whatsoever on their day-to-day lives, and the abilities of others are so radical that they sometimes become invalids for fear that their powers may hurt someone."

Bisset looks down, eyes skipping left and right. "And anyone can be an Alpha-Omega?"

He nods. "Anyone at any time. Just yesterday, actual smoke started coming out of the palms of a ninety-year-old woman on the floor above us. Scared her half to death, but she was breathing it without any harm to her lungs. We had to evacuate patients in the rooms around her for fear of smoke inhalation. The only way we can contain it is to have her wear latex gloves."

"That's...highly unusual."

"Tell me about it. Thankfully, I was here at the time; I'm the hospital's A-O specialist."

"So you know all there is to know about Alpha-Omegas?" Her voice becomes eager.

A one-sided shrug. "Not all there is to know about them, but a great deal, yes."

Bisset pauses before framing her next question. "You said that A-Os are physically altered by their gene, but is it possible that they're altered mentally as well?"

"Well, I'm sure they have to change the way they think in order to—"

"No no, what I mean is, is it possible that the A-O gene can change a person's mental state?"

"Force them to become unstable?" He takes a deep breath. "It's entirely possible. Scientists are still conducting studies on people with active A-O genes and uncovering new information every day. With the way genes affect a non-powered person, I don't see why not."

"So you mean to say that some Alpha-Omegas have no control over the way they act, the things they do and say?"

"It's...possible." Head nod. "I don't see why not. There are several illnesses and disorders that leave a person unable to control their speech and actions. But I get the feeling you're talking about more than occasional vocal outbursts and muscle twitches."

Bisset nods.

"Well, we're not abundantly clear on how an active A-O gene might impact someone with an existing motor or mental disorder. Just like having a disorder can be what activates the gene, it might be possible for an active gene to lead to a new type of motor or mental disorder that hasn't been discovered yet."

Bisset chews on her bottom lip. "I see. Thank you." She stands and calmly walks from the room.

"Wait."

She looks back, a bit of...hopefulness on her face.

The man stands. "Aren't you going to say goodbye to your cousin?"

Bisset looks from the man to the patient as she presses her lips together. "He's asleep."

He looks back at the man in the bed. "So he is. Listen, I know we just met, but if you're ever interested in getting a bite to—" He looks back and sees that she's gone. His eyes scan the room. He frowns. "Of course."

The nearest Noir approaches him barefoot, kneeling down and cocking his head. His visage is twisted in a furious mask. He slams a fist into his twin's face.

The original Noir feels a phantom pain in the side of his cheek and flinches. He looks up at Furious Noir.

"The fuck were you thinking, estupido? Injecting yourself with that faggot's blood. Now you probably got AIDS or some shit." His fingers work themselves into grinding fists.

The original Noir cracks his lips, stops, and looks confused. A sudden pain bolts through the side of his face and he suddenly feels the full force of the punch. A string of thick blood mixed with spittle leaks from the side of his mouth.

"Things don't work the same as they do when you're awake." Another Noir snatches a washcloth from the sink, wets it, and walks over with it. He hands it to the original Noir. "We need to talk." This Noir is calm. Calm Noir.

"Oh, really?" Original Noir presses the cloth to his mouth. "Thought you wanted to beat the shit outta me."

Calm Noir looks down at the puddle of blood. "We do...Well, *you* do, but not for the reasons you think you do. Do you?"

Little Noir steps forward before sitting down cross-legged in front of his hallucinating self. "We think that you've forgotten."

"Forgotten what, lil' ese?"

He grins from ear to ear. "Why you are the way you are. Why you kill the people you kill."

"I know why I do what I do." Original Noir gets to his feet, touching a finger to his split lip. He walks around the kitchen island to the sink...and sees another version of himself hunched on the floor with his arms folded over knees pinched up to his chest. His eyes are wide and move with furtive rolls and flicks. "Who the hell—"

"—are you?" Nervous Noir finishes. "You're a man who doesn't—" His eyes dance to the left, orbs trembling in their sockets "—who doesn't believe in rehabilitation, doesn't believe that some people can get better. That's who you are." He takes a quick gander at Original Noir before averting his eyes. He sniffs and bobs his foot.

"You remember our Uncle Benito?" Little Noir now has a toy truck and rolls it back and forth on the floor. When next he opens his mouth, his voice is more mature, harsher with a bit of an edge. "You got your allowance today, didn't you lil' grillo? Mind letting your Uncle Nito hold a few dollars until he gets back on his feet? Need to buy some blanco feliz."

"His pet name for coke." Original Noir shakes his head. "He was hacked up into lil' pieces when his dealer caught him shaving too much off the top."

"Don't forget your cousin, Beto." Nervous Noir wipes at his nose with the back of his wrist. His voice shifts when he speaks again, eyes focused on the floor. "There's just something so...pure, so clean about the way that girl's skin feels. When I touch her, it's like sliding my hands against heaven. And her hair...ah, Dios. I'd get a spinal tap every day just to have the scent of her hair in my nose until I die."

Original Noir looks at him with his lips parted as the memory unspools in his mind. "I didn't know it at the time, but he was talking about the little girl who lived across from us on the street. They never did find her body after—" He snaps his teeth together.

"Don't forget about Mr. Jerome across the street." Furious Noir's thick lips lift in a vile smirk. Voice shift. "I did it and I'll do it again. I'll kill that man a thousand times over if I have to. You even so much as look at him again and I'll dig a grave for you right next to him. You're my wife, act like it."

"The infection you want to rub out as a man is the same one that surrounded you as a child." Calm Noir puts his palms on the back of his head and watches his own expression. "That level of fucked-upness affected you. Badly. You never had a positive role model. Sure, they all wanted to get help, be rehabilitated, but sooner or later, they were back up to their chests in the tar as it sucked them down into that bottomless abyss."

Original Noir looks at him obliquely. "Never knew I was so articulate."

Calm Noir shrugs an eyebrow. "You're not."

"Some infections only affect the people who are already marked." Nervous Noir is jittering. "But others, others affect others, infect others. Bystanders, those who shouldn't have to suffer because of someone else's neurosis." He steals a glance at Original Noir and instantly looks away when he sees himself staring back.

"You make it sound like a single period in my childhood is what made me the person I am now." He shakes his head. "Can't stand that shit, people who aren't half as traumatized as they think they are who blame a fucked-up adult life on their childhood instead of having the cajones to let that shit go and regain agency over their lives." He looks at his doppelgangers. "This some kind of mental intervention? You all want me to shake my wicked ways?"

Calm Noir looks up. "No, we don't want you to stop. We want you to keep doing exactly what you're doing. We want you to go after more A-Os like Matthew."

Adam grips the armrest as Dr. Hannigan continues.

"—rather normal for a man your age to have a low sperm count. Now, that doesn't mean that it's impossible for the two of you to have a child, but it does mean that it will be exceedingly difficult for you. There are all sorts of alternatives out there, and I think that the two of you will make wonderful parents and an absolutely beautiful baby." He nods. "I'm going to make a few calls to some of my associates who specialize in fertility and see if they have any openings or contacts you can get in touch with." He spreads his hands on the desk. "In the meantime, the two of you should keep trying. I know that's not the glimmer of hope you were looking for, but I'm sure you can find it in yourselves to enjoy the effort." He smiles. "Be right back." He leaves them alone.

Maggie clears her throat and wrings her hands, fingers sliding over her wedding ring. She blinks and gives her eyes to the bookcase before looking down at her lap, up at her husband.

"At least now we—"

"I had a physical before we were wed three years ago and I was perfectly fine. Perfectly." He slowly turns his head to her. "I don't understand what's changed."

She reaches out a hand and allows it to hover hesitantly over his before gripping his limp fingers. "You weren't an instrument of God three years ago."

Adam's body seizes and she can see the veins in his neck working furiously. "Are you blaming God for our situation?"

She pauses before responding. "All things are made possible through him, Adam. If he doesn't want us to have a baby, then..." Her eyes slowly slide away.

He grips her fingers. "I am the Sovereign of God, His spiritual hand made flesh, I am His will and I believe—no, I *know* without a shadow of a doubt that He wants this blessing to continue." A beat. "For that to happen, we must have a baby."

His wife's eyes cloud with wonder. "Do you even care about the child, or do you just want to achieve some empty immortality through your offspring?"

He says nothing. He says nothing for a very long time.

She jerks her hand away.

"How could I not have heard of something like Alpha-Omegas?" Bisset walks past the hospital cafeteria. "Have you and The Dragoness been blocking or altering my memories?"

"I haven't." Seraph floats next to her. "Unfortunately, I cannot say the same about The Dragoness. But I can tell you that you've been blessed by the Most High, not by genetics."

"Blessed to have angels and demons roaming around in my head. Is that how the Most High blesses people now?"

Seraph loosely folds her arms across her chest and looks ahead. "There's still much of this that's unknown to me. I told you, there are some things I still can't remember."

"Then it is possible that I could be an Alpha-Omega." As they pass, she looks in on a woman holding the hand of a giggling little girl sitting in a hospital bed. "Can't help but question if...I was like this before."

"Like what?"

She glances at her divine reflection. "Fractured. Did I shape the way my gene manifested, or did my gene shape the way I manifested?"

"The feather or the wing."

They walk out of the hospital and into the chill of the early evening. The breeze catches Bisset's tight curls and sends them billowing back as she waits for a van to pass before heading for her car. She unlocks the door, slides in, and stares out the window. Seraph appears in the backseat in the rearview mirror.

"I don't know what your fate is, Bisset, but I do know that it's something you mold, not genetics."

She looks in the reflection at her reflection. "But you just said that the Most High—"

"Gives you the tools, but it's you who must manifest the construction. It's the same way that an artist can have the talent, but not the will to create." She looks out of the window and back. "There is someone who might be able to help you, another instrument of the divine."

"Who?"

"I don't have a name, only a powerful sensation. What I do know is they have a light that resonates on the same wavelength as our own. I've been able to feel this individual for a few days, and wasn't sure of what it was until now." Her lips lift. "Maybe whoever it is is helping me to remember who I am. And I think they can help you, Bisset."

"Do you know where this person lives?

A head shake. "I only know where I felt the light last, I don't know if they're still there."

"Can you feel them now?"

"Yes."

Bisset drops her eyes to the steering wheel for a moment. She slides the keys into the ignition and starts the car. "Show me."


Sovereign is flying through the night sky over Oswyn when he hears it.

"NO! GET OFF ME! MMPH! NO! STOP! PLEASE—MMMPH— STOOOOP!"

He hovers in the air for a split second, pinpoints the sound, and shoots off in a streak of platinum white. He lands in an alley of cracked and badly repaved cement. A bare-legged man struggles beneath the weight of a heavier, grunting man viciously thrusting and forcing himself in and out of him.

"Yeah, take it, fuckin breeder! Just the way you want it!" The bigger man raises a fist, loosely slugs the slightly smaller man in the back of the head, and raises it again before he feels iron fingers around his thick wrist. His thrusts cease and his mind trip-hammers conflicting messages through his bewildered eyes.

He is careening back into the wall and the world becomes a smear.

Sovereign streaks toward him. "Monster!" Sovereign grabs him by his bubble vest. "Filthy demon!" He slams a fist into the man's face, pulling his punch so the jawbone only fractures. "If it were up to me, I'd see you dead!" He slams the rapist's spine into the brick wall.

"DEAD!" He lets go of the man and watches as he slumps to the ground, blood drooling down his broken face. He raises his eyes to Sovereign, setting something off.

*WHAM!*

The rapist hears and feels his skull fracture around his eye.

"Look at me again and I'll blind you, I swear." Sovereign's arms quiver and his vision seems to bleed. His fist is furious in motion again. Something collapses and gives way beneath the blow. He sees that he has buried his fist, wrist, and most of his forearm in the wall. "Leave. Now." The words are shoved out through packed teeth.

The man pulls his jeans up from around his ankles and limps awkwardly from the alley, spatters of blood marking his path.

Sovereign tugs his arm from the ruin of the wall and turns back to the man gathered in a puddle of limp limbs, quivering, and tears. He kneels down close to the other man, but doesn't touch him. He quenches his platinum flames. "Sir, are you oka—" He shuts his mouth and rephrases. "Are you hurt?"

He's clutching his legs to his chest, covering his lower body as best he can with his rigidly curled hands. Eyes hollow, mouth trembling, head wobbling no.

"I don't want to touch you. It can sometimes be traumatizing for someone to be touched after they've...after they've been..." The word looms unspoken between them. The man flinches anyway. "I'm going to call an ambulance." He pulls his phone from his jacket pocket.

"I'm not—I'm not gay." Tears. "I was jus' walkin' home from a bar when..." Words slur and Adam realizes the man is more than a little drunk. He visibly struggles to hold back tears of embarrassed rage, sniffing, hardened expression crumpled and compromised as the realization of what just happened eases through the cloud of his inebriation. "I'm not gay, man." Furious head shake. "I'm not."

"I'm sorry." The uttered words are weak. His call is answered. "Yes, this is—" Adam looks at the man. "I need an ambulance at the alley on the—" He reads the fading street sign twenty feet away. "—south end of Peoria, a man's been attacked." He listens. "I'm sorry, but I can't give you that information. Please, come quickly." He ends the call.

114

"What if he gave me something?" The man squirms on the bare concrete biting into his naked flesh. He can feel cooling wetness running down his thighs. "What if he infected me with some disease?"

"Then I'll see to it that he pays." Adam starts to put a hand on his shoulder, thinks better of it when he notices the flinch.

The man finally looks up at his savior. "What's your name?"

His lips part and utter only air for a moment. "Sovereign, call me Sovereign."

"Name's Ryan." Lips tremble around his hesitation. "Will you wait with me? 'Til the ambulance arrives?"

"I'm not going anywhere, Ryan." He reaches out and carefully clasps the other man's quivering hand.

Hesitation simmers in Ryan's tear-stained gaze, in his very bones as he looks down at the normal fingers covering his. He looks back up, confused. "Were you on fire a second ago?"


Bishop Martin rounds the table with a tray of tea with sugar and honey in tow. He sets the tray on the table before easing down into the seat across from his guest.

"There we go. Do you take sugar and honey with your tea, Miss Torres?"

She brightens. "Just sugar, please. Three teaspoons will be fine."

The older man pours two cups. "The person you describe can only be Brother Kensie, the newly-blessed Sovereign of God."

She watches as he scoops sugar. "Brother Kensie." The name makes her mind hum. "Yes. I, uh, I'm going through a bit of a tough time and I heard that he might be able to help me."

"Yes, Brother Kensie has made quite a transformation; I'm surprised we haven't heard about him in the news with all he's done lately."

Bisset accepts the tea. "Thank you. I understand that Adam is an...an instrument of the Most High?"

"Oh, yes. He bursts with the Holy Light at the utterance of a single word. Quite a magnificent sight to see with these aging eyes."

He sips. "If you don't mind my asking, Miss Torres, what is it that you need Brother Kensie's help for? Maybe I can provide you with a bit of assistance."

She sets her cup in her palm, dancing her eyes while she blows on the steaming liquid and looks down into her lap. "Well...It's a bit of a—It's really a private—You'd think I was crazy if I told you."

He lowers his cup on the table and looks at her. "Oh, I doubt it. I've heard and seen much in my years. I'm a man of God, yes, but I also have an open mind and an open heart. What is it that's bothering you?"

Bisset swallows. She studies him for a moment before continuing. "Have you ever been visited by demons and angels, Bishop Martin?" The words are whispered.

"Why, yes, more times than I care to count. Some of them are angels and demons of the heart, and others are of the mind. The angels all leave behind seeds of wisdom, and the demons leave seeds of faith...after they attempt to corrupt the fruit on the vine, that is."

"Have you ever seen the demons and angels so vividly that you could swear they were real, only no one else could see or hear them?"

"Physical manifestations of the two are extremely rare, but not unheard of." He nods.

"There's a demon in the room with us right now, she calls herself The Dragoness." Her eyes flick over the bishop's shoulder. "And as soon as the sun rises that demon will be replaced by an angel named Seraph. The Dragoness has made me...do something that I feel nauseous just thinking about. But at the time, it felt right, seemed like the only option to bring about a positive change."

"And did it?" His voice goes soft.

"Yes."

"But at the cost of a bit of your soul?"

She nods.

"I see. That's the way the devil works. He twists our philosophy until we're uncertain where ours begins and his ends. He wants us to believe that the two are hardly separate, that they are, in fact, one and the same." He holds up a finger. "But we must remember that evil is evil, no matter how right it may seem."

"Is it still evil when the end result is two people reconciling their marriage?"

The bishop pauses for a long while. "An outcome of good brought about from an evil deed doesn't make the end result just. Evil is evil is evil." He regards her. "Yes, I can see that you will need Brother Kensie's help. Let me give you his address." He reaches for a pen and paper.

"Bishop Martin, you said that Adam bursts with the Holy Light at a single word, did you mean that literally?"

He looks up at her. "Yes, he says the word and it's like...it's like a star is born inside of him. A silver-white glow wreaths his body and his eyes...have mercy, *his eyes!*" He holds up a hand, looking up at the ceiling as he conjures up the memory.

"Do you think that he's an Alpha-Omega?"

The bishop comes back. "Alpha-Omega." He spreads his palms. "Perhaps he is, perhaps he is not. Or perhaps this is simply God's way of casting a spear of light into the heart of the world. Humanity has come to trust the words of scientists more than the Holy Word." He drops his hands. "And that, Miss Torres, is truly a sin and a shame."

Furious Noir's body jitters with pent up violence. He paces the room like it's a cage. "The infection is still the same, but people ain't. Now they got abilities, superpowers 'n' shit." He stops and points at Original Noir. "Somethin's shakin' up the board. You gotta shake with it or your ass gets tossed off." He bends down and swipes up the used needle, waggling it in Original Noir's face. "It's all in the blood, baby, all in the blood. Blood is death and life, blood is the difference between them and you. Gotta become what you behold." He grins and taps the needle against Original Noir's forehead. "An' use it to your advantage."

Original Noir looks down at the red dot on his arm. "You tellin' me I got McCain's abilities now?"

The furious one smirks. "Guess you'll find out when you wake up. *If* your punk ass wakes up."

"If you do have McCain's abilities, you're gonna need more."

Little Noir has found crayons and construction paper and sits on the floor drawing a picture. A stick figure stabs knives into another stick figure's wrists. The red crayon is almost a nub. "Not all of those with the infection can be defeated with claws."

Calm Noir prepares a blunt on the coffee table. He looks up as he sprinkles green herbs on the paper. "But you gotta be careful that the infection doesn't spread to you as well. Can't be takin' any unnatural powers; shootin' laser beams from your dick or anything like that. Anything that exists naturally in nature is fine. Just—" His eyes drop as he rolls the blunt "—be natural."

Nervous Noir gets to his feet with apprehension, holding his arms close to his body and making himself as small as possible. "You probably shouldn't inject too much blood at one time either." He hunches his shoulders as his doubles look at him. "I'm—I'm just sayin'." He scratches quickly behind his ear. "You know, you're still human at the end of the day. Don't know what all this will do to you." He looks at Original Noir's chest. "Could kill you."

Furious Noir suddenly whirls and shoots his foot out and up at the bookcase, viciously snapping his foot down on a shelf with a grunt. The shelf snaps in half and his foot continues, driving down into the three other shelves. Books tumble into a pile as a jagged crack splinters the middle of the case.

The Noirs stop and stare.

Furious Noir curls his upper lip. "Fly was on the..." He swipes his hands angrily through the air. "Fuck it. Look, man, there's a lot more than crazy ass genes floatin' in blood. All kinds o' diseases waitin' to attack you and fuck your body up. You ready to deal with that?"

"I know a guy who can test the blood for me before I inject it." Original Noir slips his eyes at his calm self toking away.

"Wanna hit?" His voice is strained as he holds his breath.

"This is a hallucination, wouldn't be worth it."

A shrug and an exhale of a thick, white cloud. "Could do more than you ever imagined." He holds out the blunt.

The familiar thick scent fills his nostrils like cotton. "What the hell." He reaches for the offered blunt.

"Got your hit right here."

Original Noir turns——and a furious fist slams him in the face.

He's knocked out of his dream and back into consciousness. He sits up with a gasp as the remnants of a phantom pain collide through the side of his skull. He looks around his empty apartment, looks out the window at a night-drenched Mercurmont.

He crawls to the couch. The empty needle sits as it did in his hallucination, plunger depressed. He looks at his arm. A throbbing red dot at the crook of his elbow. His eyes trail up to his palm and he uncurls his fingers, turns his hand over. His nails are normal. He feels...something just beneath his cuticles. He flexes his hand.

His fingernails lengthen and harden into sharp, four-inch claws.

Noir's eyes go wide. He clicks his claws together experimentally, enjoying the sound they make. He suddenly spins and swipes at the couch.

Slashes like silk.


The Rapist tenderly touches the bandages wrapped around his head, wincing at the piercing throb that shoots through the left side of his skull. "Platinum fucker."

A chirp trills from his pocket.

He answers his phone. "'Ello?" He wipes at the dried blood flaking on his chin.

"Slow down, man. Yeah, I did what you asked. Why'd you have me stalk this guy for so long if you hate him so much?...That's sick, man, that's real fucked up...No, I only did what he asked...His *body* was asking for it, dude! Straight guys don't walk down alleys in gay neighborhoods unless they're DTF...Well, yeah, I mean, I blew my load in him, but I didn't finish the way I wanted to, something showed up...No, no, I mean, it looked like a man, but he was...he was all lit up with platinum light...Platinum! Yeah. Yanked me off of your boy and threw me into a wall before he beat the shit outta me." He adjusts the phone to his other ear and presses a bag of ice to his head. "I dunno, I yanked my pants up and got outta there before he killed me."

His front door erupts in an explosion of splinters, brass, and wood.

The platinum fucker stands in the demolished doorway.

The Rapist drops the phone from his jaw, a spike of pain forcing him to snap it shut. He knocks a chair over as he teeters back, holding his hands up, boulder biceps bunching underneath his tight shirt. "Hold up, man, you can't just come in here like that. *Thisisagainstthelaw!*"

"And raping someone isn't?" Sovereign walks into his house. His fists curl and flash-burn silver-white. "You should have cleaned up your wound before you returned home, or at least traveled by car. Your blood trail led me right to you."

"He—He—he wanted me to. You didn't see his face, the way he walked." He snatches a butcher knife from a cutting board and brandishes it in a quivering hand. "You didn't see his face!"

"But I heard his screams." Sovereign knocks the chair out of the way and steps closer.

The Rapist looks at his chest before stabbing him.

The blade snaps clean off in the middle.

Sovereign grabs the wrist of the hand holding the knife, twists sharply, and hears the snap of bones sing out in harmony with the man's cries of agony. He grabs the man by the shirt and plops him down in a chair. The Rapist cradles his wrist, biting down on his bottom lip as his face contorts in pain.

"Da—dafuq are you?"

"I'm Sovereign, and that's more than you need to know." Sovereign squats down until he's eye level with him. "Why did you do it?"

"Someone paid me to do it, mess with his breeder confidence."

"Who?"

"Some guy named Herman. He had me watch Ryan for a few weeks before I went through with it."

Sovereign frowns. "Why in God's name would anyone want you to do something like that?"

The Rapist shrugs, eyes screwed up in pain. "I don't know. He paid me five thousand dollars. I didn't ask too many questions."

"You're demented, the both of you."

"I know, man." He pauses, his expression shifting the

slightest bit. "Can you help me?" Massive chest heaves.

"I can't, but I know someone who can." He reaches into his pocket and pulls out a small Bible and a cross. "You've been targeted by the Devil, cursed with two afflictions...at least. You knew what you were doing was wrong, but your love, your destructive love of money made it all clear." He puts the cross around The Rapist's neck. "But God will direct your newfound clarity to the truth, the *only* truth."

He opens the Bible and prays over the whimpering, quivering, crying man.


Leo rubs his palms together and listens to the faint opening of John Coltrane & Johnny Hartman's "Lush Life" coming from the neighboring room.

"Nervous?" Marlon sits across from him.

"No, I..." He lowers his eyes, smiles. "A little."

"Glad you decided to come back and give this anotha shot." He crosses his legs. "I'd much rather we do this in a regular group session, but some o' the others were a little shaken by your first visit. I figure if you and I have some one-on-one time, we can ease you into this before bringin' you back into the fold."

A nod. "It's fine, I understand."

"So tell me what's been goin' on in your life lately."

"Well, I took a leave of absence from my job; felt it best I give myself time to get control of my curse before I go back." He runs his hand over his scalp. "Since I don't know how long that will take, I need to bring in a regular paycheck to keep from using more of my paid time off than necessary. I may have to go back to waiting tables." He laughs to himself. "God, haven't done that since college."

"Any luck finding anything?"

"The positions either don't pay enough or are in a work environment where I can't risk a flare-up." Head shake. "Can't risk the exposure, either. I hear that not all of the experiments being performed on A-Os are entirely voluntary. Might find myself shoved into the back of a windowless van some night."

"Awful." Marlon shakes his head. "Have you been practicin' your abilities, tryin' to control 'em?"

Leo's eyes narrow slightly. The air burns in a thick blob of silver-blue in front of a book on the table. The small force field pushes against the book until it tumbles from the table. "Getting a grasp on reducing the size of my fields and manifesting them for longer periods of time."

Marlon nods. "Seems like you're gettin' the hang o' this."

"Yeah."

"...Still hate yourself for bein' an A-O?"

Leo rubs a hand across his jaw and doesn't respond for a moment. "I—" He exhales frustration through his nose. "I realize it's just a matter of me accepting this thing I have, this thing I can do, but I don't know why I can't do that." He looks at Marlon. "Why can't I do that?"

"I ain't no psychologist, but maybe it's not just your A-O gene you're havin' trouble acceptin'."

A crease in his brow. "What do you mean?"

"Maybe all o' this is tied up wit' something else." Marlon inscribes circles in the air with twirling index fingers. "What else is goin' on in your life that could be holdin' you back?"

Leo blinks, lips parted and eyes lowered as he presses his mouth closed. "I yelled at my parents."

"What about?"

"They sheltered me when I was growing up. I know they had the best intentions for me when they did it, but when they cut me off from a part of the world that I would have to eventually grow up in, it...stifled something in me, something that should have been strengthened over the years."

Marlon scratches his knee. "I don't follow."

"Do you know how difficult it is to grow up as a biracial kid?"

"No."

"Neither do I."

"So you would rather have had it rough growin' up? Had people starin' at you and sayin' stuff outta the sides of their necks?"

"No."

"'S what it sounds like to me. Leo, you gotta understand that your parents did you a mercy by shieldin' you from all that mess. It wasn't a failin' on their part, and it doesn't make you weak, makes you blessed. Now what the hell's weak about love? Sometimes it takes more strength to look past somethin' that's starin' you in the eye rather than face it and acknowledge its existence."

Leo lifts his head.

Marlon continues. "You're a biochemist, so you have to realize that things have layers, that there are these—these tiny, indelible connections that make up a molecule or a cell or whateva. Same thin' with us. We're connected to our parents through our blood, our noses, our hair, our personalities, our allergies, our smiles."

A grin tilts Leo's lips. "You're saying I'm blaming my parents for being an A-O, for hating a part of myself."

A nod. "You're so wrapped up in self-loathin' that you haven't stopped to take the time to figure out the root source o' the emotion."

"But I love my parents. I mean, I genuinely love my parents."

"You sure?"

"I'm positive." The words burble out around a small laugh.

"But why? Why do you love your parents? Do you love 'em because you have to, do you love 'em for makin' you feel weak, do you love 'em for givin' you an active A-O gene?" A shrug. "Why, Leo? Why love?"

"I can't explain it. I don't think it's something I can put into words, even though it's burning inside my brain." He licks his lips. "I think about them and how they've been there with me, been there with each other through so much and no one left. No one got tired and just threw in the towel like so many other couples do." Head shake. "No, I take that back, they did get tired, but they never gave up; not on each other, and not on me."

"So why do you feel this way about 'em now?"

He swallows. "They gave me everything I needed, but now I...I feel like they left the job half-done, left me without a core component, something they knew I'd need eventually."

"That likely wasn't done on purpose, Leo. They had no idea their son would become an Alpha-Omega, that you'd feel like you needed hardship to survive in your life."

No sound.

"Know what you gotta do now, right?"

"Yeah."

"Gonna be difficult, harder than splicin' genes with a butter knife." Marlon grins, corners of his eyes wrinkling.

"Yeah."

"But ya gotta do it."

"...I know."

Time is suspended in silence.

"What else?"

Leo looks at Marlon. "What do you mean?"

The other man spreads his hands. "Somethin' this life-changin' can't be centered on one thing. What else about your bein' an A-O rubs you the wrong way?"

"Thought you said you weren't a psychologist."

"I'm not."

"You're starting to sound like one."

Shrug. "Either way, I'm here to help. But let's focus on you, what else about who you are is keepin' you from bein' who you wanna be?"

Leo scratches at his head. He looks away. He rubs his hands together. "I've always struggled with my identity, figuring out who I am."

"Okay, keep goin'." Marlon interlaces his fingers and leans forward on his knees.

"I was at a point where I felt I was finally living a life instead of just trying to build one. When I found out about my gene, I was right back at square one feeling hollow, like joy forgot my name and address."

"Your A-O gene smashed through every brick of your diligence."

A nod of agreement. "I've been thinking about making an appointment for a consultation at the Johnson Family Boundless Joy Clinic downtown, seeing if they can help me find my way back."

"Nothing wrong with reachin' out for help, takes a lotta strength to do that."

Leo scratches at his scalp. "I just want things to be how they were. It wasn't the most favorable situation, but I made the best of it."

"Why can't you make the best o' this one?"

He scratches at his scalp. "Too old."

"'S a cop out, Leo."

Leo snaps his head up. "You don't know me."

"From what you've told me, you really don't even know yourself."

He shakes his head and scoffs. "There's only one person in my life who knows me."

"And who's that?"

The sun rises on his face. "Francie."

"Girlfriend?"

Nod.

"She doesn't care how many heritages I have swimming in my blood, she doesn't care that I'm a genius, she doesn't care that I'm an Alpha-Omega. She cares that I hate zucchini, she likes it that I listen to the radio while I'm taking a shower, and she doesn't mind that I keep the light on to read while she sleeps next to me."

"Francie's your lifeline."

"I love her. Maybe more than I love myself."

"And if she weren't in your life?"

Leo glances at him before studying the healing stab wound on his palm. He lifts his eyes to Marlon. "If Francie weren't in my life, I might have aimed that pair of scissors at my heart."


Bisset shakes her head again, attempting to rattle the voice from her brain. "I doubled the dose of my medication and I still can't get your voice out of my head." She walks faster down the sidewalk, squinting to focus on the house numbers as she passes.

"You can't block the truth, Bisset." The Dragoness's disembodied voice blots the inside of her ear. "No matter how many pill bottles you empty, I'll still be here, inside. Seraph and that tottering old fool want to change the very foundation of who you are. Why can't you see that?"

"Probably because you won't let me."

"I agree that my methods are extreme, but only because they

have to be. You can't give anyone a gentle nudge anymore, you have to shove them off the cliff. The services I perform, that *we* perform, are necessary and you know it." Her voice softens. "I am who you naturally are just as you are who I naturally am. You have to understand that you, Seraph, and I are one and the same. Three points that form a single, perfect line that never ends." A chill shudders down Bisset's spine. "Extricating me from your soul will be like hacking off an arm. And for Seraph, it will be the equivalent of slashing off one of her wings."

"You're desperate."

"Not for my safety, for yours. You think your mind is twisted now, just wait until I no longer exist, until I'm no longer there to counter Seraph's advice. If she is the superego, then I am the id. One cannot and should not exist without the other. Balance is required."

Bisset's hands curl and she clutches at her head. "SHUT! UP! JUST SHUT UP!" Her throat feels raw as she heaves air.

The Dragoness is silent.

Bisset is silent.

The street is silent.

After a moment, the frazzled woman gathers the filaments of her sanity and continues down the sidewalk.

2156 Saint Paul Street.

A modest affair coated in yellow paint with a small table and set of chairs arranged on the spacious porch. Bisset walks up the walkway, up the front steps, and feels something stirring below her feet. It resonates deep in her chest behind her sternum. She stops and curls her fingers at her chest. "Seraph?" A force propels her.

She knocks.

No answer.

She knocks again.

No answer again.

She looks out at the street in anticipation. She walks to the edge of the porch to peek around the corner and sees that the garage sits empty, waiting just as she does.

She sighs and runs a hand through her curls. Eventually, she sits down in one of the chairs and waits. She rocks and waits and rocks and waits and her eyes drift shut until—

—there is a hand shaking her shoulder.

"Miss?...Miss?"

Bisset jerks awake, arms coming up protectively. A man with brown-blond hair and blue eyes. There is a silver-white haze wavering around him that vanishes when she tries to focus on it.

"Can I help you with something, miss?"

Bisset's eyes flick up from the muted glow at his chest to his eyes. "Are you Adam Kensie?" She removes a stray curl from her face.

"Yes, I am. Can I help you?"

"Adam Kensie, the Sovereign of God, right?"

Adam frowns. "Did someone from the church send you?"

She nods her head. "Bishop Martin."

Confusion melts. "Oh, well...What can I do for you, Miss—"

"Bisset, Bisset Torres." She takes a deep breath. "What do you know about exorcisms?"

## FADE OUT

## DOMINION CITY - CENTURY HEIGHTS - OFFICE OF THE JOHNSON FAMILY BOUNDLESS JOY CLINIC

LEO tries his best to swallow his nerves as he sits and fights the urge to squirm in the lush confines of the fine leather chair. Anita and Charles Johnson sit across from him, both with generous smiles heaped on their faces and patience powering their serene stillness.

"Take all the time you need, Leo." Anita nods her head with a measure of reassurance. "We understand that not everyone is so willing to open up about what brings them to our offices."

Leo swallows and nods, blinking a few times and wishing he could blink away the haze obscuring his mind. He thinks about Francie, thinks about experiencing joy and happiness, genuine joy and happiness unfettered by the chains of *what if*. He thinks about what his life would be like to exist in a perpetual state of bliss, one where he loves himself for being an A-O, one where he has nothing but pure confidence in his ability to find a job and take care of himself and Francie, one where he feels nothing but pride when he thinks about the way his parents raised him. It's enough to force the words from his tongue and lips, to speak his truth. "I want to get to a place where I've made peace with the fact that I'm an A-O." He lifts his head and looks the two in the eyes. "I want to learn how to be optimistic while still being in touch with reality. I...I want to find myself at peace. I've been making some progress in the last few days but..." His knuckles pop as he rolls his fingers into fists. "It never seems to last."

Charles unlaces his fingers from the knee of his crossed legs, rests them on the chair's armrests. "We appreciate you opening up to us, Leo. The first thing I want to do is reassure you that we have nothing but your absolute best interests in mind. I also like to tell our potential patients that I have an extensive background in clinical therapy, so it's not as if it's only my A-O abilities that qualify me to do what my family and I do."

Leo nods his understanding.

"During consultations, we also like to ask why people choose to come to us rather than a traditional therapist or consider medication," Anita asks.

Leo flicks his eyes to her. "Honestly, I'm not sure I have the patience required to work through the steps of traditional therapy." He grimaces as his hand goes pins and needles for a bare second before releasing an involuntary tic of energy, setting the scar on his palm to tingling.

"That's quite understandable." Charles rubs fingertips over the leather of the armrests, lifting his eyes from Leo's hand.

"Well, let us tell you a bit about what you can expect if you decide to allow us to help you unlock your bliss." Anita rests her elbows on her knees and leans forward a bit. "On the day of your appointment, our son, Miguel, and daughter, Annabelle, will be here since our ability only works when we're all together." She holds an upraised palm to the plush reclining chair with a lengthened seat across from them. "We'll have you stretch out on the chaise longue with some soft music of your choice piping through a pair of earbuds while we surround you. Miguel and I will place our fingertips on your temples to close the circuit and start the process."

Leo listens with rapt attention.

"Most of our patients say it feels like being immersed in thick, warm molasses when the unlocking process starts, much like drifting off to sleep." Charles smooths his hands out over the air as he speaks. "Afterward, you'll likely feel like you've heard the best news of your life. I say *likely* because it's different for everyone, but that's the general frame of mind our patients report."

"Are there any side effects?"

Anita shakes her head. "Only unbridled joy." She grins, giving him a preview. "Since the effect of our ability only lasts about a month, what we encourage our patients to do is ruminate on what brought them to us in the first place. While we can bring you the peace you desire, we can't completely eliminate the root cause of your discontent. By concentrating on what's blocking you from experiencing your own joy, you're actually able to change the way your brain responds to those thoughts, the chemical concoction brought about by that frame of mind. When the effect of our ability wears off, you'll feel and think differently about your psychological obstacles."

"A bit like the effects of MDMA or psilocybin when used on people who suffer from PTSD."

Charles casts his gaze to the side, considers. "Yes, actually. That's a perfect way of putting it."

Leo rolls his lips over his teeth, mulls over the torrent of possibilities, thoughts, and impossibilities tumbling and thundering through his skull.

"Take as long as you need to think things over." Anita's voice snips his rushing stream of consciousness. "While we realize how fantastic this all sounds, we also recognize the fact that it's a monumental decision."

What she doesn't know is that Leo has already made up his mind; he's going under the mental knife. He's going to let the Johnsons help him find his ever-elusive jubilation and invite it (or drag it) into his reality by any means necessary. Or unnecessary.

Leo's going to find out what it's like to vomit rainbows and sunshine every time he opens his mouth.

# EPISODE FIVE: *JUXTA-*

Adam opens the doors of the abandoned church, casting it in a shroud of glittering sunlight. He flicks on a light switch and the house of worship is blanketed in a weak, winking glow that quickly stabilizes.

Bisset follows behind him, nose curled. "Why here?"

"I wanted to conduct our sessions in a private place, but still in the presence of the Lord." He goes over to a massive overturned pew and uprights it with barely a flexed muscle. He does the same to another and rearranges the two so that they are facing one another. He wipes off enough dust for them to sit.

Bisset parts her lips with a small *ah* sound. Her expression fractures into a sullen one.

"Are you okay?"

"I'm fine, it's just..."

"The Dragoness?"

She shakes her head. "Seraph. She can be a bit forceful when she wants to."

"Can you tell me what she's saying?"

"She can speak to you through me, if you want."

"Really? It doesn't hurt you or anything?"

Bisset shakes her head.

Adam nods. "Okay, then, but only if you're sure you want to."

"Anything to help me with this." Her body goes still, her eyes empty before their brown edges are traced with a golden outline. A smile blossoms on Bisset's face...on Seraph's face. "Hello, Adam. It's a pleasure to meet the owner of this magnificent light I've felt. God is quite pleased with you."

A little smile caresses his lips. "You've talked with God, Seraph?"

She laughs and he shivers in its wake.

"God talks to all of us, but most simply choose not to listen."

His head hangs. She reaches forward and grabs his hand. "Talk to me, Adam."

He licks his lips, sliding forward in his seat. "We're trying to bring back God's word, the followers of the Apostolic faith and I. God's teachings have been broken apart and distorted; taken in by some denominations and denounced by others. I want to bring all of His children back to Him and show Alpha-Omegas that they are part of this world, but not of it. They need to know that they're soldiers in the army of the Lord."

Seraph squeezes his hand. "I've felt your light for a while, Adam, it's one that almost rivals that of the angels." She shakes her head a bit. "But from what little Bisset and I understand of them, I'm not sure Alpha-Omegas are part of God's plan for this world."

Adam's head rocks back, hand slipping from her touch. "Why do you say that?"

"Their fantastic powers do seem like gifts from On High, but that isn't to suggest that they're divine vessels...like you and Bisset."

"But I believe they are. They're simply lost children who need help finding their way, like Bisset. Mankind has slowly averted their eyes from God, but they still feel His power in their souls." He pats a palm to his chest. "They might not acknowledge what is it, but they feel it." He is silent for a moment. "I believe that I and people like me are meant to do great, marvelous things together in the name of the Lord."

"Instruments of the Most High."

"Put on this Earth to gather a symphony, and God shall be our conductor." He hesitates away for a second. "May I...may I ask you something?"

"Certainly."

"Why did you choose to inhabit this body?"

"I'm honestly not sure that I did. Maybe Bisset choose me, whether she wants to admit it or not."

"It seems as though great things always happen to the most ordinary people. Why do you think that is?"

"Those who think they have purpose in their life are often blinded by their final destination. But those who have no corporeal goal are often able to see the web for the weavings, the small intricacies that bring everything together. Your faith in your fellow man and in God is unshakable. I have a feeling that you haven't even begun to explore what God has planned for you."

Adam's mouth suddenly goes dry and his expression falters.

"What is it?"

"God doesn't want me to have a child." His chest rises and falls as he takes shallow breaths. "When I first found out that I was blessed to be the Sovereign of God, almost immediately I knew that I was supposed to pass on this blessing to my child to lead the next generation. But I just found out last week that my...that I can't...that it will be nearly impossible for Maggie and I to have a child."

"Your not being able to procreate right now isn't as monumental as you might believe. Things change, Adam. You know that just as well as I."

His eyes plead. "But I wanted to give Maggie a son or a daughter, a beautiful baby that we created together. One of the things she's wanted most in life is a child." A helpless shrug. "And I can't give her that."

"But you can give her so much more. You can give her your love, your trust, your loyalty. You may not be able to have a child of the flesh, but you can have one of the spirit." She lightly touches him below the collarbone. "What's the use of dwelling on what you can't give her? It only weakens your love and your light."

Adam nods. "You're right." He lifts his head and his lips along with it. "It's nice to be able to talk to someone else about all this, someone who knows what I'm going through."

"You feel you can't talk with Maggie or your friends?"

It takes a moment for him to respond. "I really don't have any friends outside of church. As far as Maggie, I used to feel like I could talk to her about anything and everything."

Bisset dips her head to the side a bit. "What changed?"

His eyes meet hers. "I became Sovereign, and now I'm not human the way she is anymore. I feel like I've gained just as much as I've lost."

"Or maybe God is just making room in your life for the blessings he's about to shower you with."

The words seem to seep and steep into his soul, coloring it with clarity and brightening his expression.

Bisset grins. "Look at us. You're supposed to be helping Bisset and here I am consoling you." She rubs the back of his hand.

"Maybe you can help me cast this demon out of Bisset."

The angel's smile weakens. "The more I understand of her, the less I think of The Dragoness as a normal demon." She rolls her shoulders a bit. "But I'll do anything that I can to help Bisset."

A frame is suspended in mid-air, covered in a shimmering silver-blue glow.

"A little higher to the left."

The frame bobs higher and glides smoothly to the left.

"Now, the artist asked that it be tilted just slightly to the right."

The frame dips slightly to the right, resting on the small hooks embedded in the wall.

"Perfect."

Leo lowers his hand and the glow slides down the frame as he dissolves the force field. He studies the myriad of colors, shades, and multi-faceted hues splashed and dashed on the crooked canvas as he walks over to Marlon. "What is this all about again?"

"The DC Art Museum is hostin' a show here. Local and nationwide artists reveal their depictions of Alpha-Omegas." He takes in the various art selections decorating the walls of building. "They're calling it Apocalyptic-Origin." His eyes pause and take in the sculpture of a horrific demon with the white wings of an angel and the hands and feet of a human with a grotesque twisted phallus dangling between its legs. There is no face.

"I never really got into art." Leo cants his head, scrunching his eyebrows together.

"That's probably cuz you use the other side of your brain."

"You mean the logical side?"

The other man shrugs. "Some of these artists may think it's illogical to shove your eyes into a microscope every day."

Leo scoffs. "Hasn't been every day lately."

"Still ain't found work yet?"

"Nope."

"Real sorry to hear that." A smile peels on Marlon face. "Either way, I sure 'preciate you givin' us a helpin' hand these past coupla days." He turns and walks into the small kitchen.

"Just trying to keep myself busy. Francie hasn't said anything, but I know she gets tired of seeing me on the couch with a biochem book every time she comes home."

"Least you ain't glued to the TV, mess will corrode your brain." He peels open the fridge door and takes out two bottles of water, passing one to Leo.

"Thanks." He twists the cap open and swigs.

Marlon lowers the bottle and wipes at his mouth. "You know, the curator of the DCAM said somethin' 'bout needin' some help. Could be just right for you."

Leo frowns at him after a sip. "I just told you I never really got into art."

"Yeah, an' you also just told me you ain't found work yet. I wish I could pay you for the work you do here, but our budget is pretty stringent. I've got Addie's number, you want it or not?"

Leo sighs, swallows.

He reaches into the side pocket of his khakis for his phone.


# EXCERPT FROM LAMAR KOEHLER LIVE:

"Good evening, America, and thank you for joining me for another episode of *Lamar Koehler Live*. I'm your host, Lamar Koehler.

"Tonight, I'm joined by a family that upon first glance looks very normal, very mundane. But the Johnsons are anything but that. In actuality, the Johnsons are a family of Alpha-Omegas who share an ability. Please join me in welcoming Charles Johnson, his wife, Anita, and their children, Miguel and Annabelle. Welcome to the show, everyone."

"Thank you, Lamar. How are you?"

"I'm very well, thrilled to have such wonderful guests joining me tonight. Now, Charles, your family has been in and out of the media in the last few weeks, and that has got to be a hassle for all of you."

"Oh, it is. But we're slowly getting used to having people photograph us and ask us questions when we're out and about in public. But one upside to the exposure is that it's actually helped us and our small family business based in Dominion City."

"Could you explain to us what your business is?"

"Sure. What my family and I do is we make people happy. Literally. We've recently discovered that we each share an active A-O gene that allows us to take away a person's inhibitions that block them from achieving their dreams and allowing themselves to be truly happy."

"Anita, how did you and your family discover this ability? I know you said earlier before the show that it only works when all four of you are in physical contact."

"It's a bit of an odd story, actually, but it usually is when you're talking about A-Os. Ah, we were all gathered for family dinner and Miguel had invited his friend, Cristobal, over to join us. Cristobal was having some family problems, so we wanted to get him out of that environment and take his mind off of things. We all joined hands for prayer and Cristobal was sitting between Miguel and Annabelle. While Charles was saying grace, Cristobal clutched Miguel and Annabelle's hand to his chest, and the only thing that I can think of is that their hands must have brushed together which...activated our gene. There was this flow that went through all four of us, and I could actually feel that flow go into Cristobal."

"How did it feel?"

"It felt like...like light, and happiness, and...purity. It's hard to describe, really. After that, Cristobal just couldn't seem to stop smiling all throughout dinner. He was laughing and just being a kid, something we hadn't seen him do since we'd met him. It was the best feeling in the world, for him and for us."

"And that's when you decided to make spreading happiness the family business?"

"Well, that came a bit later. We all sat down and talked about what happened with Cristobal and eventually realized that this gift only manifested when all four of us are together."

"Fascinating. I know that since you've started the Johnson Family Boundless Joy Clinic, your lives have changed drastically, and not just with the exposure. Miguel, you actually bought your first car in full with your own money, correct?"

"Yes, sir."

"And it wasn't just some used bucket of bolts! This was a top of the line car, a BMW."

"Right."

"Wow. And Annabelle, you bought prom dresses for every girl in your class?"

"Yes, sir, I did."

"You did an excellent job of raising these two, mom and dad."

"Thank you, Lamar. We're just glad that all of this attention hasn't gone to their heads. We've always stressed to Annabelle and Miguel that they're no better than anyone else, and now that they've become public figures, it's even more important for them to remember that."

"I have to ask, how do you feel about charging people for happiness?"

"Charles was a licensed clinical therapist before his partners decided to shut down the practice. We feel charging our clients is no different than a therapist charging a client to help improve his or her life."

"And it's not as if we're charging some outrageous fee. The effect of what we do lasts about a month or so before a person needs to decide whether to come back for another treatment."

"I see. Have you heard the latest news reports about you?"

"What news reports are you referring to, Lamar?"

"Do we have the repo—We do? Can we put that on the screen, please? Thank you. According to multiple news sources, several of your former patients are now in the psychiatric ward or have committed suicide after receiving treatments from you. One woman actually died with a smile on her face. The wife of a former patient of yours is claiming that her husband nearly crushed her to death with a hug after returning from a session with you. Do you have anything to say about this?"

"...Where did you get these?"

"From multiple news sources. You can check them if you like, they're perfectly legitimate. Do you have anything to say about these accusations?"

"We're finished here. Come on, let's go."

"Thank you for joining us. That was the Johnson family, ladies and gentlemen. Spreading happiness with just a touch. We'll be right back."


The Johnsons are on the TV. The TV is on mute. But their smiles and their laughter need no audio to convey their message. A camera quickly pans the live studio audience before swiveling back to the talk show hostess. Charles smooths his fingers across the back of Anita's palms. Anita absently runs a hand through Miguel's shaggy hair. Annabelle crosses her legs and smiles at no one in particular.

But no one in the drug den pays any attention to the muted television set. They are too busy weighing out kilos, sampling the product, and calling to confirm meets and negotiate sales.

"An' I tol' you dat you ain't even gettin' another abe until you pay me my money." The man with an orange bandana wrapped around his forehead scratches his thigh with the barrel of his gun. "Hit up the towers on Sherman." He sniffs and paces across the torn tiled floor. "In Mercurmont, you dumb mothafucka! Fuck, no wonder you punk ass bitches can't sling this shit right, you don't even know where to peddle your shit." He stops, raises the large gun to the phone. "'Ey yo, you got one mo' time to call me a wigga before I blow you and your bitch crew's heads off. You feel dat?" He lowers the gun. "A'ight. You got twenty-four hours to brin' me my money or I'm comin' after you." He whips the gun forth and back. "Naw, betta yet, I'm comin' after your fam. Make your moms suck my dick before I put a load an' a bullet down her throat. Believe dat." He hangs up before lighting up a cigarette.

"Beedrow and his crew givin' you the run around?" The man in the tight tank top slouches on the couch. His red-glazed eyes follow the man with the bandana as he starts pacing.

"As fuckin' usual. Gave 'em a week to sling that package. A whole week!" He whirls suddenly and angrily extends the arm holding the gun, muscles quivering. "I keep givin' these fuckas chance after chance after chance to prove 'emselves and I wind up takin' it up the ass like some lil' bitch. Ain't havin' dat, man."

"And you shouldn't." The man in the tank top uncurls his hands and shows his palms. "Gotta start makin' examples, show these cats that Wayne King don't play."

"Das right, man, das right." Wayne nods his head. "Where we at?"

The man in the tank top jerks his head at the activity behind them. "Gettin' another re-up ready for the south side. Plannin' a sell with Magnet." He scratches the back of his shoulder. "Hate dealin' with that cat."

Wayne sits down next to him, wrists dangling over his spread knees. "Why?"

"Cuz he's weird as shit. Dude comes to the meet with a fedora cocked to the side wit some faggot ass feather stickin' out."

Wayne's knees bob. "Mag digs those film noir flicks. Tryin' to bring dat ol' skool style back."

The man in the tank top scrunches his eyes together, a mass of wrinkles creasing his forehead. "The fuck is film nur?"

"Film noir, mutha fucka, *film noir*." He stares at him, hisses between his teeth. "You fresh lil' homies don't know nothin'."

"Well, break it down."

"A'ight, look, film noir is a style of movie dey made back in—"
*c r e a a a k*

"The hell was that?" Wayne and the man in the tank top turn to look on the other side of the couch. The young woman with the ponytail looks up at the ceiling.

"De hell was what?"

"Shh."

The man in the tank top glares at her. "Man, I know this lil' bitch didn't just shu—"

*crreak*

"Heard it dat time." Wayne stands and looks up at the ceiling.

Everyone in the house does the same.

"Think it's rats?"

"We got ridda the Mickey Mouse club last week."

"Then what the fuc—"

Four crude lines scour through the ceiling. Eve—*RIIP!*—ry hand scra—*RIIP!*—mbles for a—*RIIP!*—weapon. The claw marks form a rough square. Then, the ceiling cutout suddenly explodes down on them, showering them in wood, paint chips, and bent nails. Noir bursts out from the jagged hole upside down, claws bared, before flipping his body and landing on his feet in a crouch. He smirks as dust and debris kiss his shoulders and the top of his shaved head, swirling around him. "I'm the fuck."

The man next to him lunges for one of the guns on the far table. Noir quick steps to him, grabs him by the wrist and yanks his arm back and up before slashing his hooked claws out once, twice where the man's arm connects to his shoulder. His claws scrape through bone and muscle with vicious ease. The man's arm suddenly comes free in shreds and threads of tendon and flesh as the man stumbles backward, catching himself on his remaining hand. Noir roughly boots him in the side of the head.

The man in the tank top takes up the crowbar at his feet and starts swinging. It makes Noir laugh as he dodges left and right in the steps of a familiar routine. "Did this number just last week, 'cept my partner was a much better dancer." He quick ducks. "Like to do these little spins on the balls—" He pistons a fist into the man's groin, forcing a hoarse groan between tight lips as the man brings his knees and thighs together. "—of his feet." He absently shoots a kick back at the woman rushing him from behind before swiping his claws at the man's throat. Blood squirts and blurts from the severed artery in his neck.

He spins on the stumbling woman just in time to see her yank a blade from her waist. She thrusts. Noir jerks his head back and the tip of the blade scratches a line across his cheek. She jabs low, starts to slash high. Noir captures her wrist as it's in motion before twisting it while cranking it out at her side at an agonizing angle, feeling bones grind together. He presses his claws into her wrist, forcing the blade from numbed fingers. He flings her into Wayne just as he raises his gun. They go down in a thrash of limbs.

*B L A M !*

A shot rings out behind him and the bullet *thunks* into the wall.

*B L A M !*

The spot where Noir stood just a split second before.

*B L A M !*

Noir vaults over the back of the couch, body parallel to the ground, and brings his knees up to his chest before launching them out into a brutal missile kick. The gunner wearing a backwards baseball cap is flung back on top of the table, crushing a bagged eight ball and reducing a brick to powder. Noir rolls off of the couch and fetches him up by the shirt and heaves him over the couch.

Wayne and the woman are on their feet, standing next to each other.

Noir takes two quick steps before jumping up into the air, planting his left foot on the back of the couch and slashing his right leg out. *W H A M !* His boot lashes out at the woman's face, cracking across her cheek, but she doesn't fall. Noir's body is spinning in the air. His other le flashes out. *W H O O M !* Wayne takes a sole to the head. Noir brings his right foot up as he comes down, dropping it solidly on the gunner's neck as gravity calls him back.

*C R A C K !*

He buries a clawed hand in the woman's soft stomach, forcing her mouth open and her muscles to constrict reflexively around the hand twining through her entrails.

*B L A M !*

The passing bullet gnaws across his right ear with a burning bite. He withdraws bloody fingers from intestines and slaps the gun from Wayne's hand. He dives for the falling gun as Wayne reaches for the second gun at his back.

Time swims languid like syrup.

A hand snatches a gun from the crank-dusted floor. A hand wraps around the grip of a gun tucked into a waistband. A shoulder hits the floor and the body twists. An arm whips out along with a gun barrel, aiming.

Time slams back like a concussion.

Noir stares up into the barrel of a gun as Wayne looks down into one. The—

B      L      A      M

Wayne looks confused. Noir breathes evenly. Wayne's eyes roll up at the neat bullet hole blown through his bandana. The puzzle comes together in his eyes, ears flicking as a bit of brain leaks out from the messy hole in the back of his head. He collapses forward with a loud thump.

Noir collapses on his back as blood pulses through his veins. *In* his veins.

Wayne's veins give a final surge, leaking blood from the hole in the back of his skull.

As Noir stands, he puts a hand to his grazed ear. "Hijo de puta!" He snatches up a bandana on the back of an overturned chair, wads it up, and presses it to his ear. He scans the bodies, making sure all of them are expired, and the TV snatches his attention. He searches for the remote and thumbs the MUTE button.

"—ered us a reality show just last week." Charles Johnson shrugs. "I don't know if we're going to take it, it's still on the table."

"All I have to say is wow." The blonde talk show hostess laughs. "Well, if you do accept, you'd not only be the first Alpha-Omegas to have their own reality show, you'd be the first American Alpha-Omega family to have a TV show. No pressure or anything!"

"As long as it doesn't interfere with the family or our business, it's definitely something we would consider." Anita Johnson removes a strand of hair from her eyes. "This is a chance some people never have but many deserve, and we feel that it's our duty to—"

Noir scoffs. "Someone should do *me* a favor and kill them." He looks down and remembers that he has a gun in his hand. He raises it and pulls the trigger. The TV gives a dying snap, crackle, and pop accompanied by a small burst of sparks spouting out of the bullet hole.

Noir taps the barrel against his thigh as he turns and leaves.

Several handfuls of several seconds pass.

He comes back, stomps over to the table resting on three legs, and snatches up a gym bag bulging with tight rolls of money wrapped almost lovingly in rubber bands. The door creaks as it closes behind him for the final time.

Someone steps out of the room behind the TV. The glaring light makes a pair of pristine shoes shine as they walk across the blood-blessed floor. The bullet that killed the TV has buried itself in their chest, but they don't seem to notice it.

Fingers, fine-boned and delicate, slip into the side pockets of designer slacks. The person stops and studies the tableau. They then bend down and touch Wayne King's cooling wrist. Death courses from one corpse into another. The bullet is pushed out with a *pling*, flesh healing beautifully around the wound. They look down at the hole in the silk shirt.

Giorgio studies the opening and frowns.


Fiery reds interspersed with dramatic golden hues suffused with dashes of white. In the corner a single blob of blue rests solemnly, looking up at the racing streaks of green and brown with envy.

"Isn't it prosaic?"

Leo clasps his hands and rubs his knuckles. "Isn't art supposed to burst with imagination and creativity?" He swallows the large lump in his throat.

The tall woman at his side looks at him, glossy black banana curls atop her head swinging and bouncing mightily. "Yes, but the lack of spirit is a testament to art itself. The candid quality doesn't immediately assault your eye. You spend hours looking at it, wondering what the artist is trying to say until...you finally figure out that there's nothing to hear."

Leo shakes his head. "All I see are colors and shapes strewn together on a canvas, Addie."

"You see through the eyes of a scientist." Addie steps behind him and grips him by the shoulders, her mouth at his left ear. "We all think ourselves as fools to art, afraid that the artist's true message isn't the one we leave with. The truth is that the message is what you see, with your own eyes." Her hands leave his shoulders, her mouth his ear. "Now, Leo, I have a phone conference. Mr. Morente should be here in a little while to pick up the Vusay, it's all ready for him in the receiving room." She throws him a smile. "Why don't you idle here for a moment and see if anything speaks to you, hmm?"

He nods.

"Wonderful." She breezes off.

Leo walks over to a sculpture wrought from wood and iron. He steps back to take it all in. His chest rises and falls in a low breath.

"Don't think Addie was being literal when she said the art would speak to you."

Leo turns to find an older man in a jumpsuit slightly slumped over pushing a mop and bucket across the floor. He scratches at the rough stubble across his hollow cheeks, adjusts the frayed cap on his head. "What's your name?"

"Leo."

"Clint. I'm the janitor." He squeezes water from the mop. "As you can tell."

"Nice to meet you."

Clint goes about mopping the floor. "So who are you, Leo?"

He looks away from the sculpture. "Sorry?"

Clint stops mopping, stretches up to his full height, and dramatically widens his eyes. "Who. Are. You. Leo?" He grossly over exaggerates each word. "What. Did. You. Do. Before. You. Worked. Here?" His eyebrows reach for the sky, neck stretched out as he gives a limpid little smile.

"Oh, I was a, uh, I was a biochemist."

"Biochemist?" He pops his head back. "Don't they make good money?"

"Yes, we, uh, we do." He slides back a step.

"The hell you doing working here, then? Mix the wrong chemicals and blow the place to hell?" A jittery little guffaw twitters past his dry lips.

"No, I'm just figuring some things out." He tries to go back to the art.

"Hmph. I heard that before." He slaps the wet mop on the floor. "Said the same thing when I quit my job with NASA." A shrug. "Somehow, cleaning up little kid vomit and buffing floors is so much more satisfying than pulling down six figures."

Leo glances at him, but says nothing.

"Hear anything yet?" *Swish. Swoosh. Swish.*

"Actually looking more than I'm listening." His lips barely move around the words.

"Ain't gotta be a smartass." He looks up from the wet floor. "Someone could dab a single dot of paint on a canvas and sell it for a cool million." He dunks the mop in steaming water. "Have folks in those little hats, you know, the ones with the little stems, have them all in a tizzy trying to figure out what it represents."

"Berets." He doesn't look away from the sculpture.

Clint stops mopping and starts staring. "Wha?"

"Those little hats with the stems you were talking about, they're called berets."

A side of his mouth wrinkles. "Well, you are a smart little whip. Still don't explain why you working here." Mopping calls his attention.

"I told you I'm—"

A dismissive wave. "Yeah, yeah, son, save it. Just mopped this floor, don't need your hogwash all over it."

Leo looks at him. "And why are you here?"

A genuine chuckle. "Told you, got tired of working with NASA."

## RADIO SHOW EXCERPT:

*"Thanks for calling, you are on the air. Who's this?"*

*"This is Noa, from Phosphorous Park."*

*"All right, Noa from Phosphorous Park, speak your piece."*

*"I think that the Johnsons should stop what they're doing and make an honest living like the rest of us."*

*"So you don't think that they should be making people happy?"*

"I'm not saying that at all. What I am saying is that it's dumb to charge someone for something that they can get for free, and it's even dumber to pay for it."

"You don't think people should have the option of being happy and satisfied without having to pop a pill or going to therapy?"

"No no no no! In those cases, the person needs to figure out why they're unhappy in the first place. We've become so accustomed to a quick fix and it sucks, it really does. I don't have anything against Alpha-Omegas, my girlfriend's one, but I do have something against exploitation. The Johnsons, this so-called normal American family, are just using us to look like the Jesus Christ family."

"I see."

"And after watching my man Lamar Koehler last night, I looked into what he was talking about, about how several of their former patients have snapped. The man is on to something. Many of their patients, clients or whatever, are wearing crazy coats now, babbling and foaming at the mouth with huge drooling smiles on their faces."

"That could be a completely unrelated circumstance, Noa. Maybe complete happiness wasn't what they really wanted at all and they couldn't handle it."

"I'm sorry, man, but that doesn't make sense to me. When was the last time you weren't happy with being happy? I'm not disagreeing with you that being happy isn't nice, just that it doesn't solve all of the problems in the world."

"But it doesn't hurt."

"No, it doesn't."

"Who knows why some of those people committed suicide, Noa? Maybe they were in a rush to see what the afterlife is like. Some people commit suicide on accident. I know I wish some people would kill themselves just so I wouldn't have to put up with them anymore!"

"And maybe the Johnsons are giving these people pure satisfaction, but I don't think life is meant to be lived like that. You can't—no, you shouldn't be happy all of the time."

"And why not, Noa?"

"You just shouldn't, man. Can you imagine how weird it would be if everywhere you looked all you saw were people smiling and laughing?"

"Brings a nice image to mind."

"It shouldn't. We're human; we were given all of these different feelings, all these different muscles in our faces, muscles that were meant to convey a whole lot of emotions and expressions."

"But you have to remember that the Johnsons aren't human, not in the conventional sense, at least."

"Yeah, but I'm sure they still remember what it's like to be human. They weren't born Alpha-Omegas...okay, so they were, but they didn't know what they would become until a few months ago."

"So what do you think we should do about them?"

"I don't know, but we need to do it fast, man, need to do it fast."


"I'mhappyI'mhappyI'mhappyOhI'msohappysohappysohappysohappy happyhappy."

Beady brown eyes dart here and there on the other side of the metal door, white paint flaking and peeling around the bars on the windows.

"How long has he been like this?" The young woman slides trembling fingers down her folded arms, trying her best to hide the tears in her eyes.

The woman in the white coat glances down at the clipboard. "Since about five o'clock this morning. We've done tests on him and he seems to be fine except for above-normal levels of serotonin and dopamine in his system."

"So the only thing that's wrong with my grandfather is that he's obscenely happy?"

"Essentially, yes."

The granddaughter touches fingers to her lips. "I've been hearing about what that A-O family does, but I was hoping it was some kind of publicity stunt." She looks in the small square window. Her grandfather looks back.

"I'm happy, Lisa! I'm happy!"

"Yes, grandfather, I know, you're crazy happy." She gives a forced reassuring grin. "Is he in any danger?" They take a few steps away from the door.

"His body can't keep up with the chemical demands of what they've done to him. We've tried sedating him in an attempt to get his brain to slow down producing the chemicals, but it doesn't work."

"Will he..." She swallows. "Will he make it?"

The doctor taps the clipboard against her thigh. "If we can't figure out something soon, it could lead to permanent brain damage."

"I guess being happy for the rest of his life won't be the worst thing."

"Not to him at least."

"How many other patients in here are former clients of the Johnsons?"

"We've admitted eight over the past two days."

"Damn."

"We're running out of rooms." She presses her lips together. "Happiness and satisfaction have always been a human desire. Now that we have what we desire we—"

A ragged scream of ecstatic joy rips through their ears.

They hurry to the door.

The old man has his fingers dug in his eye sockets, digging fitfully for his eyes as twin trails of blood run down his stretched cheeks and into his open mouth. "I want to see it! See it! Let me see it!"

The man bleeds and laughs and is obscenely happy.


Night has taken over Mercurmont. Cars clog the streets as moving bodies blanket the cracked sidewalks.

Noir walks alone.

He passes through an abandoned lot on the way home, hands shoved in his pockets as the unseasonably warm, fetid air brushes across shoulders bared in the tank top. The zipped bag of money rubs against his thigh.

He walks into a cone of flickering piss-yellow light and kicks the large rock at his feet, sending it bouncing and clattering off the metal beams discarded and decayed in a pile.

"You gon' follow me all the way home, amigo?" He doesn't turn, doesn't stop, doesn't seem concerned in the slightest.

"What did you gain by killing them?" The voice slithers from the strip of shadows behind him.

"What did I have to lose?"

The sparse tufts of grass around his feet yellow, crinkle, and curl before withering and wilting to brown. Now Noir stops. "The fuck?" He whirls and sees the man behind him. Loose brown curls, bright yellow-green eyes, delicate razors for cheekbones, well-dressed.

"You doin' this?"

The other man only stares, hair buoyed beautifully by the corrupted breeze.

Noir drops the bag, lunges forward, and shoots his fist out in a cross. The man dances back in a lazy sway. Noir uses the wasted momentum to fling his other fist out in a hook. The man absently catches it and Noir suddenly feels his captured wrist go numb, the sensation sinking into muscle, bone, and nerve.

"Amazing how smoothly you can move when you don't have rushing blood and adrenaline to distract you." He pushes Noir away. "But you haven't answered my question: why did you kill those men and that woman?"

Noir glances down at his wrist just as the sickly purple and yellow bruising around his aching arm fades back to brown. "I killed 'em because they were bad boys and girls. What were you doin', hidin' somewhere, pretty boy? Sure you saw the whole show, the guns, the scales, the lil' baggies...the drugs." They regard each other, Noir's fingers curling and uncurling in slow anticipation.

"You don't believe that the quality of your life is lessened by taking the lives of others?"

"Not if they deserve it."

"And if they don't?"

"Then I don't kill 'em." His lip curls. "I only kill people that need killin', so why you all in my face?"

The man smiles. "I'm doing you a favor."

Noir's lips part and his eyebrows draw together. "Got your lines mixed up."

The well-dressed man's hands go behind his back. "Have you ever thought about doing something else with your life, Mr..." He rolls a hand through the air with a flourish.

"Call me Noir."

He lifts his chin a touch. "Poignant."

"Thanks. Now who the hell are you?"

"Giorgio Quintero." He wears an expression of consideration as he brings a hand up and rubs the tips of his fingers and thumb together. "At least that's who I was."

Noir breathes through his nose.

"Have you ever thought about doing something else, Noir? Have you ever felt that you were wasting your life, throwing it away?" He leans forward, eyes shining in the streetlight. "It's not like you get a second chance at this."


"Only what I allow her."

Adam studies her for a moment. "If you're sure."

"I am." Bisset nods and leans her head back. Her eyes go distant and her body goes rigid. Her eyes *flash* golden with smoky verdant swirls before flicking back to their natural brown hue. She tilts her head forward with a smile that doesn't touch the rest of her face. "Adam." Bisset's voice is now sultry, low, and cooing.

"The Dragoness?"

"In the honey-brown flesh."

"I heard that you wanted to speak to me."

"I do."

"Concerning what exactly?"

"Why do you wish to change my hostess, to change Bisset?"

"Bisset came to me in tears—"

"That's a falsehood."

"Not all tears are physical. You have ripped her mind to shreds, made it so that she can't live a normal life. You have tarnished Bisset's light with your unholy sickness."

"And you're just the man to take that blight and cast it back into the chasm of Hell from whence it came, correct?"

"Yes." He grits his teeth around the word.

"Mmm. That's not it, not really. Why do you really want to change Bisset, Adam? For her...or for yourself?"

"You don't see what you're doing to her."

"And you won't let yourself see what you *will* do to her. You only want to feel that warm rush, that ecstatic spurt of pleasure you get from helping people. You simply want to feel good about helping someone who isn't even aware of how truly blessed they are because of misguided and jealous people like yourself."

"You are quite the temptress."

"I only tempt with the unpolished truth."

"You twist the truth. I'm looking into the eyes of a serpent; hypnotic and full of deceit." He leans forward and stares into The Dragoness's eyes. They blink once, snapping to captivating green and gold. They blink again, snapping back to empty brown cavities. "I'll extend this offer only once: Get out of Bisset Torres's body, serpent. Right now."

The Dragoness's tongue slips out to slick across her lips. "You don't seem to understand this relationship. I can't extricate myself from this body anymore than you can. You are your body, your intestines, your cells, your thoughts, your desires. For some reason, humans can't wrap their big little heads around the idea that everything is connected, that separation doesn't exist. It's simply something else that they manifest to make sense of the world. Time, reason, philosophy. Nothing but walls. All of the lines are connected, Adam."

Adam stares at her, saying nothing. "You're refusing to give this woman her freedom?" The words are whispered.

"For someone who's more than human, you're not very incisive." She blinks and leans forward as she twists her head a bit to the side. "Is God yelling too loudly in your ears for you to hear me?"

Adam goes to the pulpit and comes back with a dusty bottle of anointing oil. His gaze never leaves hers as he unscrews the cap and puts his thumb over the opening and tilts the bottle. "I cast you out in the name of the Father, the Son, and the Holy Spirit." He smears oil in a horizontal line on The Dragoness's forehead. "I command you out of this body, out of this mind, and out of this soul by the power of God and His son, our only savior, Jesus Christ." He smears a vertical line on The Dragoness's forehead. "I exorcise this wicked demon by all of the Holy Power in me." He presses his thumb in the center of The Dragoness's forehead, gripping the side of her head with his fingers. "Back to the Inferno, I command thee!" His eyes ignite silver. "Back to Hell, I command thee!" His body explodes in a swath of silver incandescence. "BACK TO THE INFERNO, I COMMAND THEE!" His clothes press against his skin as a sudden hot gale flashes into creation between them. The Dragoness's curls are whipped and stretched back behind her.

"I CAST YOU OUT, SATAN! I DENOUNCE YOU AND ALL THE EVIL THAT YOU HAVE BROUGHT ONTO BISSET TORRES."

The Dragoness's eyes drift closed, her breath hitches...

And she sneezes.

The wind falters, dying away along with the silver glow around Adam's body.

The Dragoness's eyes open. Unimpressed.

"Finished?"

Adam glares at her. "Only for tonight."


Addie leans forward in her chair. "Are you sure, Leo?"

A nod. "I'm sure."

She flattens her palm on the desk. "I know this isn't exactly in your chosen field, but I can see that there's a lot going on with you. It's all over your face, the tightness in your shoulders, your voice."

He cants his head sideways. "You can see all of that?"

A soft smile. "Not everything has to be studied under a microscope."

He sighs. "It's just that I don't feel this job is right for me...not right now."

"Or maybe it's just the job you need right now. Something new, not too demanding, something that throws you out of your comfort zone."

"I'm sorry things didn't work out how Marlon thought they would."

Addie braces her chin on her palm. "I've known Marlon for a while; his instincts are almost as good as mine. If he thinks working here can do you good, then he's probably right." She sips tea from the steaming mug on her desk. "So why do you think you shouldn't be here?"

He scrunches his face together. "I can't tell what's going on in half of these pieces. How am I supposed to describe it to other people? I don't know what I'm talking about."

She waggles a finger at him. "Many people have come to realize that most of the time it's the experts who don't know what they're talking about. They have too much know-how to look at something subjectively in a new light. Take you for instance. You think that art and science couldn't be further apart from each other. In reality, they're very much the same."

Leo frowns.

"All of the cells and atoms, the nucleus and all of the protons and neutrons, all of them are essential to the body. Without one, it just wouldn't work properly. All of the small things create the whole." She arches her eyebrows. "See where I'm going with this?"

"Yes."

"Good. Now, Mr. Morente has just arrived and he's interested in looking at the new Karthesier piece up front before we conclude our business. I'd like for you to show it to him."

Leo's face drops. "What? No, I—I can't."

She stands. "Yes, you can. He's not a pretentious bastard. He enjoys hearing different perceptions. In fact, he relishes them." She opens the door. "Come on." Her banana curls bounce as she nods her head at the door. "Don't make me yank you out of that chair and wrinkle up that nice shirt."

Leo stands with a groan. He walks with Addie out of the office and into the gallery. A man with silver hair beneath a dark green fedora stands with his back to them. His lightly wrinkled hands are clasped behind him, head tilted up at the wood and iron sculpture Leo had been studying earlier. Addie gives his arm a pat.

"Mr. Morente, such a pleasure to see you." He turns, removes his hat and beams as they embrace. He looks older than he moves.

"Ah, Addie, my beauty. Looking wonderful as always." He holds her by the elbows with tender care.

"Why, thank you. Mr. Morente, I'd like you to meet our newest employee, Leo Kennington."

Leo holds out a hesitant hand, glancing at it for a second and willing his tic not to manifest. "A pleasure to meet you, sir." His power obeys. For now.

The older man shakes his hand. "No need to be so formal. You think just because I own over twenty art galleries in America and teach at an Ivy League college you have to bow down to me. I bow down to you." He gives a slight bow and a guffaw.

Addie laughs. Leo gives a hesitant nod.

"The Karthesier is just this way." Addie leads them deeper into the gallery toward the Native American exhibit. "How was your flight?"

"Adventurous." The old man beams. "We ran into turbulence halfway through, twisted my stomach into knots. Oh, it was wonderful. As we were passing over Colorado, we stumbled into a storm. Skeins of lightning decimating the sky with the wind whipping the clouds into all sorts of frothy shapes. And just on the other side of the sky the sun was peeking out for a look. I didn't know whether to be frightened or awed." He holds his hands up as his eyes take him back. "So I was both."

"You should be a writer, Mr. Morente." She smiles at Clint as they pass.

The janitor tips his hat at her and slides a smirk at Leo.

"I've given it some thought. I think I'm too old to start something new. If you can't fully commit to something, then don't even bother starting, I always say."

"You've got, what, twenty, thirty more years left in you?"

"Give or take ten or fifteen."

"Actually, with the advances they're making in pharmaceuticals and medical science, it isn't entirely unlikely that you can squeeze at least thirty more years out of your life." Leo nods behind them.

"I hope Brandon Harriott doesn't get wind of that little fact." Morente's shoulder shake with hi chuckle. "He's one toe in the grave and, sometimes I'm tempted to give him a good push and grab a shovel."

"Here we are." Addie stops at the painting to the left. "Well, I'll go and draw up the papers. Leo here will answer any questions you may have. If you'll excuse me, gentlemen." She gives Leo a smile, Mr. Morente a nod, and clicks out of the room on her high heels.

Mr. Morente steps closer to the canvas. "Exquisite detail,

don't you think?"

"Um, yes, very nice."

He puts outstretched fingers close to the piece, but doesn't touch it. "And the shading and points of color here, very subtle, but quite effective." He shakes his head. "I've heard that Karthesier once spent seven months perfecting a single brushstroke. Seven months. Can you imagine, Leo."

"I once spent seven months growing a plant cell."

Mr. Morente looks over his shoulder. "I'm sorry?"

"Nothing, didn't mean to interrupt."

"Quite alright, my friend." He holds his chin between his thumb and index finger. "What do you think of the expression on the woman's face?"

"Well, I really don't know too much about—"

"No, no, you do. Art imitates life. You have experienced life, right, young man?"

"Yes." The word is hesitant, unsure.

"Then you've experienced art. Now, tell me what you think of this representation of life."

Leo looks over his shoulder to see Clint leaning silently against the wall with a hand smoothing down the broom handle. He shakes his head. Leo turns back to the Karthesier.

"She...she has this look on her face almost as if she's...as if she's waiting for something. The expression on her face says one thing, but it's—it's the eyes that I'm noticing." His voice drops. "There's a certain...dullness to them." He takes an involuntary step forward as Mr. Morente takes one back. "There's a line just here." Leo points. "Almost like an endoplasmic reticulum. Maybe she's trying to cover up her true feelings."

"You have quite an observant eye."

Leo blinks rapidly. "Thank you."

"Who are you, Leo Kennington?"

Leo looks over his shoulder. Clint is gone.


Adam shuts the door behind him and turns to find Maggie sitting on the couch with a book in her lap. He goes to her and kisses her on the lips before going into the kitchen.

"How was your day?" Adam peels open the refrigerator.

"Wonderful. I went to the park with a few of the other sisters and we flew kites." A grin splits her face. "Haven't done that since I was a child." The word freezes her expression and gradually crumbles it.

Adam comes back into the living room with two bottles of water. He passes one to her and twists the cap off the other.

"So, where were you?"

"I was with a friend." He sits down across from her and puts her bare feet in his lap, massaging them.

Maggie glances up. "What..." She smooths her hair. "What kind of a friend?"

"A woman named Bisset, she came to me for help."

Her eyes don't waver. "Came to you, or came to Sovereign?"

"Mmm, both I suppose." He reaches for the bottle of water on the table.

A slow nod before going back to her book. "What did she need help with?" Her eyes roll across the page.

"...I really don't think that she would be comfortable with me telling you."

She cocks her head, no longer focused on the page. "I'm your wife, Adam." She looks up at him.

"I know that, honey."

She flicks the book shut. "Don't do that, Adam."

"Do what?"

"Don't sit there and be a—a *man* about this."

His fingers stop kneading her soles and he lifts his shoulders. "I don't understand where this is coming from."

"You're out all day with another woman, a woman I don't even know, and you come home and don't tell me anything about her?"

"Maggie, you know that I would never do anything to tarnish this marriage."

"I know that." She tosses the book on the table and snatches her feet from his lap.

"Then where is this com—"

"I want to see, to hear some kind of reaction, Adam! We haven't even looked each other in the eye since we came back from Dr. Hannigan." She claws a stray strand of hair from her face. "Does it even bother you that we can't have a child?"

Adam goes still. "How could you ask me that?" The words fall like hollow notes. "I've yearned and prayed for a child almost as long as you have, you know that. How can you sit there and ask me that question?"

Her tone eases. "Because you act as if you don't care that you—that *we* can't conceive a child."

"Dr. Hannigan said there's still a chance."

"A very small chance, an *extremely* small chance."

"Maggie, where is your faith?"

She shakes her head. "Where's your sense? We just weren't meant to have a child. It doesn't matter how hard you want something, if it just wasn't meant to be, then it wasn't meant to be."

Adam suddenly finds that he can't look at his wife. "So what do we do now?"

She rubs her fingers across her lips and looks out of the window. "There's adoption."

He shakes his head with conviction. "Absolutely not. The only child I want to hold in my arms is one who is a part of me, the fruit of *our* love." He runs a hand through his hair. "What's the use of dwelling on something we can't change? I don't want to fight about this." He slides closer to her. "We—we may not be able to create a child of the flesh...but we can create one of the spirit. One that exists in our hearts." He takes her hand, kisses it and cradles it. "Can you hear it, Maggie?" He whispers. "Can you hear our child laughing?" He presses their bodies together. "Can you hear it?"

She is silent for a moment, forehead pressed against his. "I want to, Adam." Tears glimmer. "God, I want to."


Bisset stands and watches the shadows stretch and unfurl on the wall of her darkened apartment. She feels The Dragoness emerge on the edges of her consciousness.

She sways out of the murk, sheathed in nothing but air and

bare confidence. Her hair is straight and shimmering, skin glowing flawless and supple, eyes glistening in the pane of light. She stands a few feet away from Bisset, a shaft of shadow shading her breasts.

"I like him."

"Who?" Bisset doesn't even turn to acknowledge her.

"Adam." Bare feet pad on the floor. "He's so..." A deep inhale. "*Light*." She wrings her lips into a grin and partially hoods her unfocused gaze with her eyelids.

"I really think he's going to be able to help me get rid of you."

The twin in her head snorts. "Yes, it worked so well when he tried to exorcise me." She rests her chin on Bisset's shoulder. "Guess that proves I'm not a demon."

"Guess so."

The Dragoness grips her hostess by the arms. "Then what am I, Bisset?"

Bisset stands silent and still.

"Exactly. You don't know." She glides fingers soft and warm down Bisset's arms to her forearms. "I hear a bit of hesitation in your voice. You're no longer convinced of what I am, of what you are."

Bisset takes a breath through her nose.

"But I'll do it for you."

"What?" Bisset seizes still.

The Dragoness' unbinds herself from Bisset. "You heard me. I'll prove to you what a vicious demon I can really be. You should have accepted the terms you were initially given, it would have made all of this uncomplicated."

Bisset turns.

The Dragoness isn't there.

"*Remember when you let me speak to Adam, allowed me to take control of your mouth?*"

A nervous swallow.

"*You really shouldn't have done that.*"

Bisset's hands start to move of their own accord, moving slowly to the buttons of her shirt, undoing them slowly one...by...one.

"*Now I'm learning how to take full control of your body, of our body,*"

Bisset slides out of her shirt. The cool air caresses the bare skin of her stomach, slipping around to kiss her spine. Her hands find her pants.

*"You desire this, Bisset, you desire me and all that I represent."*

Bisset tries to stop her arms from starting to remove her pants.

*"Now I'm going to give it to you."*

"S-s-stop this. You don't have my permission to do this."

*"I am your permission. As you sat there in that pew making doe-eyes at Adam, I could feel your craving. Curling, licking, and stroking its way in your head. You and I both saw what was behind those silver eyes. That man isn't as righteous as he thinks he is. And we're just the ones to show him that."* The Dragoness suddenly appears in front of her in an exact mirror image.

Bisset stands in nothing but her underwear.

She shudders as her arms, hands, fingers reach back for her bra. "No, this isn't—STOP IT!"

Her fingers stop. Her reflection straightens.

"I only want you to experience yourself...unfettered...in all your natural glory." The Dragoness vanishes, leaving behind nothing but an afterimage of her golden-green eyes that slowly fade in the air.

Bisset's breaths shake and tremble as her eyes dart around her apartment.

She scrambles to find her medication.


Forty-seven years of age cross her visage like a story etched in wrinkles, laugh lines, creases, and a pleasant sense of weariness.

Anita Johnson isn't sure that the story is a true one.

She slowly smooths her fingers through her straight auburn locks. Her face turns in the mirror, crow-feet framed eyes analyzing every crevice on her face.

Charles spits out white toothpaste foam. "Honey, I've told you, you've got beautiful, and perfect, imperfections."

His wife wrinkles her nose and shakes her head. "I saw that picture of us in *The DC Domain* yesterday, I've got grandma hair." She turns to him. "I want you to be honest, didn't your mother have this hair color the last time we saw her?"

Charles pauses with foam dripping slowly from his lips as he takes in her hair. He slowly turns back to the mirror and shoves the toothbrush in his mouth, scrubbing at his molars.

Anita groans, dropping her hands. She goes to the bed, plops down, and wrings the bedspread in her fists. She welcomes the throbbing pain that comes when she bites down on the inside of her cheek.

Charles comes out of the bathroom wiping his mouth. "Anita, it's not that big of a deal. We've finally got enough money rolling in that you can have any hair color and style you want."

She jerks her head at him. "Charles, it's not the damn hair in the picture! It's the article that was next to the picture." She sucks in air. "They're saying that our gift either kills people or makes them crazy. Just yesterday Julius Banks started laughing and couldn't stop, he nearly asphyxiated."

Charles kneels at her feet and takes her hands. "What happened to him wasn't our—"

"YES, IT WAS!" Her eyes are wide. "It was. We damaged that man, Charles. This family mentally damaged that man, I know it." She rocks slightly. "I thought our gift was supposed to help people realize their dreams." Charles's arms are around her, squeezing her, his shoulder cradling her head. "What have we become?"

The doorbell chimes.

"I'll get it." Annabelle from downstairs.

Charles glances out the window at the cars parked in the guest parking lot.

Blood drains from his face and his limbs slacken.

"Annabelle, don't—"

Downstairs, Annabelle Johnson opens the door with a smile that's obliterated when she sees who it is. A gloved hand smashes into her freckled face and shoves her inside of the condo. The intruder walks over the threshold and slams the door shut.

The welcome sign swings back and forth on the door.

**FADE OUT**

# DCBN Newscast - 7:05 A.M. October 22nd:

"**GOOD** morning, I'm Carmen Alexandra with DCBN News. Earlier this morning, the Johnson family was discovered savagely murdered in their new condo in Cade District.

"Authorities found their bodies around five o'clock this morning after a neighbor arrived home and noticed a suspicious woman coming out of their residence with what looked like blood on her jacket.

"I'm here at the scene, and, while we'd like to spare you the grisly details, we do want to let our viewers know what happened here. What I can tell you is that the family's wrists were slashed, and each of them had a note nailed to the chest that reads, quote: *As unto others, so unto yourself*, end quote.

"So far offic—Detective. Detective West! Carmen Alexandra, DCBN News. Can I get a statement from you? Are you able to tell us exactly what happened in there?"

"From what we were able to gather, we know the murderer was either invited in or let in, probably by Annabelle Johnson, as hers was the first body we found upon entry. From there, the murderer moved on to Charles and Anita before killing Miguel up in his room. The ME has found traces of an as-of-yet unknown chemical in their bloodstreams, we figure that's what killed them."

"So the murderer slit their wrists out of sheer spite?"

"The exacerbated mutilation to the corpses was a message. The person or persons obviously didn't like what the Johnsons were doing."

"And what about you, detective? Do you think the Johnsons

deserved to be murdered?"

"No one deserves to be murdered, Miss Alexandra."

"But surely you must have an opinion on all this one way or another. This family has been in the news for weeks, and now their deaths will cause even more of a frenzy. What are your thoughts?"

"I think you should focus more on the story at hand and less on the sensationalism. Now, if we're done here, I have four murders to investigate."

"Actually, I just have—"

"You have a good day, Miss Alexandra."

"Detective West...DETECTIVE WEST!...Godda—"

"Still live, Carmen."

"Oh, I—The Johnsons were a family of Alpha-Omegas with the ability to grant what was many people's greatest wish: to be happy. In their short time in the limelight, the family made great strides in repairing ties between A-Os and non-powered Americans, ties that some say had become either tangled or destroyed since the discovery of the A-O gene.

"The next question on many minds tonight following this grisly crime is simply: what next?"

# EPISODE SIX: -POSITION

**THE** television set blips off.

Noir stretches out on his couch and stares at his reflection on the dusty screen. "When I said someone should kill 'em, I was just jokin'...a lil'. Whoever they are, what that sick fuck did to that family is beyond fucked up." He shakes his head. "Damn." He grabs the lit cigarette from the rim of the open beer can on the table and takes a long drag. He exhales from his nose and rolls his eyes up to his houseguest. "You smoke?"

Giorgio studies him from the well-worn leather armchair, one leg flopped over the other knee with his elbows on the armrests, posted up like royalty on a secondhand throne. He sniffs delicately. "Not anymore; the deep-seated craving has left me."

"Oh, word?" Noir pinches the cig between his thumb and index finger and raises it to his lips. "Woulda figured you thought yourself well-above such a pedestrian habit."

"Just yesterday I witnessed you brutally murder a handful of people and now I'm watching you cringe at a simple newscast."

Noir closes his eyes and massages his forehead. "I don't kill kids. Ever."

"So it's the souls of little Annabelle and Miguel that's got you smoking out of frustration?"

He shrugs and brings his hands behind his head, scratching at his scalp. "They were a good family, helped people."

"There were allegations that their powers drove people mad, made them kill themselves."

A crooked eyebrow. "Least they died happy, hellava lot more than what most people get." A scoff around the cig. "Lot more than what most people deserve. If you're gonna go out, might as well do it with a smile in your face and a song in your heart."

The animated corpse goes silent before—

"We should investigate the murders."

Noir gives him a look. "Pretty sure we were watching the same news report, deadbeat Dan. 'Member those guys in the creased black suits flittin' around in the background goin' in and out o' the house, tapin' up yellow party streamers? They're called the police. They investigate the murders, not us."

Giorgio stands, goes over and slaps Noir's feet from the tabletop. "Now we're investigating them, too."

Noir looks up at Giorgio with smoke and a smile curling from his lips. "Why?"

The living dead man winces and looks down at his hand painted in sunlight. He goes to the window and yanks the curtains closed. "It's been almost two weeks since I woke up in a woman's bed with her corpse next to me."

"Wait, lemme get a pen and paper to write this down, could

become the next bestseller."

"Nearly two weeks since I died and the kiss of a necrophiliac brought me back to unlife. In that time, I've watched my mother have a conversation with my sister and ask herself if she loved me, if she's sincerely saddened by my passing. I've hallucinated that I talked to God, who looks like me, and learned that death and decay bring me life and I bring death and decay to life."

Noir rubs at the wrist Giorgio had grabbed.

"My Alpha-Omega gene killed me and brought me back to give me a second chance to live my life right." He looks at Noir, eyes glittering like emeralds dipped in golden dust.

Noir deposits the finished cig in the can. *Hsss.* "That why you were yabbin' at me about the quality of life last night? You don't want me to waste my life like you did yours?"

Giorgio ponders. "Yes."

Noir gestures out the curtained window and leans forward on his knees. "Got a whole city o' people equally, if not more, demented than my ass."

Giorgio tips his head to the side. "I've got time. It's not as if I'm going to die any time soon."

"Unless the gene that killed you and brought you back to life offs you again and makes it stick this time."

Giorgio goes still and seems to step out of time.

"Din think about that, didja?"

Giorgio walks back to the chair, but doesn't sit. "Death doesn't hold the same meaning for the living as it does the dead. Our brothers and sisters with blood still streaming warm in their veins only know that when a person dies, they're gone. No more. But to us, it simply means leaving." He sits. "And when something leaves, it has to go somewhere."

Noir stares at him, specifically, at the crook of his arm beneath the delicately rolled-up sleeves of his linen shirt.

"What?" Giorgio looks down at his smooth, normal-looking flesh.

Noir shakes his head and reaches for another cigarette.

"Someone is killing God's divine creations, and that doesn't sit well with us."

Adam swallows and nods from where he sits on the other side of Bishop Martin's desk. "The death of the Johnsons."

"The *murder* of the Johnsons." The older man jabs a finger at the air, stabbing emphasis into the word with a pinched brow.

"The police are doing all they can to bring the murderer to justice."

Bishop Martin leans forward on his desk, interlacing smooth fingers before him. He weighs his words before breathing them into existence. "I truly hate to contradict you, Brother Kensie, but I really don't think the police will invest that much diligence into this investigation."

Confusion coats itself across Adam's face in light brushstrokes. "And why is that?"

"Because none of them realize what a blessing the Johnsons a...were." He curls a finger over his mouth, taps his lips. "To them, that family is nothing more than four corpses. They don't realize what a vital weapon the light has lost." Gray eyes gleam in deep sockets. "We need to make an example of the perpetrator, punish them. They have to face God's judgment." A beat passes. "Your judgment, Sovereign."

Adam shakes his head. "God's judgment is the only judgment that matters."

"And maybe God has seen fit to bless you to carry out His judgment, His will. Maybe it's time that Sovereign went public, showed the entire world who he is. Starting with Dominion City."

The younger man rubs the sweat building on his palms over the knees of his dress pants.

"I feel that God is telling us that now is the time to act, the time to respond and make our voices heard, His voice heard." Sunlight pouring through the windows behind him halos his head in gold. "I've been talking about it with a few other members of the congregation; we think you should let Dominion City, and especially the murderer, know that we of the Apostolic faith won't tolerate those who interfere with God's work. There's no telling if something like this will happen again. We need every soldier we've got in the trenches for this war, Adam."

Adam hears Dr. Hannigan's words resound in his head as he explains the chances of him and Maggie successfully conceiving a child. He recalls Bisset's poorly restrained distress when he first stumbled on her on his porch, Seraph's uncertainty about them banishing The Dragoness. He feels the remnants of Alan's doubt at the thought of being able to love himself again. Each of them instances of Satan interfering with The Most High's perfect plan. Resolution burns like fire confined in his bones.

"Alright, I'll talk with some of my connections at the police department and see what I can find out."

The response makes the bishop smile. "Praise the Lord."


Perry rubs his forehead in frustration. Images of the Johnsons' bodies look up at him from his desk.

*Blood soaked into the carpet.* He can still smell the lingering copper scent at the crime scene.

*Brains scooped out of their skulls.* The image doesn't do the real thing justice.

*Limbs splayed out on top of one another.* A family that died together.

He wraps his fingers around his mouth and takes a deep breath through his nose. He looks up, raises his voice. "'Ey, Birkoff, hand me that file there, will ya?"

The older officer turns, yellow-white mustache twitching underneath his bulbous nose. "You actually lookin' into this, West?" He hands over the thin file. "Waste of your time."

"Not called an investigation for nothing." Perry opens the file and scans the paper.

"Tomato, potato. I'm just here for the overtime." He slurps from his coffee mug, red-rimmed eyes blinking blearily.

Perry rolls his eyes up and peers over the rim of his reading glasses. "Are you—Jesus, Birkoff, it's ten o'clock in the morning."

Shrug. "Had to sling back five shots of bourbon and jack off twice just to get up this morning. Otherwise, I wouldn't be here to not give a damn about this case." Slipshod grin.

Perry shakes his head and goes back to the file with a pen in hand, underlining there, circling here.

The man in the slightly wrinkled suit plops himself down in the chair on the other side of Perry's desk. "That family deserved to die."

Perry scans the page. Stops. He makes a note.

"They helped people, yeah, but they also fucked a lot of people up, put them in hospitals and loony bins. I say they should do the same to all those other genetically awakened motherfuckers." *Sluurp.* "Why this, huh? Why did nature, or God, or evolution, or who-the-hell-ever have to throw this shit down at us? Incurable disease wasn't enough?" *Sluurp.* "War wasn't enough? People killing each other over fucking nothing wasn't enough? Why the hell do we need people who can blow your brains out with a touch?"

"Maybe it's all going exactly how it's supposed to." Perry picks up a highlighter and highlights.

Birkoff breaks off mid-*sluurp.*

"Heller believes that humans weren't meant to live as long as we do. Says that all these mass killings and tragedies are nature's way of getting the course of life back on track and that this flesh and blood existence really isn't the end for us." Perry looks up as he speaks, swiveling slightly in his chair. "A few years ago I would've just nodded and smiled at him, but now with people doin' things that belong in a sci-fi book..."

Birkoff sniffs and raises his mug to his mouth and sips silently this time. He smacks his lips. "Still doesn't mean I'll help find the blessed saint who did this." He gestures at the images. "If I do, I'm shaking his hand and giving him a medal."

Perry uncurls a finger at the badge swinging from a chain around Birkoff's neck. "That's a symbol, Detective Birkoff, not a shiny accessory."

The other man's eyes widen. "And how long have you been waiting to use that one?" He shakes his head and gets up. "Leave the theatrics to the heroes with actual powers, West." He leaves.

Detective Torv walks up to Perry's desk, eyes following the slightly staggering Birkoff. A chuckle and a smile roll across her face. "Why is it that every time I see you you're having a...*disagreement* with someone?" She braces herself on the back of the vacant chair.

Perry looks at her, lifts his shoulders, and looks back at the file. "Can't help it if half the city's police force is either lazy or apathetic or apathetic about the fact that they're lazy."

"And yet here you are."

He scoffs. "Gotta keep the homefires burnin', light the way home."

She sits down and looks at the pictures. "This might be the same guy who killed McCain? Has his signature sliced all over the bodies."

Perry closes the folder and tosses it on the desk before rolling his head back and stretching his arms. "Could be. It all looks straightforward but..." He shakes his head and bites his lip. "There's somethin' 'bout this one tha's botherin' me. Somethin' 'bout the way they were murdered. Different...essence from McCain." A hand through his hair. "Gonna need to see the ME report again."

# END OF THE FUSE NEWS SHOW – 5:18 P.M. OCTOBER 22ND:

"Welcome to *End of the Fuse*, I'm Mick Douglas. Earlier today, the bodies of the Johnsons, a recently renowned family of Alpha-Omegas, were found horrifically murdered in their home in Dominion City. So far, authorities have no leads or suspects in this vicious attack, but we're not here tonight to talk about their lives so much as their deaths and what they entail.

"I'm joined by psychologist Sarah Fain, Alpha-Omega equal rights advocate Malachi L'Grange, and the national spokesperson for Common Sense, Frank Peizeki. Welcome, everyone.

"Now, Frank, I know you and Common Sense have had quite a few things to say about Alpha-Omegas in the past year. I want to ask what you think about all of this?"

"While what happened to the Johnsons is tragic, Mick, I'd be lying if I said something like this was unexpected."

"Care to elaborate?"

"Sure, Mick. When you set yourself up as a public figure and put yourself, your family, and your life in the public eye, you have to be prepared for the consequences. It's not all about smiling and laughing and hugging on camera, you have to be aware that there are sharks in the water and they want to eat you alive. The Johnsons simply weren't ready to swim."

"Sarah?"

"I have to disagree with Frank—"

"Of course you would."

"Frank, come on now."

"—I think the Johnsons were an accurate and unblemished portrayal of not just an American family, but of *any* family. They weren't trained or fed what to say and what not to say on camera, at least not to my knowledge, and it made their lives very genuine, very real. And I think we could use more of that."

"More realness?"

"More realness."

"What do you think, Malachi?"

"Whoever did this *has* to be made to pay. Period point-blank."

"That's one opinion."

"Let him speak, Frank. Go on."

"Thank you. I admit that I don't think it was right for the Johnsons to charge people for their services; it doesn't make other Alpha-Omegas look good. But I do think that it was very brave of them to be willing to be basically stripped naked in front of us."

"Are you an Alpha-Omega, Malachi?"

"Frank, what does that have to do with anything?"

"It's a legitimate question, Malachi. You are an advocate for equal rights for A-Os, after all. Are those your own equal rights you're fighting for? It's a simple question."

"And so is mine. What does that have to do with anything?"

"It may make you a bit biased. I know it hits me just a bit harder when I hear good or bad news about a fellow Christian, and I know you must feel the same way being a man of color."

"...I don't—I can't believe you would say something like that. Alpha-Omegas are just like—"

"Ahh, I wouldn't go that far, I wouldn't go that far."

"Recent studies show that Alpha-Omega brains, bodies, everything mostly operates the same as in a norm—ah, non-powered human. Now, sometimes their physiology does have to adapt to their abilities, but other than that, you could pass one on the street and not know it."

"And that's the part that worries me, Sarah. I want to know who my enemy is. I want to be able to point them out in a crowd. I want them to wear a red flag that says DANGER TO SOCIETY in bold letters."

"What makes you think they're your enemy, Frank?"

"There's no kind of social restraint when it comes to them! I'm sure we remember Sean Pierce a few weeks back. Killed twenty-three people and hospitalized thirty-two when his A-O gene manifested. And what happened to him?"

"What happened is he killed himself."

"*Nothing!* Not a blasted thing! This is America. You break the law, we break the rod of justice over your back. You take a life, you receive punishment; you don't go on a talk show and talk about how sorry you are."

"Frank, you're saying you don't think Sean was sorry?"

"Yes, Sarah, I honestly do think he was sorry, believe it or not. I think he was sorry someone didn't kill him. The Johnsons can't say the same."

"You are way out of line, Frank. You do know this is live and being broadcasted to thousands of viewers, right?"

"Mick, I'm just telling it like it is. Sarah here was just sharing with us how the world needs to be more genuine. I'm not one of those people who acts one way in front of the camera and another way when the spotlight shuts off."

"But to say something like that is just horrible. Do you hear what you're saying?"

"Malachi, I hear it loud and clear. It's your right to idiotically idolize them just as it's my right to justifiably persecute them. Who gave them the right to just give people happiness? They may have had the power, but that didn't mean they had the right. Happiness is something you have to earn, that you have to work for. You can't just wake up one morning and make an appointment for happiness. The world shouldn't work like that, and I think it's a shame that it does...well, that it did."

"I do have to agree with you on that last part."

"Thank you, Mick."

"But I don't agree with anything else you've said."

"Glad to see you invite people on your show whom you don't get along with."

"Frank, you said you think people like Malachi here are simply trying to justify the existence of A-Os by making them out to be larger than life people—"

"Except they aren't people."

"Okay."

"Even though I don't have a special ability, I still feel that I'm...*authentic*. I may not be able to destroy an entire building with a single blow, but I do know what it's like to have to work for something rather than have it handed to me because of a genetic abnormality. It's almost like like affirmative action."

"Alpha-Omegas and non-powered humans are equally destructive and equally defined by the same standards as you or I."

"You keep believing that, Sarah. Whatever helps you look in the mirror each day."

"Have you ever considered that A-Os are the next step in human evolution? And what is evolution if not normal?"

"Did you not hear the part where I said I was Christian? I don't believe in evolution. God got it right the first time, there's no need for us to change and adapt."

"Relations between non-powered humans and A-Os have to be—no, they *desperately need* to be improved, or this is going to get messier than it already is."

"Okay, I'm gonna have to play referee and host here and say I think that's enough. Don't want anyone coming to blows. Let's read a few emails and try to calm down."


Noir tries the knob to the condo door.

Locked.

He holds a hand up and springs his claws, rearing back to swipe. A cold hand encases his wrist. He looks over his shoulder to see Giorgio shaking his head.

"You got a key or somethin'?"

"No." The undead man releases Noir's wrist. "No one thought to leave one in my coffin with me." Giorgio steps toward the door and touches his fingers to the knob. Brass flakes and tarnishes away to a darker brown that withers to russet rust. Years of decay takes place in seconds. Something crumbles and loosens inside the lock and the entire thing falls to the carpet with a hollow thud. He pushes the door open and steps inside.

"The Johnsons' place is one floor up, why are we here?" Noir remains in the hallway.

Giorgio looks around the massive, empty condo, breathes in the smell of new paint, cleaned carpet, and pine-scented wood polish. He goes down on one knee and spreads his fingers on the hardwood, sliding fingertips down the cream walls.

Noir raises an eyebrow. "The fuck you doin', man?" He takes a final look up and down the hallway before ducking in and quietly closing the door. Glaring white streetlight is bisected by the open blinds. He realizes. "You used to live here."

Giorgio looks over his shoulder in the condo mired in murk. "You don't realize how much of an imprint you leave on a place." He stretches up to his full height and leans against the island in the kitchen. "I lived here for five years. Brought home countless women, several hundred bags of designer clothes, and hosted many a party with quite the assortment of narcotics."

Noir gives a quick shrug. "Sounds like a typical resident of Cade District to me: drowning in white privilege, young, pants always around your ankles." He crosses his arms over his chest.

"But I don't want to be that anymore."

"From what I understand, ese, you can't. Kinda dead now. You're very alive, but still very much dead." He walks over to the window. "You said it yourself, this is your chance to do it over. You don't like who you were before—" He peeks out between the blinds. "—change it." He turns.

"I am...I have."

The other man spreads his arms open. "Then what the hell we doin' here?"

"Remembering." A breath. "Remembering why I died."

Noir regards him silently for a few moments. "You think you died because you were fuckin', snortin', and smokin' your life away?"

"And maybe the Johnson's died for the same reason, because they weren't living the right life."

A scoff. "Maybe they'll come back from the dead, too."

Giorgio looks at him.

Noir holds his hands up in surrender. "I'm just sayin'."

"Don't mock me."

"I ain't mockin' nobody here, just statin' my opinion is all." He lowers his hands. "Now, if you're finished floggin' yourself, the crime scene you wanted to check out is an elevator ride away."

One book shuts. Another book opens. A page is flipped. Eyes search. A page flips back. Eyes scan. A book shuts. Frustration grows.

Perry growls and clenches the pencil in his hand nearly to the snapping point. The pencil and his nerves have a lot in common.

"What the hell is this drug in your system?"

He leans back in his chair and looks out of the eastern window of the J.V. Berto Public Library. The table is scattered with medical notes, scribblings, and various descriptions of pharmaceuticals. A fine trembling trills through the table. He looks at his illuminated phone screen as it vibrates across the wooden surface. Walter.

A little sigh slips past his lips as he snatches up the phone, slides out of his seat, and quick-walks to an empty hallway.

He snatches off his reading glasses as he presses the ANSWER button.

"'Ey, Walter." His voice is pitched low.

"Hey, just calling to see how the case is going. I know you can't give me intimate details, but...you know."

He leans against the wall. "Case is going nowhere fast. Some things don't add up right and I can't figure out what the hell it is."

"It'll come to you. May help to take a break and come back

and look at it with fresh eyes."

He massages his temple with a knuckle. "Maybe."

Hesitation on the other end. Then... "Do—ah...Do you think it might be the guy who attacked Matthew?" The stitched-together sentence is unleashed in rush. "I've written down what I remember about him; I don't mind helping. Probably should—"

"I don't think your guy did this." Perry shakes his head. "But I can look over what you've got. Entertain every possibility and all that."

"Alright. Come home safe, Perry. I'll go pick up the new John Scalzy book for you, give you something to take your mind off things for a little while."

The sentiment tugs at the sides of his mouth. "Thanks, Walter. I really appreciate that."

"Anytime. See you when you get home."

END

He looks at the blank screen of his phone for a moment, unfocusing on the date and time on the display to notice his framed reflection, his framed smile. He pushes away from the wall and goes back to his chair and the table scattered with fragments of frustration.

"Excuse me, but are you Detective West?"

He looks up to find an attractive man with brown-blond hair and vibrant blue eyes. A golden cross glints at his collarbone.

"Yes, can I help you?"

"My name is Adam Kensie, I'm a parole officer. Miller down at the precinct told me where I could find you. I saw you this morning on the news report." His Adam's apple bobs. "I'd like to help you with your case." He looks down at the medical reports and books cluttering the table.

Perry stares at him, studies his face. A slow blink.

"And how exactly can you help me, Mr. Kensie? Do you have any evidence you'd like to present?"

"Not...not quite." He pulls out a chair and sits. "You see, me and the members of my church believe that Alpha-Omegas are God's divine instruments in His army." He opens his palms on the table. "When we heard that the Johnsons had been brutally murdered, the

**173**

news fell on us like something physical. The fact that someone—"

West's phone buzzes again. He holds up a finger and answers it. "Detective West here."

"Detective, this is Vincent Cooper down at the city morgue. After I completed the toxicology report on the Johnsons, I was able to figure out what the strange chemical in their blood is."

Adam folds his hands on the table.

"What is it?"

"A drug called hectaphan. In medium doses, it causes paralysis, but the unique thing about it is that after a few minutes, it starts to thin the blood. The Johnsons were paralyzed when they were murdered, that much is obvious, but what I found odd was the amount of blood from their wounds."

Perry partially slides a photo from underneath a folder.

"With the amount of Hectaphan in their systems and the way their bodies were positioned, there should have been more blood...a lot more. Unless—"

"They were dead before the drug was administered."

Adam rolls his eyes down, head cocked forward a bit, motionless.

"Exactly."

Perry scribbles a note. "Any other cases you remember where Hectaphan was used?"

"Uhh, usually only murderer investigations, kidnappings, the occasional rape cas—"

Adam's head flashes up.

"Detective, I think I may have something for you."

Perry stares at him with agitated curiosity.


# DOWNTOWN – 6:49 P.M. OCTOBER 22ND:

He ambles down Lynord Street, iPod in hand, thumb scrolling to find something *just right*. No Etro Anime. Just listened to Zero 7. Maybe some Van Hunt later. Jeff Buckley?

Janelle Monae.

Yes.

He scrolls down to "Many Moons," cranks it up, and starts bobbing his head.

"Hey."

His hips start twitching at the opening quick-tempo drum groove.

"Hey."

His lips move, eyes squint shut, fingers snap.

"HEY!"

A hand on his shoulder that whirls him around. A finger jabbing sternly into his sternum.

"You need to burn that shirt."

He looks down at his shirt that reads ALL GENES ARE NOT CREATED EQUAL! BE HUMAN. He looks up. "You new in this country? I've got the right to wear whatever I want."

A fist from nowhere.

A kick to the ribs.

His earbuds are knocked from his ears and Miss Monae's lyrics bleed out faintly.

That's when he notices the second shadow and the second set of fists and feet that begin to beat the shit out of him.


Giorgio looks for clues at the crime scene while Noir searches for things to swipe.

"Would think that with all the money they came into they would have a better selection o' things to choose from." Noir opens and shuts the drawers of the bureau in the bedroom. He slides a drawer open and his face lights up, much like the diamond earrings in the small open case. "Ooo, sparkly. Mrs. Johnson had *reeeal* good taste." He snatches up the earrings, goes to slip them into his pocket, slows when he sees Giorgio watching him. "What?"

"We're here to investigate, not pilfer the belongings of the deceased."

The earrings disappear in his pocket. Noir points at him. "No, *you're* here to investigate, I'm here..." He swipes a pair of cufflinks. "...for immoral support and to steal shit." He waggles his eyebrows.

Giorgio shakes his head and slips into the next room. Noir slips into the closet, emerging a second later with slightly bulging pockets. "Find anything?"

Giorgio narrows his eyes in concentration and holds out a hand. "There's something...I'm not quite sure. It's...tugging at me." He slowly moves into the living room.

Noir follows after. "Let's hope it's somethin' I can sel—I mean a clue, let's hope it's a clue."

# DOWNTOWN – 7:02 P.M.

It's snowballed into a brawl. A righteous one. A woman jumps on this man's back as he shoves that man who accidentally elbows this woman in the face as she stumbles back from a flailing fist thrown by that woman into his jaw as he drags another woman roughly from her scooter.

"HELL OFFA ME!"

The woman with the golden-red hair slams on the breaks and boils out of her car.

"HEY! ASSHOLE!" Her pointed nail jabs at the man with the busted lip. "Take the fight somewhere else."

"SICK OF PEOPLE LIKE YOU!"

He wipes at his lip with his already bloody t-shirt, grabs her by the blouse, and slams her onto the hood of her giant SUV. She protests and flails, but his striking palms and shoving hands stamp out her disputes.

"FUCKING FREAK LOVER! GONNA BEAT YOUR ASS!"

Someone cracks a steel pipe across the back of his skull. He drops to the street and does not move, he only bleeds.

"THEY'RE AN ABOMINATION IN THE EYES OF—"

A motorcycle sails through the air and crashes beautifully through a storefront window. The owner rushes out.

"SAID THE SAME THING ABOUT YOUR PEOPLE!"

The pistol in the store owner's hand turns a few heads, but not enough.

"BREAK THIS MESS UP RIGHT NOW!"

Traffic has stopped on Lynord. Horns are honking, doors are opening, and voices are shouting.

"HE'S GOT A GUN!"

That's when someone gets hit by a car.

That's also when the same Alpha-Omega with superhuman strength who threw the motorcycle picks up a minivan and flings it into the crowd.


Adam hurries after West out of the car.

"Detective—" He shuts the door. "Detective West, if you would just wait for one second."

"Why? You wanna explain to me why you didn't report this bastard?" He stalks up the walkway.

"I told you, he's not a sinner anymore. I've shown him the way." He screeches to a halt as the other man suddenly whirls on him.

"You think a rapist stops being what he is because you lay hands on him?" Head shake. "And people say I'm crazy." He advances up the steps and knocks on the newly installed door. The door frame still bears a few cracks from Sovereign's last...visit.

"He only did that because he was paid to do it. I'm helping him deal with his transgressions. I'm a parole officer, I do this for a living."

"Then you know damn well you shoulda reported him the moment you knew who he was." West knocks loudly again. "DCPD!" To Adam: "I should bring your ass in with him."

Adam goes rigid. "I'd advise against that."

"No matter what you believe, Mr. Kensie, you aren't the law. And neither is God."

"God is greater than the law."

West's mouth and the door open at the same time.

Whirling heads, a shocked silence, a little yelp.

The door shuts. West kicks it open before it fully closes

"Not you again, you platinum motherfucker!" The Rapist sprints down the hall, moving surprisingly fast for a man his size.

West runs after him as Adam shouts *the word* and soars behind him.

A door slams and locks. The door is demolished by a platinum fist.

*BLAM!*

*Ting!* Off of Sovereign's chest.

*BLAM!*

*Tang!* Ricochets from his shoulder.

*BLAM!BLAM!BLAM!*

The bullets *pling* and *plang* away from silver-ivory flesh.

*Cchk.* The Rapists frowns at his gun. Aims again and pulls the trigger. *Cchk. Cchk. Cchk.*

He looks at the gun. "Aww, fuck." He looks up to see Detective West's foot slicing through the air and folds as it takes him in the softness of his temple. "Ow! Fuck!" He withers and whimpers as he touches the throbbing spot on his head. "They lied! Said you wouldn't be able to trace them back to me."

"Who told you? Trace who? Speak up, dumbass." West boots him in the abdomen.

The flames enshrouding Sovereign blaze once more before they *fwoosh* out of existence. Adam steps forward. "Kicking him is unnec—"

The other man's finger is in his face.

"One more word and you're down there with him with my heel on your throat. I don't care if you can break me with one finger."

Adam shuts his mouth.

West turns back to The Rapist. "Now, start from the beginning."

The Rapist starts crying.

## DOWNTOWN – 7:06 P.M.

Leo cradles Francie to his chest as pandemonium rages out of control around them. A glass bottle smashes against the pavement at their feet. Four men gang up on one, cussing and kicking, taunting and teasing, breaking and bloodying.

"Still think all A-Os should be put in a box and gassed?" One man punctuates his words with a boot stomp to the shoulder. "Huh?"

Approaching sirens serrate through the distant air. A car has caught fire in the middle of the street. A woman holds up her fists and roars victory at the flames.

A squeal of tires.

The harsh sound of vulnerable flesh impacting with unforgiving metal.

A minivan sailing through the air directly at Leo and Francie.

Leo looks up as the vehicle's shadow blankets them.

Instinct.

He throws a hand up and wraps a force field tight around the soaring minivan. A silver-blue outline surrounds the vehicle and it *jerks* to a stop as Leo grits his teeth, holding both the force field and the van in place several feet in the air.

The nearby crowd cowers and covers their heads.

Leo seems to realize what he's done and dissolves the force field, dropping the van in a relatively clear spot on the street.

He looks down at Francie.

"You okay?"


Giorgio kneels down in the living room, white tape outlining the deaths of the Johnsons. He presses a hand to the carpet, seemingly unmoved by the drops of dried blood.

Noir clops down the steps from the second floor, sitting on the bottom one with his elbows on his knees. "Find what you were sniffin' for, Fido?"

Giorgio closes his eyes. "I...I think so. Yes. There's something wrong here." He spreads his fingers. "This family didn't die correctly."

"The hell you talkin' about?"

He opens his eyes and looks at the other man. "This might sound odd, but it's the only reasonable explanation. Or as reasonable as things can be when you speak of death." He glances down at the carpet, opens his mouth and says—

"It was all a ruse. The Johnsons and their wholesome family image, it's all bunk." The Rapist rests the back of his head against the wall he's fallen against. "They're not even American."

"Then where're they from?" West pulls a notebook and pen from the front pocket of his dress shirt, jots notes.

Head shake. "Dunno. What I do know is they're an experiment."

"What kind of—" Adam begins and ends at West's glare.

"What kind of experiment?"

"The kind where you find out how people react to the life and death of a normal, well-known American family."

"The Johnsons weren't normal."

He scoffs and a bubble of blood froths from a nostril where Perry decked him earlier in an attempt to unsnarl the truth from his unwilling tongue. "Not yet they aren't." He sniffs. "In a few years, Alpha-Omegas will no longer be exotic, they'll just be run-of-the-mill. Average." He wipes his nose and examines red smear on the back of his wrist.

"You said they wanted to find out how people would react. Who's they?"

The Rapist starts to laugh and then starts to hurt and clutches at his chest. "Think you broke something."

"Good, you deserved it. Now answer my question before I break something else."

"They, uh—" Wince. "They call themselves *Libera Mentis Machina.*"

West pauses before translating. "Free Mi—No, Unfettered Mind Machine."

The detective looks from The Rapist to Adam as they stare at him. "My mother made me learn Latin to teach me about patience and attention to detail." To The Rapist: "What's their end goal?"

A shrug that turns into a cringe. "Dunno. One of them approached me and asked if I would kill this family for seven thousand dollars."

"You told me you wanted to get help." Adam ignores West's glare.

The Rapist looks up at him. Then he smiles. "You're hot as fuck, but you're also dumb as hell, you know that, Mr. Platinum? I only let you smear that oil on my forehead and mutter those prayers to get you out of my face and out of my life. It's not like I'm actually going to stop getting paid assloads of money because of some dumbass overgrown child's obsession with angels and shit." He laughs in Adam's face. "I got student loan debt and an IRA to take care of. Bouncer jobs don't pay what they used to, especially when some of the rowdier folks are A-Os and I'm not."

West holds up a hand before Adam retorts. "Why the smoke and mirrors? Why make the murder look like some kinda ritual?"

The Rapist blinks up at both men. The smile carves itself deeper and he opens his mouth and says—

"The Johnsons aren't dead." Giorgio curls his fingers into his palm and lifts it from the carpet.

Noir sits still and silent for a beat. "Get the fuck outta here."

## DOWNTOWN – 7:15 P.M.

Bisset stands in the middle of the swarm.

The Dragoness bathes in the chaos.

A man runs at her screaming and yanks his fist back.

The Dragoness overrides Bisset's mental block and catches the man's knuckles in her palm before tossing him high into the air into the flames of the burning car.

His howls are like a spice that makes her shudder, fingers stroking the air before sliding down her tongue.

"You see, Bisset? You see what their suffering has erupted into?" She walks calmly down the street.

A woman beats a man with a bat.

"What will the end result be this time? A final realization they're a community that needs to genuinely come together? Death for those who deserve it?" She jukes back as someone falls to the concrete, stepping nonchalantly over the body. "A riot is just the spark needed for great and much-needed change to take place."

She steps inside the swing of a man with a crowbar about to attack an injured man cringing on the sidewalk. She plucks the crowbar from his grasp. "Too much." She whacks the crowbar against the side of his temple, dropping him before dropping the crowbar with a clatter. She turns and kneels before the injured man with a bleeding gash on his arm, caressing his sweat-kissed cheek. "Too little."

She curls her fingers into a delicate fist and rams it into his nose.

A geyser of blood and screams.

"Just right." She stands and walks away. "Suffering must always be administered in just the right amount."


Adam and Perry watch as a paramedic helps The Rapist out the front door.

"Preston Caulley." West shoves his hands in his pockets.

"What?"

"His name's Preston Caulley."

Adam watches as Preston turns his head a bit and gives a half-assed wave before slumping into the arms of the man helping him down the steps. "We should have made him tell us who these...Unfettered Mind Machine people are."

A sidelong glance from the detective. "Ten minutes ago you regarded that man as a child of God, now you're turnin' your back on 'im? What kind of Christian are you?"

"The man lied to me, to himself. He doesn't want to change, he doesn't know how."

Perry clears his throat, massages his knuckles. "We'll drag him through the ringer once he's properly recovered." He pauses a beat. "Why'd you do all this?"

Adam looks back at him. "Because God wanted me to. I think the time is right that the rest of the world knows who Sovereign is and who he stands for." He holds his chin a bit higher.

A stare. "You do understand you're an Alpha-Omega...right?"

"Detective West, I'm a Sovereign of God. That's all I am, have been, and all that I will be until God sweeps me up into His arms and calls me home." He looks straight ahead.

"Whatever you say...*Sovereign.*" West begins to walk out of the house and stops. "By the way, they're constructin' a special set of holdin' cells made of reinforced titanium down at the precinct for A-O perps with enhanced strength." A smile, a two-fingered salute. "Take care o' yourself, Mr. Kensie, and stay the hell outta my way."

Adam watches him leave before going over to the table. On it is a pocket-sized Bible. He opens the cover.

*May God bless you and guide you on the path of Righteousness.*

*Brother Adam Kensie*

He shakes his head and stuffs the Bible in his right side pocket. In his left is his own pocket-sized Bible.

He leaves.

# DCBN NEWSCAST – 9:03 P.M., OCTOBER 22ND

"A massive riot broke out downtown this evening, resulting in several dozens of people being injured and at least four killed. The cause of the riot is believed to be related to A-O and non-powered human relations. Lynord Street, one of the city's busiest thoroughfares, has been blocked off until the damage can be repaired, which may take as many as three weeks. We'll be sure to provide you with updates as they become available.

"In other news, a break has been made in the case regarding the homicide of the Johnson family. Thirty-four-year-old Norma Gargis confessed a few hours ago and has been arrested and charged with four counts of first degree murder. While being detained, Gargis said that, quote, I only wanted to do to them what they did to my grandfather. Fair exchange is no robbery, end quote.

"Now, let's go to the weather."

Noir shuts the door behind him, swiftly swiping crisp bills from one hand to the other as he counts.

"'Ey, man, made a pretty penny from all o' that crap." He wraps the wad of Benjamins in a thick rubber band. "How do the undead celebrate? They have any zombie strip clubs around here. Wanna go out for a few shots o' quicklime?"

Stop.

Search.

Silence.

"Giorgio?"

# FADE OUT

## SOME NOWHERE

THE day is windy, trees yielding to the streaming squall pressing against them. The trees are in well-maintained lawns. The lawns surround rows of houses that all look just the same. Neighbors wave to each other and stop to converse as they check the mail, wash their cars, walk their dogs, go for a jog.

Suburbia.

Charles and Miguel Johnson are flying kites in the backyard, a red diamond and a blue and yellow triangle stretched tight as they slide and glide in the breeze, ribbons fluttering in their wake.

"There you go, dad. Good job." Miguel looks over at his father's kite as it whips a loop in the air.

"I'm supposed to be the one teaching you how to fly a kite." Charles smiles as he tilts his face up to the sun. He plays out more string and watches the kite soar higher. A small frown smudges his expression as the kite flies free. He remains where he is on the ground. Not moving. Trapped. Caged.

"Parents learn from their kids all the time." Miguel squints at the sky. "Just because you're older, *much* older, doesn't really mean anything."

"Yeah, but it should." His father wipes the frown from his face and replaces it with a smile.

An hour passes. Kites crash back to the earth only to be lifted into the air again. Conversation is made, jokes and laughs are traded as life goes on. Soon, Miguel tires of the charade.

"Dad?"

Charles suppresses a sigh. He recognizes the tone in his son's voice. "Not now, Miguel." His low words are snatched away by the fitful breeze.

"But, dad, I just want to know when we—"

He jerks his head down from heaven. "Miguel, I said not now."

Miguel says no more.

It's then that Charles notices the man with glasses wearing jeans and a pullover leaning on the back gate as he watches the kites.

"Miguel, go inside. Now."

His son opens his mouth to protest, but sees the man on the fence, now waggling his hand in a wave. He drops the kite string and hurries inside the house.

The man unlocks the gate and saunters into the backyard as soon as the door shuts behind Miguel. He tugs his sleeves up to his elbows and beams at Charles as he stoops down to scoop up the kite string as it's dragged along the grass.

"Wonderful weather for this, huh?" He grins broadly as he watches the kite.

"That's the reason we're out here, Damon."

"So I see."

The wind whips.

"My boy wanted to ask me how long we would be staying here."

"You'll stay here until we decide what to do with you."

"The world already thinks the Johnsons are dead, what else do you want with us?"

String unravels. "You and your family are a loose string, Charles. Know what happens to kites with loose strings?" He looks over at the other man. "They fly away."

"We agreed to come to the U.S. for your organization's ideals. We've helped you with your experiment, you can let us go."

The side of Damon's mouth curls. "You helped us plant the seed. Now we have to start reaping. And remember, when it came time for you and your family to be brought in, you struggled. You were going to run as soon as you saw our vehicle parked outside your house."

"We weren't ready to go back." His Northern speech pattern chips and a Ukrainian accent trickles through.

"That proves to me that you aren't a man of a your word. Nor are you a man who accepts his fate." He tugs on the kite string.

Charles drops his arms and drags the kite down. "I've heard stories about Americans and your secret organizations." He adjusts his American accent back into place. "You don't seem to be very keen on keeping your promises either."

"Everybody's got a knife up their sleeve." The kite loops once, twice in the air. "Oh, nice." A look of glee. "Did you know a massive riot recently broke out in your old backyard? Right on Lynord Street. Four confirmed deaths and several more injuries. All because someone broke into your house, scooped your brains out, and slit your wrists. Supposedly."

"Isn't that what you wanted?" Charles' kite spirals back down to the ground.

"A result is all that *Libera Mentis Machina* wanted. I'm just a lab assistant, but I know the lead scientists would have been pleased with anything." The kite blocks his view of the sun as he winds the string around the spool. "My associates and I only want to study the shared psychology of society. Not our fault if they kill each other in the streets. Something tells me those people were just waiting for something like this to happen so they could get all that rage and bile out." The kite settles on the green grass. "You and your family still have your powers, just make each other happy." He lifts a shoulder and drops it as he politely hands the kite to Charles.

"Our powers don't work like that."

Damon knits his brows together. "Oh. That's a shame." He claps Charles on the arm. "Well, see what you can do about Mrs.

Geller next door. Her husband just passed."

Charles watches as Damon opens the gate, closes it, and locks it back before throwing him a friendly wave and a charming smile.

The man looks at the kite in his hands. He clutches it tightly before snapping the fragile wooden frame. Charles Johnson goes inside to his family.

# EPISODE SEVEN: *TAKE IT BACK*

"As with several of his other paintings, Gamez blends two seemingly unrelated events and transforms them into something closely tied together." Leo steps to the right and points at the painting. "Here we have a man in a grocery store reading the label on a carton of ice cream. And on the other side we see a couple walking hand-in-hand with the woman smiling as she looks at her companion." He draws his attention to the tour group, a miniscule smile etched on his face. "What's the connection?" A pause. "Anyone?"

"Both the ice cream and the man go straight to the woman's thighs."

A ripple of laughter suffused with a few disdainful glares.

Leo smiles, drawing his hands behind him just as his power tic releases a warble of force. He manages not to wince this time. "Not quite, but you are close. Here, Gamez is saying that deciding whether or not to buy a pint of ice cream is no different than deciding whether to be with someone who you may or may not even love.

Choosing to buy the ice cream may not be as dire of a choice as choosing to love or not to love, but both of them require equal amounts of consideration. Is it worth it? Will it make me happy? Will I regret it in the morning? Is this really the one that I want?"

"Will it taste good with chocolate syrup and cherries?"

Another gaggle of guffaws and shocked expressions.

"Riiight." Leo draws the word out. "Gamez is looking for some kind of reaction, almost like one you would get in science. Things should be moving, people should be pondering why one thing happened instead of another.

"Okay, I think that's enough handholding for now. If you'd like, you can explore the rest of the art and exhibitions scattered throughout the museum. I know many of you are interested in Sammy Doherty's 'Orion's Fall' collection, which is located in the northeast section of the third level. If you have any questions, feel free to ask me or anyone in a blue vest. Thank you."

A round of applause sings out before the group fractures.

Addie walks up next to him with her hands behind her back, banana curls bobbing and swaying as she smiles and thanks visitors. "Another excellent job, Leo. You've really developed quite the knack for this."

"Thanks. I just stopped worrying about sounding like an idiot and focused instead on keeping the visitors interested and informed."

"You don't always get eaten when you throw yourself to the wolves." She pats his arm and follows the throng of people heading for the elevator.

Leo walks down the hallway, greeting other employees as he passes, stopping for a quick word with Helen in the New Artists room. A voice turns him around.

"Does it hurt?"

Clint is changing the bag of the trashcan in the hallway.

Leo stops, considers, and slides his hands into his pockets. "Does what hurt?"

The other man looks up, well-worn cap casting a shadow across the facial hair on his lined face. "Bendin' yourself out of shape like you do." His fingers flutter fluidly as he ties the bag. "You walk around grinnin' and jokin', showboatin' like you happy here."

Leo regards him. "And what makes you think I'm not?"

"The way you look when no one else is lookin'." Shrug. "People ignore me. I see stuff others don't." He leans the bulging bag against the wall and pulls out a roll of trash bags from his back pocket. "You look at all that still art and I study the movin', breathin' livin' art." A wink. "Now that's organic for ya."

Leo watches as he peels the bag open and snaps it down, filling it with air as it parachutes open. "And what is this canvas saying to you?"

He stuffs the bag in the trashcan. "You're forcin' yourself to be happy here. Maybe there's someone in your life that you want to please. In order to please them, you gotta please yourself...or at least pretend to." The top of the trash bag is tugged tight around the rim and tied into a knot. "Still ain't answered my question yet, son."

"Which one?" Leo scratches under his eye with a thumbnail.

"The one I asked when you first started workin' here." He slides the trashcan back into place. "Who are you...little mixed boy?"

Jaw muscles flex. "I'm not a boy."

The other man belts out a splintered guffaw. "Still showboatin'. I know a wall when I see one; thrown up plenty o' 'em myself." He lifts his cap up only to tug it back down. "When you gonna tear those walls down, Leo, let people see the real you?"

Silence swirls.

Leo finally speaks. "Do you know why I put up with your shit, Clint? Why I stop to listen to every ignorant thing that comes out of your mouth?"

Clint waits, blinking. The tip of his tongue flicks out.

"Because I need your steaming shit. I need your adolescent accusations. I need to look at you and the dumb expression on your face every day as you try to bait me." A slow smile. "Thank you, Clint. You're giving me exactly what I need."


Belwine Park is surrounded.

The perimeter of the park is surrounded by Dominion City, buildings, bustle, and Broadway Street barely held at bay by the walking path. The grounds of the park are surrounded by tents, booths, and kiosks. The center stage is surrounded by a swarm of people, more streaming in by the second as a middle-aged woman steps up to the podium and speaks into the microphone.

"My name is Joanna Banks, and I'd like to start off by saying thanks to all of you for attending the Johnson Rally." A deep breath. "The catalyst for this rally occurred three days ago when a riot sparked just five blocks from where we're standing. The cause of the riot wasn't the tragic death of the Johnson family, it wasn't anger, or prejudice, or misunderstanding. It was silence."

She looks out at the audience.

"Silence is deadly. It's a poison that burns through us before we even know it's there. Alpha-Omegas and non-powered humans have to start communicating with one another. We can no longer glare at each other from opposite sides of the street. We can't support each other in secret, afraid of what our neighbors will think of us if they knew how we really feel. It's your right to speak against just as it's your right to love and accept. I'd like to open the floor now and get a discussion going. There's no specific topic, I just want you to come up and let us know how you feel about the way the world, your world, is changing around you. Because no matter what you think or how little you care, this. Does. Affect. You. Who would like to come on stage?"

Giorgio leans against a tree, standing in the deep shadow cast by the canopy of leaves and branches. The sun sets to his left, golden half-sphere peeking out between the towers of the Oleander Hotel and The Lavender condominiums. He watches as a middle-aged man with shaggy hair and red-tinted glasses makes his way on stage. The man accepts the microphone from Joanna's small hands into his own, turning enough to let Giorgio and the rest of the audience see his palsied left arm slightly twisted and curled toward his chest.

"My name is Freddy, and I'm a freak." A few uncomfortable bubbles of laughter froth up in the audience. Freddy slightly ticks the corner of his mouth up. "People often look at me with pity or veiled disgust in their eyes, and they do that because that's how they've been programmed to feel." He takes a breath and rubs at his palsied limb. "Anyone who doesn't look like everyone else is often automatically pitied. I don't need your pity, but you may need mine."

He places the microphone on the podium. Then Freddy disappears.

The audience cries out in communal confusion.

"I'M OVER HERE!"

Heads whirl as one. Freddy waves to the crowd from the information booth fifty feet from the stage. He vanishes.

"HERE NOW." The row of food tents one-hundred feet from the stage.

"Up here." The words spill from the speakers. Freddy is back on stage. "When I said I was a freak, I didn't mean because of my gimp arm...well, I did a little, I guess."

More laughter that Freddy joins in with this time.

"I'm a guy who can barely move his left arm and has a top speed just above Mach two." He waves to the crowd as he ambles off stage.

Joanna shakes his hand. "Thank you, Freddy!"


"Adam? Adam, I—I think I may need your help. I shouldn't have done it, but I did and now it's—I thought I could do this, but I can't. I just wanted it all to stop. Please...Call me when you get this."

Bisset's eyes slip to and fro. She listens. She waits. She watches.

No Seraph.

No The Dragoness.

The empty pill bottle and the phone slide from her hands. The bottle hits the floor with a *thock*, bounces, rolls. She can almost feel all eight capsules churning in her gut, blocking the voices in her head and administering peace to her mind.

The smile starts out as a twitter, the laugh a burble. Both swell into full conception. She slides off the toilet seat, clutching her sides as laughter pulls and pushes at her muscles. Tears ease down her stretched cheeks. She rolls back and forth on the floor.

Unbridled delight.

Bisset opens her mouth to say something, seals her lips, and shakes her head. She stands from the floor and looks at herself in the mirror. Her reflection looks back. One face. Her true face. Her true self. No ivory feathers, no golden-green eyes. No perfection. No imperfection. Just...

Bisset.

Her hand quivers up to the reflective surface, reaching tentatively. She touches her lips, her nose, slides her fingers across her cheeks and curls. A bittersweet burst of laughter and tears. A deep breath flows into her mouth.

She reaches over and twists on the hot water to the shower before starting to disrobe. She steps in and shuts the sliding door and lets the water spray over her body. Steam reels and rises around her, surrounding her. She enjoys the sounds of silence pounding her head while the water pounds her flesh as she suds her body up, rinses off, steps out, and towels off.

"So this is what it feels like to be in your own headspace." The whispered words ring hollow in the small bathroom. "This is what it feels like not to have voices in your ear telling you things you don't want to hear."

No response.

"This is who you are, Bisset. Not an angel sent to save everyone and not some seductress created to cause suffering. You're a normal, ordinary woman."

Her stomach growls.

"A normal woman who needs some food."

She stops toweling off her legs.

No response.

No. Response.

No.

Response.

She swallows the small lump in her throat as blood pumps gently in her ears.

She suddenly feels very much alone.


Leo wipes at his mouth as he exits the cafeteria, tossing his napkin and sandwich wrapper in the trash as he pulls his tie from over his shoulder. He pushes the door open and steps out into fresh air, a setting sun, and the soft distant sounds of Century Heights.

He looks up at the architecture of the Dominion City Art

Museum and can't help but smile at the slanted angles, curves, and sharp lines that shape the unusual seven-story building.

He reaches into his pocket to pull out his lip balm when he snaps his fingers, remembering something. He backtracks and takes the path to the Abstract Building instead of the path to the Sculpting Square. He punches the code into the keypad and walks in.

*A flicker of movement*

He stops and softly walks backward to the room where the employee lockers are housed. He peeks inside the pool of murk and watches as Clint yanks open a combination lock and peels the door open. He reaches and rummages inside, tip of his tongue worming across his thin lips. A crooked smile twitches across his mouth as he pulls out a woman's wallet, peeling it open and taking a few bills.

He jumps when Leo clears his throat.

Leo snaps the light on and watches Clint fumble and drop the purse. Bits of paper, tissues, tampons, and a clinking change purse spill out.

They both stand still, staring.

"This is the part in the novel where your character makes up a dumb excuse for why it only *looks* like he's stealing."

Clint starts to reach down for the fallen purse, stops. "Why? I am stealin', ain't no use lyin' about it." A jittery chuckle. "Lyin' is your job."

"At least I have one."

The janitor takes a step forward, wad of cash still in his hand. "Com'on, man. You know these one percent mutha fuckas ain't go' give us nothin'. We gotta take what we want. That's real affirmative action."

Leo puffs out a wry laugh. "Earlier today you referred to me as 'little mixed boy.' Now we're working class brothers in arms?"

A dismissive wave. "I was just teasin' you, tryin' to make you tough. You may be mixed, biracial, mulatto, or whatever, but you white as a snowflake." A shuffling step. "Please don't tell Addie you saw me in here. I need this job." He lifts his cap up and tugs it back down in a nervous gesture. "Please, Leo."

Leo looks up in the upper right corner. Looks back.

Clint wrings his thin hands together. "You said yourself that you needed me and the shit I put you through, you said you 'preciate it. If I get fired, who's gonna give you that, huh?"

Leo blinks and clears his throat.

"Come. On. Man. *Pleeeaaasse.*" A finger bobs at the row of lockers. "That was Janae's purse I took money from. You know how that bitch is, snobbier than a housecat."

Leo doesn't respond. He looks at the bills peeking out from the side pocket of Clint's work pants.

"Ohoh, this? This is from Ira's purse. You know she just got a raise, so she can stand to lose a few dollars. I ddn't take all o' their money, just a few bills so I can take the bus home and buy my dinner. Can you believe I been workin' here for four years and they still ain't give me a raise?" His hand wipes down his mouth.

"I'm not even going to try to follow that line of logic."

Clint's twisted grin droops. "So whatchu gonna do?"

Leo regards him for a moment. Then the turns on his heel and walks out of the door.

"'Ey! Thanks, man!"

Clint isn't thanking him an hour later.

An hour later, Clint is in Addie's office watching himself on a computer monitor as he breaks open Janae's locker. Addie pauses the feed with a keystroke and looks up at him where he stands on the other side of her desk.

Clint tugs his cap off and scratches at his head. "When'd you install the new cameras?" He gently slaps his cap against his thigh.

"Recently. Apparently, you never noticed them." Addie dips her head at the frozen image on the screen. "I don't think it's your responsibility to clean out employee lockers, Clint."

"I'm—I'm sorry, Miss Addie, I am." A slippery smile. "It's just that I've fallen on hard times now. My wife got laid off, my mother's back in the hospital, and my kids only get one meal a day."

"Hard times? That's your excuse for stealing?" She crosses her arms and leans back. "We've all fallen on hard times, but most of us make do with what we have."

His eyebrows stitch together. "Miss Addie, I been working for you for four years. Four years." He holds up fingers. "And in all that time I haven't gotten a raise. Do you know how many extra hours o' work I put in? Off the clock! Do I have to remind you o'—"

An upraised palm. "No, Clint, you don't. I know how hard you work here, and I do realize that you should have been given a raise long before now. But you should also realize that you've been here since the museum first opened. Most museums go under almost as soon as the doors open. We're very lucky and extremely blessed to have what we do here. Five years ago an artist like Sammy Doherty wouldn't even think of Dominion City as a place to showcase his art. We're only just now starting to come into success. On the video you mentioned that Ira just got a raise, so you know we're starting to bring in a solid profit. You could have—you *should* have come to me about a raise...even though I was going to give you one next week."

Clint fumbles and falters for words.

Addie nods. "I was, Clint. I was." She places her hands on her desk and looks down. "I know I should have approached you about it much, much sooner than this, and I do take a bit of responsibility for where we are now. I'm truly sorry about that, but still the fact remains that you stole, Clint. I'm going to have to terminate you; effective immediately."

"But, Miss Addie I—"

"Please don't force me to call security." She shakes her head, thick curls swinging along with the motion. "I'll have someone clean out your locker and meet you outside."

The bottom of the man's lip quivers. He jerks his hat off and wrings it in his hands. He stops with his hand on the doorknob. "Who told you?"

Addie looks up with a sigh. "You need to leave this office right now."

Clint looks from her to the computer screen where the feed is still playing. The image shifts to a different angle. In it, Leo is looking up at the camera.

Something burns in Clint's eyes as he shoves the door open.


The brunette accepts the microphone from Joanna with a smile. She clears her throat and steps up to the podium.

"I'm Susan. That's not my real name, but it is the name I'm

giving you. I wasn't going to come up here today, but I felt that I had to get this off of my chest so it would stop festering inside of me."

A hush.

"A-Os aren't human. That's what a lot of people say, that A-Os aren't human. That might not be what they are, but what they've become is a cause. No, no, please, don't applaud. Being a cause isn't always a good thing if that's the only thing a person sees you as. You're something to take up, a reason or an ideal. It's good that there are people out there who want to fight for you, but it's bad when all they see you as is something to fight for, something to take up arms for. What I mean is that some people are against Alpha-Omegas only to have something to argue against. They don't care about restricting rights, they just want to disagree with someone about something, go against the grain. It's the same with people who see Alpha-Omegas as their equal. They understand A-Os have to work for a living, have to struggle, have friends and family. Those people also understand that it's become the social norm to accept anything as long as it doesn't harm anyone. You *have* to accept a person who isn't like you, because that's your role in the world now, that what's expected, for you to openly embrace everyone and their ideals. Do you really want someone that narrow-minded fighting for your cause? A-Os know they aren't human, and some of them don't expect to be treated like them. They just want to be seen as beings. Not as something to rally around."

Only a few people applaud as she walks off of the stage and continues out of the park.

"Um, thank you...thank you, Susan." Joanna musters up a smile. "Is there anyone else out there who has something to say?"

A flurry of hands.

"Yes, you there in the light blue polo shirt. No no, the brown-skinned gentleman with the hair twists. Yes, you. Come on up, sir."

Giorgio brushes against several people as he walks past them, pulling miniscule traces of sustenance from the collection of dead skin cells dusting their vibrant bodies. A few people sway drunkenly behind him, but none seem to notice what is taking place. The dead man stands in the middle of the crowd, a hollow cork bobbing in an ocean of life.

The brown-skinned gentleman with hair twists in the light blue polo shirt waves at the crowd. "Hello out there. My name is Tyler. I actually want to start by addressing what Susan said about Alpha-Omegas being nothing more than a cause. I'm not necessarily against any certain group of people; none of my friends look like me, they don't come from the same social or financial background as I do, and they certainly don't all dress like me. That being said, I'll admit I don't think Alpha-Omegas should be allowed to live with norma— excuse me, non-powered beings. I'm not talking about *all* Alpha-Omegas, just those with dangerous abilities.

He paces.

"Think about how many people die from accidental gunshot wounds, how many people are stabbed to death, poisoned, hit by cars, choked, beaten. We all know that there are Alpha-Omegas out there who are capable of so much more than that. Many of them don't even realize it, and even more can't control their abilities. We may be restricting their rights by putting them in special facilities, but I would rather have them hate me than have them out on the streets accidentally killing the people we love because no one wanted to step on anyone's toes and tamper with anyone's civil liberties. Isn't life one of our civil liberties?"

A voice from the crowd: *"You can't make someone do something against their will!"*

"Yes, you can. You can. A blind person may not believe you when you tell them that the grass is green, but that doesn't mean it isn't true."

*"He's right."*

*"Just because a person has a point doesn't make it the right point."*

*"I agree with Susan. This man is just using A-Os as exploitation."*

Someone flings a shoe at Tyler, whacking him on the head.

*"Hey! The man has a right to speak his mind."*

*"I didn't come here to listen to this bullshit!"*

A boisterous storm boils over the ocean of life.

Thunderous protests swell in the air. Tension crackles and crawls like lightning.

A bolt strikes Giorgio, igniting a memory.

*His bare arm scraped across the carpet as a volley of sound struck his tympanic membrane.*

*Incessant.*

*Insistent.*

*Irritating.*

*Giorgio groaned as a wave of nausea bludgeoned the shores of his nerves.*

*"Answer your damn phone, G, I'm trying to sleep." The neighboring lump in his bed yanked the covers over a head of tousled black and blonde curls.*

*The shock is syrup-slow, contorting his face into a narrow-eyed, press-lipped, furrowed-brow expression. It looked horrible.*

*"I told you to leave when we finished."*

*"What can I say, you're a charmer. No man's ever lasted as long with me as you did."*

*"Where the—where's my phone?"*

*The lump rolled back and forth. "Just follow the ring, G, just follow the ring." She yawned. Then she snored.*

*Giorgio stumbled out of the bed, picking his way over empty champagne bottles, condom wrappers, clothes, and underwear. A square light flashed beneath a pair of lace panties. Giorgio flung them and the little baggie caked with a white powder residue away and stabbed the ANSWER button before picking the phone up.*

*"He—" Nausea bubbled from his gut up into his esophagus. He fought to keep his throat closed and the vomit down. "Hello." Palm to his forehead.*

*"Giorgio?"*

*"It's too early in the morning to play the name game. Who is this?"*

*"It's your Uncle James. How are you, son?"*

*"Hungover with an aching need to empty my stomach at both ends. What is this about, unc?"*

*"Well, I—I hate to call like this; it's been a few months since we've seen each other. I—"*

*Rattling sigh. "How much?"*

*"What?"*

*"James, please, let's discard the rigmarole. How much money do you need? Is my mother being characteristically disingenuous about her generosity?"*

"She can't help me with this."

He grabbed a cigarette, shoved it in his mouth, and looked for a lighter. "Like she ever can." Not on the desk. "Look, I know we're family and we're supposed to be there for one another…" On the nightstand? "…but I don't feel like caring at the moment. So tell me what it is that you need and I'll tell you whether I'm feeling like a bastard or a saint." By the—yes. He flicked flame and lit his cigarette.

"Giorgio, I've got chronic kidney disease and—"

"Oh, God." The nicotine triggered heaving. Giorgio raced/stumbled to the bathroom.

"I know, son, I—I know. Your mother should have told you."

Giorgio set the phone on the edge of the sink and vomited violently into the toilet bowl, a few chunks trickling down the edge onto the floor. Words blended with splashes, hiccups, burps, and heaves. Giorgio wiped at his mouth with the back of his hand, coming away with a line of drool. His uncle's last words seemed to blare out at him.

"—gio, I need a kidney from you."

Giorgio stopped, hand about to run through his curls. He crawled to the bathroom sink and pulled himself up until he could lean against the biting cold marble. He gingerly picked up the phone with both hands

"I'm sorr—" Burp. "What?"

"You're the only person in our family who might be a match for me. Your mother's is too little. The doctors would bring you in for an examination and—"

"Would I have a scar?"

"—then you—What?"

"Would. I. Have." Roll of nausea that passed. "A. Scar?"

"Only a small one. You wou—"

"No." He rested his forehead on the mirror, rolling his bleary eyes up at his bedraggled reflection.

"…What? Giorgio, son, I am going to die unless I can find another kidney. You only need one, so it's not like I'm really robbing you of anything."

"Except you are!" He slammed his palm on the mirror. "Giorgio Quintero will not and cannot have a scar. Do you hear me?" He took the phone from his ear and yelled into it, sliding down the sink as his muscles slacked. "I have three more days in sunny Tahiti, and I intend to stay the remainder of those days drinking, tanning, fucking, snorting, smoking, and shopping. Nowhere in there is there time for scarring or recovering."

"Giorgio, you can save my life."

"That doesn't mean I will. Unfortunately for you, I seem to be feeling like a bastard today. Goodbye, uncle, and good luck."

"Giorgio, please! I'm begging you! Ju—"

He tossed the phone in the toilet water with the vomit and staggered back to bed.

Thunder rumbled outside.

The memory burns away to the present. Chaos licks its lips and makes ready to pounce.

Giorgio lifts his hand and brings a bit of death essence to bear.


Bisset takes a sip of her lemonade and spears broccoli with her fork. She looks out over the floor of the restaurant before bringing the utensil to her lips. Couples, groups, crowds, trios, and parties. Everyone has someone.

Bisset studies them, tries to find the signs of disease and decay sloughing through their bodies. She squints her eyes and sees a dull red glow buzzing between a man's ears. It fades as she focuses. Seraph's gifts are gone.

"How's your meal, miss?"

She jumps a bit as the server breezes by. "Oh, it's delicious."

"Excellent." The man smiles and walks away with a sway of apron strings.

She puts her fork down, holds her hands in her lap, and bows her head. "I shouldn't have taken all of those pills, I know that. But I just—" She looks up to see no one is looking back. "—I just wanted to be alone for a while. The two of you are always...always talking, always there." She continues. "At first, I hated it, was confused because I thought I was going crazy." Head shake. "But I realize now that I feel crazy without your voices in my head." Pause. "Are you there? Seraph? The Dragoness?"

She listens. She looks.

A man sits in tears as the woman next to him throws her eyes around them, clearly embarrassed. Her lipsticked mouth moves in small, hushed tones between nervous smiles. She pats his hand.

"HOW THE HELL AM I SUPPOSED TO CALM DOWN WHEN YOU JUST TOLD ME YOU'RE LEAVING ME!" Tears trickle from the man's scrunched eyes. "HUH?"

She slaps his hand in rough pats. "Shahid, please don't do this here."

Sorrow crescendos to anger. "Why not? You did. Gina, I loved you. I wanted to start a family with you." He slams his fist on the table, rattling dishes and sending quivers down the hanging tablecloth. "I was willing to look like a damn fool for you in front of my boys, and I don't do that for anybody. ANYBODY!" Hot air fumes from his nostrils as he stands. "Tell me why?"

She sits calmly with her legs crossed. "Not here, Shahid, wait until we get back home."

"We don't have a home anymore, Gina! You just fucked it up. Fucked it all up."

Gina grabs her purse. "I can't do this right now." She leaves.

Shahid collapses back into his chair, covers his mouth with a hand, and breathes through his nose, eyes roving. "Mama told me she would do this, she told me." Hand goes to his head. "But I wouldn't listen. Was too in love to listen." He closes his eyes. He feels a hand on his shoulder and looks up at Bisset.

"Dry your eyes, Shahid." She kneels down. "It's good that she left, she granted you a kindness many don't receive until it's too late." She squeezes his hand. "This experience will make you stronger. This period of suffering will do you good."


Clint comes at Leo in a righteous fury just as he is getting in his car.

Leo turns, sees him, and locks the doors.

"GET OUTTA THE CAR!" A fist bangs on the roof. "I SAID GET OUTTA THE DAMN CAR!" Face in the window, hands pressed to the glass. "I JUST LOST MY JOB BECAUSE OF YOU, SNITCH! I NEED THIS JOB!"

Leo fumbles for the car key, sticks it in the ignition. The engine turns.

"CUT THE CAR OFF!" Gear shifts down to D. "YOU AIN'T GOIN' NOWHERE, MUTHA FU—" He jumps in front of the car and slams his hands on the hood. "YOU AIN'T GOIN' NOWHERE! NOWHERE!"

Leo puts the car in R and quickly backs up...into a wall. He feels a familiar tightening of his skin, loosely registering it starting to gleam a faint silver-blue around the quivering of his hands.

"GONNA BEAT THE BLACK AND THE WHITE OUTTA YOU, ASSHOLE! AND ANY OTHER COLORS YOU GOT IN THAT SNITCHING BODY O' YOURS!" He stomps forward, body strung tight.

Leo starts to panic. "Clint, listen to me, I di—"

"I KNOW WHERE YOU LIVE, LEO! I'M GONNA COME TO YOUR HOUSE AND BEAT ON YOUR GIRL! FRANCIE IS MINE! TELL THAT BITCH I'M COMIN' FOR HER."

Leo stops panicking. The gleam sharpens into something solid, focused. He shoves panic into the passenger seat and gets out of the car.

Clint hurries forward.

Air blurs.

The first flung force field only makes Clint teeter back. Leo adjusts and makes the next more powerful. It knocks the man on his ass. Leo gestures forcefully. "Get up!" The force field smoothly constructed beneath Clint props him up. Leo jerks his hand out and smashes another in Clint's face. Blood.

"Never."

Force field to the stomach.

"Ever."

To the jaw.

"Threaten."

Wrapped around the throat.

"Francie."

He walks forward with each word, each hurled mass of nigh-invisible energy, until he is inches from Clint. The ex-janitor raises an arm, punches, and howls as his arm careens into solid force an inch in front of Leo's face.

Leo tightens the force field around the other man's throat, making a squeezing motion with his trembling hand. Clint's eyes bulge as he tugs at the collar of near-nothing around his neck. His mouth gapes, tongue fishing at the air. Blood vessels scratch themselves across his eyes.

Leo drops his hand, drops the force field.

He gets in the car and drives.

Carefully.

It takes three tries for him to unlock the front door of his apartment. His hand quivers a bit as he steps inside, keys rattling as he puts them on the hook. He stops.

He goes to the fridge and grabs a reusable bottle of water, chugging it down before pressing the cold empty bottle to his forehead, cheeks, and the back of his neck. He breathes. And breathes. And breathes. And watches as Francie comes into the kitchen. He goes to her and holds her tight.

He isn't aware that he is crying until he starts sniffing and feels the tears, the deep sobs in his throat.

She holds him tight. "Leo—Baby—Leo, what's the matter? Tell me. Here, sit down, sit down." She grips his hand as they sit at the dining room table. She waits patiently for him to speak.

"I almost killed him, Francie, I almost killed a man." He drags his forearm across his nose, smearing snot.

"Who?" She snatches a paper towel and wipes his nose.

"Clint."

"That asshole who's been giving you trouble at work?"

Nod. "He got fired today and blamed me for it." Deep breath. "I was about to leave when he came up and start—started banging on my window threatening me. I tried to leave, but I was too shaken." Deep breath. Fewer tears. "Then he started threatening you and I just—I don't know, Francie. Before I knew it, I got out of the car and hit him."

She looks at his hands.

"No, not with my fists." He swallows and starts to calm down.

"You used your powers."

Nod. "I was doing things, making shapes I didn't know that I could. It scared me. But it scared me even more that I almost killed him. That man's life—Francie, that man's life was in my hands and I almost—I almost—" A torrent of tears. Francie holds his head on her shoulder and rubs his back.

"But you didn't, Leo. All that matters is that you didn't."

Muffled words. "What am I turning into?"

"Babe, this just proves that no matter what you think, you're still human. You're still Leo. And I still love you." She rubs a hand through the buzz of hair over his scalp. "I hope you're not getting snot all over my top, I just bought this."

A laugh she feels in her bones.

She kisses him on the head. Twice. "It's going to be okay."

"What if he presses charges?"

"There's no physical evidence that you laid a finger on him. No blood is on your hands. I'm going to start the shower for you. Scrub yourself down and we'll talk about it more. Okay?"

He lifts his head and nods. "Thanks." He pecks her on the lips.

"My pleasure, love."

Minutes later he stands naked in the bathroom. He braces himself up on the sink and takes in a lungful of steam-soaked air. He feels better. Then he glances up and looks in the mirror where the thick tide of condensation has started to obscure his reflection. The beginnings of his smile curdle when he sees himself. He quickly turns away and steps into the shower.

Water beads his body, sluices down his frame.

"It's okay."

He turns and lets the stream of water hit the back of his neck.

"It's okay,"

He turns and the water hits his face.

"It's okay.

He opens his eyes and sees the tiles on the wall.

"It's okay."

His fist lashes out at the wall and the force field he's thrown over it ripples as it absorbs the impact. There is no pain.

"It's okay."

His fists crank and piston as he assaults the wall, water shivering and leaping from his skin. He opens his mouth, tosses his head back, and just before he screams, wraps the entire bathroom in several thick layers of force.

He steps out of the bathroom ten minutes later.

Francie looks up from her paperwork. "How many times did

you drop the soap? Sounded like you were making beats in there."

"Just let it be."

Giorgio's fingertips brush the back of the man's neck closest to him. Death essence flows frigid over his skin, penetrates muscle, and injects itself into the man's stomach and intestines. Organs churn.

The man suddenly starts vomiting uncontrollably. He vomits, spews, projects, hurls, and retches.

Giorgio swipes a hand across a woman's shoulder. Her entire left arm locks tight, then starts spasming. Her body convulses and tries to twitch itself apart. She collapses to the grass.

A cold palm presses to a young man's back and suddenly he starts hacking in a violent fit.

Giorgio walks, spreading disease with every few steps. Cries of protest turn to cries of concern.

"Are you okay?"

"I NEED HELP OVER HERE!"

"Sit down here and just try to breathe."

"DOES ANYONE KNOW CPR?"

A little girl with a glowing ivory dot on her brow presses the cone of radiance to the seizing woman's forehead. The woman's limbs slowly release their fit.

A teenage girl kneels over Freddy's body. She holds his hand and has a phone tucked between her shoulder and ear. "I don't know! His eyes just turned yellow and there's blood coming out of his nose." She presses two fingers to the pulse in his thin neck. "It's weak. Pleasejusttellmewhattodo!" Freddy's gaping eyes roll up at her, his hand clutching at hers. "You're fine, Freddy, an ambulance is on the way, just keep breathing. Breathe with me."

Giorgio watches the two and is about to move on when he sees him.

Noir.

The Hispanic man kneels down next to Freddy and the girl. He puts a hand on her shoulder. "He gonna be okay, miss?"

She holds the phone to her ear with one hand and grips

Freddy's palsied hand with the other. "I don't—I don't know. They should have some kind of emergency services here." She looks out at the concerned citizens. "Do you know what's going on?"

"No. Some people just suddenly starting getting sick. Strangest thing." Noir pulls his hand away from cradling Freddy's neck, his fingers curled around something. "I'm gonna see if I can find him some help."

"Thank you." She gives him an expression of gratitude before speaking into her phone. "Yes, I'm still here."

Giorgio watches as Noir puts a hypodermic needle into a small case and slips it into a pocket. He gives the panicked crowd a cursory glance.

Gazes collide.

Noir smirks.

Giorgio arches an eyebrow.

They step forward.

Noir rolls the sleeves of his black long-sleeved shirt up over his forearms. He holds a hand out. "This your work, Mr. Morgue?"

"Some of it, yes." He regards his work as the two of them stand on an isle of serenity. "The sickness was my doing, the overwhelming concern is simply human nature at work."

"Wanted to prevent another riot from breaking out, huh?"

A slow nod. "Sometimes the best way to break a cycle is to stop it from forming."

Noir folds his arms over his chest. "So you just go 'round town doin' good deeds for the masses? Solvin' murders, breakin' up would-be, could-be riots?"

"I'm simply letting things be."

A scoff. "Lettin' things be? Hombre, to let things be, you gotta let things run their course. Stop interferin'."

This time Giorgio smirks. "That's not quite what I was referring to."

"Run it by me again, then."

A relative silence.

Giorgio looks up at the darkening night sky, at the stars barely seen over the lights of the city. A man runs between them.

"Don't tell me you're tryin' to score points with the peeps

upstairs." Noir shoves his hands in the back pockets of his pants.

Giorgio drops his chin, momentarily closing his eyes as a breeze tumbles through his curls. "No, Noir, I'm not. Honestly, I couldn't care less about God, his Heaven, or his fallen angel's little hell. I'm not trying to do right with my new life, not this time. I'm just doing it differently." He opens his eyes. "And if doing it differently gets me into Heaven, then fine. If not..." Shrug.

Noir shakes his head and turns.

"What was in the needle, Noir?"

Without turning. "A favor."


The wall plucks at her attention and she stares.

Phones ring.

Machines beep.

Voices mumble.

Keys clack.

Work takes place.

Bisset sits at her desk in the office and stares while her computer screen blinks at her. For all the sounds, it seems that she hears nothing.

Left

Right

Center

"B—"

Small grains of fabric.

"—ss—"

Steel edges casting back a distorted reflection.

"—et"

Monotone puff of the vent, blowing air into the room. What would happen if it stopped working? Just suddenly stopping pum—

"Bisset!"

Yanked. Slammed. Jerked back.

"Yes. What?" Her hands flurry for her keyboard. She looks up and sees Oscar standing there. "What is it?"

"You okay?"

She manufactures a reassuring smile. "I'm fine. Did you need something?" She rolls back a bit in her chair.

"I was wondering if I could borrow your stapler. I was joking around with Brendon earlier and threw it at him. Now he won't give it back."

She silently passes him her stapler.

"Thanks." He walks away. Comes back. "Are you sure you're okay? I was standing there for a second and it just looked like you were...like you were waiting or listening for something."

Rapid nod. "I'm just on this new medication. Still getting used to the side effects."

"Still having those really bad migraines?"

"Yeah, but they're getting a little better."

"I hope it's nothing serious. I mean, do you wanna—" He reaches for a spare chair on the other side of her desk. "Do you wanna talk about it? I'm pretty much finished for the day."

A gentle protesting hand. "No, no. Thanks, Oscar, but I'm okay. I'll get used to it after a while."

"You sure?"

"Yes."

"Okay then." He raises the stapler. "I'll get this back to you in a second."

Rigid smile.

She licks her lips and sits for a second, doing and hearing nothing. She looks over her shoulder and sighs before picking up her phone and pressing two numbers. "Hi, Delores, it's Bisset. I really hate to do this, I know I'm a little behind on running those background checks for the new tenants, but I'm really not feeling too well. Would it be alright if I left a little early today? I'll put in some hours this weekend to get caught up."

She listens...and hears this time, but it's not the voice she wants to hear.

"Thank you, thank you so much. I really appreciate this. It's just my head is all over the place. Yeah, sure. Thanks again."

A half hour later on her patio she watches the sun slide down past the Western Scraper on the edge of the city. The building is burnished in radiance, clouds suffused with effulgent golden light that gently scatters itself across the sky. Bisset turns...

...and sees nothing and no one standing in the living room.

She quickly goes to the bathroom mirror, opens her eyes wide, and looks for any traces of emerald or gold. She looks in the edges of the mirror for glimpses of her other self.

The sobs creep up on her, hijacking her body and wrenching her to the floor. She presses her hands to the cold tile and can almost feel the remnants of the tears of joy that had once blessed the floor. She brings her hand to her mouth and tries to force the cries back, but they refuse to be dammed. She wraps her arms around her knees and rocks.

Hands on her shoulders.

She looks up and sees a familiar countenance. The Dragoness does not smile and she does not speak. She only holds, squeezes, and listens to her hostess' sobs. Bisset struggles against her at first, slapping at hands that might not be there. Eventually, she settles into her own arms and calms.

They both open their mouths.

But neither speaks.


Leo's thumb taps as he walks across the pavement, bulging garbage bag in one hand and phone in the other.

**Don't worry about it. I'll pick up your dry cleaning.**

*Send*

He bumps into someone and drops his phone, immediately manifesting a small, malleable force field underneath it. "Oh, excuse me. I'm sorry." He bends down and retrieves his phone. "Guess you shouldn't text and walk either."

The shorter man has thick brown waves for hair, a smooth boyish face, and full lips. "It's alright, man." His voice is deep. "Your phone okay?" He turns to the large receptacle next to him, pulls out a trash bag, and lobs it in the dumpster.

"Yeah, it's fine." He takes in the man's familiar uniform. "You the new janitor?"

"Yeah, name's Simon." He takes off a work glove and holds his hand out. "Simon Ashcroft."

"Leo Kennington, nice to meet you."

Simon stares at Leo as he puts on his glove. He darts his gray-green eyes down at the bag in Leo's hand.

"Oh, sorry." He hands the bag over. "Take care, Simon." Wave.

"You, too, Leo."


"*Ascension!*"

Adam ignites in a burst of platinum flames. He blasts off the top of the skyscraper roof, scorching silver-white as he flies. The burning building is a beacon.

He hears the swell of Coldplay's "Viva La Vida" in his head.

He smashes through a window on the top floor, scans the room, and listens. Smoke smothers the air. Flames flutter spastic. A cry resounds from down the hall. Sovereign shoots off in that direction and finds a man cowering in the corner with his arms up, clothes singed, and face smeared with soot.

A section of the ceiling collapses.

Silver flames blur.

The beam smashes on Sovereign's spine as he stands hunched over the man. He looks up at his blazing savior in awed confusion. He swallows. "T—thank you."

Sovereign gives a curt nod before scooping the man up in his arm and flying out of the smashed window. He descends to the ground and deposits him in the arms of the nearest person he sees. "Get this man some help. Is there anyone else in the building?"

The woman helps the rescued man sit down. "Tami and Maya are still on the...the seventh floor, and I remember seeing JT on the sixth before the fire started."

Sovereign swoops back inside. He finds a woman with one foot perched on the edge of the seventh floor window sill as another woman reaches for her from her position on the floor, foot twisted at an unnatural angle. The burning walls seem to close in on them.

"Maya, what are you doing?"

The woman looks over her shoulder as her disarrayed hair flares in the breeze blowing through the window. "I'd rather break both my legs than be burned alive."

"Don't you dare leave me like this!"

"I'll come back with help, I promise." She lifts her other leg on the sill.

"Maya, no!"

Maya jumps.

Sovereign hears bells ringing in the Jerusalem Tower in the distance as he locomotors forward and gingerly picks Tami up from the floor. "Hold on to me." Her arms hesitantly wrap around his neck, pausing at the sight of the silver flames. He holds her close before leaping out the window. He grabs Maya by the wrist just as she drops past the second floor. He guides her to the pavement before gently placing Tami next to her. "See about her leg." He pushes off and flies for the sixth floor.

"JT!"

Roaring flames respond.

"JT, are you up here?"

He walks through fire, kicking open doors as he hurries from room to room. "JT!"

He finds him seconds later. JT is slumped over a desk, the remainder of his body burning. Fire consumes flesh. The blaze burns wicked and wild, stirred by the wind coming in through the shattered windows.

"Oh, God, no." Sovereign knocks a massive falling beam aside with a negligent sweep of his forearm. He flings a mahogany desk from his path. He sees the man is charred beyond all recognition. His mouth cracks open and a whimper slips through. Hungry flames lick at Sovereign's flesh, but find nothing to burn. Silver-white shoulders slump and suddenly weakened knees give way.

Three minutes later Sovereign slowly soars out of the window with JT's remains in his arms. A crowd gathers around him as he sets the blackened body on a stretcher and allows an EMT to cover it.

"I'm sorry I couldn't save him."

Silver flames burn away to flesh and blood.

Adam turns and finds microphones, tape recorders, cameras, flashes, and phones in his face. Questions and voices gnaw at the air around his ears.

Coldplay pierces through the dissonance. Who would ever

want to be king, indeed?

Only then does he notice the partially burning banner.

5TH ANNUAL NORTHWEST REGIONAL NEWS REPORTERS CONFERENCE

"Who are you?"

"What's your ability?"

"Do those silver flames hurt?"

"Can we sit down for an interview?"

"How long have you been doing this?"

"How did you know about the fire?"

"How does it feel having not saved everyone in the building?"

Adam holds up his hands and steps back only to have the pressing blockade of flesh roll forward.

He looks up at the sky, beseeching. Bishop Martin's words come back to him.

*And maybe God has seen fit to bless you to carry out His judgment, His will. Maybe it's time that Sovereign went public, showed the entire world who he is. Starting with Dominion City.*

He glances back up at the open sky, then down again as his phone chirps in his pocket. He pulls it out a bit and looks at the screen.

BISSET

He slides the phone back in his pocket.

He looks into the camera, at the waiting faces, at the tape recorders clutched in hovering hands.

*Maybe it's time that Sovereign went public, showed the entire world who he is.*

"My—" He swallows the lump in his throat. "My name is Sovereign, and I'm an instrument of the Most High."

*Starting with Dominion City.*

**FADE OUT**

# Dominion City – A hospital in Cade District seven years ago

"SHE'S wonderful."

Jenny Weisman cradles the baby girl in her arms. Her husband, Glen, bends down with a grin and rubs a thumb across the infant's forehead. "Hello there, little Lisa. Welcome to the world."

Small blue-gray eyes crack open along with a small mouth in a yawn.

"Aw, she's bored already." Glen waggles his finger in his daughter's grip.

"There's so much for her to see, so much for us to do."

Lisa's eyes roll around curiously, little fingers absently squeezing her father's. She looks up at her mother and opens her mouth.

"Hey, baby, I'm your mother."

Little eyes roll to Glen.

"And I'm your da-da."

Little Lisa looks from her da-da to her mother and back to her da-da.

Jenny laughs. "I think she understands us."

Little Lisa blinks with her little lips puckered in curiosity.

"We've got a little scholar on our hands." Glen makes a face at his baby girl.

Little Lisa slowly lets go of his finger.

*Five years pass*

"Lisa?"

"I'm upstairs, daddy."

Glen clops up the stairs to his office as he puts on his cufflinks. He looks down and sees his daughter sitting inside a ring of books.

"What are you reading, sweet pea?"

"One of your old math textbooks." She doesn't look up. Instead, she scratches through a set of numbers with a pen and scribbles a set of her own. "Several of these solutions are wrong. Did you know that, daddy?"

"What does a five-year-old know about advanced calculus?" He smiles and bends down. He examines what she's written...and the smile slowly drips from his face. "Where did you learn this formula, sweetie?"

A little shrug. "I just know." She scratches out a three and replaces it with a five.

Glen looks at the pile of books around her. Literature. Politics. Anatomy. Accounting. Appliance manuals. All of them slashed with blue ink. He smooths a hand over his daughter's hair. It's the same color as her mother's. "We'll talk about this later. Right now, I still have to fix your lunch and pack your backpack before I drop you off at the academy." He stands.

She looks up at him, little lips parted. "I did all that after I fixed breakfast for mommy and I. We had chocolate chip pancakes, Eggs Benedict, and french toast with honey." She glances aside, considers. "I should have said mommy and me, not mommy and I."

Glen pauses his flitting fingers as they tie his tie. "You don't need anyone to take care of you, do you?" He smiles.

*Today*

"Lisa, why don't you wait until your dad comes home and let him do that."

"I can do it, mom." Lisa picks up one screwdriver, discards it, and trades it for another. She picks up the smaller pole and attaches it to the two larger poles. The pages of the discarded instruction book flap in the breeze.

Jenny watches from the porch as her daughter assembles her new swing set. Disbelief mixes with concern on her face. "Lisa, you really should just—"

Lisa turns around with a wrench clamped in her mouth. "Whaish et, mum?" Metal mangles her words.

"Nothing. Let me help you." She steps out into the yard.

Lisa spits the wrench out into her palm, points. "Okay. Can

you hand me those pliers there, please?"

Jenny picks up a tool.

"No, not those. The tool—Next to it—No, other si—Yes, those." Her mother hands her the pliers. "Thanks, mom."

Jenny sits and watches her daughter.

That night, Jenny grabs her designer purse and matching jacket and walks for the door. "Glen, we're going to miss the previews if you don't hurry."

"I'd rather miss the previews than miss the movie. Watching previews is like looking at a meal you won't be able to fully enjoy for several months." Glen shrugs into his blazer as he hurries down the stairs.

"If I wanted logic, I'd stay home and watch the science channel." She kisses him on the lips.

"Where's Lisa?"

"Waiting in the car."

"Did she finish her history report?"

"In the car on the way home from school." Her hand hovers near the key hook by the door. "Where are my keys?"

"Did you check it?"

She frowns at him. "The keys?"

"Lisa's report. Did you check it?"

"Of course I did. Now, have you seen my keys?"

"No." He grabs his keys from the peg. "Probably stuck inside that chasm of a purse of yours. We'll look for them later."

They lock up the house and step into the garage...

...and find little Lisa behind the wheel of the silver Lexus. She rolls the window down, waves, and honks the horn. "Come on, pokies. We won't have time to get overpriced snacks and drinks if you don't hurry." The engine's purr rumbles up to a growl as she presses her little foot to the gas and giggles.

"Lisa Persia Weisman, get out of that car right now." Her mother jabs a finger down at the ground.

Lisa looks confused. "What's wrong, mom? I can drive us there, it's not that far."

"Lisa, listen to your mother and get out of the car. And don't touch any of the buttons."

Lisa looks at them while she turns on the headlights and windshield wipers and activates the hazard lights. She throws the car in reverse and peels back into the driveway before shifting back into park. Jenny and Glen can make out the tip of her head before they start running for the vehicle.

Her father wrenches the door open. "Get out of the car right now, Lisa! I mean it! This isn't one of your toys!"

"I don't play with toys, dad! I'm seven!" She takes off her seatbelt and hops out. Glen reaches in the car and removes the key from the ignition. "It isn't like I took the car out around the block by myself. You never let me do anything."

"That's because you're a child and can't do whatever you want." Her mother bends down and runs her fingers through her daughter's hair. "You're phenomenally smart and extremely intuitive, but you're still a child. Your dad and I have to take care of you, watch over you."

She plays with her mother's hair. "But I don't need you to take care of me. I wake myself up, clothe myself, feed myself, do my own homework, and everything else. I don't need you."

"Honey, you do need us." Her father kneels down. "We're your parents."

"I know that, dad. I need the two of you, I just don't need parents." Her mouth twists down. "I don't understand why you're upset at me for taking care of myself."

Jenny looks at her daughter, at a younger version of herself, and begins to cry. She sniffs and wipes at her eyes. "Lisa, baby, you don't have to take care of yourself, not yet. Let us do that for you."

"But who takes care of the two of you?" Blink.

Glen looks at his wife, takes her hand. "We take care of each other. Sometimes I'll cook and sometimes your mother will wash the dishes. You're our responsibility."

Lisa looks at her parents in wondrous confusion. "But...that's not taking care of each other, that's just helping each other. I don't understand."

Her father opens his mouth. Closes it.

"Why are you crying, mom? Is this conversation making you upset?"

"No, sweetheart it's just—" She shakes her head and looks down.

"We just don't want you to grow up so fast, that's all. Your mom and I are just a little shaken. We love you, you're our little star."

Little Lisa scrunches up her face. "Star? I'm not a mass of gas. I don't generate energy by thermonuclear reactions."

Her father's eyes glisten.

Little Lisa wraps her arms around her parents and consoles them. Little Lisa takes care of them.

# EPISODE EIGHT: GOD'S TALENT

Preston Caulley thumbs his nose and sniffs as he waits.

Sunshine cascades through the high window and paints the warden's office in golden tones and warm hues. He stretches his hand out to catch a ray, curling and uncurling his fingers as if the light is tangible.

The door opens.

He snatches his hand back.

Detectives Torv and West walk in. Perry removes his suit jacket and loosens his tie. He grabs a chair from the wall, drags it closer to Preston, and plops down. "How ya doin' in here, Preston?"

Jill leans against the wall, arms crossed.

"I'm in prison. How do you think I'm doing?"

Lifted eyebrow. "Just being polite is all. But hey, at least it's nice and warm in your cell. It's pretty frigid outside."

"Frigid?"

"It's a word." He takes a notepad from his pocket. "Use your copious amounts of leisure time to take a little trek to the library. I have a few book recommendations if you'd like."

Preston stares at the man's little smile before looking over at

Torv. "She the bad cop?"

Perry smirks. "Detective Torv is here to serve as a witness to the interrogation. Procedure and all that."

"I appreciate being seen as the bad cop." Jill tugs her gloves off.

Perry gives her a look.

"What? I don't look threatening?"

Perry tries to hide his expression as he takes a pen from his shirt pocket.

"I've told you everything I know about the Mind Machine people." Caulley tugs at the links of chain binding his cuffs together.

The detective leans forward. "Funny thing about verbal information; you tend to glean new details the more you recite it, or, in my case, hear it. Unless you've been lying all this time and simply memorized the whole thing." He rolls his lips over his teeth and gives the other man a poignant stare. "You're not lying to me about any of this, are you, Caulley?"

He stretches his hand out in the sun again. "No. Like I said earlier, one day last month, a woman approached me, said she had heard about me and my, uh, my reputation."

"As a rapist for hire." Perry scribbles.

Preston tears his eyes from his sun-soaked hand. "I don't just rape people, detective."

"Well, congratu-friggin'-lations, pissant. What'd the woman look like?"

Sigh. He draws his hand back. "Early thirties, long brown hair. She had a sort of hometown girl face, like she should be modeling for cosmetic companies or something." Eyes unfocus in memory. "Brown eyes. She was...in good shape, I guess. I mean, she was wearing a sharp little business suit."

"She give you a name?"

"No."

"So what did Miss Mystique say to you?" His pen is poised.

"She told me that she represented a group called *Libera Mentis Machina*, that they wanted the Johnsons to fade away before they caused any more trouble. You probably heard about the side effects of their happy trips."

"Making loons out of people, yeah, I've read about it."

"Well, one of the Johnsons' former patients was waiting in the car the woman was in. She brought him out and this guy was, I mean, he was fuck-nuts crazy." His hands weave the story. "He just kept smiling with glazed-over eyes and babbling about being all warm and fuzzy. I mean, he actually said warm and fuzzy. But that was before he peed himself...and started laughing about it."

Perry winces.

"Anyway, the woman told me who he was and asked me if I wanted to save a lot of lives."

"And of course you said yes because you're just that kinda guy."

"Exactly, I—" He stops, catches the sarcasm and continues. "Anyway, I really don't care about helping people. The only saving I care about is my savings account." He scratches at his stubble. "Plus, I wanted to see what it was like to kill someone."

"But you didn't really kill the Johnsons."

"Yeah, but that doesn't mean I didn't kill *someone*. I mean, that's why I'm in here, right? Because I killed four people."

"Don't forget all the men you raped. Sometimes leaving someone alive in pain is worse than killing them."

"I'll have to write that on my cell wall."

"So, Miss Mystique told you that you wouldn't be killing the real Johnsons. Did she tell you what would happen to them, where they would be taken?"

"She said she wanted to take them home."

"And where is that?"

Shrug.

"You didn't ask any questions, didn't wonder if this brown-eyed woman was really who she said she was?"

"She was dangling seven-thousand dollars in my face."

"You killed an entire family for seven-thousand dollars?" Head shake. "You're a tenderfoot."

"I'm a sick man."

"No, you're not, you just want to be. You're an average white guy with flights of fantasy. I could sit here and tell you a few things about yourself you probably didn't even know, but I'm not. You probably want someone to tell you that you are what you aren't."

"You should have been a profiler."

"And you shoulda been a thirty-something discontent sleeping in his parents' basement." Perry doesn't look up from scribbling.

"Whatever. How's the 'hero'?"

Now Perry looks up, confused.

"The platinum guy. What'd he call himself? Savior? Admiral Asshole?"

"Sovereign. I don't know how he is, and I honestly don't care. Man's about as delusional as you are."

"And yet he's still flying free." He leans back, taking a lingering look at Jill's hair caught up in a bun held in place by two hairsticks. "Rather take my chances in here being someone's muscle prag than put up with him. The Lord can't help everyone, no matter how hard he squeezes the world in his heavenly hands."

The detective flips through his small notebook. "The woman who confessed to the murders—" His eyes rove and roll. "Norma Gargis. What's her part in all of this?"

The inmate opens empty hands. "They didn't let me in on the cast of this production before opening night. Maybe she actually wanted to kill the Johnsons and hated them enough to take credit for my work."

Perry leans forward with his elbows on his thighs. "You have any idea where this organization is headquartered?"

"No."

"Any idea what their endgame is?"

"No."

"They mention anything else, any future machinations?"

"No."

Perry studies his face. His wrists go limp. "Spit it out."

Caulley slashes his eyes to the other man. "I don't have any gum."

"But you are chewing on some information. Tell me now before I call the COs in here."

Inhale. Exhale. Frustration. "While I was in the Johnson's house, I noticed this thing, a device."

"What kind o' device?"

"I think it was some kind of tracker. I found it taped under the toilet tank lid."

"What were you doing looking in the toilet tank?"

"Because that's the last place anyone checks when they're looking for something valuable."

"Why didn't you take it?"

"Didn't see the value in it."

He scribbles. "So how did you know it was a tracking device?"

"It had a map on the screen with a little glowing dot. That doesn't scream tracking device to you?"

"We didn't find any device of any kind when we investigated the scene."

He slouches. "Like I said, last place anyone checks."

"Alright. Anything else you want to tell me?"

"No...But there is something I want to ask." He leans forward on his thighs, mirroring the other man. "How good are your reflexes?"


The flash of the bulbs is almost bright enough to rival Sovereign's flames as he stands at the pulpit. The packed pews of Dominion City Apostolic Faith Church seat the congregation as well as reporters and photojournalists. Sovereign has dimmed the intensity of his platinum flames to make it easier on the eyes of those gathered, and to make it easier to photograph him.

He speaks.

"The Devil walks the earth. We see the prints of his cloven hooves all over this city; the riots, the murders, the hate, and the debauchery that overflows our streets like sewage. Satan is blinding us from the truth. He wants us at our neighbor's throat, at our brother's throat, at our own throats so that we're focusing on the wrong thing. None of this is about who's human and who isn't, it's about who is righteous and who lives a life of sin. We need to realize that all of us, *all of us*, are living in sin. But God is here to give us salvation. And I'm here to help Him.

"For those of you who don't know, my name is Adam Kensie,

and I'm also the Sovereign of God. At first, I didn't want to make my presence known to the public, but now I realize that someone who represents the Holy Light cannot work in the shadows. I do this not for the fame or the publicity, but because it is divine will. I was chosen by God to gather His children, His army, and guide them back to the flock. Alpha-Omegas are instruments of the Most High and nothing else. They are not experiments, they are not celebrities, they are not evil or unnatural, they are simply misguided children.

"Science has led us to believe that our holy brothers and sisters are abominations, mistakes or jumps in this absurd theory they call evolution. The media wants us to believe they should be regarded as gods. Brothers and sisters, Alpha-Omegas are blessed, pure and simple. They are blessed with God's talent." He beams brightly.

"Maggie, could you come up here, please?"

Maggie walks down the aisle amidst pulses of light and flickers of sound. She steps up to the pulpit and takes Sovereign's hand. "This is my wife, my angel, Maggie." He gently squeezes her hand. "I don't know who I would be if she hadn't come into my life. I may be the Sovereign of God, but this woman standing next to me is an angel made flesh." He kisses her softly and cameras snap like an ocean of sparks.

"Sovereign."

A magnified voice from the back of the church.

The lovers break from their kiss. Sovereign looks out at the crowd and sees a waving hand attached to the body of a man in a dress shirt and golden vest that almost matches his hair.

"Yes?"

"Aza Softly with the Dominion Voice. Can I ask a question?"

"Of course, but only if I can ask one first."

"Shoot." His voice booms pleasantly.

"What kind of vocal training allows you to throw your voice like that? It sounds like you're using a microphone."

A smile in the distance. "I'm one of the soldiers in the army you speak of. I guess you could call me the bugler."

"Your blessing magnifies your voice."

"Yes. Now, may I ask my question?"

"Of course, Aza." He rubs a flaming hand down Maggie's shoulder.

"How much are they paying you?"

The church rings hollow.

A rapid series of blinks. "I'm—I'm sorry?" Nervous chuckle. "I don't know what you mean."

"I think you do. This is all a stunt, something set up by the church to try to bring people back to God, except this time, the church brings God to the people. You're another charlatan, Mr. Kensie."

A rumble of retorts.

Sovereign holds up his hands. "No, no, please, let's hear what this man has to say. Elaborate, Mr. Softly."

"You're mixing fear and hope and pouring it into these people's hearts. Those who believe have renewed faith because they think you're a herald of the Second Coming while those who don't believe are wondering if there was some truth to all the biblical rhetoric they've brushed off all these years." A stabbing finger. "You're a fake, Mr. Kensie." He strikes a hand through the air. "Actually, you aren't entirely. I saw the shiny flames just like everyone else and I do believe you are something...you're an Alpha-Omega, like me. But you're not my commander, you're more like my brother."

Sovereign leans heavily on the podium, his mouth inches from the microphone. "And you are a thief and a corruptor, Brother Softly. You take the gift the Almighty has given these people and you twist and tarnish it. You seek to turn their eyes from the light. But I have news for you, *brother*, I have enough faith for you and for them, and there's plenty left over inside my heart. I will not allow you or anyone else to let this congregation stray from the path to Heaven."

"*AMEN!*"

"I am the Sovereign of God—"

"*YES!*"

"—and you are fighting in this war whether you realize it or not."

"*HALLELUJAH!*"

"Don't let the Devil fool you, pull the wool of slaughtered

lambs over your eyes. Even if I am delusional, it's the best delusion to have. I have delusions of victory!"

"*VICTORY!*"

"Divine glory!"

"*GLORY!*"

"Of God's love and grace!"

"*LOVE AND GRACE!*"

Aza Softly cries out, but his amplified tones are obscured behind the oceanic swell of call and response.

"Why did you become a detective, Mr. West?" Caulley stands by the window looking out at the prison yard as inmates play basketball and lift weights despite the bitter chill lacing the air. "Of all of the professions in the world, why this one?"

Perry tucks his pen away. "I'm not here to answer your questions, Preston."

Preston scratches at his nose with his thumbnail, hands held awkward in the handcuffs. "What about you—Torv, isn't it?"

Jill adjusts her stance  "I hate mysteries. Not knowing something eats at me...like a cancer. I don't know why you are the way you are, and that bothers me."

"Keeps you up at night?" He walks to the middle of the room.

"Not anymore. You're where you belong now."

"You people ever feel vulnerable in the field?" Preston divides his glance between the two of them as he steps away from the window and shuffles closer to them, chain linking the cuffs on his ankles singing out a jingling refrain. "There're individuals out there who can take a bullet and keep coming at you." He holds out his manacled wrists. "Some bad guys can snap these things like straws of hay." He drums his fingers together. "Think about how much safer the streets would be, how much safer you'd be personally, if you had an Alpha-Omega or two on the force." Pleased smirk. "Couldn't stand it if I were you."

Perry drapes his jacket over his arm.

The prisoner looks the man up and down, wry smirk twisting his lips. "Do you know why I asked you that question earlier, West?"

"The one about my re—"

Caulley explodes into motion. He folds into himself while corkscrewing his upper body halfway around, aims a tight elbow at the detective's midsection, chains jingling all the while. Perry quicksteps back, dropping his jacket to the ground and snapping out a sharp kick at the prisoner's head. The bigger man crumples into a roll under the blow. He braces bare palms against the linoleum floor and sweeps his massive legs out, catching the detective at his ankles and spilling him onto his shoulder. Breath heaves out.

Caulley scrambles to Perry, all dragging legs and quick-clawing hands, and pinches his head between bicep and forearm. He flexes. Perry chokes, struggles, flails.

That's when Jill reaches up for the hairstick twined into her blonde locks, yanks it free along with a cascade of glossy hair, and rams the sharpened piece of wood precisely into Caulley's exposed carotid artery.

A bit of blood splashes both detectives as Caulley releases Perry and slithers back on elbow and feet, wry smirk fracturing into a quivering one as red liquid trickles down his neck. He reaches up and pulls the hairstick out. And plunges it into the other side of his throat. Still, he maintains his smirk. Stab. Smirk. Stab. Smirk.

Still.

The detectives look at each other as the COs rush in like a uniformed tide.

Jill looks from the blood spotting her hand to the large corpse. "Please tell me he didn't want us to do that."

Perry really wishes he could.


The car's headlights flash once before it lets out a polite beep as Adam activates the alarm. He steps onto the sidewalk into the flow of pedestrians, offering anyone who makes eye contact a quick warm smile. Recognition lights up in the eyes of some, breaking through the brief haze of confusion and they point, request a handshake, or offer a "praise the Lord." Others share the same expression of recognition, except they offer sneers instead of smiles. One woman feels the need to stop and ask him if he's ever considered speaking to a therapist. Adam tells her that praying to God is all the therapy he needs.

He takes the scorn and the adoration in equal strides.

His mind flickers back to when he was thirteen and his parents told him that there would be people who would persecute him for his faith just as they persecuted Jesus. "Let your faith be your armor and let God sort out the rest," his father had told him. "Some people simply do all they can to resist the word of God."

His mind flickers forward into the past to when he first became a parole officer. He'd wanted to focus on parolees who had found God in prison and were transitioning out of two prisons, one of the body and another of the soul.

Adam remembers the scoffing, the barely restrained laughs, the poorly concealed looks of disdain. He also remembers when those expressions shifted to ones of barely restrained amazement when his efforts proved successful.

The memories fill him to the brim with courage and conviction, radiating out of his eyes and thrumming through his every step. Let them question his sanity. He knows The Most High has him in the cradle of his never-ending love and mercy.

He pulls open the door of the coffeeshop, scans the floor and sees the young woman with thick brown and blonde curls. She waves and beams at him. He walks over to her table.

"Cheryl, how are you?" They shake hands.

"Great, Adam." She gestures at the laptop on the table. "Just trying to find work."

"Excellent! Any calls back so far?"

She nods as she takes a quick sip of coffee. "Even set up a few interviews." She sets the cup on the table. "But there is another job I was thinking about applying for, but I'm not sure if I'm properly qualified."

"Oh, really? Which position?" He leans his elbows on the table, folds his hands together.

She stares at him for a moment before responding, uncertainty glazing her gaze. "I was thinking about being a minister." A beat. "Like—like you."

Adam fights to keep his expression under control. "A minis—

Cheryl, I admire your drive and your commitment to spread the word of God, but..." Hands open. "I hate to say it, but right now you need to focus on getting a job that pays you. That's part of your parolee agreement."

She looks as if he told her she has to go back to prison. "Adam, you're supposed to help me get my new life on track. You of all people should understand my decision."

He starts to reach for her hand, stops and curls his fingers into loose fists. "And I do, I truly do, Cheryl. But right now, you need to think about getting your daughter back, getting her life on track. I absolutely love the fact that you want to be minister, but right now, the system isn't set up in a way that that's considered a valid form of employment." Head shake. "I'm sorry. I'm doing my best to change things, but it's a slow process."

Cheryl shrugs. "At least teach me how to do what you do, teach me how to be like Sovereign and get people riled up and encouraged about the word of God. Help me become a holy vessel like you."

It's there in the middle of Tia's Teas & Coffees that Adam wholly understands the concept of the word *ramifications*. It's at that moment he also understands why superheroes cling so tightly to their secret identities.

Perry hold his phone to his ear as he steps out of his car, rolling his eyes down and giving a subdued wince at the dried blood spatter soaked into the fabric of his shirt. "Know it doesn't improve our public reputation, but I think we got all we were going to get out of Caulley." He listens as he walks from car to the inside his apartment building. Loosely stitched eyebrows. "This has gone all the way the mayor?" More listening. "Commissioner Moskovitz, I ca—*we* can handle this." Clenched fist as he steps into the elevator. "How 'bout if I work with the FBI instead of just handing the case over to th—" He reaches over to stab the button for the fifth floor. "I'm not disagreeing that they have better resources, and I'm not disagreeing that the Johnsons could be anywhere by now." The elevator smoothly climbs higher as his mood steadily drags lower with each passing floor. "Alright." He lifts his free hands in surrender. "I'll get the case file together to hand over tomorrow."

Walter is sitting at the kitchen table when Perry opens the door. His years of experience interviewing witnesses, suspects, and criminals make it easy for him to see that Walter is in the middle of an emotional battle, one raging just underneath his skin, digging trenches into his facial expression, setting off small explosions in the form of fidgeting fingers, claiming casualties in the form of aborted thoughts tearing holes through his mind and hemorrhaged hesitation leaking from an uncertain gaze.

"'Ey." The word drops from Perry's lips with a bit of his own apprehension.

Adam drops a bit of his apprehension as Bisset finishes her account. He takes her hand. "It sounds like you were able to handle everything fine on your own."

She looks down, then up. "I shouldn't have taken all of those pills. I could have killed myself."

"But you didn't. You know now that you can take care of yourself when you need to."

She shakes her head. "I didn't, Adam, I didn't take care of myself. The Dragoness was there to help me."

Adam pulls his hand away a bit. "The Dragoness was—She gave you comfort?"

Nod. "She just held me. I resisted her at first, but..." Sigh. "She's right, we need each other."

Adam gives her hand a tight squeeze. "No, Bisset, that's the Devil talking to you, twisting your mind. You don't need The Dragoness at all. For anything." His eyes dance through hers. "Where was Seraph during all of this?"

"The sun had just gone down."

"What did The Dragoness say as she held you?"

"Nothing, she was just there. She rubbed my back and held my head on her shoulder."

Slow blink. "Strange, she's never shown signs of compassion before."

"In her own way, she has." Bisset looks down, looks back up.


Walter looks over at Perry closing the door behind him, sets mail, keys, wallet, and lip balm in the bowl on the table by the door. "Hey."

Perry sits down next to him. "Looks like I'm not the only one who took a haymaker to the metaphysical face." He doesn't pause when he rests a hand on Walter's shoulder, squeezing it. "You okay?"


"Why are you doing this?"

Adam studies his palms. "I don't know, Bisset, I—"

She holds up a hand. "You can call me Seraph for now."

"There's a lot happening. The public knows that I'm Sovereign, I'm starting to gather followers..." He looks up with distress. "There's so much for me to do, so many people depending on me." He wipes his hands down his face. "I have to do it."

"Creating a child isn't something you have to do, it's something that you want to do." Pause. "Does Maggie know how strongly you feel about all this? Why you want to have a child?"

Sunset starts to slide in.

"She does, but...It's less like our faith is being tested and more like our faith is being defined, chiseled into something we're both trying to recognize."

"You're undoubtedly and mightily strong, Adam, but you're still a man, still human. You don't have to prove your strength to anyone, including yourself. People look at you and know that you've been touched by God. His light is spilling from your pores, your eyes, every fiber of your being."

"But still, I can't fail."

"You're not infallible." A hand on his cheek. "You've got to find it in yourself to fly away from this limited scope of belief. Elevate your mind to match the level to which God has elevated your body."


Walter elevates his head to look the other man in the eye. "I can't stay here, Perry. I really want to, but...but it's just not a good time for me."

Perry slides his hand up from shoulder to neck, massaging it. "Mind if I ask why not?"

"I just got out of a relationship; not in any way that's typical, but it's ended." Breath puffs past his lips. "And I'm starting to fall for you."

The massaging continues.

"I don't know if it's mutual, but I do know it's not healthy. For me, at least. Not right now when I need to be working on myself by myself."

The massaging slows to a stop. Perry withdraws his hand. "Bad timing, I guess."

"Yeah." Walter starts to reach for Perry's hand on the table, stops. "And I feel like I might be interfering with your work."

The detective smiles. "If anything, you're helping."

"And now it's time that I help myself."

"Don't wanna get in the way of that." Perry looks down into his lap, wipes a hand down his mouth, sniffs. "Glad you're stepping outside of your fear."


"I'm afraid."

"Afraid of what?" Seraph leans forward and takes his hand.

The man breathes, sits, contemplates, and bounces his foot. "I'm afraid that God will no longer find me worthy...that He'll take away His blessing, take away His shining light." Adam closes his eyes and draws in a deep breath, letting it out in a low sigh.

"Maybe the reason you're so eager to have a child isn't only to ensure salvation for the next generation, but to also plant the seed while it's still spring, while you still have your blessing."

A nod. "Is that wrong?"

The sun's final ray slips away.

Bisset's eyes ignite green-gold and her posture changes to something liquid and feral. She takes her other hand and caresses it down the back of Adam's. "It's only wrong that it's so right. A child is a stamp, a representation, or a footprint. But you have to remember that sometimes children are the exact opposite of their maker. The child of the Sovereign of God could be the Antichrist." A slow smile. "Light and darkness inhabiting the same flesh, something I know nothing about."

Adam looks confused at first, then he notices the lack of sunlight in the room. He snatches his hand away with a sneer gnarling his lips.

The Dragoness leans back in her seat, crossing her legs at the knee and resting an arm across the back of the chair. "I'm not the only one in this abandoned house of worship with two sides. In public, you couldn't be more courageous, more commanding. But when the flames are extinguished and the enraptured eyes vanish, you're a quivering little boy, afraid and alone."

"Like Seraph said, I'm still a man."

A slender hand flaps at the air. "Don't get caught up in *her* wayward wisdom. She has a tendency for downplay. You're more than a man, Adam, you can feel it. Maybe the little angel is jealous of you because you're closer to God than she ever was."

"We share the same light."

Her lips spread. "If that's true, then you should have sensed it when that light fled this body." She leans forward. "It should have left your skin freezing." She peers. "Did you feel anything like that, Adam? Did feathers tickle your cheek as Seraph left? Did your soul cry out as she fled?"


Walter elbows him in the ribs. "Not crying over me, are you? I know I'm the catch of a lifetime, but, damn."

Perry's face lights up. "I won't lie, I was startin' to feel a lil' sumthin' for you, too." He lifts his head to look the other man in the eye. "You're a great guy, Walter, and I think you're a helluva lot more capable than you think you are." He leans forward to give him a quick peck on the cheek. "Glad I'm still able to help someone in this city."

"You did more than just help me."

"Stay with me as long as you need to until you feel you're ready."

"You can stay with us as long as you need to until you feel you're ready to face your wife, your truth, and your self." The Dragoness luxuriates in Adam's frustration.

He doesn't stay.

Adam presses the page down against the rooftop winds and continues reading aloud Hebrews chapter eleven, verse five.

"'By faith Enoch was taken from this life, so that he did not experience death; he could not be found, because God had taken him away. For before he was taken, he was commended as one who pleased God. And without faith it is impossible to please God, because anyone who comes to Him must believe that He exists and that He rewards those who earnestly seek Him.'"

His eyes look out over Dominion City, at the specks of people rushing across crosswalks, at the lights burning in apartment and business buildings. Moonlight melts down the reflective surface of the Parcell Spiral.

"How many of you are earnestly seeking God?" The roiling wind whips his words. He reads on. "'By faith Abraham, even though he was past age—and Sarah herself was barren—was enabled to become a father because he considered him faithful who had made the promise. And so from this one man, and he as good as dead, came descendants as numerous as the stars in the sky and as countless as the sand on the seashore.'"

He clutched a hand to his chest and blinked back tears. The next scripture is a bit choked and raw.

"'All these people were living by faith when they died. They did not receive the things promised; they only saw them and welcomed them from a distance. And they admitted that they were aliens and strangers on earth. People who say such things show that they are looking for a country of their own. If they had been thinking of the county they had left, they would have had opportunity to—'"

A shriek and the staccato sound of twisting metal as a bus slams into something.

Adam's head snaps up and he looks down at 16th and Gateway. He squints his eyes and can barely make out the features of a man...stepping out of the large crater crumpled into the front of the bus. He does not wobble and he does not appear to be injured.

Instead, he walks to the side of the bus and deadlifts it with his bare hands, raising it over his head. He roars, leg and arm muscle cording tightly as he prepares to throw the bus.

Adam slips the small Bible in his back pocket and drops from the edge of the roof.

Wind whistles.

Vision streams.

Gravity grabs.

*The word* is uttered.

*"Ascension!"*

A blaze of silver glory engulfs his body and gives him the power of flight. Sovereign brings his arms to his sides and slices through the air in a rush of platinum, a silver-white brushstroke coloring the air.

The man holding the bus frowns as his ears pop, thick eyebrows knitting together. The air screams and smudges seconds before two fists slam into his gut and he is knocked back into an aging phone booth in a crash of glittering glass and mauled metal.

Sovereign hovers back to the bus and catches it before it lands on its side, gently setting it down. Passengers scramble out as he turns and advances on the man pulling his short frame from the demolished booth. His flesh, shimmering slightly in the nearby neon light, is whole. He twists his neck to the left and right, bones cracking. "You came."

"Explain yourself."

"Okay." The man runs forward, drops his shoulder, and plows the both of them into the empty bus, using Sovereign to cushion him from the worst of the impact. The vehicle rocks back at the titanic mass, tires roaring as they scrape across the street.

A crowd gathers.

Sovereign slams an elbow on the man's back. Flesh rings out in a song of struck steel, but his opponent does not bend, budge, or break. Again Sovereign rams an elbow into his back, putting all his strength into it. The man's grip loosens and Sovereign shoots out at his chest with both feet, sending him flying back through the air...straight into the crowd packed with fragile forms.

A silver streak.

Sovereign fetches the man behind the back and under the arms before his dense flesh careens into anyone, platinum palms pressed to the back of the man's head. "Stop this!"

"I can't yet." He shoves both their bodies down into the pavement and pops Sovereign in the mouth before he can recover. The smaller man whirls out of the platinum grasp. Fingers curl into a fist and piston forward. Sovereign bats the fist aside and delivers a right cross, left cross, right in rapid succession from the ground. He's in motion as the man fires off another punch at his head. The blow shatters concrete.

"Why are you doing this? This isn't how your blessing should be used."

The man stomps over and yanks up a streetlamp in a shower of sparks and snapped wires. He swings. Sovereign is about to dodge when he sees the people behind him. He steps forward, folds his forearms over his head and takes the full force of the blow. The pole warps and wraps noisily around his body. His opponent drops it and uproots a metal bench. It becomes an airborne missile. Sovereign jumps twelve feet into the air and catches it before it hits someone. "Will all of you please clear the area!"

The crowd barely stirs. Some people stand with their smartphone cameras pointed at the fray.

The Sovereign of God sighs and turns back just in time to avoid a headbutt. He hops back, grabs the man by the sides of his head, and rams a knee into his face. The man stumbles backwards and almost falls. He stalks forward.

Sovereign holds a hand out. "This is unnecessary. Stop this foolishness."

"Not. Yet." He backhands the silver man clear across the street. He lands roughly and the entire block quakes, skipping and bouncing back as he plows deep divots in the concrete.

A whisper. "God, please forgive me for what I'm about to do." Sovereign swoops for the empty bus, digs his fingers into the back end, picks it up, and takes to the air until he hovers over the crazed man.

"You wouldn't dare."

Sovereign dares. He uses the bus as a battering ram,

bludgeoning it down on the man's head, seeing his mouth drop and his eyes widen as the bus's shadow expands around him as it rushes closer. His skin loses a bit of its lustrous sheen.

The bus accordions in a raucous refrain as it kisses pavement and flesh. Concrete cracks and rips. The crowd gasps and steps back as bits of debris showers the area. The smell of gas tinges the air.

Sovereign waits a moment before picking up the ruined remainder of the bus, half of it snapping off. The man is on his back, a bit of blood oozing from his nose and mouth, his hair now streaked with oil. The grin he gives Sovereign quivers.

"You passed."

The silver sight of Sovereign is snuffed out. Adam steps into the crater, kneels, and gently lifts the man's head. "Passed what? What was this about?"

He points a broken finger at the crowd. "I had to prove it to them, the non-believers. You are the Sovereign of God, Adam Kensie. I know that, and now they do, too."

"SOMEONE CALL FOR AN AMBULANCE!"

People continue to stare, record the spectacle on their phones, text, and talk to each other or the person on the other end of the phone. A few people look at each other. A stooped-over old woman with a walking cane finally calls 911.

"Can you feel your arms and legs?"

He licks blood from his lips. "I think I may have broken a bone or two, but don't worry about it. I only partially reverted my body back to flesh and blood before you hit me."

"You shouldn't have done this." Adam wipes at the blood on the man's face with his shirt.

The beginnings of a shrug that twists into a cringe. "Too late. Hate that we had to tear up the block and ruin a bus, but it was worth it. Can't always be cordial when you're talking to people, sometimes you have to scream." Cracked smile. "Or hit them with a bus."

Sirens wail in the distance.

"Sovereign?"

Adam looks down at him.

"Pray with me?"

He nods, clasps the man's hand, and prays. He lifts his

supplications for forgiveness, healing, and Truth. Adam raises his eyes to heaven, but sees only stars against blackness, skylights, and the flash of cameras in the corners of his eyes.


Perry steps into Commissioner Moskovitz's office. The two men in black suits stand with their hands behind their backs, postures stiff and faces politely blank.

"Detective West, I'd like you to meet agents Acevedo and Beecher."

Acevedo's grip is as hard as his face. Beecher's eyes dance rapid in his skull; analyzing, cataloguing, and filing.

"We'd like to extend our thanks on behalf of the FBI in regards to your work on the Unfettered Mind Machine case." Beecher withdraws his small, soft hand behind his back.

"Thank you."

"We'd like to go over all of the files and notes you've gathered so far and cross-reference them with our data banks, see if any matches turn up." Acevedo scratches at his nose.

"Absolutely. I've got time now if you'd like."

"That'd be ideal."

Perry leads them down the hall. "I, uh, I was wondering if it would be possible for me to assist you with this case. Not asking to be right there in the thick of it with you, I could just—"

"We've already assembled a team." Acevedo stops at a water cooler and fills a cone cup. He looks at his partner. "You want?"

Beecher shakes a hand.

Perry waits while Acevedo finishes three cups, crumples the cone and tosses it. They move on. "I realize I may be getting in over my head here, but I'd really like to offer my help in any way I can." Perry stops at his desk and collects folders and notes. "This case means a lot to me, an' I'd really like to be there w—"

"Is this everything?" Acevedo nods at the small pile.

Perry's forehead wrinkles. "Yeah, that—" He rubs at his mouth. "That's everything. Wish I had more."

A muttered "me too." Acevedo opens the blue folder and stuffs the loose notes and slips of paper inside. "We'll be in touch.

Thank you, detective." He brushes past him.

Beecher holds back. He glances over his shoulder at the door man as he walks down the hall. He looks back at Perry. "I'm really sorry about my partner. He's still kinda new at this and thinks he has to be a gaping asshole to everyone whose first name isn't agent, deputy, or chief."

"It's fine."

He scratches at his balding head. "I'll, uh, I'll see what I can do about getting you on the team."

Acevedo stops at the far end of the hall, looks back.

Beecher clears his throat, glances down, and rubs beneath his lip. "Look, I, uh, I've heard about you being, you know—" Whisper. "—gay and all, and I just..." Quirked eyebrow. "I was wondering if—" He closes his eyes and exhales through his nose. "Fuck it." He retrieves his phone, pulls out a card from the case. "I live just outside of Neon, with the rest of the family. Give me a call sometime if you want." He sets his card on Perry's desk, sticks his hand out for a parting handshake that lingers a few seconds more than necessary, and leaves.

Acevedo shakes his head as his partner catches up. "Please tell me you did not give him your number." He walks.

"So what if I did?" He looks over his shoulder one last time. "He's damn attractive."

"And your ass is still legally married to that hateful bitch of a soon-to-be ex-wife of yours."

"I sign the divorce papers tomorrow."

"And you'll be getting your ass plowed five minutes later."

"God, I hope so."

Perry braces himself up on his desk and watches them leave. He catches Moskovitz's eye, quickly looking away and plopping himself down in his seat. Moments later Moskovitz eases himself down in the seat across from the detective.

The commissioner's mustache wriggles. "Say it."

Perry interlaces his fingers and loops his hands over his head. "Say what?"

Grey eyes roll. "You look like someone just gutted you and stole one of your kidneys without so much as a happy ending."

Perry snorts, swings his hands down. "Might as well have. I've been working that case since the beginning and I'm expected to be totally compliant when the FBI waltzes in and plucks it out of my fingers."

The commissioner spreads his hands. "They have more resources than we do, they can solve it faster." Beat. "You've never had a case taken away from you, have you?"

Head shake.

"Not used to just rolling over and taking it when someo..." He trails off, ticking his eyes down and clearing his throat. "What does it matter who solves it as long as the case is solved?" He stands. "There's still a chance the FBI will bring you in and ask for your perspective on finding this—this underground cabal." He starts to leave, stops, turns. "And don't go doing anything that might cost you your badge." He raises a finger. "Don't need the director of the FBI gnawing on my ass because of one of your little tantrums."

Perry watches him leave. Just as he watched Acevedo and Beecher leave after they took something from him, something that he simply handed over.

As he sat on his ass.

Detective Perry West grips his armrests, his jaw muscles flex and tighten. Then he gets up off his ass.

## *EXCERPT FROM LAMAR KOEHLER LIVE:*

*The image wavers and wobbles as the man in it holds the bus over his head.*

*The air whines and people in front of the camera step back.*

*"They shooting a movie or something?"*

*"Where are the wires holding the bus?"*

*"That's an Alpha-Omega, you dumb**BLEEP**."*

*A silver missile blurs the air and the man with the bus is slammed back by a powerful force.*

*The bus starts to fall.*

*A man burning platinum catches it.*

*"Is that that guy?"*

"What guy?"

"That guy that was on the news earlier. At tha—WOAH!"

"That guy" is tackled back into the bus, crumpling it like sheet metal. Seconds later, a body comes flying out of the wreckage towards the spectators. "That guy" turns into a silver-white smudge and wraps the other man in a body lock.

"Holy**BLEEP**, that's Sovereign!"

"Who?"

"The guy that was on TV at that church."

"That's not—Is it?"

Sovereign slams a series of punches into the other man's jaw before evading the concrete-shattering blow.

"Damn that guy's strong."

"And he's so little."

"That's how deceptive A-Os are. Sneaky little freaks."

"Hey, lady, my grandma's an A-O."

The crowd surges back in the image as the shorter man swings a streetlight at Sovereign, sparks flying from the shattered bulb. The camera jerks up as Sovereign catches a thrown bench. The silver-white man turns to the camera.

"Will all of you please clear the area!"

"And miss this? Is he serious?"

The battle continues.

"This event took place earlier tonight in downtown Dominion City. Thankfully, no one was injured or killed. The Alpha-Omega male fighting Sovereign has yet to be identified, but he has been released from the hospital with only minor injuries.

"Up until now, Alpha-Omegas have been seen as many things: neighbors, family, friends, coworkers. They have been persecuted and protected, reviled and respected. But tonight, they have become something else. They've become feared.

"We've known since their debut that there are Alpha-Omegas with terribly destructive powers, and we're once again reminded of the threat these genetically reawakened beings can pose to our safety.

"Not all Alpha-Omegas seek to make peace with the non-powered community, and not all of them wish to live normal lives.

The idea of super-powered criminals worries me, frightens me. But the idea of an Alpha-Omega like Sovereign, one who seeks to protect us, gives me great hope.

"I only pray the world is well-prepared if war should break out between Alpha-Omegas. I pray we're prepared, and I pray even more that we'll survive.

"Good night, America."

# FADE OUT

# EPISODE NINE: "WE'RE JUST ORDINARY PEOPLE"

*I don't normally break the fourth wall like this, but there's someone else watching them, Adam, Bisset, Noir, Perry, Giorgio, and Leo. An A-O with the ability to cast out their mind to read and manipulate the thoughts of others. I've felt them as I've been narrating this story, scratching and buzzing and prodding at the edges of my omnipresent awareness. I don't know what this person wants, their thoughts and activities are mostly shielded from me, but I have been getting more psychic flickers these last few episodes.*

*The Great Orchestrator approaches the podium.*

*THUM-THUMP*
*THUM-THUMP*
*THUM-THUMP*

Alien blood pumps and propels itself through Noir's veins. He cocks his head to the side, listening to the pulses of life throbbing away in his arteries. Individual notes hammer at his heart. Matthew

Maddrox McCain's legato tenor *THUMP* is complemented by Freddy's staccato bass *THUM*.

There's a song in Noir's heart.

A puff of laughter from his lips.

"The blood is clean."

The song collides with its coda.

Noir looks over at the man with hay-colored cornrows as he brings his head back from the eyepiece of the microscope and looks over his shoulder at Noir. "Don't know how in the hell your body is doin' it, probably your A-O gene, but you've managed to...*hybridize* blood together without any harm to yourself." He rests an elbow on the table. "You've also got two different blood types now, which is physiologically impossible."

"A-O blood ain't normal, padre." Noir sways and lifts a shoulder. "I am O positive, that might have somethin' to do with it."

Padre lights up a clove cigarette and removes the slide from the stage. "The fuck were you thinkin' shootin' up another person's blood without lettin' me check it first?" Smoke slithers thick from his nostrils as his Western drawl slithers thick past his lips. "Ain't no tellin' what the hell could be incubatin' in you."

Noir lifts a shoulder. "Long as I burn through the candle before the flame sputters out."

"You shoot up some poet's blood, too?" The man hands the syringe back to Noir. "Just because the blood's okay don't mean it's okay. Might be something there that I can't detect." He takes a drag. "How's your health, your other abilities?"

Noir puts the syringe in the foam-lined case before slipping it into his pocket. "Health is fine. No pain or nothin' when I pop my claws. Can only do short bursts of speed, though. Streak longer than a mile an' it feels like my heart's gonna go ka-blooey."

"Streak?"

"'S what I call it when I move at super-speed." He sniffs.

Padre grunts. "And yet the guy you sucked the blood from didn't seem to have any problem."

"That's 'cause his body was wired for it, genes an' shit shufflin' around so his ass could handle it even with his gimp arm."

The man's eyes rove over Noir's fit frame. "Ain't a complete dumbass after all. Look, brother, you need to wait a few weeks before you shoot up any more blood, see if there're any long-term effects. What was the other poor fool's ability?"

Noir points at his eyes. "All in the peepers. Woman could see heat signatures, see in the dark, had sharper vision." Smirk. "Pretty sweet, huh?"

The other man goes to the sink and rinses off the slide. "You kill her?"

"Jus' knocked her out is all. No harm."

Padre turns around, taps ash, shoves the cigarette back in his mouth, and peels off his latex gloves. "Yeah, you just popped the bitch unconscious and stole her blood. No foul play there."

"Exac'ly, man." He puts his hands on his waist. "Anythin' else?"

A finger kissed with powder jabs. "Yeah: don't shoot up that blood. As a matter o' fact, you need to get rid of the junk and stop whatever the hell it is you're doin' to your body, cause at the end of the day, you're just fuckin' yourself in the head."

Noir holds his hands up in surrender. "Alright, man. Damn." He pulls a thick envelope from his back pocket, throws it onto the desk.

He wipes his hands on a towel, eyes on Noir. "Where?"
"What?"

He takes the black cylinder from the corner of his mouth. "Where'd the money come from?"

Noir steps forward and reaches for the envelope. "Look, man, if you don't wanna be paid for services rendered—"

A hand around his wrist.

This close, Noir can feel the heat from the cigarette. Padre's hands are dry and gritty with powder.

"Jus' tell me where you got the money from."

"Coupla pussy pushers on Elizabeth. They were purposely infectin' Johns with HIV. That, and I sold some of my rare Magic cards."

Eyes slide to the money. Eyes slide to Noir. His wrist is free. "Never pegged you for a nerd."

"Never go the way they expect, 's how you keep 'em off guard and on their toes." Noir leaves.


Bisset rolls over in bed and sees The Dragoness stretched out on the other side. Her reflection looks over her naked shoulder out of the window to watch the belly of the sky burn with the approach of sunrise.

"Astonishing, isn't it?"

Bisset turns over. "It's too early in the morning for this."

"Too late at night, you mean." She rolls over on her back and slides fingertips down her stomach. "How does it feel knowing your little savior might become a fornicator to achieve his goals?"

The sleepy woman looks at her over her shoulder with bleary eyes.

"Oh, Bisset, don't look at me like that." Hands beneath her head, legs crossed. "It's like Seraph said, he's a man. A deluded man who thinks he's both more and less than he is." She rolls her head to look at Bisset. "But a man nonetheless." A finger slides down between her breasts. "And men have needs, desires, just like everyone else."

The sound of Michelle opening and closing her door bleeds through the walls.

"Aren't you going to protest, tell me he's not like that at all, that he has the best intentions at heart?"

"You talk like you've already been rooting around in my head for the answer to that question."

"How does that make you feel?"

"Why should it make me feel anything?"

Scoff. "Because the man whom you're putting all this hope and faith in seems more concerned with his own problems and less with yours." Giggle. "The masses would be horrified if they found out he might be infertile."

"As long as he can still help me."

"You shouldn't pretend to be so apathetic. I feel what you feel, a modicum of it at least." Pause. "But I have to admit that there's a part of us that finds his...firmness against changing admirable. Adam is who he is and doesn't hold any qualms about it whatsoever."

"You in love with him?" Bisset's words are muffled against

the pillow.

"I don't know love, darling, only suffering. You should take a message from him. You've been seeing him in that dank church for some time now and you're no closer to getting rid of me than you were the day I slithered out from your consciousness."

Bisset pulls the covers up.

"I'm not saying this to upset you. I only hope that one day you can accept me as you accept Adam and Seraph. Then, and only then, will you be rid of me. Accept yourself and I fade away." She puts her mouth close to her hostess's ear. "The universe demands balance, Bisset, don't tip the scales in favor of chaos."

Bisset rolls over just as the first ray of sunlight pierces the horizon and trickles into her apartment. The Dragoness vanishes. She turns back and finds Seraph floating cross-legged and angelic at her bedside.

"Good morning."


"You're not."

"I am."

"But, Perry—"

"Jill, my hands are tied, and I can't do shit else through the proper channels."

"Why can't you just let the FBI handle this?"

"Because it's my case and I have to finish it. Did you find his number?"

"Yeah."

"That quickly? Where?"

"In the phone book."

"Who the hell still has a landline at his age? And he's actually listed?"

"Not as Sovereign, of course. As Adam Kensie."

"Figured he woulda changed his number as soon as he...came out."

"Probably screens his calls, tells people he's out saving lives and souls and to leave a brief message."

"Alright, I'm calling."

"You're sure about this?"

"Nope."

"Insane."

"Yes, is this the Kensie residence?...Excellent. You must be Maggie. Sorry to be calling so early in the morning, ma'am. This is Detective Perry West with the Dominion City Police Department. I was wondering if I could speak with your husband concerning an ongoing investigation...Oh, no, he's not in any trouble or anything. After all he's done to help out this department and the city, I couldn't even bring myself to write him a citation."

"Want to remove your mouth from his di—"

"Adam, good morning. Detective Perry West here. Look, I just wanted to call and apologize about my behavior before."

"Don't roll your eyes like that."

"I'm sure you can understand my need to protect people, keep them safe from undue harm. I think the reason I butted heads with you so hard is because you remind me of myself a bit. I just hate it that I let my emotions get the best of me like that. The Devil must have got a hold of me for a second. "

"You should've been an actor."

"Yeah. Right, I know. I know God forgives me, I just hope you can, too. But I was also calling because I really think we can solve this case together. Two guardians, one with a badge and the other with the power of the Almighty behind them. *Libera Mentis Machina* can't even comprehend the righteous wrath that's about to fall on them. So, do you think you can fly over to the Johnsons this evening?...No, that's fine, I understand. You've got a pretty full schedule, can't save everyone."

"You're guilt-tripping the Sovereign of God? I think you just broke a commandment."

"You can? Okay, great, see you at six...God bless you, too."

"He's not just some tool you can use like that."

"'parently, he is. Can't go back to that crime scene alone. If they do catch us, I'll just tell them I was doing the Sovereign of God a favor by helping him find the Johnsons."

"And if they ask why you didn't call in Beecher and Acevedo?"

"I'll tell 'em the truth, that I wanted to finish what I started.

Even if they don't believe me or want to arrest the both of us for interfering, you think the public will allow their holy roller and his faithful assistant to be thrown in jail for doing the right thing? I think not."

"I'll cover for you the best I can. Get in, snag the tracking device Caulley told us about, and get out."

"Open and shut case."

"Better hope it doesn't shut with your ass hanging out the door."


The plunger depresses, igniting a spark at the tip of the needle. Scarlet lava devours the stream of blood in his body. Pain cascades and vision fades to points of light and synapses delight in the sense of pleasure and pain that strain at nerve fibers.

Noir tugs the needle from his arm, shaking his vision and senses free of vertigo, and focuses on the muscular woman standing in front of him with her dukes up.

"That some kinda drug you shoot up there, Jose?" Her voice is gritty and grating. She pivots, twists, and slugs him in the jaw.

A galaxy explodes behind his eyes.

He feels the birth of a bruise next to the one on his cheek that throbs like the one on his ribs. The pain pumps into rage. He knocks her head around with a wild hook before bringing his aching fist back in a backhand blow. He kicks her in the stomach, folding her over, and slams a knee into her nose. She stumbles back into the glass display case on the wall.

"Hateful-ass bitch."

"You come and attack me at my job and have the nerve to call me a bitch!?" Her lip curls, her head shakes.

Noir's eyes start to itch. Then they feel as if sand has been poured into them.

The woman splits into two, the second a perfect, fully clothed duplicate of the first. One grabs him from behind and the other slams her fists into his gut. He starts to weep. A jab thunders into his cheek. Something cracks and agony sears the side of his face. Uppercut to the chin. He involuntarily chomps down on his tongue and blood gushes in his mouth. He opens his eyes and sees nothing.

Gripping hands on either arm, propulsion, weightlessness in the air. A sudden wall. His skeleton jars and jangles as it slides down. Fingers grip the back of his head before ramming his skull into glass. A moment of resistance that lasts and lasts and lasts before shattering like the glass. Shards slice and blood flows. Still, he is blind.

Noir flexes his hands and sprouts his claws. He slashes. She blocks with the back of her wrist and plows her fist into his solar plexus.

The blow brings back his vision. Her body is molded in reds and yellows that plume out from her core. He ducks under her fist and throws a body shot to her ribs while throwing his foot out behind him to land a blow on her twin's nose. He's busy trading blows with one while the other picks up a metal mannequin and drops it on his head, her massive arm muscles bulging under her compression shirt with the strain. He streaks out of the way at the last second and the metal mass slams into her other self.

His vision winks out and leaves him in darkness. "Mierda!" Noir shakes his head to no avail.

The two women grunt as they charge him, large boots clomping over hardwood. He times it just...right.

*SLASH!*

"Ah, shit!

*SLASH!*

"Mother fuck!"

He blinks and his vision returns and is so bright that it nearly blinds him again. Light fixtures are like phosphorus suns jabbing luminance into his eyes. Hammering blows stain his brilliant vision. Blood dots the collar of his shirt in vivid relief against the white fabric.

Two turns to three.

Now there are six fists, six feet that want to spill his hybridized blood.

Noir's vision blips back to normal just in time to see the grimaces, twisted smiles, and bared teeth interspersed between stomping boots and bare knuckles speckled with his blood. He curls up in a ball and tries his best to protect his head as the tip of a boot cracks into his spine.

A gleam of yellow-green eyes.

A man's soft hands grab one of the duplicates by the sides of the head. The hands do not squeeze or twist or yank. The long fingers of those hands twitch once along with the woman's body. Her hands drop to her sides, her mouth agape and her eyes suddenly blank. The flesh around the fingers darkens to gangrenous green and black for a mere second. She collapses and does not move.

Giorgio glides to the next duplicate.

Every vein and artery in her body floods with blackness, death, and decay. Small black lightning bolts strike in the corner of her eyes, pupils dilating to onyx holes that stare into oblivion. She convulses, joints locking, popping, and locomotoring to a stuttering, spasmodic beat. She gurgles in time to her jerks.

Giorgio glides.

Before his hand can land, Noir drags his hooked claws deep across the woman's exposed stomach and rolls out of the way as her insides become her outsides. He lays on the floor for a moment to catch his breath and see how many bones are broken, how many aches are aching, and how many toes he cannot feel. He rolls his eyes up to Giorgio.

The handsome man's skin has gone deathly pale with an unhealthy tint. His body is gaunt, cheeks deflated and his once beautiful hands reduced to skin wilting on bones. A curly lock of hair flutters to the floor.

Noir rests his cheek on the cool tile and slides his eyes shut. "'Ey, G. You look like shit warmed over." A grimace mars his mouth as he clutches his ribs. "And tha's a compliment." He spits out a glob of blood that hangs on a thin string from the corner of his mouth.

"I used too much death essence, withers me back into my true self." His jaw clacks and cracks. "Still learning the limits of my..." He bends down to the eviscerated corpse. "...abilities." He grips the disemboweled woman by the forehead. Her skin goes a few shades paler as her built muscles and feminine curves seem to melt through her thinning flesh. The once tight top now hangs loose. Teeth work free from her open mouth to click onto the floor.

Giorgio Quintero siphons her death and spins it into his un-life.

Noir squints up at him with one eye, the other now swollen shut. "Nice. Think you could heal me like that?"

"The process would kill you." He takes a handkerchief from his pressed slacks, dabs it on his pink tongue, and wipes at Noir's forehead. "My place isn't too far from here, I'll take you there and get you patched up." He bends down and gently helps the broken man to his feet.

"Get tired of sleepin' in unmarked graves? Where you hangin' your tombstone now?" He clenches his teeth in pain as he's hoisted up.

"A luxury townhouse my mother owns, in the same building as my old condo and the Johnson's old residence. She goes there by herself every few months when she needs some time to slough out of her human skin and lounge around in her scales. I'll take you there and then get some medical supplies." Giorgio carries him out of the building.

Noir notices the expression on his face. "What?"

Giorgio looks down at him as he turns the corner. "Do you...You wouldn't happen to have any money on you for cab fare, would you?"

Noir grimaces. "Not unless you can pay with Bitcoin."

The undead man stops them. "Are you serious?"

"Don't tell me you're one o' them narrow-minded assholes who doesn't think bitcoin is just—"

"No, I just know you're the son of Amaury and Eva Minadeo; it took me a moment to recognize you after we first encountered each other. The wealth your parents have amassed over the decades makes mine look like the scroungings of rusted coffers and plastic piggy banks."

Noir grimaces again for reasons unrelated to his pain. "Fuck."

"Surely you have a few tufts of diamond-encrusted lint in those perfectly distressed and woefully out-of-style cargo pants of yours." Giorgio continues toward the nearby curb. "Did your parents disown you and cast you out of their house, pull your suckling lips from the considerable teat of their largesse? Is that why you're doing this?"

"Guy's not allowed to walk his own path in life?"

"Not in those boots he's not."

A sigh. "Hand me my wallet in my back right pocket. Think that bitch mighta fucked up my shoulder and arm."

Giorgio reaches. "Like you couldn't have your arm replaced with a top-of-the-line titanium prosthetic." He pauses. He squeezes. "How the hell is your ass cheek this firm and plump? What's your workout routine?"

Leo opens his arms, eyeing the scar on his palm, and lets the wind swallow him. Rushing air pushes him back as he stands on a manifested force field platform that juts out from the edge of the rooftop of the Stratus Building.

He looks down at the fifty-story fall. Looks up at the clouds sheathing night sky and stars. He takes deep breaths of the chilled air, shoulders slumping, and lays out on the hovering disc with his hands beneath his head and thoughts rushing his brain. He thinks of the life he might have had and the person he might have been had the Johnsons lived long enough to unleash his full happiness potential. Their touch might have reduced him to a blathering, drooling husk with a permanent grin, but there are worse ways to be out of touch with reality.

"What made you change your mind, detective?" Adam is behind West as they walk down the hushed hallway.

"Honestly, Mr. Kensie, I haven't changed my mind about you at all. Still think you're an Alpha-Omega with a savior complex lying to yourself and to everyone else you meet." Scoff. "Sovereign of God."

"I'm not the only one here with a savior complex."

"Not gonna argue with you on that."

Adam stops. "I could leave. Walk away right now instead of helping you with this case. You called me because you need me."

West pauses and turns. "You're right, I do need you, but you're not gonna leave. You can't." He scratches at his nose with a thumbnail. "If there's a chance you can save the Johnsons, then you'll take it." He spreads his hands. "That's who we are."

Adam stares at him. "So you're just tolerating me?"

Shrug. "People tolerate me and my crap all the time. Respect isn't always tantamount to like."

"You respect me?"

"I respect what you're doin', but not how you're doin it." He heads toward the elevator. "Comin' or not?"

Adam sighs. "God give me strength."

He follows.


Leo is now stretched out on his stomach with his chin resting on top of his hands looking over the edge of the force field down at the miniscule cars and the tops of people's heads fifty stories below. His tongue dabs at the corner of his mouth.

He thinks about dissolving the force field and plummeting fifty feet. He wonders if he would pass out before he hit Platt Street.


Noir is reminded of the first time he tousled with an A-O. Matthew Maddrox McCain. The night ended then the same as it did today: in bandages, pain, and a great deal of cursing.

"You got any mota around here, niño bonito?"

Giorgio swipes at the nearly invisible gnat biting at his neck. "What?"

"I called you pretty boy."

"I'm aware of that. What is mota?"

The Puerto Rican man rolls his good eye up. "You know the Spanish equivalent for 'pretty boy' but not the word for weed?"

The undead man goes back to his ministrations. "I spent a wondrous season with the most beautiful Latina my eyes have ever had the pleasure of drinking in." He dabs alcohol in a cut. "Beautiful hair spun from velvet, long legs the color of shimmering cinnamon." He sighs. "Enough to make me feel alive again."

"Do you?"

"No, I said it was only enough to ma—"

"Tipo, do you have any weed around here!? I know you said you used to smoke 'n' snort it up back in your glory days."

"No, I don't." He smoothes a large Band-Aid over the cut.

"Can you even get high anymore?"

He pauses. Considers. "I'm not sure." He resumes his work. "I haven't tried."

"Can you still get drunk?"

"Have yet to make an attempt." His hand bats at the gnat.

"All o' your plumbin' workin' down there?"

His brow furrows. "What are you—" Eyebrows lift. "Yes, of course my...*plumbing* is working."

"How? I mean, you don't have any blood, so how do you get har—"

"If you don't stop talking, I'm going to add a fresh bruise on your head."

Silence.

"Why did you attack that woman at the clothing store?"

"Crazy chick was plannin' a killin' spree during a shoppin' spree next week."

"You've been watching her?" He wipes at the slash of blood on Noir's arm.

"For a few days now. Had a dangerous need to drop a deuce and I stopped in the store to use the can. Overheard her in the ladies room next to me talkin' to someone on the phone about takin' out everyone in the store." He shakes his head. "Thin-ass walls."

"She could have been venting her frustration. A threat isn't always an imminent one."

"Waited for her until she came out, saw the look in her eyes."

"And what look would that be, pray tell?"

"The look that says I'm about to seriously fuck some shit up. You see it once and you never forget it, looks the same on everyone. May not know what it is when you notice it, but you know it ain't good. That, and I followed her to a gun shop. People that vent usually don't ask to test out a shotgun."

Giorgio leans back. "All done." He hands him two aspirin. "Take these."

"Thanks, doc." He gently eases himself up. "Why were you

there?"

"Feeding." Giorgio leans back against the couch. "There's a small graveyard not far from the store. I heard your little skirmish just as I was about to replenish."

Noir stands up and starts walking around the spacious townhouse. "So death is what keeps ya goin'?"

Nod.

"How does it feel to...eat death?"

He rubs tenderly at his mouth. "My skin freezes before it's set aflame for one glorious second. It's like being submerged into a tub full of ice and gasoline and lighting a match." His hand swats. "Damned bugs."

"Hmm." Noir juts his bottom lip out. "Sounds really relaxin'." Fingertips rub over the black walnut desk. "Mind if I ask why you live in the same buildin' as your moms? Not like this neighborhood is lackin' in high-end real estate."

The other man gathers used cotton balls and bandage wrappings. "She wanted to keep me close, within her reach, always has. She made her offer practically diabetic by taking care of my rent and throwing in new furniture."

"Think my moms would be fine with me livin' off planet. Not that she wants to get rid o' me or anythin', just that she knows how much there is to see and experience in the world. Don't want her baby missin' out." Noir peers out the peephole at the door, starts to pull his head away and looks back. "Gotta be fuckin' kiddin' me."

"What is it?"

"Just saw an old friend and that white guy that's been on TV tellin' everyone he's God or some shit like that."

"Adam Kensie?"

He tears his eye away from the door. "Yeah."

"What are they doing?"

Eye back to the peephole. "Gettin' on the elevator. My guess is they're goin' back to the scene of the crime."

"The Johnsons' apartment?"

"Unless there's another murder conspiracy goin' on in this buildin' I don't know about."

"I'm curious as to what it is they're looking for."

Noir looks at him with a smirk growing beneath the cuts and bruises. "Let's find out."


Leo's eyes flutter and he re-solidifies the platform below him that he has been slowly and unconsciously weakening, softening, and dissolving along with his will.

He swallows the lump in his throat, wipes the tears from his eyes, and takes a deep breath of oxygen, focusing on the way it makes his lungs expand and the way his blood pumps through arteries and veins to keep him alive. Keep him alive. Keep. Him. Alive.

Desperation soaks his mind, seeping into his thoughts like drops of oil in water. Maybe the Johnsons left something in their condo that can do what they no longer can.

He takes a few minutes to mentally gather himself before heading downstairs.

Cade District isn't too far away.


Detective West shuts the door behind them, flicks the overhead lights on.

Adam looks around the apartment. "Except for the police tape on the door and the tape outlines on the floor, it almost looks like they just stepped out." He picks up a family portrait. "What exactly are we looking for?"

West walks down the arched hallway. "I got Caulley to talk, told me that he found a tracking device here." He raises his voice from a room in the back. "Figure maybe it can lead us to *Mentis Machina*." Scrape of porcelain. "Jackpot."

Adam follows his path down the hall. In the bathroom, West has removed the lid from the toilet tank and waggles a small handheld device between two fingers.

The sound of the front door being kicked open ripples down the hall.

Adam races back to the living room, door vibrating in its hinges as it swings back, rusted and tarnished knob clattering and rolling on the floor.

In the doorway. Two men. One with curly brown hair and the other with a shaved head wrapped in bandages.

Adam opens his mouth to say *the word*. The bandaged man blurs and is suddenly behind Adam with a bandaged hand around his mouth. "Next time, don't advertise the secret power word on TV."

The brown-haired man calmly closes the door behind him as best he can.

Adam brings his elbow back hard. The bandaged man shoves a curse out between hard-packed teeth as he backpedals and holds a hand to his ribs, sinking to the floor. He braces himself on a knee and relearns how to breathe around the shafts of agony.

Adam opens his mouth and inhales—

—and chokes when he's punched in the larynx. He sees a wavering Detective West in his vision raise his gun and fire at the brown-haired man.

The apartment's acoustics capture the reverberating gunshot and resonate them throughout the living room.

The bullet catches the man in the shoulder. He winces more in agitation than in pain. Another bullet to the stomach. Chest.

"Will you please stop doing that? This shirt is Delgadar and you're riddling it with holes."


_____ diverts a sliver of attention away from the fray and spreads it to the minds of the other residents in the building. _____ calms their mounting hysteria at the sounds of the gunshots, shuffles their thoughts and massages their tension into something more docile. _____ implants the suggestion that they all heard fireworks in the park next door. Damn hoodrats. _____ goes back to the regularly scheduled telepathic programming.


Detective West slides his aim to the wounded man. "Don't think your injured buddy here is as resilient as you."

"Better make that first shot a killin' one." Claws sprout from the ends of bandaged fingers.

"Am I the only person in this room without an active A-O

gene?" The detective eyes the sharp talons, the warped bullets being ejected from swiftly healing flesh, at Adam holding a hand to his throat.

The bandaged man flicks his fingers, making his claws click. "You don't know, detective, could wake up tomorrow a new man...or woman...or child. Never know what wacky power you could get."

Perry's grip tightens on the firearm. "How'd you know who I am?"

"You could say we've met."

"Pretty mug like yours is hard to forget."

"He knows."

Three heads swivel to the handsome man.

"He knows the Johnsons are still alive. Don't you, detective?"

Perry shuffles his feet, gun wavering uselessly. "How do you know that?"

"The dead tell no lies, but in this instance, they do." He glances around the room. "They're both quite faint, but the essence of death and the essence of life clinging to this residence don't match. The people who lived here and the people who died here aren't the same."

Perry finally lowers his gun, looking at it as if it's a plastic toy. "He's right." Eyes cut from bandaged man to bullet-ridden man. Jaw muscles flex. "The Johnsons were taken by a highly-protected secret organization called *Libera Mentis Machina*, Unfettered Mind Machine. As far as we can tell, they're a group of scientists or something that performed an experiment, wanted to see how the world would react to the life and death of America's first prominent A-O family." He taps at the side of his thigh with his useless firearm. "We recently had one of their agents in custody, told us about this tracking device the family had stashed here."

Noir limps carefully over to the couch and leans against it. "Why give up the goods so easily? At least let me buy you dinner before you spread your legs."

Perry does his best to hide his annoyed grimace. "All four of us obviously want to figure out what really happened to this family." He holsters his weapon. "Got our own personal stakes, but..." Shrug. "No reason we can't all eat at the same table."

"Fair enough." The handsome man gestures at the device. "But what do you plan on doing after you've tracked them down? If this...clandestine organization is as powerful as you seem to think, then I doubt that even a person with your resources could disassemble them if they're experimenting with A-Os and elaborately staging murders."

"I might not be able to shrug off gunshot wounds, but I am super-stubborn. Gonna gnaw at me for the rest of my life if I don't even try to save these people...assuming they're still alive." He looks over Giorgio's shoulder at the family portrait of the Johnsons.

"And you're so choked by ambition that you would foolishly risk not only your life, but the lives of the Johnsons to please your lofty aspirations?"

"I'll help him." Adam clears his throat a few times. He swallows and speaks. "These people are interfering with God's plan, penning in and separating his holy flock. It's time we visit the lion's den."

"This lion probably has a lot more to fight with than fangs, claws, and a ferocious roar."

Noir braces himself up on his elbow. "So we just—

Giorgio swivels his head over his shoulder, curls catching the gleam of the lights beautifully. "There's someone in the hall."

Noir's image smears as he streaks out of the living room and into the hall. The sound of struggling. The sound of rubber slamming into a body accompanied by a glare of blue-white light. Noir staggers back into view in the doorframe. He starts to blur forward, is suddenly fetched up and bound tight in a thick coating of blue-white jelly. He hovers back into the condo, followed by Leo, who's thrown up a protective force field in front of him.

Perry snaps his gun up out of reflex, lowers it when he notices the half-sphere shielding their new arrival. Shoulders slump. "There a gahdamn A-O flash mob scheduled here tonight?"

"Guess I'm not the only one out searching for bliss tonight." Leo slides his eyes across the remaining three men in the living room.

"You here to sign up for the Johnson rescue mission, too?" Noir gives another fit of struggling in his bonds.

Leo's conjured manifestations flicker and fade as his

concentration takes a direct hit. They stabilize a second later as he resets his stance. "The Jo—" He swallows the rising lump in his gullet, tries to clear it from his throat. "The Johnsons are alive?" He's a parched man who's heard the whispered and everlasting promise of water and salvation.

Adam flicks a glance at the others before quenching Leo's thirst with a single word. "Yes."

Leo's eyes flutter, throat works, pulse throbs, mouth dries. "How sure are you?" He releases Noir from his bonds, dissolves the force field in front of him.

Perry finally holsters his firearm. "You mind telling us who you are and what you're doing here before we share any more information with you?" He slides his way past Leo, giving him plenty of space, steps to ease the door closed again after poking his head out and looking in either direction down the hall.

"I'm Leo." He looks from over his shoulder at the detective to the other men in the room. "I was thinking about undergoing treatment from the Johnsons."

Noir fold his arms over his chest. "You have heard that people go batshit happy from their joyful noise, right?"

Leo looks down, pitches his words low and packs them to the brim with conviction. "It's worth the risk."

Adam cradles his throat as he speaks."Is your life truly so unful—"

"Adam." Perry cuts him off. The two make eye contact and Perry gives a small shake of his head. He continues when Adam gets the not-so-subtle hint, striding over to the kitchen for a glass of water instead of finishing his sentence. "If you were under the impression that they were dead, what are you doing here?"

Leo raises his eyes and looks around the condo. "I thought maybe they left something behind that might help me."

"A final grasp for a final straw." Four head swivel to Giorgio as he speaks. He glides backward and eases himself down on the fine grain white leather couch, folds one leg over a knee with a motion that's all easy grace and breezy elegance.

"Something like that."

"We don't really have time to sit here and discuss this over tea, gents." Perry pulls the tracking device from his pocket and bounces it in his palm. "Gotta get moving if we're gonna do this."

Noir shakes his head and allows a huge grin to split his face. "You locos ain't serious, are you? Ain't no way of knowin' what you're walkin' into. Could be a damn fortified military base or some shit like that." He knuckles his eyes.

"Among other such perilous horrors." Giorgio tucks a stray strand of hair behind his ear.

"We've got someone with super-speed and claws. Adam can protect us from anything *Libera Mentis Machina* throws at us. I might not have superpowers, but I can shoot the shit outta something. This well-coiffed man-twink here's got his—" Perry's fingers flutter at the undead man. "—devastating *GQ* cover boy looks and bulletproof thing goin' on." He turns to Leo. "And I know we just met, but I've got a feeling we could damn sure use whatever it is you can do."

Leo narrows his eyes. "You're pretty quick to trust for a police officer."

Head nod. "Right now, yeah. Truth is that I need people with abilities like yours to see this thing through. But if you help us, you might be able to get that Johnson special you seem so hard up for." He dips his head to the side and twists his mouth along with it. "Would be a textbook-perfect irresponsible bastard if I intentionally put civilian lives in danger, but...I feel like it's you all who's gonna be protectin' me on this one. I just hope it's worth it."

Leo licks his lips. "You and me both."

Adam massages his throat and winces as he swallows around the pain still throbbing there. "So are you with us?"

Leo considers the alternative, pores over the emotions gnawing at and plaguing his peace of mind and sending him to the roof of the Stratus Building. "When do we leave?"

Detective West tosses the tracking device in the air and catches it. "As soon as we do a little recon. Friend of mine should be able to get us satellite coverage of wherever the hell it is we're going. Let's reconvene at my place." He heads for the door.

"You all go on ahead." Adam polishes off his glass of water. "I'm going to see about getting us some more help."

Bisset's palm leaves Adam's cheek stinging.

His head snaps to the side. He lifts fingers to his face and they come away with blood. He looks at her hand and sees/imagines her red-stained nails sliding back to normal length.

"There's my answer." She takes a step back into her kitchen.

"Bisset, I understand how you feel—"

"THE HELL YOU DO, ADAM!"

He steps inside and closes the door.

"Have you not been listening to me for the past month? The Dragoness is not some resource you dig out of the box when you think it's convenient. Do you honestly know what you're asking of me?"

"Yes."

"No, Adam." Her eyes search his. "I came to you for help because I thought I was possessed by a demon. You could bathe this entire city with the tears I've cried.

"I've told you what The Dragoness does, what she whispers in my head. I told you that she's starting to take control of my body. And here you are asking me to let her loose for people who may or may not be alive."

"I'll be there with you, Bisset."

"How about you be there *for* me, let The Dragoness take control of your body and do as she damn well pleases." She spins around and walks stiffly to the counter, bracing herself up as best she can. "Be quiet."

"I didn't say anything."

She shakes her head. "I was talking to Seraph."

Adam starts to take a step forward, but withdraws his foot at Bisset's expression. "What does she say?"

"She thinks I should go with you. She says this could be what The Dragoness needs to—to calm down." Her chest heaves. "All three of us are supposed to be one and the same, but I still feel like I don't know who I am."

"Maybe Seraph and The Dragoness don't know who they are either."

She stops rocking and turns around.

"Or what they can do. We need all the help we can get. We don't know what we're going up against and we—"

She faces him. "She's smitten with you."

Frown. "Who?"

"The Dragoness. She tells me how much she admires your tenacity, your *vim*, as she put it." She feels the heat from Adam's body. She grabs his hand and places it on her breast.

He jerks back.

"What's the matter, you don't like black women? Don't want a biracial child as the next savior of the world?"

"Bisset, please, you're speaking out of anger."

A scoff accompanied by faux confusion. "I wonder why. You don't want to use my body, you just want to use. My. Body." She shoves him back into the door. "I am sick to death of everyone trying to use me, of everyone wanting something from me."

"Please, listen to me, Bi—"

"Get out."

"There's a family that needs—"

"I'm drowning in needs, Adam. Part of me *needs* to hurt, part of me *needs* to heal, there's a part of me shoved in the back of my fractured mind that *needs* to schedule a damn tire rotation for my car. But right now, the only thing in the world I need most is peace."

Adam slides a look out of the window and back to Bisset. He eases back toward the door, reaches behind him, twists the knob, and leaves.

Bisset watches his stretched shadow underneath the door. The shadow ripples and Adam slips something underneath. The shadow glides away.

Bisset picks up the loose piece of paper.

Perry West
215 E. Washington Ave. Apt. 344


"Okay." West slides his finger across the laptop's touchpad and clicks on the attachment. It begins to download. A few seconds later a detailed map fills the screen.

"Yeah, I got it. Thanks, Beecher." He stops tapping keys. "Uh, yeah, I don't know, it's kind of a bad time for me." He listens. "Not exactly." He looks at Walter's jacket draped on the chair across from him. "It's...convoluted. Sure, I'll keep in touch. Thanks again." He ends the call and turns back to the three men in the room.

"Was he able to find the location on the tracking device?" Giorgio leans against the wall.

"Yeah." He scoots his chair back and adjusts the angle of the screen. "It looks like *Libera Mentis Machina* is holed up about five hours from the city." He points. "In Thornebriar." A detailed overhead view of a cluster of houses, streets, and dots fill the screen.

Noir leans closer, holding a hand to his ribs. "Thornebriar, Thornebriar, Thornebriar, I think I've—" He squints. "Isn't that like command central of suburbia purgatory?"

West nods. "Exactly." He taps the touchpad. "Everything checks out except—" He breaks off when he sees the screen has gone gray. "Slow piece of shit, com'on." Gray. Gray. A closer image. It's blurry at first, but resolves in a few seconds. "Finally. Now, everything looks okay except for this section here." He taps a key and the image zooms in on the western section of the community. The houses in the area look strangely disjointed and somewhat smudged. "Normally, this part of the layout wouldn't raise any eyebrows, but a recon satellite took a scan of the place."

"What did it find?" Leo studies the map.

"That's just it, it can't find anything. The place is shielded up tight. No radio or cell phone transmissions, nothing on radar. It's like the area was swallowed up whole and all that's left is the image."

"Sounds like what we're looking for."

Walter walks in with Adam behind him. "Found your friend here on the doorstep."

"'ey." Perry throws Walter a smile.

"I did all I could. I wasn't able to convince my, uh, my friend to help us. I'm sorry." Adam shoves his hands in his pockets.

Walter looks from Perry to Adam, Adam to Perry. "I feel like we all mean different things when we say friend." He dips his head at the man with the disgustingly perfect cleft in his chin. "He in your homo ho-tation?"

Adam stops.

Noir stops.

Walter spots the man who killed his old boyfriend.

And stops.

"My God."

"Oh, my God."

"Madre de Dios."

Adam looks at West, expression snarled into disgust. "You're a homosexual?"

Walter hurries down the hall. "Suddenly have to pee." Noir limps after him.

West's eyes follow Walter before swiveling on Adam. "You have a problem with what I do in my own damn house?"

"God sees and hears everything!" He points down the hall. "You are tainting that young man with your debauchery. Had I known you were a homosexual, I would have never approached you. Never!" He runs his fingers through his hair in agitation. "It is a vile, vile sin."

In the bathroom:

Walter shuts the door behind Noir. "The fuck are you doing here?" The hissed words ring hoarse in the confines of the room.

"Not killing your new boyfriend, if that's what you're worried about." He leans against the door, running his tongue over his teeth. "So you're exploring the daddy types now, eh?"

"You have to leave. Now. Seriously."

"Take it down, dude. I'm not doing any favors today, at least not here."

"Do you know how many nights I couldn't sleep after what you did to Matthew? I sat awake scared shitless that you were gonna come back and kill me."

"Do you know how long it took for me to heal after your crazy-ass *abusive* boyfriend carved me up?" He jabs a finger into the smaller man's chest. "Still have a scar on my stomach."

In the living room:

"—throw that Bible rhetoric at me, Adam. Get that crap outta my face." Perry swats a hand through the air and goes back to the laptop.

Giorgio and Leo watch.

Adam advances on him and shoves the laptop onto the floor, shattering the screen. He stomps on it, crying out with each frenzied step. Loose keys fly like teeth, shards and fragments of plastic break off and skitter along the floor until the machine's guts are exposed. "This!" He jabs a finger at the mess. "This is one of the problems that needs to be rectified. Technology. Humanity advancing down the wrong path." He steps towards West. "This is not the way to God." His furious blue eyes bore holes into West's gaze. "The destruction of His great works by people like you is one of the reasons there's so much evil in the world. You masquerade as a man of the law, but you—"

**BAM!**

The world tilts, whirls, and flashes as pain cracks through Adam's jaw. He crumples to the floor along with a spatter of blood from his mouth.

"Get the fuck outta here." West stands over him, massaging his bruised fist and breathing heavily through his nose.

Adam stands on feet that wish to sit. He wipes at his mouth with the back of his hand, swallowing a glob of blood. It's the second time he's bled today. He looks at West.

"God bless you."

"GET. OUT!"

He leaves.

West looks at Leo and Giorgio.

"Anyone else got anything to say to the faggot?"

Giorgio goes to the window with lips sealed. Leo picks up a book on the coffee table.

The heavy clomp of boots sounds from down the hall moments before Noir stops at the edge of the living room. Giorgio has opened the window and leans against the sill with his hand in the breeze. Leo's eyes don't move on the random page of the open book. Perry has a bottle of beer tilted up, glugging away.

The wrecked laptop remains in a jumble of its own electronic intestines.

"Can't take you pendejos anywhere without you showin' out." A glance around the room. "Adam gone to pray or something'?"

The beer bottle is slammed down on the counter. "Adam's

gone home to nourish his grievances along with his mouth."

Noir's eyes land on the bit of blood on the floor. "You didn't."

"I sure as hell did."

"You sure as hell did." Leo turns the page.

"We can't do this without him, man." He starts counting off fingers. "He's got the strength, the speed. That glow thing could come in handy if we need light." He stops, thinks. "But if I can get the hang of my new peepers I can—"

"We can still do this." West polishes off the bottle and pops open a new one. He takes a long pull before continuing. "I can bring in some of the guys on the force on this—"

"And tell them there's a very substantial chance that they could die on this little rescue? That they may be going up against Alpha-Omegas who mean to do them a great deal of harm? Explain to them that they'll be fighting an organization we know next to nothing about?" Giorgio looks away from the window.

Perry lowers the bottle. "You don't know them like I do."

"I'm sure that if they wanted to lend you a hand, they would be here right now, detective. But they aren't, are they? We're all you've got, and Noir is right. We need Adam and anyone else he can convince to help us." He steps away from the window. "Leo, how powerful are your force fields?"

Leo looks over his shoulder. "I haven't stopped anything larger than a van."

"*Libera Mentis Machina* has the capability to disguise their presence from a recon satellite, you can be sure they won't skimp on the defenses for the base. Guns, missiles, assault vehicles." He turns to Noir. "How fast can you move?"

His mouth hangs, eyes blink. "Well...you saw how fast I took out Adam." He slowly crosses his arms. "Haven't really tested my top speed."

"And I'm still discovering the limits of my abilities. No one here is ready for this; none of us are prepared, and we don't have time to train."

Perry sets the bottle aside. "Why didn't you bring any of this up earlier?"

The undead man cracks a smile. "I suppose I underestimated

the fortitude of your convictions and sterling intentions."

"We just met, but I get the feelin' you're not used to fightin' for what you want." Perry walks from around the kitchen counter. "The chance that we survive is just as high as the chance that we could live."

Giorgio holds up a finger. "Actually, the chances of our...well, *your* deaths are—"

"Let me finish."


"You should have let him finish, Bisset."

"Why?"

"Adam has faith in us. He could have gone to someone else, but he didn't."

"Because he wants to use us—you. Why are you taking his side on this anyway?"

"We've never shown him what we can do, how strong we really are, and yet he's somehow able to see a strength in you that you can't even see yourself. Open your eyes."

"Why? I see the same thing whether they're open or closed."

"I can show you."

The world seems to stop revolving.

"Let me show you what I, The Dragoness, we, Bisset, can do."

"You're trying to trick me."

"I swear by all the suffering and strife in this world and all others that I'm not. You take control of me this time."

Bisset opens her eyes and sees herself swathed in a sheer black dress trimmed in gold and emerald scales, feet bare, hair straight and sleek, eyes green-gold.

"Be in me, Bisset, be in me." The Dragoness opens her arms.

Bisset faces her reflection. She takes a step forward and The Dragoness mirrors the movement.

A second step.

A third step.

On the final step, Bisset collides into herself.

Unchained strength soaks deep into her muscles, tightening underneath supple skin that shimmers. Her nose becomes unclogged as scents and smells spiral in like light into a black hole. She opens her eyes and ears for the first time and sees the world in details so sharp they almost slice, sounds so vivid they seem to slide and quiver around her.

Her shoulder blades itch along with the tips of her fingers. Her mouth tastes of ashes and stale heat.

Large leather wings suddenly burst from her shoulder blades as long hooked talons the color of emeralds rip through her fingernails.

**POWER** she has never felt before, and yet she knows is rightfully hers to inherit, is a tsunami swelling from her core.

Bisset/The Dragoness opens her mouth, tongue flicking over the sharp fangs, and loosens a blast of green-gold fire that roils up her throat, from her stomach and tickles the paint at the ceiling, making it bubble and burst.

"Freedom!"

The force of nature charges the window and shatters it in a baleful blast of glass and metal. She stretches open her wings and feels the air engulf her, embrace her. She slides her eyes shut and lifts her head back as her hair whips around her. She flings arms open, clutching her fingers into fists.

"FREEDOM!"

The Dragoness/Bisset flies upward into the clouds, blasting through the flimsy atmospheric constructions painted in hues of gray and night.

"Feels natural does it not?" The Dragoness/Bisset opens her eyes wide to the air slamming into them.

"I never thought that...Is this how you feel all the time?" Bisset/The Dragoness finds it hard to speak around the undiluted ecstasy and divine fire burning through her being.

"Until this moment, I could only feel a bare fraction of our true self, just as you could only touch a bare fraction of yourself."

"My God." Bisset/The Dragoness runs her fingers through wind-whipped tresses.

"No, *you* are the goddess."

Bisset/The Dragoness shoots back down to Dominion City in a rampant tailspin. She slowly closes her eyes, lets her body go limp and luxuriates in the peaceful feeling of madness.

At the last moment, she flips her body and lands on the roof of the Stratus Building. She does not look down at the city below her, instead, she looks out at the stars, the sky, and the great lake of skyscrapers.

The Dragoness/Bisset breathes deep. "The air is so sharp...so sweet." A grin as the wind swirls around her wings. "Feels like taking my first breath."

A hush. A pause.

"You really think we should help Adam?"

"This isn't about Adam, this is about us. Adam can barely govern his own life, how can he expect to help you with yours? We do this for ourselves, including Seraph." Arms cross. "I'd like to show you what we're capable of, and we can't safely do that in the confines of the city; too many people, too much suffering concentrated in one area. If Unfettered Mind Machine is truly as disreputable as Adam says, then we can be sure no one will mind if we...cut loose."

"You don't care about saving the Johnsons at all."

"No. That family has done more to harm than heal the people they come in contact with. Whatever happens to them will be well-deserved."

"Even if we save them?"

"Even if we save them."

Bisset/The Dragoness walks slowly across the gravel slung across the rooftop. She crouches down and takes a large fistful in her hands. She squeezes gently. The rocks crumble to powder that whirls away in the wind.

"When can I do this again?"

"Whenever we'd like, as long as the sun is below the horizon."

She looks out.

"Hope the Unfettered Mind Machine isn't afraid of the dark."


Adam presses a button on his key fob, unlocking the doors of his car. "I don't understand why those people persist in their sin. If they aren't concerned with the risk to their souls, they should at least be concerned about the risk to their health." He stalks as he mutters to himself, shaking his head as he steps off the curb.

"Adam?" The familiar voice whirls him around. The familiar face stops him.

"Suzie." His agitation disentangles itself from the muscles of his forehead, untwines from his intestines. "Such a blessing to see you." He holds his hand out.

"You, too." They shake. "You live here now?"

Adam looks back at the apartment building and a spark of his smothered ire stokes back up. "Oh, no, I was just..." He dismisses the rest of the sentence with a sweep of his hands. "It's going to make me upset all over if I dive back into it." He rests his back against his car. "How have you been? Parole and everything going okay?"

She nods, thick violet and neon pink dreadlocks bound at the crown of her head swaying. "Absolutely. I've been seeing someone lately who's been a massive help in keeping light in my life, creating a healthy space where I can generate positive change."

Her joy is infectious. "That's beautiful."

"Yeah, so's she."

"Is this a...a therapist." Adam loosely crosses his arm.

"Girlfriend. Her name's Amala."

The response vaccinates the joyous disease, heaps cinders on smoldered emotions. "Oh...Suzie, I thought that you were fully giving your life over to God when you were released from prison." He pushes away from his car. "I don't want you to—"

"Adam." His uttered name locks his words behind his lips. " I appreciate everything you've done for me since I got out, but we both know that it takes more than a parole officer with a heart of solid platinum and a mountain of good intentions to keep people like me from going back in. Be one-hundred percent honest with yourself: is all that Amala's done to help me, to help you help me, totally eclipsed by the fact that she's gay?"

He shuffles his stance. "What exactly is it that's so fantastic about this...woman?"

Suzie pretends not to notice his verbal stumble. "She's a damn A-O she-ro, for one thing. She can create, like, these teleportation portals. Uses them to help people in the neighborhood get to and from work, kinda like a ride-share service, only faster...and free." She gestures at the building in front of them. "She also helps people move, helps the elderly residents get to and from the supermarket and their doctor's appointments. She even saved a bunch of people in that shooting at Northwest Dominion Community College a few months ago."

Adam clears his throat. "Sounds like she's...like she's doing the Lord's work."

"She asked if I could introduce her to you, Sovereign, I mean."

Adam jerks his head back, confusion layering his features. "Really?"

"Yeah. I told her you're my parole officer, and she sees you on TV; thinks you're Superman come to life."

"You didn't tell her my beliefs about—" He swallows. "About her chosen lifestyle?"

"*Our* lifestyle." Suzie gnaws off the words. "No, I don't want to disappoint her." She eases hands on hips. "I don't have to tell you that the world is changing, Adam, but I do feel I have to help you when and where I can just like you're helping me." She cleaves her eyes to the side a moment before sliding them back to him. "Why is it that you're willing to save the souls and support the lives of former criminals, but at the same time you still act like almost everyone who's anything but...normal and Christian are vile demons from the pits of Hell?"

Stillness and silence.

"You've gotta decide what your philosophy's gonna be now that you're a hero, Adam. Saving lives is different from savings souls. With souls, you've got time to lead the person back on track. But with lives..." Head shake. "You don't have the luxury of time when it comes to lives, you can't ease your way into things and get a sense of someone's intentions while they're tumbling out of a burning building." Shrug. "As far as you know, you might have already saved a gay person's life."

Adam raises his palms in front of him. "I love all of God's children, Suzie, I truly do; sinner and savior alike. I agree with you that Amala's decision regarding her sexuality doesn't demean what she's done for you or anyone else she's helped. What I'm struggling with in my soul, what I've always struggled to wrap my mind around ever since my parents first sat me down and talked to me about homosexuality and gender confusion is why certain individuals who...identify as members of that community are so extravagant in their displays." His face twitches as he struggles to keep disgust off his face.

"The word *flamboyant* is used to describe the gay community for a reason. And I can see where you're coming from, but you and people who look like you don't have a history of needing to hide who you are, of having to wall off an entire part of yourself when you're out in public out of fear for your life."

He drags fingers through his hair. "I know that nor—that heterosexual people have it much easier in the world, but is there truly such a need to always, *always* essentially shout in everyone's face to make yourself seen, to make yourself understood?"

"I'm guessing you don't personally know any gay people, at least not any who are open."

Eyes to the building where Perry lives. "That changed a few minutes ago, actually." Eyes back to Suzie. "I don't want gay people to die from HIV, and I don't think they have themselves to blame for the endless turmoil and mental torment they endure when they share their identities with other people. I just want to help bring the flock home to God. But maybe...maybe God is telling me that just as he's changing the world, His shepherds have to change how they tend to His new flock." His eyes slip shut as he exhales. "I have to remember that shepherds not only lead and guard the flock, they feed the flock as well. Maybe it's time for new spiritual nourishment."

Suzie takes a step forward, reaches for his hand, squeezes it. "And that's exactly what you're providing, Adam. You just need to make some tweaks to the recipe."

"Sometimes I don't know if God has broken me and is putting me back together in a new spiritual form, or if I'm whole again and everyone else around me is shattering and being recreated with a clean heart."

"If you're broken, you have to be open to receive the people God puts in your life to help bless and renew you. And if you're whole, you have to be open to the people God wants you to bless and renew." Shrug. "And most of the time, the people on either side of the equation aren't at all who or what you think they should be."

Noir sits on the curb with a black cigarette dangling from the corner of his mouth. He bobs his foot, arms wrapped around his knees. He takes the cigarette from his mouth, blows smoke, and scratches around the bandage on his neck. "The hell is takin' 'im so long?"

"He had to get a van with heavily tinted windows." Leo sits behind him cross-legged in a cone of electric light on the steps of Perry's apartment building, a glittering force field sphere buoyed between his hands.

Noir looks over his shoulder. "The hell for?"

Leo glances over at Giorgio leaning against a pillar with his arms crossed loosely over his chest. "Exposure to the sun's rays at certain hours of the day does horrors to my skin, as does extreme cold."

Noir stares as smoke trickles past his lips. "Princess. Anything else you allergic to?"

Giorgio continues to stare down the street. "We have a five-hour ride ahead of us, maybe I'll tell you on the way there." He looks at Noir and flashes him a condescending smile that lasts a solid second before it flutters from his face.

"Whatever." Noir brings the cigarette to his lips and watches Leo squeeze the shimmering silver-blue orb between his palms, the muscles in his forearms cording. The sphere remains intact...for seven seconds before disintegrating into winking shards that vanish as they fall. Leo starts again. "Perry's little pep speech change your ways? You were all set to walk out an hour ago."

"It's not as if I have anything else to do but brood and sulk in your absence." Lids slide halfway over yellow-green eyes.

Noir flicks the cigarette butt and watches as it spins end over end into the street. "Any wonder why we've become such fast BFFs?"

A full-sized police van turns the corner, busted headlights flaring over the three waiting men. It grinds to a noisy halt at the curb and the engine is cut. Detective West opens the groaning door and pops his head over the roof. "Let's roll, party people."

Noir stands and rubs at his chin as he inspects the vehicle. His raw burst of laughter cascades down the street.

Giorgio takes three hesitant steps forward, wincing all the while. "This absolutely has to be the most grotesque vehicle I've ever laid eyes on." He looks at Perry and gestures at the eyesore on wheels. "I wouldn't be caught alive in this malformed monstrosity."

Leo brushes past them and opens the side door. It cracks open a foot and grinds to a halt. He forces it open the rest of the way. "At least it's clean on the inside." He gestures to the interior. "After you."

Giorgio rolls his eyes and gets inside...carefully. "My brain must be more decomposed than I thought."

"Ah, com'on, deadbeat. Slap on some chrome platin', hydraulics, and a coupla subwoofers on this bitch and we'll be ridin' in true style." Noir hops in behind Perry and leans back as he adjusts his seat back. "How ya like me now?" He bobs his head to his own mental beat.

Perry reveals a small grin as he slides back behind the wheel.

Leo gets into the decrepit vehicle and almost closes the door before getting out again and looking down the street.

"Do you have to go tinkle again?" Giorgio leans forward from the backseat.

A female voice.

"I'm not too late, am I?"

Brown skin, tight curls. The smell of lilac and...the faint smell of something burning.

"Is Adam here?"

Leo looks inside of the van and finds a lack of help. "Adam, uh, Adam took off a while ago." He scratches at the back of his neck. "Are you his backup?"

An outstretched hand. "Bisset."

"Leo." They shake. Leo gestures inside of the van. "That's Noir, in the back is Giorgio, and Detective Perry West will be our chauffeur for the evening."

Bisset waves and forces a smile. "I don't really know if I should—I mean, since Adam isn't here maybe it would be better if—" She looks to the side and appears to listen. She looks down for a moment before looking back up. "Let's go." She climbs in. Leo slides the door shut behind her before climbing into the front passenger seat.

"Thanks for helping us out, Bisset." Perry starts the van and clicks on the radio. David Bowie's "Heroes" bleeds from the speakers.

Shrug. "Nothing on TV but reruns."

The van slides into drive and putters down the street.

Silence except for the squeaky seat springs each time they roll over a bump or dip.

"So..." Noir rubs his palms over his jeans.

Three heads turn and a pair of eyes look at him in the rearview mirror.

"Who's payin' for gas?"

## FADE OUT

## THORNEBRIAR - NOW

THEY execute the plan under cover of darkness.

Charles Johnson maneuvers the family van from the driveway, lights flashing across the kitchen window as loose gravel crunches beneath the tires. He shifts gears and starts down Pleasant Street.

"We should turn back." Anita glances in the mirror at the reflection of the diminishing house. "We should turn back now, Charles."

Charles reaches over and grabs her hand. "That's just your nerves taking over. I'm going to need you to keep it together." He looks back in the rearview mirror at Miguel and Annabelle. "We all do."

"We're gonna escape and everything's gonna be fine, Mom."

Miguel sticks his head between the driver's and passenger seat.

Anita sips in a deep breath. "Sit back and put your seatbelt on, Miguel."

He smiles and complies.

A newly waxed black truck gleams under the streetlight and rolls to a stop next to them. A middle-aged man beams as he waves a hand out the window. "'Ey there, Charles. Pretty late to be driving, don't you think?" He nods at Anita.

"Hey, Ty. We all suddenly woke up with a hankering for ice cream; thought we'd go down to the Swift Mart and pick up a few pints."

Ty's smile relaxes at the edges before fully unfurling again. "All of you woke up at the same time with the same craving?"

Charles shrugs and smiles. "Guess that just proves we're all related."

Ty nods as his eyes flick to the young Johnsons in the back. He pats the outside of the truck door with two staccato smacks. "Well, alright then. Just wanted to stop and say hello before I head home." He eases away.

"Hey, Ty?"

The black truck stops with a slight shriek of bad brakes, rolls back a foot in reverse.

"Yeah?"

"How's this graveyard shift working out for you? Gwen and little baby Stephani probably feel like they never see you." He reaches for his wife's hand.

Ty scrunches his face up. "It's going to take some getting used to."

Anita reaches for Miguel's hand.

"But until she can get back on her feet and working again, it's what I have to do to support my family."

Miguel reaches for Annabelle's hand.

"You know how it is."

"Yeah, I do." Charles reaches out with his free hand. "Send Gwen and Stephani my love."

"Will do, Charlie. You all take care, and don't eat too much ice cream."

They shake hands.

Ty shivers and his eyes flutter shut. His manufactured smile turns into a genuine one that nearly splits his face. He begins to laugh, fingers wrapped tight around the steering wheel. "What did you—Oh, I love my wife. Even when she's hitting me with her tiny little fists because I don't want to have—" His eyes widen, his mouth cracks open. "And, oh oh oh, it makes me so happy when Stephani laughs after she poops. It's so cute. You should come over sometime and I'll show you."

He looks over and sees that the Johnson's van is turning the far corner. "Am I—" He squints his eyes as a wave of laughter attacks his stomach. "Am I drunk? I'm only this happy when I'm drunk, so I—I musht me." He pauses. "Musht be. HAHAHAHAHA!" He shakes his head. "Gotta call Damon, tell him that they're escap—escaping."

He puts the truck in drive, accelerates—

—and bumps over the curb and careens into a tree when tears blur his vision and laughter grips his sides.

Anita whips her head back at the crunch of glass and metal echoing up the street. "We hit him too hard."

"He would have alerted Damon." Charles presses the gas. "He still can."

"Is Ty okay?" Annabelle looks up at her parents.

"I'm sure he's fine, baby."

"Maybe we should go back and—"

"NO!" Her mother lowers her voice. "Ty isn't who you think he is, he isn't your friend. None of these people are."

A wink of headlights ahead.

Charles starts to lift his hand to wave at Mrs. Devereaux when she suddenly jerks the wheel, pumps on speed, and sends her station wagon barreling into the van.

A jarring *C R A S H !*

The van cuts a tire-scrubbed arc to the side, rubber screeching. Charles corrects the vehicle and the wheel before they both spin out of control. The van *vrooms* down the street.

"Is everyone o—"

His head is whipped backward as Mrs. Devereaux rams the nose of her car into the back of the van. Charles presses the gas, looks in the mirror, and can barely make out the murder smoldering in the elderly woman's eyes. She pulls back a bit before zooming up next to them, wisps of silver hair flying loose beneath her scarf. She jerks the wheel with her shrunken wrinkled hands and slams the car into the side of the van, rocking it. She pulls back before repeating the maneuver.

Anita clutches the door handle and looks back at her children and their terrified faces. "Charles."

"A little occupied right now." He grits his teeth as the van lurches violently to the side again, nearly off of the road this time.

"Charles, the children. You have to."

"But she's just—"

Anita reaches over and jerks the wheel to the left as hard as she can. The large van veers over and bulldozes the small car, forcing it across the small parking lot of the post office and straight into a wall. The hood of the car accordions. The little old lady's upper body is whipped violently forward and the airbag affectionately cushions her liver-spotted head as it inflates with programmed insistence as the seatbelt holds her in its loving embrace. Fluids bleed and blend underneath the car. Mrs. Devereaux does not move.

Miguel gapes at his mother. "You just killed Mrs. Devereaux."

"Miguel—"

"She was just an old lady."

"She was trying to kill us, Miguel!" Her American accent slips away from her tongue. She ignores the inertia pressing them into their seats as they whiz around a corner. "I am so damn tired of people threatening the lives of my family. We are getting the hell out of here, and we're doing it tonight."

Had Anita not been wearing her seatbelt, her face would have gone straight into the dashboard from the van's rubber-scorching halt.

She looks out the window at Damon standing in the middle of the street with a half-pint of mint chocolate chip ice cream in hand. He licks the spoon clean and sticks it down in the carton. He lifts the bulging plastic bag in his other hand.

"I've got plenty here for everyone if you'd like to come out and join me." He gestures at the stretch of grass on the other side of the pavement. "We can all sit out here and have a nice little chat." He puts a spoonful of ice cream inside his mouth. Swallows. "How does that sound?"

"Don't think I won't run you over."

Damon blinks. "Take them out."

"Oh, God."

The air buzzes with a ballad of bullets. Punctured tires hiss as they deflate.

"Get out of the van."

"I'm not—"

"You must have me confused with a man who repeats himself. Anita, you first."

Anita grinds her teeth. Then she notices the glimmering red line cutting through the air. She looks back and notices the red dot trained on her daughter's forehead. She gets out of the car. Damon gestures to his left. Anita walks over to his left.

"You next Miguel." Damon points to his right.

Miguel gets out of the car.

Annabelle is next, followed by Charles. Each of them stands at least five feet away from the other, red dots pinpointed at their heads.

Damon licks dribbling ice cream from his hand. "Thornebriar can't let its favorite family leave for vacation without a proper send off." He smacks his lips. "We've got a new experiment that's just perfect for you." He points at the carton. "Are you guys sure you don't want some?" He looks in the bag. "I've got Chunky Monkey, strawberry swirl, aaannnnd, ah, this new blue mystery flavor, if you're feeling adventurous."

No one accepts his offer.

Damon lifts his brow. "Fine, I'll give them to the assault team when we wrap up here." He scrapes the bottom of the carton. "I should probably tell you what we've got planned." He puts the top back on and licks the spoon, setting the empty carton and bag at his feet. "We're trying to see if we can duplicate the powers of an A-O in currently-non-powered humans as well as other A-Os. So far, our results have been varied." His eyes go distant. "Don't know how I managed to finish that half pint with those *grisly* images still in my head." He grins. "But anyway, we'd like to see if we can replicate your powers."

"We make people happy. I don't see how that could be of any value to you and your organization." Charles shuffles his stance.

Damon starts to put his hands in his pockets, notices the sticky film of ice cream clinging to them, puts them behind his back instead. "Think of happiness as a drug that you'll do anything to have. You'll steal another person's happiness to make it your own, you'll lie and say you're sad so that loved ones spend time and maybe even money trying to make you happy. Some drug addicts won't hesitate to kill if anyone comes between them and their next fix." He bends down and reaches into the plastic bag. "People think drugs like cocaine and meth are the real hardcore narcotics." He pulls out a slim gas mask. "But...when you get right down to it, drugs are all about emotion, wanting to feel something, even if that something is all-consuming nothing." He adjusts the straps on the mask. "Emotion is the real drug we need to declare war on. Wipe that out and you solve all your problems." He slips the mask on. "Release."

A muffled *pfft* streams through the air, a trail of ivory smoke marking its arched path. A gas canister lands, clatters, and rolls at Damon's feet, spewing a sweet-smelling chemical. A fit of coughing laces the air.

Annabelle grabs Miguel grabs Charles grabs Anita grabs Damon. The cloud of gas glares golden. Damon smiles behind his mask. He looks down at Anita and her family as they fall to their knees and succumb to the gas's soporific effect.

"Not going to work. If I were any happier, I'd positively burst."

Anita's head seems to float to the ground. Damon's retreating image cants to the side before fading along with the rest of her vision to nothing.

# EPISODE TEN: *On the Verge of Greatness*

## Part 1

Booming bass barrages the inside of the van.

Noir bobs his head in the passenger seat, flat palms stirring the air in time to the synchronized beats pumping through the speakers. He bites down on his lower lip and draws his eyebrows closer together as his body moves to the music.

The volume is suddenly yanked down to something a bit more tolerable.

"The fuck you doin', man?" He drops his hands and looks over at Leo in the driver's seat.

"Can't concentrate with the music so loud." Leo massages his head as he switches lanes.

"Concentrate on what, drivin' in a straight line? That was my jam, dude." He slumps in his seat. "Can't go disruptin' me when I'm jammin'."

"I like Chase and Status as much as the next person, but not when my head is pounding as loud as the music."

Noir slides him a look. "You know Chase and Status?"

Leo returns his look. "Yeah." He looks back to the road. "'Eastern Jam' is one of my jams, too."

Noir grins. "Fuckin' love that song. I actually got a bit o' choreography mapped out. Impresses the ladies and some of the fellas when I hit the clubs. Who else you like?"

Shrug. "All kinds of groups. One of my favorites at the moment is Electric."

Parted mouth. "The Electric Company?"

Nod.

"Duuuude! I love their sound. I really like the rhymes in 'Life Is a Struggle.' Could listen to it all day."

"Do I take this exit or the next one?"

Noir scrambles for the directions. "Uhhh, next one, 241."

"The message in 'Levitation' just spoke to me. I must have

listened to that song twenty times a day when left my job at the lab."

In the backseat, Bisset glances out of the window and watches as her reflection subtly shifts into Seraph. "There's something you should know."

"What?"

"Mmm, wha?" Perry lifts his head beside her, bleary eyes fluttering open.

"Nothing, just talking with myself."

Perry's mouth cracks open, then shuts along with his eyes.

Seraph seems to glow in the window. "Someone is watching us, someone with telepathic abilities." She glances somewhere in the van. "I can feel their presence right now."

Bisset looks toward the front of the rickety van, watching as Noir and Leo share a laugh. She looks over at Detective West snoring softly. She starts to look behind her at Giorgio, but can feel his eyes boring into her. She drops her head and thinks aloud instead of speaking aloud.

*"Are they doing more than watching?"*

"I've felt them attempt to brush our surface thoughts a few times."

*"Only an attempt? Why?"* Bisset frowns.

"Most likely because merely gra—"

A sudden force bludgeons the doors of her mind.


_____ tries to pry into the woman's mind. They touch upon the surface and are immediately caught up in a cataclysmic crash of images. A man covered in light. A woman covered in blood. Smiling. Crying. Joy. Anguish. A couple hugging one another. A couple stabbing one another. A baby. A corpse. A blooming bud. A withering forest. The smell of incense and rose oil. The smell of desiccation and death. _____ is horrified by the purity and delighted by the filth.

_____ grits their teeth and feels a string of drool edging down their chin. The telepath laughs and cries, feels as if they are dying by living. They open their eyes and see roses and skulls, feathers and blood, eyeless decapitated heads wrapped in a child's first laugh.

_____ yanks their mind away before it is obliterated.

Bisset darts her eyes around the van as the psychic force fades away.

*"Did you feel that?"*

"They were trying to force themselves into our mind."

Bisset looks over her shoulder as Giorgio rips his eyes from her and looks out of the heavily-tinted window. He stares intently at the dark-injected images scrolling past the glass.



Consciousness crests in a collection of sounds, smells, and sensations.

The sound of the TV.

The smell of warm blueberry pie.

The sensation of having been knocked the hell out by chemical gas.

Charles lifts his head...too quickly, closes his eyes and waits while the world whirls. He tries again, movements slow this time, and sees he's back home in his easy chair.

On the television, Buffy is pummeling a bleach-blond vampire in a black trench coat. Anita is looking at him from the couch with Annabelle's still unconscious head cradled under her arm.

There is no sign of Miguel.

A teenage girl sits on the loveseat with her legs drawn up beneath her, digging into a thick piece of blueberry pie.

"Whrz—" He wipes at the drool on his chin and works his thick, fuzzy tongue in his dry mouth. "Whrs—Where's Miguel?" He rubs at his eyes. He starts to get up.

The fork in the girl's hand clatters on the plate and she suddenly has a gun pointed at Charles. She doesn't take her eyes from the TV screen. "This is one of my favorite episodes, Mr. Johnson. Sit down."

Charles lowers himself drunkenly into his seat. "Tina Rhodes? Aren't you a babysitter?"

"Why do you think I'm here?" She slowly lowers the gun next to a bedazzled cellphone.

"Anita, where's Miguel?"

Helpless shrug. "He wasn't here when I came to."

The man looks at Tina…and sees two of her. Seconds pass before the images waver together into one. "Where's my son?"

She bites down on pie, eyes glued to the screen. "He's in the garden."

Blood drains from Charles's face and he nearly passes out again. "He—he's where?"

She reaches for the glass of milk on the table and takes a gulp. "In. The. Gar. Den."

Anita's eyes widen and she stops stroking her daughter's hair. "Young woman, I don't find that amusing at all."

She presses the bottom of her fork down on piece of crust. "Wasn't supposed to be. Miguel's in the garden."

"Stop saying that." Charles wrings his hands into fists.

Tina finally seems to notice him. "You asked."

"Damon wouldn't take Miguel to the garden. He wants us alive." His breath accelerates in and out of his nostrils. He shakes his head. "Where is he? In the bathroom?"

"Dammit, I already told you, he's in—"

Charles launches himself up from his seat, ignoring the volley of vertigo. "Stop saying that!"

The plate clatters and shatters to the floor as Tina rises from the loveseat with the gun aimed at his head. "Mr. Johnson, you need to sit down right now. I'm one of the few people here who actually likes you, but I will put a bullet in you."

"Do you know what these people, *your* people, do to a person taken to the garden?"

"Sit down, Mr. Johnson."

"I swear to God if one hair is out of place on my son's head…"

Anita starts to stand. The gun swivels to her. "Down!"

Anita lowers herself. "Charles, if you would just—"

"She just told us our son was taken to the garden! We're being held prisoner by a fourteen-year-old girl with braces and you want me to—"

"I'm counting to four."

"Charles, just—"

"Take me to my son."

"One."

"Charles—"

"Get that damn gun outta my face and bring me my son!"

"Two."

"Mom...whuz goin' on?" Annabelle groggily lifts her head.

"You're going to have to shoot me if—"

"Annabelle, baby, don't move. Tina point the gun at me. Just—Just point the gun—"

"Three."

"Tina?" Annabelle scrunches her face.

"Four."

The front door opens.

The characters on the TV screen fall silent along with everyone in the living room.

The sound of sneakers scuffing across the floor.

Charles starts to run for the front door, but stops when Tina steps in front of him.

"You're testing my patience, Mr. Johnson." She flicks the barrel of the gun down. He sits.

The sneakers stop.

A few seconds pass before Miguel steps into the room with his hands in his pockets, looking healthy and hale. He stands there for a second...then he starts to cry.

"Go to your father." Tina lowers the gun.

Miguel fairly falls into his father's embrace, sobbing and clutching at him with his arms. Charles puts his hand on the back of his son's head, eyes closed and tears streaming. "Oh, thank God, Miguel." He presses his son against him for a full minute before holding him by the shoulders. He slides his hands down his son's thin arms. "Did they—" He stops when he reaches Miguel's bandaged wrists. He looks down and the world zooms back as if distancing him from what he is seeing.

His son has no hands.

His son has no hands.

His son has no hands.

Horror grabs his gut, grips his lungs, and forces his mouth open. "Miguel, what—where are—why—" He looks into his son's eyes, at the stream of tears rolling down his wracked expression.

"They said that our ability is in our hands." The words are whispered through quivering lips.

Madness massacres reason. Charles throws himself at Tina. He ignores the pain cracking up his knuckles as he cracks the young girl across the cheek. Incoherent words writhe past his lips along with spittle. He hammers down on her chest with clenched fists, blood misting the air.

A small fist slams into his temple.

Sensation scatters, vision becomes pixelated and vague.

Tina grabs a finger, yanks back.

*CRACK!*

"AUUGHH!"

She kicks him in the face, knocks him on his back, and grabs his foot with one hand on the heel and the other by the toes of his shoe. She wrenches.

*SNAP!*

"AAHH!"

She relaxes as he contorts with pain. He rocks back and forth, keeping the pain back behind clenched teeth. Then Charles is suddenly lunging at her neck. He bites down.

The high-pitched scream from the fourteen-year-old girl shatters the air. Blood erupts from the small hole bitten in her tender flesh. Charles yanks his head away, spitting out the gobbet of flesh. Blood soaks into his polo shirt.

Anita opens her mouth, but her words are blasted away along with the back of Charles's head when Tina puts a bullet through it.


"Heavenly Father, I'm coming before you again asking for guidance and wisdom. I've recommitted myself to leading your children back to your heavenly gates, but I feel as though you're telling me that I also need to recommit myself to being a soul brimming with radiant love that's free of judgment, that I need to be a light that warms and shines the way home. I ask for forgiveness for the words I spoke to Detective West and Suzie earlier today. I know that I can't change either of them, only you can do that, but it's my deepest prayer that they see the light and free themselves from the pull of iniquity.

"If it's still your desire that I work with the others to save the Johnsons, please show me the way to them. I open my mind, my body, my soul, my everything to your guiding hand, dear God. I ask that you please show me the way."

Silence.

"Yes, I feel Seraph's light. Praise God. I'm on my way."

"*Ascension!*"


"Try it now."

Leo twists the key in the ignition and pumps the gas, groaning when nothing happens. He gets out of the van, shoes sifting through the dirt coating the abandoned road. He points at Noir as he walks by. "Next rescue mission we stick to the map. Don't care how *awesome* your sense of direction is."

The other man rolls his eyes.

"Thing's on a half tank of gas. I don't understand why it's not working." Leo puts his hands on his waist and watches Perry as he studies the cords, tubes, wires, plastic, metal, and oil-streaked surfaces of the engine.

"Just because it has gas doesn't means it's gonna go, Mr. Biochem." Perry fiddles with connections under the hood.

"What do we do now?" Noir sits on scraggly patch of grass with his arms flopped over his bent knees. He touches flame to the cigarette between his lips. He looks out in the distance, squinting his eyes a bit as he does his best to keep from shivering.

Perry shakes his head. "Got four super beings here and not one of you can fix the engine...or fly to get help." He runs the back of his wrist across his forehead. "Anyone get a phone signal yet?"

Heads shake in the negative.

"I could use my speed, run to get help." Noir expels smoke. He blinks and narrows his eyes at something.

"Last building I saw that didn't look condemned was more than a mile back. You can't blaze that far, can you?" Perry hunkers down closer to the engine.

"I don't call it blazing, call it streaking." He taps ash.

"What?"

"I said, I call it streaking when I run super fast, not blazing."

A grin cracks. "Yeah, I've known a few people who run really fast when they streak, too. Usually they're running away from me."

Noir mutters something under his breath and resumes staring out at the horizon.

Bisset steps out of the van with a bottle of water in one hand and a ratty rag in the other. "Broken down in a dead zone with no cars or road in sight." Scoff. "Someone out there really doesn't like us." She looks out at the open field.

Perry wipes his hands on the offered rag. "Thanks." He tilts his head at the van, lowers his voice. "Giorgio okay in there?"

"He mostly stared out of the window the entire time. I try to talk to him, but he doesn't say more than a few words."

"Maybe he should drag his cadaver-ass out here and see if he can bring life back to this old heap."

A raised voice from inside the van. "I'm dead, detective, not deaf."

"Does anyone see that?"

Eyes dart to Noir. Eyes dart to where Noir's eyes stare.

"It's called the horizon." Perry points. "That's a cloud, and that bright thing there, which I really hope you're not lookin' directly at, is the sun."

"I'm bein' serious, cabron." Noir's eyes are coated with a light neon blue sheen. "There're...waves in the air. I think it's something on the electromagnetic spectrum. I can almost hear it." He tilts his head to the side.

Leo steps away from the van. "Electromagnetic? Could be what's messing with the phone signals and the engine. What else do you see?

"Just blue waves in the air."

"Can I help you folks?"

They turn.

A police officer approaches them from behind, arms rigid on either side of her waist. The gun and laden utility belt cinched around her hips don't hinder her movements at all. She studies them from behind a pair of aviator sunglasses.

"We're just having a bit of car trouble is all." Perry tucks the rag in his back pocket.

Her head doesn't move, but maybe her eyes do behind the tinted glasses. "Maybe I can give you a hand." She walks toward the van, tugging a pair of black gloves from her fingers and slipping them through her belt beside her gun. She keeps her glasses on.

Perry steps aside and watches as she checks the oil, fluid levels, and the engine. She twists her head this way and that, looks up and sticks her arm down as she fiddles with something.

Then—

Noir. "Get back!"

Bisset. "Watch out for her hands!"

The officer casts her hand out. Solid, oily darkness blasts forth from her smooth palm. It billows into Perry and savagely catapults him back, arms and legs pinwheeling in the air.

Leo flicks out a hand of his own and catches the flying man with a soft force field cushion. Perry lands gently, sinks slightly, and bobbles on the silver-blue construction. A large black stain clings to his shirt.

The woman steps away from the van while slicing a hand in Noir's direction. A crescent of onyx jets out from her fingertips. The cigarette tumbles from Noir's lips as he rolls out of the way. The scythe of dark energy embeds itself deep in the dirt, soaking the grass in an oily gleam.

The woman's arms piston in a parade of punches. A volley of black blobs with violet tails pepper the air. Noir blurs, streaks, and slithers out of the way. He avoids most of them, but not all. One slams into his shoulder, whirling him around. Another takes him in the hipbone, forcing him to his knees.

Perry runs up behind her and launches his foot out at the small of her back. The blow causes her to stumble forward and he takes a sidestep and kicks out at the back of her knee with his right foot. It buckles inward and forces her to the ground. Perry lifts his foot for an axe kick that never lands as the woman thrusts her open palm down and shoots out a wide mass of black concussive force at the earth. The recoil of the massive power jets her body into the air. Back bent, she twirls head over heels, popping West in the chin with her heel as she flips over. She lands on her feet, spins on Perry, and strikes out with both fists to fire another wide net of midnight force.

Leo lifts a hand and curls his fingers. A concave force field flashes into view around the detective and shields him. The morass of black colliding with shimmering silver-blue emits ripples of sickly yellow-green in the air. Leo concentrates on keeping the integrity of the field intact. The woman cranks her head at him, eyes sightless behind her glasses. Fingers spread and darkness dives forward in a wide tide. Leo makes the field around Perry wider.

The woman suddenly jerks her right hand in his direction and sends out a stream of darkness.

Leo grits his teeth and swings his left hand up close to his body, blocking the stream with a plate-sized shield over his chest. The stream swells wider. The tide rolling towards Perry grows stronger, following him wherever he goes. Leo broadens the field protecting him, sweat popping out from his pores and sliding down his forehead into his eyes. He blinks rapidly.

Noir is a colored streak in the air racing towards the woman.

Without letting up on either attack, she twists her hips and throws a leg out along with a vicious explosion of dark power. Noir's blurring form becomes solid as he's knocked to the ground.

"Perry, roll to the left!"

Perry rolls to the left.

Before the woman can redirect her stream, Leo sweeps his right arm to the left along with the force field and uses it to knock the hand pointed at him aside. He hardens the shield in front of his body and shoves his left arm out along with it. She takes the driven force field in the side and is slammed harshly to the ground. She rolls to her knees. Her sunglasses sit shattered on the grass, revealing sunken pits of obsidian weeping black mist masquerading as eyes.

She begins to raise her hands, fingers laced with tangled black ribbons.

Bisset steps in front of her, lifts an upraised palm and lets loose a blinding cascade of luminance.

The light gradually settles, soft motes of ivory and gold dotting the air.

The woman is sprawled on her back, unconscious.

Giorgio peeks out from the van. He looks up from the

senseless woman. "That was a fantastically fine pair of Apollo sunglasses you just destroyed."

Damon watches as the uniformed cleaners clear Charles's body from the living room, shaking his head.

A footprint etched in blood mars the floor.

Damon goes into the kitchen, returns with a wet rag. He stoops down and rubs at the blood-smeared spot. "I'm truly sorry about your husband." He goes down on his hands and knees and rubs harder.

Anita takes her eyes from Tina, who sits on the couch gingerly touching the bandage on her neck. A ghastly bruise has blossomed just above the collar of her shirt. Her swollen lip barely disguises the slip of a smile gracing her puffy mouth.

"Sorry doesn't bring Charles back, and it doesn't give back my son's hands." Anita holds her children close by her sides.

Damon stops scrubbing and looks up. One of the cleaners crosses in front of him and starts sopping up the bits of brain staining the easy chair. "Charles was more than a subject to me, Anita, and I'm being sincere when I say that. As for Miguel, that decision was out of my—" He looks down, shaking his head. "I know you think that what this organization is doing is awful, and it is. I'm not going to sit here and give you some tangled mess about how we're really not all that bad." He sniffs. "Sure I don't have to remind you of what life was like in your home country." He touches a knuckle to his lip. "*Libera Mentis Machina* wants to make the most of the way the world is being tested right now, put the data to good use, and you and the rest of your family have played an essential part in doing that. What it means to be human is being redefined, and you've all helped mold that definition."

One of the cleaners places a bucket of water next to him. Damon whispers his thanks and dunks the bloody rag in the steaming water.

"Our organization was formed by a group of psychologists and scientists a few years back."

"You've told me this before, Damon."

"And I feel like it's the ideal time for a refresher, Anita." His grin is subdued this time. "Instead of looking at an individual patient, we wanted to study and treat an individual group." He wrings the bloody rag out. "Society." He scrubs at the last stubborn streak. "Some think that looking at society as a whole to determine how people think isn't as effective and accurate as examining individuals." Finished, he drops the rag in the bucket and rests back on his heels, palms on his thighs. "You'd be surprised at the hive mind people share. Look at religion, politics, fashion, social class, literature. All of them molded into the same shape from different pieces of clay."

"This is starting to sound more and more like a tangled mess."

He blinks behind his glasses, lifts them to wipe at his eyes. "Bear with me just a second longer. How many times have you been influenced to buy something, say something, think something, or live a certain way by another person? Either on TV, in a magazine, or in real life." Pause. "Now, think about that idea being shared by millions and millions of people, all on the basis of its appeal." He scratches his thigh. "Alpha-Omegas are being regarded with so many emotions. Some people hate you, some fear you, others love you, and there are those who hope they will become you. In our experiment with your family, we took all those separate strings—" He holds his hands up, fingers spread. "—and wove them together into this assortment, forced them to interact each other, to intertwine." He interlaces his fingers, brings his palms together. "And the result is the truth. People revealed how they really felt about you and your kind. There were deaths, riots in the streets, protests." He looks at her and holds up a finger. "All because of one special American family. That's what *Libera Mentis Machina* does, we bring the light to the truth."

A knock sounds at the front door.

Everyone stops.

Damon holds his hand out. "It's your house."

Anita slides her eyes to Tina before looking down at her children.

"They'll be fine. You're just going to the front door." Damon washes his hands in clean, warm water.

Anita slowly gets up and goes to the door to find the mailman.

"Afternoon, Anita." He smiles. "Was asked to deliver this message to Damon. He's here, right?"

Anita's mouth parts. She nods and accepts the letter. The mailman tips his hat. "Have a good one." She watches him bounce down the stairs, whistling all the while. She closes the door and walks back to the living room where she hands Damon the letter.

"This came for you."

"Thank you." He dries his hands and opens the envelope, scanning the letter inside. He looks up and shakes his head, eyes on Anita. "One of your own has fallen." He takes his phone from his pocket, presses an icon and waits. "Tell Eric to open the Cavity." He ends the call and perches himself on the arm of the couch. "You all may want to hold on to something for this.

Noir squints and chews on a blade of grass in the corner of his mouth. His eyes flash gold.

"I can see the outline now. Pretty swanky community, gotta admit. Looks perfect for privileged, gentrifyin' white folks."

"Any visible defenses?" Perry and the others stand behind him. Giorgio watches from inside the van.

"Ahh...no. Got a weird-ass heat signature comin' from the perimeter, though, prob'ly some kinda gate." He chews on grass and rubs his chin.

"How are we getting in?"

Perry looks at Leo. "You're the one with the big brain, you figure something out. I got us this far already."

"No need to argue, gentlemen." Bisset gives a slight head shake.

"We're not arguin, we're just havin' a discussion."

"Guys." Noir's brow creases.

"All I did was ask how we were getting in. Is this how you thank me for saving your life?" Leo lifts his shoulders a bit, opens his palms.

"Guys."

"Didn't know you were looking for payment."

"I'm not, detective. I'm just saying that a pinch of gratitude wouldn't go amiss."

"GUYS!"

Electricity crackles and snaps in the empty air. Something shimmers in the distance. Thornebriar gradually wavers into view in all its suburban splendor.

"Noir, did you—" Perry looks over at him.

Noir shakes his head, lips parting as a curiously warm wind snatches the blade of grass from his mouth.

A brilliant, blinding flash of emerald soaks the air accompanied by a sucking squall that seems to emanate from the light. The air whines and shrieks, whistles and rages rebelliously.

Ears are covered, bodies are wrenched forward by untamed winds. The group is almost yanked from their feet before Leo stretches out his arms and throws a half-bubble around them. The van rocks, wavers, and eventually tumbles over into the green light emanating from the center of Thornebriar.

"Giorgio!" Bisset reaches for him, but is restrained by Noir.

Perry yells over the tempest. "Leo, can you catch him?"

Leo shakes his head. "It's taking everything I've got just to keep this shield up."

The emerald luminance bends and wavers the edges of reality, swelling and growing as it consumes houses, minivans, tricycles, trees, and flowerbeds. The battered police van slams into the now-visible concrete street once, twice before being swept up into the void, disappearing in a sizzle of light.

The roaring winds dissolve into whispers along with the turbine whine knifing through air and ear alike. All is quiet. The emerald light eventually coalesces into a massive dome covering the entire suburb.

Leo drops the barrier. "Where did Giorgio go?"


Rain lashes the inside of the void.

Verdant lightning rends the sky outside the van and forces Giorgio's eyes to squeeze shut against the sparkling vividness. He waits for his vision to righten itself before he crawls from the backseat and tries the sliding door.

It grinds out protest.

He grips the handle and trickles death essence over the metal. It corrodes and rusts as he yanks on the handle again. Something inside the door pops as it slides open. He steps out.

And sees a line of soldiers with assault rifles aimed at him.

The rain soaks through his clothes in seconds, matting his once lustrous curls to his forehead, water dripping from his lips. Green lightning casts light on the five women and men in black body armor in a semicircle around him. A man with an umbrella stands behind them. The two gunners in front of the man part on a silent cue as he walks forward, rain speckling his spectacles. His eyes slide to the van.

"Did you come alone?"

Giorgio drips in silence.

The man repeats the question several times in several languages until he bats a hand through the rain-soaked air. "Finish him off, Vin, single shot to the head." He turns and walks away.

Raindrops drip from the barrel of Vin's rifle as he squeezes the trigger, muffled *brap* of the gun ruffling through the rain. The bullet slams into Giorgio's forehead, jerking his head back a bit.

As the bullet drills through his dead brain, it dislodges the memory of a song: 311's "You Wouldn't Believe."

Rifles waver when he doesn't fall and die like he's supposed to.

The man with the glasses pauses when he doesn't hear the sound of a corpse splashing down on the pavement. He turns. The bullet pushes itself from Giorgio's forehead and *plinks* down into a puddle. The man with the glasses lifts his eyes from the ejected bullet. "Alpha-Omega."

Giorgio starts to shiver in the freezing rain. He looks down at his skin and sees that it has taken on a deathly pallor, veins standing out vividly beneath his flesh. "My name is Giorgio Quintero. I'm here to rescue the Johnsons."

Rain bounces on the umbrella and the man gives Giorgio his profile. "Are you now?" He turns fully and takes a single step forward. "Are you the one who killed Twiggy?"

"The police officer with irreproachable taste in sunglasses? A rather vibrant name." He puts his hands behind his back. "And yours is?"

"Damon. Are you the one who killed Twiggy?"

Lightning illuminates the pause.

"I suppose I am."

Damon whips out a gun from the holster at his back and shoots the man twice in the gut. Giorgio folds forward on his knees and grimaces at the sudden flare of phantom pain. Seconds later there are three bullets glistening in a puddle. He rises.

"I apologize." His voice is a wheeze. "Was she a close friend?"

"We were close to completing our experiment with her. You've just washed months of diligence down that gutter." He points at a gutter. "How did you find this place?"

A soaked smirk. "The dead see everything, Damon."

"Not everything." He gives Giorgio a once-over. "You don't really strike me as a man who would risk his invulnerable life to save a family he only knows through television interviews and magazine covers. Make it plain for me, why are you really here?"

Giorgio slicks water across his cracked lips with his tongue. "Why do any of us care about the life and death of this family?" He wafts back to sit down on the floor of the bus, out of the downpour. "I'm a dead man, and ever since I awoke in the embrace of a necrophiliac, I find that I value my death more than I ever valued my life." He puts a hand out in the rain, collecting a tiny pond in his palm. "I don't experience the same feelings, impulses, or emotions that I used to. I didn't feel anything when I learned of the Johnson's death, and I felt even less when I discovered they weren't dead after all."

Damon involuntarily slides a sneakered foot forward through a growing puddle, lured by Giorgio's honeyed words. "So what did you experience?"

Giorgio upends his palm and watches the water dribble down. "The same thing that I've experienced, that I've phantom-felt since I died: a sense of water rolling down my skin. Doesn't cling to me, but it does make me feel clean, fresh." He gives his eyes to Damon. "Anew." He pulls his hand back. "I think I came here hoping to feel something again. Maybe I thought when I reached this moment, this very second in this very time frame, my skin would grow warm and my brain would send signals to my limbs and animate me into epic heroic action."

"And now?"

Giorgio cups his chin in his palm. "Now I just feel the need to repair my undying body. Doesn't agree with this nippy weather."

Damon runs his tongue over his teeth. "I take it that bandages and alcohol swabs won't do you too much good."

Giorgio shakes his head.

"What will?"

Yellow-green eyes examine the circle of guns. "A corpse."

Damon nods and tucks the umbrella between his cheek and shoulder as he takes off his glasses and wipes raindrops from them with a small cloth pulled from his pocket. A beat. "Linda, you were supposed to be watching the Johnsons when they escaped last night."

The gun directly to Giorgio's left wavers and the woman holding it shuffles her stance.

"But Jay, you were the one who suggested that she shirk her duties to—" He slips his glasses back on. "Well, let's not air all your filthy laundry." He takes the umbrella back in his hand. "Linda, if you will."

Linda adjusts the aim of her gun in a silky twist and fires off a single shot just as Jay goes to swivel his gun on her.

Now there are four men and women with guns aimed at him. Water collects in Jay's ear canal as he dies listening to the patter of rain.

Giorgio slides out of the van, walks, and kneels at the corpse, turning it over on its back. The slack lips slide open and water collects in the mouth. Giorgio wraps his hands around the head, bows his own head...and looks up. "Am I the only person here who prefers not to have guns trained on him while he dines?"

Damon swipes a hand down.

The guns are lowered.

Giorgio bows his head again and feels the death essence growing inside Jay's dead body, feels it surging and rolling over the last vestiges of life fading from blood vessels, muscles, and organs. Death blossoms, blood begins to cool, and the heart slowly, reluctantly deflates one last time.

Giorgio strokes Jay's face, mindless of those watching him. The sensation of rain pattering on his hand and death tingling languidly on his fingers brings back euphoric narcotic memories. His eyes slip shut. Slowly, he siphons the diaphanous sludge from the corpse, delighting in the sensation trilling through him as thinning skin is repaired, slackened muscles inflate, and his lips become full and flushed.

Death brings life.

Jay's corpse withers to flaps of skin and brittle bone. Rain beats flat on desiccated flesh.

"That's amazing." Damon grips his umbrella tighter.

"That's life." Giorgio stands.

"So, shall we stand here in the rain and riddle you with bullets, fists, and feet until you stay down, or should we just cut your head off?" He slips Giorgio a smile.

"You'd better bring your absolute best if you test me...unless you're ready to die." Giorgio slicks a hand through his sodden hair. "But how about I give you a new test subject instead?"

Head full of ideas that you couldn't conceive.

## FADE OUT

## MERCURMONT

"See?"

He rolls his hand over to his palm, flexing his fingers.

The girl who looks like him squints her eyes and runs her fingers over the patterns of lines, whorls, and DNA etchings.

"I don't see anything, Mal."

He points at the faint red line running down his index finger. "Right there. I sliced my finger open yesterday, and now it's completely healed."

She drops his hand. "That doesn't mean you're an A-O." She relaxes back against the park bench, shielding her eyes against the sun while looking out at the children scampering across the playground.

"How else could I have healed that quickly, Val?"

Shrug. "You're at an age where your body is starting to change, maybe your immune system is changing, too."

"Changing into something superhuman." He curls his fingers closed into a fist.

His sister shakes her head. "You and your overactive imagination. You need to become a writer or something instead of a stock broker."

Mal goes quiet, the cloud rolling across the sun mirroring the once across his face. "Jim wouldn't like that."

She reaches for the bottle of soda next to her, unscrews the cap, and takes a quick sip. "He's our stepdad, he doesn't have a syllable of a say whatsoever in how you should live your life. Just because he's a stockbroker doesn't mean you have to be one." She dabs at her mouth with the back of her wrist. "Have you seen him when he comes home? He looks like hell. Hair all rumpled, slacks wrinkled, funk of coffee on his breath." She shakes her head. "You want to look like that in fifteen years?"

It's Mal's turn to shrug. "He's shown me some of his books, he's even taken me to the office a few times. It's not...it's not that bad." He scratches the back of his neck.

Val looks at him. "I've known you longer than he has. You had that same expression on your face when you were eleven and mom dressed you in that ugly plaid sweater and you said you loved it."

"No, really I—"

"Can't sit here."

Val and Mal turn and see a tall young man with his arms

crossed over his large chest. Veins wind the flesh-colored tree trunks peeking out from his sleeveless shirt. Another young man of the same size stands at his right with a crooked grin on his acne-dappled face.

"It's okay if you skip a day, Phineas." Mal bobs his knee.

A smile ripples and bubbles across a pock-marked face.

"Shut the fuck up, Chris." Phineas slaps a large palm into the young man's chest. He scowls back at the twins. "I told you to call me Phin." He looks Mal up and down. "Little sand nigger." He turns his attention to Val. His expression turns licentious. "'Ey, Val, when you gon' let me hit it?"

She grabs her bottle and messenger bag and stands. "Let's go, little brother."

Phin slides in front of her, hands up close her chest. "Whoa whoa whoa, you can stay."

Val glares. "You just called my brother a sand nig—" She clamps her mouth shut over the word. "You'll have sex with a girl of color, tell all of your friends you tapped a black or brown ass, but you won't date a girl with thick lips, a big ass, one who wears an abaya or a niqab, or skin that isn't the same pale-ass color as yours." She puts a hand up and steps away.

Large fingers capture her wrist. "Bring your big brown ass back here."

A small fist pops Phin under the chin, knocking his head back. Phin's eyes widen on Mal. His lips part, revealing bloodied teeth. "You fuckin' crazy, camel jockey?"

Chris's eyes swivel back and forth between the two.

"Touch my sister again and I'll kill you." Mal's fist clenches. "I'm not gonna let you pick on me anymore, I'm different now."

"You're still a nigg—"

"STOP CALLING ME THAT!" Indignant rage wraps him tight, making his body quiver and quake. "I just found out I'm an Alpha-Omega."

Chris and Phin stare at him, look at each other and laugh.

Mal steps forward, fists raised.

"Mal, don't!" Val reaches forward too late.

Mal punches Phin in the stomach...and draws his fist back as agony ricochets through the bones in his arm. He looks up and his

**299**

vision is eclipsed by a careening fist.

*BAM!*

The blow spins him around and knocks a tooth loose. He spits out blood and stands up. "Keep hitting me, I'll heal." Phin kicks him in the belly, forcing air and blood from Mal's mouth. "I'll...heal." He collapses on his knees.

Val raises her fists, but doesn't go two steps before Chris grabs her wrists and forces them down at her sides. Her anger translates into incoherent curses and snarls.

"Still gonna heal, nigger-boy?" Phin rams his knee into Mal's chin, knocking him on his back. Blood spatters the verdant grass. A blow to the skull. "How 'bout that? That gonna heal up, too?"

"I'm an Alpha-Omeg—AH!" Mal folds himself into a ball as Phin kicks him in the back. "I'll heal. I'll heal. I'll hHUUU!" Bones break.

"Mal, get up!" Val tries to break free.

The steel toes of a large boot make brutal contact with the bleeding boy's head. One, two, three, four times.

Mal Nix does not heal.

Mal Nix is not an Alpha-Omega.

Mal Nix dies two hours later at Kindred Hospital during surgery.

# EPISODE ELEVEN: ON THE VERGE OF GREATNESS
# PART 2

The setting sun slides luminescent fingers over the surface of the emerald dome, eliciting shimmering shards of light against the sprawling background of open blue sky and swaying grasses.

The beauty is lost on the four figures staring up at the swirling configuration.

"I got a question." Noir scratches at his shaved scalp, wrinkling his lips.

Three sets of eyes settle on him.

"The fuck are we doin' all of this for again?" He crosses his arms over his chest and paces. "Just 'cause you have superpowers doesn't mean you have to be a super...anything. You can just be super-normal." He stops pacing, flings his arm out. "Why aren't we being super-normal?"

Perry looks back at the massive dome. "If a helpful suggestion isn't coming out of your mouth, please keep it closed." He stares intently at Leo.

Leo blinks at him. "I'm a biochemist."

"But can't you—"

"I'm a biochemist."

"No one else here—"

"Is incapable of analyzing, hypothesizing, or experimenting."

Perry holds a hand out. "This isn't a test tube filled with mystery chemical X. This...*thing* just swallowed an entire community, it's not something to hypothesize around with."

Bisset walks up and puts a hand on the dome.

The others stop, caution, protest, and freak out.

She finds that the dome is unyielding and slick. Her brow furrows.

"What?" Leo studies the ripples rolling from where her hand touches emerald.

"It feels like oil mixed with water poured over marble."

"So basically a slicky-sticky force field?" Noir rubs at his chin. "Leo?"

The biochemist shakes his head. "Is anyone keeping score of how many times my powers have saved our asses?"

"The same powers that were given to you by a gene you

hate?" Perry kicks at a clump of grass and dirt.

Pause. "How did you know that?"

Shared stares. "Not a detective on account of how I can sniff out clues with my big nose."

"I don't—" Leo's lips seal. He incoherently mumbles something to himself before stepping towards the immense emerald jewel. He looks up...and up...and up.

"Maybe you can punch a hole in the thing or something? Can you alter the shape of your fields?" Bisset tucks a curl behind her ear.

"I'll try." He holds his hands up and closes his eyes. The air shivers, shimmers, and swirls. Silver-blue colors the air, forming itself into the shape of a large arrowhead over Leo's body. Fingers flick. Force flies.

### KEERRRSHHHZZZ!

A cataclysmic coruscation of colors, emerald smashing silver tumbling over a blue blaze. The dome flows and falters before repairing itself. Leo shapes another arrowhead field. The coloring is more vivid, the shape denser. A grunt flies from his mouth along with the construction. The very ground quakes, the air blinks in the wake of emerald lightning and skeins of silver-blue. A small fissure splits the dome, giving way to a slice of backyard and a swimming pool before emerald light quickly flows over the imperfection.

Leo wavers back on quivering legs before plopping down in the grass, sweat staining his brow, his chest heaving. "I think my head may explode if I try to make a stronger one."

Perry opens his mouth, words cut off by a sudden blaze of platinum streaking across the sky. The flames surrounding Sovereign are snuffed out and Adam falls the remaining six feet to the ground, running forward a few steps before standing before them.

Crickets chirp in the field.

Adam looks at the blank faces, lingering a moment on Bisset's.

"'Sup, dude. Glad you found us." Noir jerks his head up in greeting.

"The Lord and Seraph's light led me here." Adam flicks his gaze at the emerald dome. He looks at Perry who looks at him. "I want to repent for what I said earlier, I spoke out in anger. Now, that doesn't mean that I condone your lifestyle, but I shouldn't have—"

Perry holds up his hand. "We can talk about your skewed and staggeringly obsolete sense of the world later. Right now, we need to punch a hole through this damn thing and get inside." He drops his hand. "How strong are you?"

"I haven't really had the chance to test the extremes of my strength."

"That changes today." Perry looks back at the dome. "I think if you fly at this thing immediately after Leo fires another force field, we may be able to get through."

"Guess we know who wears the spandex in this family." Noir takes a cigarette from the crumpled pack in the back pocket of his pants and lights up.

Leo picks himself up. "I think I've got one more in me. Adam, you should fly in behind my field and the rest of us will stand behind you. If this works, we're going to have to move quickly before the tear repairs itself."

"*Ascension!*" Platinum ignites the air.

They form up behind Leo and Sovereign as another arrowhead glitters into existence. The force field blasts forward, rustling blades of grass in its wake. It collides with emerald, the explosion of light mixing with the platinum luster of Sovereign as he blurs forward with his fists stretched out before him.

**KEERRRSHHHZZ—KRACK!**

A large section of the dome shatters inward like green glass. Sovereign soars inside Thornebriar. Bisset catches Leo as he collapses and hustles him through the tear. Perry slips through and Noir blasts forward in a sudden blurring burst of super speed just as the vacuum is sealed.


Needles click. The room smells gently of flowery perfumes and musk. The cushion of the chair is cracked and bleeds stuffing. Death essence laces the air.

Giorgio looks around at the circle of elderly women with needles and yarn in hand, looping and sliding needle and thread together as quilts, scarves, and sweaters slither out from quivering yet deft fingers. The woman closest to Giorgio smiles at him, eyes twinkling behind her bifocals. He turns his head at the sudden flutter of laughter emanating from the corner. White-haired heads bend back in a chord of mirth, thighs are patted by soft, wrinkled hands.

Giorgio hardly feels the smile that slowly slips its way across his lips.

Damon grins as he steps into the room. His hands pat and embrace, his lips whisper and pull, his eyes crinkle and twinkle. He is a fabrication made flesh that walks over to Giorgio and claps him on the arm. "How're you holding up?"

"I'm overcome with a need to knit something painfully cute, but other than that, I'm fine."

Damon pushes his glasses up and turns to the room. "Ladies, I hate to stop you in the middle of your work, but it's time for swim class. Gotta keep those youthful bodies in shape."

Supple laughter coats the air. The women gather their needles and material and shuffle out the door. Giorgio jerks and looks behind him at the winking woman covering her mouth with her heavily wrinkled hands. She flutters her fingers at him as she closes the door.

"She pinched your butt, didn't she?"

"How did you know?"

"That's Mrs. Bishop. She may be old, but she has the sex drive of a twenty-year old. Can't tell you how many nights we've caught her sneaking into a man's room. It's gotten so bad that we can't even allow her to meet new male residents."

"Feisty little gray fox."

"Quite."

"May I ask you something, Damon?"

Damon looks at him.

"Why the hell does your organization have its laboratory in a nursing home?"

He leads them across the room, tapping the folder in his hand against his thigh. "In the event that we have a security breach, we don't want to make it easy for the intruder or intruders to find what they are looking for, thereby giving us ample time to hunt them down and kill them, cordially, of course."

"Of course." Giorgio sniffs.

"*Libera Mentis Machina* spent years and several large bank accounts creating Thornebriar. A majority of the people who live here also work here and are aware of our existence."

Giorgio follows him down a hallway. "But why masquerade as a suburban community? Surely not so you look legitimate."

An elderly man in pajama bottoms and a cardigan is being pushed in a wheelchair, a tank of oxygen strapped to the back of his chair. Giorgio pauses and follows him with his eyes.

"What?"

Giorgio lowers his voice. "That man is going to die today. I can feel the death essence pouring from him."

Damon watches Giorgio watching the man with a starved look in his golden-green eyes. "You don't need to feed, do you?"

He turns back. "No, but if I did, I'd know where to go." He gestures for Damon to continue down the hall. "How many residents pass away each day?"

"That's what we're going to talk about." Damon slips into the room on the right, waits for Giorgio to step in and closes the door behind them.

"We're here to talk about how many old people die?"

Damon walks to the projector in the room, opens the folder, and takes out a clear sheet with an image stamped on it. "Mmm, not quite." He walks over and closes the blinds and shuts off the light.

Darkness pervades.

A window of light. A whirling hum. A portrait of enlarged cells, black and glowing bright. One cell burns brighter than the rest.

"Giorgio, meet your murderer." He points at the brightest cell. "This is your Alpha-Omega gene."

"The one that killed me and brought me back to life."

An eye scrunches. "For all intents and purposes, you're still dead. Your A-O gene is the only thing that's animating you right now. That, and the death essence you absorb."

He switches slides.

"As you already know, extreme heat and cold and the rays of the sun at high noon corrupt what we're calling the necro-cellular regeneration process. When this happens, any death essence you've

305

absorbed attacks your body and causes you to decompose."

Giorgio sits silently.

Damon switches slides, this one of a brain. Black strands lace the outer edges.

"When we performed the CAT scan, we found that certain sections of your brain are inactive. It looks like your A-O gene was unable to reboot them upon your...redeath."

"Which sections?"

"The ones that control emotion and emotional responses."

It makes the undead man smile. "Damon, I was an unfeeling bastard before I died."

"As in life, so in death."

"I've given you what you want, and you've given me what I want, but you haven't told me anything of which I'm not already aware."

Damon lifts a finger illuminated by the cone of light. "You know what's happening to you, but you don't understand the why. You feel what's happening on a deep, instinctual level while we analyze that level from a scientific perspective." He extends his index fingers, holding them a foot apart. "Two planets residing in the same galaxy."

"I do have one question for you: Can I ever truly die and stay that way?"

Damon strokes his chin. "If you ever go long enough without absorbing death essence, you probably will, but that's not as simple as it sounds.

"When we studied you, we found that your body is constantly absorbing death essence. It's doing it right now, as a matter of fact. Death is always around us, literally. Dead skin cells, decay, particles in the air, it's everywhere. And you act as a magnet. Your body as well as your abilities are growing stronger with each passing second.

"There's more. We found strains of several viruses cultivating in your veins, some of them that haven't even been discovered yet. Our virologists actually whooped with joy."

"My body's an incubator for viruses now?"

"Yes. Me and the others think it's because of the constant influx and outflow of death, decay, and entropy in your system. Think of it as a mass of multicolored strands twisting together to form something new and exciting."

"As exciting as a virus can be."

"We think that with enough practice, you'll be able to release viruses at will, but you'll have to be careful that you don't—

"Accidentally infect someone."

Damon suddenly launches into laughter. "Think of the possibilities!"


HEAT

It swelters, swims, sweats, swarms, sticks, squeezes, suffocates, and slithers around them. Thornebriar is boiling.

Perry rips off his jacket and wipes at the sheen of sweat sliding down his forehead. "Guess we're in." He blinks moisture from his eyes and takes a gander around the alley they've landed in. A dumpster overflows, an A/C unit rattles, a door proclaims DELIVERIES ONLY BETWEEN 2 AND 5. "Weren't we looking at a backyard when we almost punched through here the first time?" He climbs to his feet, helping the others.

"The dome was prob'ly a crack in space 'n' time. What we saw was a frozen moment in time 'n' a random area in this enclosed space. Also explains why we didn't land on the other side of the dome, not literally at least, and the temperature change." Noir finds staring and narrowed eyes. "What, I ain't allowed to read and watch science documentaries?"

"We need to focus on finding the Johnsons." Adam wipes at his face and neck with his shirt, displaying the coating of sweat glued to his stomach.

"Can't just go blazing through the sky calling for them and hope they pop out waving their arms." Perry bends down to tie his shoe. "You weren't here when we were attacked by Officer Onyx. If they have guards on the outside, they definitely have them on the inside as well." He stands. "We need to figure out their defensive capabilities before we go charging in."

"And how do you suppose we do that...Detective West?" Adam folds his arms.

Perry shoots him a glare. "That doesn't sound like the tone of a man who's very repentant."

The dumpster suddenly scrapes across the alley, banging raucously into the far brick wall and spewing trash. Bisset lowers her arm. "I'm starting to regret ever stepping foot inside of that rickety van. I'm guessing that a place like this doesn't have armed guards waltzing around in plain sight." She walks to the mouth of the alley, poking her head out to take a quick look around. "They're out where everyone can see them, and they can see everyone." Her eyes rove. "Community like this probably doesn't have too many people who look like Noir and I either." She looks over her shoulder. "And Leo might even raise a few eyebrows if people look hard enough."

"Think we're on the same page, bonita." Noir smirks. "The two of us walk out there and someone is gonna catch wise. Someone who may know where our adorable little A-O family is."

"And how much trouble we can run into between here and there."

"Think you can stand holding my baby-soft hand for a while?"

Bisset puts a hand on her hip. "As long as you don't pop your claws, I won't pop mine." She shares his smirk.


Eleven minutes later, a woman's head smacks against the brick wall. Her mouth splits open as pain cracks her cranium. She reaches for her waistband, pats it, and looks down when she finds nothing there.

Perry crouches down in front of her, waggling her gun in his hand. "Misplace something?"

The woman opens her mouth, inhales, and screams bloody murder just as Leo slams a force field down around them. His words reverberate and bounce oddly in the confines. "Do that again and I put the field around your head, see how you like screaming in your own ear."

She throws herself at Leo. Noir steps in front of him and solidly punches her in the face. Blood flies back along with her head. Ripples and tremors play out on the other side of the force field. Adam slams his fists into the solid construction, mouth working, eyes furiously wide. Noir stalks toward him. "We ain't got time to be gentle! Now get the fuck off the barrier and watch the fuckin' alley!"

Adam glares at him, slides his eyes to the others. He slowly walks back to the entrance of the alley, movements tight with agitation.

Noir turns back to the woman cradling her jaw. "Where're the Johnsons?"

"Fhook you." Blood dribbles from the corner of her mouth. Her head rocks to the side when Noir smacks her.

"Same question, different answer." His fingers curl.

"Fhook you shidewaz."

Leo turns away just as Noir palms her face in his slender hand. The sickening crunch is painfully loud inside the field. Leo looks back, notices the blood spotting the brick just behind the woman's head.

"How many guards does this sheep pin have?"

Defiance.

Noir opens his mouth to bark another question. Bisset suddenly snatches the gun from Perry's hand, flicks off the safety, presses the silencer to the woman's shoulder and shoots.

The raw force of the woman's scream might have been enough to cover the sound of the shot without the suppressor.

"Where're you keeping the Johnsons?" Bisset's eyes glow golden-green.

The woman snarls...and takes another bullet in the ankle.

"Where?"

The woman's mouth cracks open, a quivering hand pressing her scarlet-soaked shirt to her shoulder. Bisset shoots her in the thigh and makes her scream out louder than before.

Everyone but the women clap their hands to their ears.

"Stop focusing on the pain and focus on the question. Where. Are. The Johnsons?"

"I-i-i-in the house with the b-bl-blue shingles on Sunny Avenue. Just a mile n-north of here. Security's light." She looks down at the blood soaking through her clothing, back at Bisset. "I'm gonna etch your face and voice in the depths of my memory. You better not leave without putting bullets in my head"

"I've told myself better threats." Bisset calmly hands the gun back to West. "Leo, do you mind lowering the force field?" Her words are steeped in tranquility.

Leo lowers the field.

Bisset walks away. Noir scuttles up next to her. "The hell was that?"

"At your rate, we would have been discovered by the time you had pulled a useful syllable out of her." Hot sunlight catches the gleam in her vacant eyes. "You went too easy on her."

"What're you talkin' about? I hit her."

Bisset stops; Noir stumbles to a halt. "That woman is a trained soldier, she's been hit before. Probably by men and some women a lot bigger than you."

Noir's mouth works, but nothing comes out.

"The others are fooled, but I'm not. I know who you really are, Noir. You're not the monster you want to be."

His lip curls. "Then who am I?"

She looks into his eyes. Hers melt from golden-green to brown. "You let me know when you find out."


The dried, shrunken husk explodes in a cloud of powder when it hits the floor, the skull snapping off and skittering to Damon's feet. He waves a hand through the dusty air. "Only five seconds to decompose this time. You're getting better."

Giorgio looks down at the crumpled cadaver. "What did he do?"

"Creased the spine of my copy of *Watchmen*." Damon eyes the hollow-eyed skull silently screaming up at him.

"I see."

Damon nudges the skull with his sneaker. "Have you ever read it? It's a graphic novel by Alan Moore. Very eye-opening, very ahead of its time, and quite insightful from a psychological point of view."

"And for that you had him killed?"

Damon bunts the skull at the wall, watches at it fractures into separate pieces. "It was a special edition copy." He raises a hand. "Let's not dwell."

Giorgio rests his hand on the foot-thick sheet of steel on the nearby table.

"From one of our old underground security doors."

"I've never attempted to break down something this thick before."

Damon tips his head on the other side of the table. "As I said, your abilities are growing stronger." He gestures at the steel. "Give it a go."

Giorgio taps the steel with his fingertip. He presses his palm against it and goes still. The alloy underneath his hand begins rust and flake, a spreading deterioration that seeps over the surface...and stops. Giorgio lifts a hand, flecks of rust sticking to his palm.

"Focus on the core of the steel. See it decaying, wasting away in your mind. Sink deep into and under the surface." Damon nods.

Giorgio replaces his hand and bows his head. Something ripples from his palm. Decay, desiccation, discoloring. They surge over the door, curling and furling flecks of steel, cracking the surface and erupting sores of rust throughout. He concentrates harder.

"Why haven't you asked me about the Johnsons, Giorgio?" Damon watches as the steel loses its luster and fades to brown-green. "Why haven't you asked anything about me or *Libera Mentis Machina*?"

Giorgio's face remains blank as his eyes roll up. "I genuinely couldn't care less about that family and what goes on behind these lace-curtained windows. And if I did, I could kill all of you with no problem and very little imagination." He lifts his hand. The steel has been reduced to peeling shades of sickly yellow, garish green, and putrid brown. He shakes flecks from his flesh.

Damon pulls a small remote from his pocket and presses a button. The TV on the right wall blips to life. The image is of an alley. The faces on the screen are familiar. "I'm assuming they came with you." Damon pushes his glasses up his nose. "Are they A-Os, too?"

"Most of them, yes." Giorgio looks away from the image and admires his work. "The true heroes have arrived."

Damon scratches at the corner of his lower lip. "We've already sent out a team to their location." He turns to Giorgio. "If they're the true heroes, then what kind of hero does that make you?"

Giorgio touches a finger to the table and a perfect circle of decay spreads from his touch. "The villainous kind."


Ten minutes have passed.

Sovereign hauls his first forward with all his might.

The green neon man floating in the air takes the full force of the blow, a platinum flare surging out from the strike, and whizzes back down to the earth in a viridian streak.

A woman on the ground points the first two fingers of her right hand at him.

Something twines itself into his intestines, tugs. Gravity reclaims him, wrenches him back to the ground. His thunderous impact is marked by a large indentation that ruins a perfectly manicured lawn. He looks over with dazed and confused eyes that watch as Noir disembowels a teenage boy with a cloud of smoke where his legs should be. The boy drops, smoke melting away to skinny legs, and does not move. Noir looks over at Sovereign, lifts his bloody claws, and waggles them.

Sovereign totters his head to the right just in time to receive a kick to the face.

Perry fires a bullet into a man that bursts into a furious flurry of snow and swirls into his face and eyes. The man reconstitutes in front of Perry and reaches out to touch the detective's brow. Perry grits his teeth as the blood flowing in his head slowly begins to freeze, torturous relief from the heat. He grabs the frigid man by the wrist and gives it a hard crank while squeezing off a shot.

An eddy of snow around the whistling bullet.

Cold sinks into his skin, muscles, and bones. The cloud coalesces and begins to reform...until it is captured inside of a spherical field of shimmering silver-blue.

Perry gives Leo a nod.

Bisset sprints past them, eyes wide as her arms and legs pump.

The tiger chasing her speeds up. The panther behind her releases a growl. The lion at her heels throws itself at her, thick sinews uncoiling as it pounces at her back.

"Have to admit, your cohorts are quite skilled...except for the man with the gun. I've seen him somewhere, but I can't quite place it." Damon scratches at the bridge of his nose.

"He was the lead detective investigating the disappearance and murder of your five-ring circus of a family." Giorgio leans on the console as he watches the bank of monitors giving aural and visual testimony to the heated fray. "He appeared on the news; you might have seen him there."

Damon's lips part in a silent *ah*. "Wonder how long they'll last."

"How much more do you have to throw at them?"

The smile on Damon's profile is illuminated by a flicker of platinum on the large screen in the middle. "Much. They haven't even reached Eric yet."

Noir streaks past the screen.

Damon looks at Giorgio. "Shouldn't you be snapping my neck and joining them? Your abilities could give them just the edge that they need."

"I'm brain damaged, remember?"

Pause.

"You wouldn't happen to have a nice merlot breathing around here, would you? I'd like to see if my taste buds are as dead as the rest of me."


A house explodes in a pillar of fire that rattles the ground. Shattered shingles pepper the air along with lengths of burning wood and warped metal. Sovereign darts out from the wreckage in a diagonal line soaring back up into the sky. "You could have killed someone!"

"All of these houses were built with underground bunkers; Damon sent out a community-wide alert as soon as your little Justice Quintet arrived." The flame-wreathed body extends its arms.

A massive *B O O M* as a plume of fire and smoke rends the air and sends Sovereign spiraling back. Platinum flames bend and twist with red, orange, and gold. Then it starts to rain human bodies.

Identical human bodies that reach and tear and seek to claw him from the sky. They grab hold of him, amassing themselves on each other and weighing him down.

Platinum flames sputter out from beneath the thrashing limbs.

Bisset ducks her head as Perry shoots an androgynous assailant in the chest as they raise tentacled hands.

"Let us help you."

She looks over and sees The Dragoness standing calm and composed amidst the incessant pandemonium. A comet cuts a screaming trail through the sky behind her.

"No."

Directly to her right, Perry cries out as a blade gnaws into his stomach. He punches a woman in the head, yanks the dagger from his gut, and holds his palm over the gushing wound. He starts to sink to his knees just as Bisset catches him beneath the arms. She puts her hands over his wound and concentrates.

Nothing happens.

"The angel is slumbering." The Dragoness hovers over them both, straightened locks fluttering in the smoke-choked breeze. She looks up at the sun. "It's daylight, and yet here I am. I'm starting to think that Noir was right, time and space are in disharmony here." She bends and touches Bisset on the shoulder, golden-green eyes going to Perry bleeding out in her arms. "We would heal your friends, but it wouldn't prevent them from being harmed in the first place." She brings her mouth close to her hostess's ear. "Let us help you, Bisset."

Perry's narrowed eyes narrow even more as he looks over Bisset's shoulder. "The hell...is that?"

Bisset stares down at Perry, at the redness staining both their hands and his shirt. Screams. Explosions. Smoke. Hollow eyes. Blood. Her tongue feels heavy and thick. A corner store collapses in on itself. Goosebumps on sweating skin. She gently lowers Perry's body.

Then she lets The Dragoness take control.

Her soul becomes effervescent and her body becomes rigid with unadulterated power. Flesh smolders with sensuous heat, her hair sizzles into straight strands of copper steel. She blinks and her eye color shifts along with her vision. Nails lengthen and harden into glimmering talons. The wind halts around her, chaos quiets, her eyes slip shut. Simmering heat waves rippling from the pavement slow their ascent.

Thornebriar goes silent.

The flame-wreathed body lowers itself in front of The Dragoness.

Her eyes remain shut. Her chest rises and falls as she samples the air. Not a muscle twitches.

The flaming form presses at her forehead with a burning finger.

Nothing.

The burning finger is held to her forehead.

Nothing.

The flame dancing at the end of the finger intensifies, brightens.

Not even a bead of sweat.

The smoky gaze in the burning face narrows.

Golden-green eyes snap open and the wind picks up slowly, languidly. Mahogany tresses wave gently, buoyed by a gale sculpted from syrup. The Dragoness opens her mouth, inhales, and screams emerald flame.

Fire burns fire.

A ragged male scream raises hairs on the arms of those watching. He staggers back as verdant flames scorch through already burning skin. The pitch of his scream competes with that of The Dragoness until the sounds collide in the air in harmonic dissonance.

The burning man erupts in an exhilarant squall of cinders and luminosity.

The Dragoness picks a bit of ash from her arm, turning her attention to the others. "There's enough suffering here for everyone."


Damon doesn't notice it as his mouth gapes open. "Who is that?"

Giorgio sips his merlot, rolling the liquid around on his tongue. "I honestly don't know, but she complements this wine quite well."

The Dragoness flings a body from her path and advances through the shower of bullets streaming from an automatic rifle. The man ejects the clip and slams another home without looking. His finger squeezes the trigger.

The Dragoness stops and revels in the sensation of being shot.

"More...*more!*" She opens her arms, throws her head back, and closes her eyes. A circle of non-powered humans surround her and spray her with murderous metal. Warped slugs *ping* and *ting* from her hardened skin down to the simmering pavement. The goddess begins to sing Emiliana Torrini's "Wednesday's Child," her rich tones pouring over the battlefield like hypnotic syrup. Without warning, the singing, statuesque woman lunges left, *slashes*, dashes right, *slashes*, streams forward, *slashes*.

The scent of blood blows through the humid air.

Five bodies fall, ruptured throats baptizing the street in liquid life.

The Dragoness gives her hands a flick, clearing them of blood, as she sensuously arches her back. Large leather wings burst from her shoulder blades and fan out on either side of her. A small *ahh* escapes her curving mouth as she pushes herself from the ground and takes to the skies.

Noir rips off another strip of his shirt and wraps it around Perry's stomach.

"Think I'm hallucinating." The words drip drunkenly from the detective's mouth.

"Naw, you ain't hallucinatin' nothin', amigo." Noir cinches the knot with care. "Everyone here just saw Bisset change into El Chupacabra." He helps Perry to his feet. "Then again, El Chupacabra was never reported as bein' so attractive...or smellin' like honey and cloves with just a hint o' cinnamon."

"Did you know she could do that?"

Noir squints his eyes. "Checked her out once when I got my new peepers. Strangest damn thing. Like I was lookin' at this...black...snake-like thing writhin' around inside o' her one minute, and nothin' but golden light the next." He watches The Dragoness smash through a launched boulder without pausing. "Knew somethin' wasn't normal about her."

The Dragoness backhands the fired missile careening at her. The projectile detonates in her face, emitting a massive ball of flame, concussion, and sound that quakes the heavens. Seconds later she flies through the smoke, unscathed except for scorched jeans and burn marks eaten through her top.

*BOOM!*

Another missile that slows her for half a second.

*BA-BOOM!*

The warhead discharges. Air is violently and noisily ripped away. The explosion echoes slowly, fading gradually as eyes watch the skies. The wind blows. Curtains are parted. The missile launcher is lowered. Debris falls from the dispersing cloud.

The Dragoness bolts out of the black-gray murk, skin unblemished, hair streaming beautifully behind her with a cloud-tail trailing in her wake. She lands with absolute grace in front of the woman holding the smoking missile launcher, rips it from her grasp with one hand, breaking several fingers in her fury, and swings it in an arch.

Bones crunch, fracture, and snap. The woman glides through the air, crashes into the ground, rolls, and does not move.

"The next person who fires a projectile of any kind at me shall be the first to experience the full force of my ire. I don't care if it's a bullet or a paper airplane." The launcher drops with a heavy clatter at The Dragoness's feet. "I've been lenient up until now."

She waits for a note of discontent.

And receives none.


Damon puts the phone to his ear and waits. He paces in front of the monitors, teeth grinding together. "Pick up the damn phone." It rings. "Pick. Up. The. Damn. Phone." It rings. "Pick up the fuc—Where the hell are you?" He listens.

Giorgio refills his glass and looks back to the battle, boosting himself up on the table.

"Send Eric out there, now." Pause. He throws up a hand. "I don't care if he has to drop the cavity around the town! If she finds the Johnsons, none of that will matter." He listens. "Fine. Make sure it's done." He stabs a finger down on the red icon and glares at the phone before flinging it at the wall. He puts his hands on his waist and scrolls his eyes over at Giorgio.

The handsome man sips. "I imagine you wish you had my lack of emotional faculties right now."

Damon seethes in silence.


Anita snatches Annabelle back from the window as the third missile goes off. She turns to Tina. "What in the world is going on out there?"

The young girl yanks her eyes from the burning cloud on the other side of the window. Nervousness raises a lump in her throat. "Si—Just sit down and shut up." Her eyes dart. Empty hands wring. "Your dumbass husband died because he thought he was in ch—" She jerks her head down and looks at her empty hands. Eyes flare wide. She lifts her head as Anita lifts the gun abandoned on the couch.

Trigger is pulled.

Bullet flies.

"*Uh!*" Tina tips back when the bullet buries itself in the side of her neck. She feels her body go limp before she collapses on her side. The world blurs. Her blood pumps from torn veins.

Anita grips the handle of the gun to keep her hand from trembling. She shoves down the sob competing with the bile rising in her throat.

Her children stare at the body. "Is she..." Miguel swallows. "Mom, is she dead?" His lips part and he folds his truncated arms around himself. "Mom, you killed—" He swallows again. "Mom, you killed Tina. You killed her."

Anita reaches for Annabelle's hand, starts to do the same with Miguel and grabs him by the elbow instead. "We have to leave before they send someone else. I don't know what's going on, but I'm hoping it's enough for us to escape."

Annabelle looks back at the shell that used to be Tina as her mother tugs her along. "Should we hide the body?"

"There's no time, baby." Anita yanks open the door and grinds to a halt when she notices the gangly boy on the porch. "Eric."

His expression is somber. "I'm sorry." He reaches behind him and pulls at the air.

The emerald dome around Thornebriar pulses into view before dropping. The temperature gradually begins to drop to something cooler as the sky flashes neon green while the air pressure rearranges itself in their ears. Day shifts to night. Eric steps off the porch, turns, and rips his hand upward.

The Cavity spills open in the air, suffusing the entire house in emerald brilliance before swallowing it whole.

Eric turns away from the dome and goes to face The Dragoness.

The bald man reaches behind him and a glossy javelin winks into his hand, the point gleaming in the streetlight. He waits until the light of the full moon illuminates The Dragoness before flinging the weapon with all his might, going into a little crow-hop as he whips his arm out and down.

The javelin splits through the air.

It nearly embeds itself in the flying woman's throat before she absently snatches it out of the air, twirls it in her delicate hand, and slings it back.

*Whhrrrrr*-squelch

The weapon goes clean through the bald man's stomach and bites into the pavement, pinning him in place.

An emerald globe enfolds The Dragoness. Gravity gives out and vertigo attempts to rob her of her senses. Emerald fades and she is suddenly flying directly into a Humvee. She slams into the vehicle, rocks it, and slides it back on two tires before her momentum completely overturns the behemoth. A crater dents one side of the Humvee and shattered glass and mangled metal litter the ground on the other side.

The Dragoness stands, the tips of her fangs peeking out from her curled lips. Her furious eyes slice through the shadows and she sees the young man standing in the garage. He glows emerald. She rushes toward him where he stands inside the garage.

Sparkling green incandescence blinds her and she's whisked ten feet back. She picks up the ruined Humvee with one hand, muscles scarcely flexing, and hurls it at him.

A green globe glitters. The Humvee vanishes.

"It was you, wasn't it?" The Dragoness flaps her wings once and hovers in the air. "It was you who made Thornebriar vanish." She vomits a stream of fire at him.

Eric glows, bursts apart in verdant motes and reshapes himself outside of the garage. "I didn't want to do it. Damon forced me to."

"You aren't beholden to anyone or anything but the limits you place on yourself." Smoke curls from her lips. "Tell me where the Johnsons are." Her voice is serene.

"Hidden."

"Mayfly, do not test me!" She lands, setting the ground to trembling. She bares her talons and shreds through the power he begins to wrap her in. He blinks and she has him by the throat. He lifts an arm and cries out when she grabs it, wrenches gently, and snaps it. "Answer me!"

He glares at her. Then he looks to the empty lot across the street and narrows his eyes. A house with blue shingles appears behind a lime haze. He looks back at her, concentrating on his breathing as she squeezes air from his windpipe.

She draws his ear close to her lush mouth. "I shall return the favor." She releases his throat, turns, and prowls for the house with quicksilver poise rolling through every step.

Eric hauls in a lungful of air just before a curved wingtip lashes out at his throat. His trachea fills with blood. Death comes swiftly.

The Dragoness walks toward the house, staring down the armed guards who raise their firearms at her. They bravely cower back, slowly lowering their weapons.

The Dragoness slinks up the warmly lit porch steps to the door, raises her hand...and knocks three times. She cleans the blood and gore from her fingers while she waits, flicking and licking her nails clean. A little smile graces her lips when a woman peels the door open.

"Anita Johnson?"

"Yes?"

"I'm here to rescue you and your family. If you would follow me, please."

Anita's brow flexes. "Who are you?"

The Dragoness blinks, pressing her lips together. "Ma'am, I just informed you that I'm here to rescue you and yours. What more do you need?"

"I need to know who you are."

The regal woman sighs and glances behind her. "I should have let them shoot the entire family." She turns back. "My name is The—Bis—" She shakes her head and her hand. "We don't have time for introductions now." She gestures behind her. "These handsome men will make sure you leave the area safely. You won't be harmed as long as you are with them. If you are, please let me know."

Leo, Perry, Noir, and Sovereign walk onto the freshly cut lawn.

"But I—"

The Dragoness spins and walks down the steps, gliding past the others. "Get them out alive."

"Where are you going, Bisset?" Sovereign reaches for her.

She stops. He stops. She turns her head halfway and looks at his hand. "My name is The Dragoness." She turns back. "I'm going to bring about a satisfying conclusion."

Her wings swell and she propels herself into the night sky. She cracks open her jaws and spews flame on Thornebriar, watching as people flee from their houses or burn inside them. She dives and smashes through Swift Mart before arching back up into the skies, trailing dust and bits of brick as she ascends.

She zips past the water tower in the center of the community and swipes a claw through steel. Water blasts out in an eager geyser of rainbow-infused mist and hydrostatic pressure.

Destruction rains along with water.

Damon leans against the console, watching as The Dragoness lays waste to the town. The Garden is on fire and the entrance to the lab is quickly filling with water. He drops his head and shakes it. After a long moment, he lifts his eyes and looks over at Giorgio watching it all with a blank expression.

"What are you going to do when she gets here?" He wipes his glasses on his shirt, hauling out frustration in a sigh.

"I honestly don't know, especially if my decision is at odds with hers."

"Do you even know how to give a straight answer?"

Giorgio twists his head at him. "What would you like for me to say? That I'll try my best to kill her as soon as she sets foot in this room? That I'll kill you as soon as she asks me to?"

Damon slips his glasses back on. "That would be an example of two straight answers, yes." He squints at the monitors, tapping keys and adjusting angles. "The hell did she go?"

The door chirps, whizzes open.

"I hope you have a good reason for not guarding the door, Bernard." Damon turns and feels his blood run cold and drain from his face when The Dragoness follows Bernard into the room.

She puts her hands on her hips. "Is it you who I have to thank for orchestrating all of this?"


The now-cool temperature begins to rise from the force of the flames. The sky is swathed in smoke and cinders. Citizens flee in the streets, cars sit idle and abandoned on the side of the pavement.

Leo blocks out most of the chaos on the other side of the force field he's wrought around them. He casts his eyes back at the remaining Johnsons. The thought of asking them if they can still free his happiness from its internal cage burns on his tongue like cinders. He takes in the shared mourning saddling their faces, shoulders, and plodding footsteps, decides against it. He'll bear it all a bit longer. Or so he hopes.

"Thank you for rescuing us." Anita wipes at her sweaty forehead. "I wasn't sure if that woman was going to kill us or help us."

"I know the feeling." Perry winces and clutches at his

abdomen when he stumbles over a bump in the road, reluctantly grateful when Anita catches him. "Where's Charles?"

The woman's eyes begin to tear. Seconds slip by. "They killed him."

Perry forces himself not to look away from her grief. "I'm sorry."

She rubs Miguel's shoulder. "We came to America from Ukraine. There, Alpha-Omegas are deified, revered for their unique abilities. *Libera Mentis Machina* contacted us and wanted us to try to bring change to America by posing as a normal American family that incidentally share a unique ability." She sighs. "We were resistant. It seems as if there is nothing but terrible news streaming out from the U.S., poisonous tentacles that reach out to the rest of the world poisoning almost everything they touch." Head shake. "Such horrors. Eventually, I was able to convince Charles that maybe we were given this ability to bring not only happiness, but positive change as well. I thought perhaps we were meant to help open the eyes of America, show you the way."

"Sometimes prayers and ideas just aren't enough."

She nods. "Progress cannot be forced. My family has...*had* the ability to make people happy, but all we seem to bring is more sadness." She blinks back something in her eyes. "Could you give us a moment, please?"

Perry nods and begins to slow his gait when Anita turns. "What is your name?"

"Perry West."

"Thank you, Perry West. Thank you." She turns with her children and continues on.

Adam sidles up next to the detective. The streets have gone silent, flames licking and flickering their way towards heaven.

Adam clears his throat.

Perry brushes a bit of ash from his arm.

Adam eyes skip left and back.

Perry looks back at Noir who squints up at the flames, eyes gleaming with a gray sheen.

"You did a good job today." Adam lifts his hand to Perry's shoulder. Drops it. With hesitation.

"Yeah, helped us out a helluva lot when I went and got myself stabbed." He touches the makeshift bandage. "Hate this."

"What?"

"Feeling weak. Helpless."

Adam shakes his head. "You're anything but weak, Detective West. You brought all of us together. None of this would have happened without you."

Perry remains silent.

"Alpha-Omegas may have special abilities, but that doesn't make them any different from you. Not in every way, at least. We all make mistakes, question ourselves and our actions. Just because I'm invulnerable doesn't make me untouchable."

More silence.

Perry opens his mouth after a while. "So are we gonna have problems in the future? Think you can handle working with a cocksucker if the need arises?"

Adam cringes. "I go where the Lord leads me."

Scoff. "I've known pathological liars who were less evasive."


"I should kill you where you cower." The Dragoness looks Damon up and down.

"Just a second ago you were thanking me."

"Only because you gave us the opportunity to show my hostess who and what we are."

Damon's eyes narrow behind his glasses. "I don't—"

The Dragoness slices her gaze to Giorgio. "Have you joined this little operation?"

Giorgio slides fingers through his curls. "The only side of the line I'm on is my own."

"You are magnificent."

They both turn to Damon.

He holds up his hands. "I hate to interrupt, but you are." He takes a step closer to her. "The way you brushed off the impact of a Hades missile at point blank range was—" His expression grows giddy. "I'd love to examine you." His head bobs. "If I could."

"Do more than look with your eyes and you'll know just how

magnificent I can be." Her eyes simmer. "Explain your actions. What's the reason for this fiasco?"

Damon shrinks at her response, slides back on his heels. "*Libera Mentis Machina* has helped just as much as it's harmed. Maybe even more so. We've caused Dominion City and possibly more of the world much grief, but we've also helped make progress. I doubt there was a single mind that wasn't changed in some way when people saw the Johnsons on Lamar Koehler." He adjusts his glasses. "We're forcing people to think, to form opinions of their own rather than let politicians and the media tell them who they should fear and who they should praise."

The Dragoness cocks her head at him. "Suffering is its own reward. Failure can be a better teacher than success."

Damon holds up a hand. "And I'm not arguing that point at all...and not because you could kill me as easily as you could bat your lovely eyelashes."

"Continue." She eases herself into a chair, back ramrod straight, and folds her hands over a crossed knee. Her wings gently stroke the air.

Damon looks from her to Giorgio. He swallows before he speaks. "Not only is the human life an experience, it's also an experiment. The whole 'learn from history or repeat it' ordeal. Perform an experiment and learn from the results. This organization was formed to experiment on the experiment, bring in more variables for more results. More often than not, people like to stay in their comfort zones, do what's familiar instead of testing out a radical idea." He holds his hands up, fingers spread. "We've been conditioned to view failure as something that's wholly about us and our ability, or lack of ability; it's quite narcissistic, really." He shows teeth. "How can we learn if we don't fail?"

"And for that reason you staged the death of a family?" The Dragoness taps at her cheek with a finger, elbow resting on the arm of the chair.

He cuts a hand through the air. "The death was irrelevant. People die every day, always have and always will, that's constant. But what isn't constant is a person's reaction and perspective to death. That's what this experiment was all about: how would

Dominion City as a whole feel about the murder of the first publicly known American A-O family?" He begins to pace. "I mean, think about what a family is, what it represents. A family isn't just a mother, father, and kids. A family is a symbol of hope, achievement...one of the greatest examples of love in the world." He grows more excited. "Some people cast away their blood family to find and form another of their very own, others come to rely on their families almost just as much as they rely on their phones. The roots of our family tree tell us who we are, who we were." His eyes widen like a net to catch the torrent of ideas. "There was a chance the Johnsons could have started a legacy, a progeny of Alpha-Omegas in every generation. Jumble in the fact that this family was *violently* murdered and you can just sit back and take notes, make observations."

"You were forcing people to feel, to react?" Giorgio stares at Damon.

Damon vibrates his hands in the negative. "No no no, we were compelling people to *think*. Why do we feel or act a certain way? Because we've been programmed to since a very young age. We hear that a person has died and instantly we say we're sorry. A person is murdered and we feel horrified. Some people bring about their own death just as some people have nothing but their own choices and actions to blame for their murder. Not all of us are good, no matter what we're taught to believe."

Giorgio looks over at The Dragoness. "He isn't wrong."

The force of nature looks from Giorgio to Damon. "His philosophy isn't entirely different from mine." She floats up from her seat. "But that doesn't excuse his actions. This experiment has leaped from your hands, from your leash, and has started spreading uncontrollably in the streets." She points at the monitors. "And I don't mean metaphorically." She drops her arm. "You hold too much power." A head shake. "But your fate is not in my hands."

Damon watches her as she glides closer. "Does that mean you're going to let me live."

"I would infect you with a ticking virus that would make you feel as if you were tripping on top-shelf acid whilst excreting your bowels and blood and vomiting all over your adorable little cardigan if you dared form something as elaborate as what you had at Thornebriar here, but I'm afraid that I might accidentally make you sneeze yourself to death instead."

Giorgio exhales a little sigh.

"And I'd let you attempt it anyway, but I can feel my hostess's simmering displeasure. We'll have to let non-powered human law sort the matter out." The Dragoness sweeps to the side, starts to lift a hand behind her, lowers it. She tosses a glance at Giorgio before speaking. "Are there any telepaths in your organization that you've sent to mentally spy on us?"

The edges of Damon's lips tug down. "Not that I know of. Unless there are and they wiped that knowledge from my mind." He attempts to grin, but it's more of a quivering grimace.

The Dragoness smothers rising cinders of displeasure, jerks her head behind her.

Damon leads the way out.

Giorgio steps closer to him. "You never did introduce me to any of the other leaders of your group. Where are they?"

"They were working on an experiment to see if they could induce a small town with collective paranoia with a series of not-so-paranormal events orchestrated by a few A-Os. I offered my professional input, but they felt I was overstepping my bounds." He pauses to take a breath. "Rather than dismissing me like they originally wanted, they instead sent me here." He waves a hand around them. "Where they felt my talents and ambitions would be of better use." A wry smile splits across his lips. "And I'm just now realizing where I got the idea for the Johnson family.

"I still have access to our considerable resources, I'm simply unable to communicate with the others." He rolls his attention back to the two A-Os behind him. "But I like to refer to them as if they still contact me. Brings me a measure of delusional comfort."

Giorgio looks back at The Dragoness. "Are we sure we don't want to kill him?"


At first, they look like flames flashing in the night.

But fire does not burn white.

Fire does not yell questions into a microphone before shoving it in your face.

Fire does not whine and click and whir.

Reporters. Police. Cameras. Paramedics. Questions. Firefighters. Lights. Vans. The press of the press. The assault of the authorities. The morass of the media.

Adam and the others stop as the refugees from Thornebriar trickle around them. Questions are thrown. Soot-stained faces are illuminated into harsh relief by the bright camera lights.

"Musta seen the flash o' light when that dome thing dropped." Noir looks over his shoulder as Giorgio, Damon, and Bisset join them.

Gazes swivel on Bisset and rest there. She looks...demure.

"The Dragoness is gone." She looks away, eyes harried. "For now."

"Are you okay?" Leo puts his hand on her back.

Quick nod. Swallow. Closed eyes.

"What was it like?"

Noir receives a shared glower for his question.

Bisset's lips and mind flounder for the words.

"Is she—"

"Leave it alone, Noir." Adam's voice brings the question to a halt as he walks past, snatching up Damon by the upper arm and hauling him along.

"What, dude? I was just askin' if she was—"

Adam whirls and rushes the other man. "Did you lose your hearing when you disemboweled that teenaged boy? I said—"

"Is that—It is! it's Adam Kensie!" One of the reporters abandons her interview with the mailman and hurries toward them, microphone jutted out in front of her. "Mr. Kensie, may I ask you a few questions?"

Mr. Kensie's ire slip-slides into a charming smile. Gripped fingers relax a touch on Damon's arm. "I'm afraid that—"

"Are you responsible for finding and rescuing the Johnsons?"

The microphone wavers in his face. The camera stares unblinkingly. More reporters trickle in along with waves of silence. Adam speaks.

"I didn't do it by myself." He turns and claps Perry on the shoulder. "Detective West here is the one who put this rescue into motion." He extends a hand at the others. "And we most definitely wouldn't have been able to apprehend the man responsible without these three men and this woman."

Damon pushes his glasses up his nose.

"Where were the Johnsons being held?"

"How do you feel about people like you being used in experiments to advance medicine, technology, and science?"

"Are these other people with you Alpha-Omegas?"

"If those are the Johnsons, then who were the people found murdered in their home?"

"Are any of you associated with the other vigilante A-Os who have started to show up throughout Dominion City?"

"Any explanation on how Miguel lost his hands? He won't tell us."

"What's the name of your team?"

The last question rings and resounds. The reporters turn their heads as one, extending their microphones, phones, and tape recorders as one.

Adam presses his lips together, looks back at the others. Leo gives a barely perceptible shake of his head. Noir smirks and quirks his eyebrows. Giorgio throws a look at a flashing camera that can almost, but not quite, be misconstrued as a pose. Bisset puts the entirety of her focus on the colossal task of breathing.

Adam takes a deep breath, forms his words, and breathes them into existence.

"We are The Furies."

The very world inhales.

**FADE OUT**

# EPISODE TWELVE: *FURIES*

**THE** very world exhales.

Dominion City sits sedated and docile. The vehicular flux on Lynord Street plays host to rubberneckers and gawkers pointing out the scrubbed spots of residual violence on the street left over by the riot a month prior. Here by Patty's Kitchen is where one woman was bashed in the face with a baseball bat for announcing herself an ally for Alpha-Omegas. There, a man was killed when he stood too quickly and took a thrown piece of pipe to the temple. And right around there was where another man was attacked by a gang of Alpha-Omega supporters.

The sun floats high in the sky and observes all as it reflects itself from the glossy glass making up the crop of buildings in the Greenback Garden. It watches the homeless rattling dirty cups and frayed hats for spare change in Mercurmont. It watches the privileged and prestigious of Cade District as they mold themselves after the pages of high fashion magazines with their small dogs in diamond collars. It sees the college kids in Oswyn awkwardly lose their virginity, whittle away at their prepackaged identities, attend class at Dominion University, and find themselves over and over and over again. It takes a peek at Phosphorus Park, replete with writers, poets, bohemians, and aspiring free spirits.

History has put down roots within this small city, dug deep into the nucleus, and begun to grow and stretch and blossom.

The sun turns its attention to Century Heights where Detective Perry West resides.

"*Gahdammit!*"

Walter presses his hands to his thighs. "Are you always this much of a...me?" He blinks up at Perry on the bed.

The other man mashes his lips together as he sits on the couch, face pale. "How many times have you been stabbed in the stomach?"

He goes back to redressing Perry's wound, wrapping the

bandage around the other man's lean torso. He lowers his voice. "What was it like in there?"

Perry lowers his arm. "A lot like home actually. Corner store. Quaint little houses. Burning buildings. Then it felt like I had closed my eyes and drifted off to sleep." He shakes his head. "Burning people flying in the sky. A man who exploded into snow and almost froze my blood." Eyes distant. "A woman with wings knocking a missile out of the air like it didn't mean jack shit."

"I'm just glad you made it out." Walter examines his work.

Perry's lips lift and he leans back on the couch. Carefully. "With The Furies to thank for it."

"Not how Sovereign tells it. They're the ones with the superpowers and they're actually thanking you."

"This non-powered human can still make waves in the universe. Damndest thing is it was Adam who taught me that I'm still in control of my world."

"You two didn't make hot, sweaty, sanctified love, did you?"

The laughter makes Perry's wound hurt.

"Hell no. That thick Bible stick shoved up his ass doesn't leave room for too much else sliding up there. We were able to reach a kind of agreement. If either of us needs the other, we're there and that's that. He doesn't bring up the fact that I'm attracted to men, and I don't mention the fact that he belongs in an institution."

"Very diplomatic." A bar of sunlight rests on Walter's face. He lifts his eyes to Perry's face, the subtle fire smoldering behind his eyes. "Looks like I triggered something there." He smirks.

The heat is doused. "What?"

Walter waggles a finger in a loose circle at the other man's face. "You and your R&B love-making eyes."

Perry holds a hand to his stomach, eases out a breath. "I won't deny it." Knees sway open and closed. "You make my dick twitch."

Walter's laugh is bright and wild. "Damn that's romantic." He swats at a swinging knee as he looks at Perry for a moment. "You know, I've honestly thought about ripping your clothes off and trying out every position with you, see if us gettin' sweaty and out of breath together is anything like the fantasies I sometimes have."

Perry's eyes widen along with his smile. "Oh, really?"

"Really." Slumped shoulders. "But I know that if I do give into that temptation it'll be that much harder to move on. Like I need to." His hand rest on Perry's knee.

Perry lifts himself from the couch, stifling a wince as a twinge of pain scrapes electric through his abdomen. He cups the back of Walter's head, molds their lips together. The kiss is a balm for the both of them, spreading through them in all the right places with warm, quicksilver ease that holds time hostage, suspends them together in a contained and self-sustained eternity, and strips them naked without the need for them to remove their clothes.

Walter eases his arms around Perry, hands sliding across the bandages as he relaxes into the rhythm of their gently working lips. Perry is the one to break the kiss, withdrawing just enough to meet Walter's gaze. "Despite all the shit that's happened lately, I still feel like I'm ready for this, or at least something damn close to it."

Walter smooths fingertips down the other man's face.

"But I know I can't be selfish, that something like this can't and shouldn't be a one-sided thing."

"I'll keep in touch with you. I hope we'll see each other in the future, but I don't want to make any promises right here and right now."

"I know. But you've got a job now, and a room in a nice house with a music producer and computer programmer."

"Cyber security engineer."

Perry lifts his hands in surrender. "I sit corrected. Anyway, I know you're gonna be okay."

Walter stands. "And I know you're gonna break down in a heap of bandages and tears as soon as I leave."

"I will if you don't leave my damn house key. Know how I like my privacy."


They chase him into the Lowe's parking lot, watching as he slips in and out of the cones of dingy yellow light. He looks over his shoulder and sees that they are now only ten feet back. His arms and legs pump harder, faster.

The world fractures and explodes when he turns the corner and is punched in the face. Reality comes back in shards that drag themselves across his skull, digging in with particular fondness around his left eye. He looks up and sees the world breaker standing over him, cracking his knuckles with a baseball cap tilted at an angle over his fresh haircut. He crouches down, reaches into his pocket, and throws a black handkerchief on the bruised man's chest.

"Got a lil' sumthin' right there." He taps at the corner of his mouth.

The other man wipes at his mouth, looks at his clean hand. "There's noth—"

*WHAM!*

His head snaps back at the punch and he feels blood dribbling from his mouth.

Mr. Manners taps at the corner of his mouth again. "Got a lil' sumthin' right there."

The man with the throbbing face wipes at the blood and turns as the people chasing after him barrel around the corner. They surround him. One of them brings the man with the tilted cap a wooden crate to sit on, brushing it off before setting it down.

The man looks at the crate with disdain. "Da fuck is this?"

The large man who brought him the crate instantly strips the shirt from his back and drapes it over the crate. "My bad, V."

V sits with his knees wide, one elbow propped on his thigh with a finger brushing his lips. He regards the bleeding man. He leans close. "Not gonna sit here and open with sumthin' poignant or clever, I'm just goin' straight for the heart." He makes a jabbing motion. "You royally fucked up one of my dens. Left alla my soldiers dead, and swiped some Gs from me, too." He rubs his palms together. "Insult to injury."

The bleeding man looks up at him with a swollen eye. " 'M sorry, dude."

V's brows knit together. He turns to a companion. "Did this muthafuc—" He turns back to the man. "Did yo ass just—" Back to his companion. "Am I hearin' this lil' punk-ass bitch right?"

"He apologized." The companion rolls his tongue over his bottom teeth.

V presses his hands together again and massages his forehead with his fingertips. "People never sorry when they need to be, only when they got to be." He looks up. "If yo ass was smart, you woulda taken da money an' split. Instead, you had to not only get yo pretty cinnamon mug captured on the hidden cameras I had installed in the house, you also had to have yo ass hangin' out on the news."

Noir darts his tongue out at the dried blood on his bottom lip.

V scoffs, mixing it with the beginnings of laughter. "Exactly how stupid are you, lil' Sanchez? Got me an' mine runnin' 'round the damn Lowe's parking lot in the middle o' the damn night. Missin' *Mr. Robot* 'cause o' yo ass." He looks at Noir. "Whatchu runnin' for in the first place? You know we was gonna catch you."

Noir looks down, balls the black handkerchief in his hands. He looks up. The handkerchief now has four holes in it from his claws. "Didn't want anyone to see me kill you."

He blurs.

The handkerchief flutters down.

The air is smeared. Someone cries out, falls down dead.

A flash of something in the cone of light that rushes the shirtless man. Claw marks on one guy's back. Jagged red lines across another person's stomach and eyes. The shirtless man begins to choke on his own blood when he finds he suddenly has a second mouth. He falls to the ground and watches as everyone else does the same. So much blood.

V aims his gun right, swings it left, spins around behind him.

He is surrounded by nothing.

"Wayne was like my brother, an' you put a bullet in his head!" His throat is ripped raw from screaming. "Blew his gahdamn brains out all on his bandana! I gave him that bandana!" He slaps his chest. "That was my fam! My brotha!"

Slick hands on his chin and on the back of his head. "I can see the resemblance, you're both wiggers." The hands jerk violently.

*CRUNCH!*

V falls, gun clattering in a pool of blood next to his limp body.

Noir looks down at the corpse and watches the last sheen of life go dim in the man's brown eyes. "Doin' *myself* a favor." He takes a step away, stops, and glances back.

He is surrounded by nothing.

His eyes simmer golden and the world is sketched in strokes of heat and whorls of warmth. Nothing shaped like a human. He starts to walk away and nearly bumps into the woman in front of him. She grabs him by the back of the head and kisses him. Her lips are like cubes of lusciously-molded ice and frost. She thrusts her tongue into his mouth and begins to leach heat from his body. She wraps her arms around him as she pulls him close and robs him of warmth.

Her eyes swell when Noir buries his talons in the side of her ribs. He jerks her away and punches her in the face, wiping frost from his lips. He scowls down at her, rubbing at his arms and trying his best to hide his shivering.

She holds up a hand as she scuttles backward. "Please don't hurt me. I'm only here to protect my family."

Another family. Another Alpha-Omega.

It gives him pause. His eyes cloud over to neon blue and sweep over her body. Nothing but ice water in her veins. Nerve endings in blue clusters. Pure white cells ice-skating throughout her body. No evidence of a baby, but no evidence to refute the existence of one, either.

He studies her face. His eyes flare red. Her heart thuds in her chest, thump-thumping from fear. Or from lying.

"Shit."

He clomps away. Pause. He clomps back and kicks her solidly in the ribs with his boot. "'S for givin' me chapped lips."


"Is this about what happened to the TV while I was gone?"

Maggie shakes her head and hesitates before sharing her truth. "I'm worried that you don't have much room for me in your new life anymore, Adam."

Her husband allows the words to resonate in his ears, in his head, soaking them in. He sinks into himself a bit, shoulders going slack. "I hate that I didn't even think about that until just now."

She reaches over to grasp his hand. "Saving people and being a parole officer have a way of eating up a lot of time and energy." She tries to reflect the humor of her words in her lips and eyes, but only partially succeeds.

Adam brings her hand to his lips, kisses the back of it. "I didn't mean to take you and your presence in my life for granted, Maggie, it's just that there's been so much that's happened so fast. I'm just trying to make sense of it all."

"We both are. I just didn't want to be the type of spouse who festers and stews in discontent, that's not healthy."

"You don't expect your spouse to stay exactly the same during the entire course of your marriage, but I most certainly didn't count on this level of change when I first envisioned the rest of my life with you, and I'm sure you didn't either."

Head shake.

"What can I do to strengthen our bond? Besides spend more time with you?"

Again she hesitates before sharing her truth. "I th—" Her truth is so heavy that it lodges itself in her throat. She swallows and tries to speak it again. "I think that it might be best that we separate for a while."

Her truth becomes a bomb that blows the bottom out of Adam's stomach, explosion pounding in his ears and obliterating the part of his brain that controls movement. It takes several breaths before he starts to pull fragments of his shattered self back together. "What?"

"I still love you, Adam, and I still want to be your wife, but..." A rapid-fire series of blinks. "The only way I can explain what I'm feeling without leaving room for misinterpretation is to say that it—it feels almost like you're having an...an affair." She raises a hand to stop his tide of protest. "Not in the way you're probably thinking. You're giving a lot of your time, your energy, and your attention to other people. More than me. I know it sounds like I'm just jealous, and in some ways I know that I am, but it's something I've felt for a while and didn't want to accept about you."

Her husband squeezes her hand, pulls it close to his chest. "Maggie, I repent. From the bottom of my heart and the depths of my spirit. I'm just trying to fulfill my divine purpose."

Maggie looks at her hand in his. "You don't have to repent, Adam; I know you have nothing but the best intentions. I just...I...I've been feeling a bit like a prop to you, like an accessory. And that doesn't sit well with me."

He moves closer to her, tightens his grip on her hand in an attempt to keep her from floating right out of his life. "Is this-- Maggie, is this about us trying to have a child? I'll go to another doctor. We can—"

Tongue darts out to wet dry lips. "We can take more tests. I'll think about adopting."

Maggie's eyes slide shut for a moment and she rubs her hand over his. "Guess I need to just show you." She focuses her eyes on the magazine on the coffee table in front of them. The object blurs, visually detaching from their reality, before a scrape of a white star flashes over its surface and drags the magazine into its gravitational center with a compact puff of air and a burst of brilliance that vanishes almost as soon as it erupts.

Adam seizes, lips parting. "Maggie, your blessing has manifested!" Elation lays claim to his face, limbs, and hands and refuses to let go. "This is wonderful!"

"No, it's not, Adam."

His joy drains. "What do—"

"What if I actually was pregnant and that—" Fingers jab at the space where the magazine used to be. "—happened to our child? What if I...what if I banished it?"

"Maggie, you—" But Adam cannot bring himself to continue, cannot bring himself to face the very-real possibility that she might be right. "When did you discover this?" He concentrates on looking her in the eyes, not allowing his gaze or mind to wander down the corridors of probability that have replaced the hallway behind her.

"While you were in Thornebriar. I was in the bedroom listening to the TV while I was brushing my hair. That political commentator Shane Chao came on spouting something about illegal immigration. I stepped out to turn it off, and as soon as I did, the TV vanished."

Her husband looks at the spot on the entertainment system where the TV used to be. "Now I understand why you didn't want to tell me when I first asked."

She nods. "It happened again with a pen and a pair of my old shoes. It takes a lot of concentration, and it seems that I can control it, but I don't want to risk any accidents."

"If you feel this is why we need to separate—"

"This just adds to it. There's an organization call FAODAS that helps the blessed control their gifts. Their nearest field office is in Denver. I figure I can spend some time there understanding how my abilities work and you can stay here and focus on finding the balance between being the Sovereign of God, a husband, a parole officer, and all the other magnificent things you are."

Adam doesn't yet seem to notice the tears sliding down his face. "Now I know how you felt when you first learned of my divine gift." He sniffs. "I wish—"

She kisses him. "This is all happening according to God's perfect will. We can't see it now, but I know that we'll look back on this very moment together in the future and see that it shouldn't have gone any other way."

"I don't want you to go." The words are whispered and restrained. The emotion behind them blares boistruous. He rests his head on her shoulder.

"We both have things about ourselves that we need to work out separately."

He lifts his head, looks her in the eye. "This is a marriage that we're in together. Can't we come up with a solution together? Maybe we can ask Bishop Martin if he can help."

She smooths a hand down his face. "I don't think Bishop Martin or anyone else at the church has the training or experience necessary to deal with something like this."

Adam drops to his knees, clasps his wife's hand to his chest again. "I'll stop being Sovereign for a while, as long as it takes. I'll put the entirety of my focus on you, on us. The other Furies can protect the city by themselves. Bisset alone can probably do the job herself once she gets The Dragoness under control, which I know she can do."

Maggie rolls her lips over and under her teeth. "I've seen what happens when one of the blessed's abilities rage out of control. With the way mine seem to work, I don't want to risk hurting someone, I don't want to risk hurting you, because I didn't take complete responsibility for the power God has given me and learn to use it the way it was intended...whatever that way is."

"I always loved you for your stubbornness, but now..." Adam looks down at the carpet. "Now I can't help but wish that I had fallen for a weaker-willed woman."


Leo is showered in celebration and adoration.

Champagne bubbles to the brim of plastic flutes, music thumps from boom box speakers, and confetti litters the floor.

Leo smiles as he brings his flute to his lips. Hands clap his shoulders, praises fill his ears, and smiles assault his eyes.

"Thank you, Leo. I feel a lot better knowing there are people like you out there to keep us all safe.

"Are you really going to keep working here after what happened in Thornebriar? Seems like being a superhero would be a full-time job."

He responds. "It's the same as one of us saving someone from a burning building."

"Now, Leo, when you say one of us, do you mean Alpha-Omegas or humans? I think the only other person here who may have a special ability is Albert. No regular human can look that well put together after coming to work hungover nearly every day."

A chorus of laughter.

Leo joins in.

Two hours later he says his goodbyes, accepts handshakes and gratitude, and heads for the door, lifting a hand to Addie as he passes her office.

"See you tomorrow, Leo. And remember, saving the city is no excuse for being late." She smiles.

He sighs and heads for the door. "Take it easy, Simon." He waves at the janitor.

"Right back atcha, tiger."

As soon as the door shuts behind him, Leo presses his back against the brick wall, slumps down on the ground, and smashes the heels of his hand to his forehead. The mask shatters. "Dammit, Adam."

Minutes later he has regained a semblance of his composure. He walks to the bus stop with his earbuds in place, the sounds of Electric's "Levitation" thumping into his cranium. He glances over his shoulder and sees that he is being followed by four men and a woman.

Leo stops and turns. "Can I help you, folks?" He removes one of his earbuds.

The bearded man in front slides his hands in the pockets of his jeans, hooking his thumbs on the outside. Leo notices the white cross inside a red circle with a drop of blood in the center permanently etched on the man's forearm. "You're one of those guys who helped saved the Johnsons." His tongue flicks out over thin lips.

Leo removes his other earbud. "Yeah."

The man holds out a hand with a cross inked on the back. "I wanna shake the hand of the man who saved members of the perfect race."

Leo examines the extended fingers, the tattoos, the genuine smile on the man's face.

A shorter man behind him with a shaved head and goatee juts his sharp nose closer to Leo's face. "Hold up a second here, Edward." He strokes at the air just over Leo's skin, takes a careful look at his hair. "You know, without the glare of the cameras, our man here looks a little..." He pulls his head back. "A little mulatto." He rubs at his scalp, cracking his knuckles. "Don't think this boy's a pureblood."

Edward grits his teeth and lifts his chin. "Was hoping my instincts were wrong this time." He shifts his stance, heavy-soled boots scraping across pavement. "Damn shame, the Knights could use someone like you."

Leo has found someone who may hate him more than he used to hate himself. Used to...used to...use—

"Niggers should stay in their place, and their place isn't on television." A fist clenched tight with racial tension careens for his face.

Leo falls to the concrete. Scuffed boots and dingy shoes fly toward his face, body, back, legs, head, neck. He folds himself into himself. *Live.* His skin burns silver-blue...and he stops manifesting the force field before it is formed. *Die.* He lets them beat him, lets them hate him, lets them spit on him, lets them purify him.

He feels the familiar bile of self-hatred swelling in his clenched throat, sour and acidic. He welcomes the bitter taste, the raw pain, the physical agony. He swallows all of it whole and prays he chokes on it.

The world crystallizes.

Mouths racked with wrath. "Stupid black motherfucker!"

The foot that knocks the air from his lung strikes slowly, surely.

Phlegm cuts through the air before hitting him on the cheek, mixing with blood. "Can't hide rancid black blood under pure white skin."

He reaches for the agony, the names, the blood. His eyes refuse to blink, to swivel, to acknowledge.

Something is ringing.

He regains control of his eyes and looks over at his flashing phone on the concrete. FRANCIE. The ringtone, Roberta Flack's "The First Time Ever I Saw Your Face," overshadows all sound.

He rolls his eyeballs in swollen sockets and sees Francie when one of his assailants shifts to the right for a better angle at his head. Her smile obliterates the past and her reaching hand rewrites the future. Disgust, hatred, betrayal, anger, and sorrow are flash-burned out of him.

The world reels away just as his hand starts to go numb.

He somehow manages to channel the tic into the the force field that explodes from every inch of his battered flesh. His attackers thrash at the air as they are violently thrown back. One is slammed into the empty street.

Leo shoves up from the concrete and runs. All the way home. Without stopping. He chases Francie's image down avenues, up streets, and across crosswalks.

Floating Francie collides into solid Francie as he throws open the door to their apartment. He wraps her up in her arms, mindless of the blood on his face, and kisses her, ignoring the burning sting from the cut on his swollen lip. He goes down to his knees and has only one question:

"Will you marry me?"

Bisset kneels down and peers into the pool of stagnant water. The wind whips over the rooftop and sets the water to a rippling refrain.

Seraph steps into the reflection and looks over Bisset's shoulder. She turns her head to see if she can see what Bisset does not see. "She's gone, Bisset."

Bisset's eyes click to her other self. "She's only sleeping. You know because I know, right?"

Seraph lifts her head to the sun.

"Say it."

Seraph keeps her eyes on the horizon.

"Say it, Seraph."

Seraph looks down at her pleading self, says nothing.

"Say it so I don't have to."

Seraph is suddenly on the other side of the pool kneeling across from a piece of herself. "If I say it, you will be saying it, Bisset. You know what The Dragoness did was an atrocity, and yet you...*we* enjoyed every moment of it."

Bisset rests an elbow on her knee, rubs at her mouth with her first two fingers. "It's not right that I...that I enjoyed killing the woman who fired that missile at me."

"But that doesn't mean it isn't okay for you to feel that way. You did it to save the lives of others."

Bisset lifts her eyes from the water, sees nothing, drops her eyes, and sees Seraph. "So if I had been on Damon's side it would have been okay?"

The angel sighs and her breath shifts the brown water to a glistening golden liquid that soon clouds back over to murk.

"Is it possible that I was emotionally manipulated by the person who's been attempting to tamper with our mind...minds?"

Seraph cuts a hand through the air. "No. Either I or The Dragoness would have sensed it, cast them out."

"Do you or The Dragoness have any idea of who this person is? Why they're watching us?"

"I don't know, but I wish I did."

"Are you sure we didn't just construct all this in our collective subconscious or something? Maybe—maybe I've got a fourth entity stuffed in the corners of my head that none of us knows about. Maybe I freed it when I allowed The Dragoness to completely take over my body the first time." Bisset blinks...and blanks out.

Seraph looks up from the water and sees The Dragoness.

Golden-green eyes catch a sunbeam. "Did you pull me from my slumber?"

Warm brown eyes with flecks of ivory regard her. "Yes. We're between two beats of our hostess' heart, slipped between the next bat of her eye and her next heavy inhale."

She slinks forward and slides her hand over Bisset's head, petting her almost. "Why?"

"Because you have exercised too much influence over her. I'm...We're losing her."

"I'm helping her realize who she is, and she's fighting it. It isn't my fault she doesn't want to heal as much as she hurts, that she wants to administer suffering more than joy."

Seraph gestures at a frozen Bisset. "Don't you see what this is putting her through?"

"Don't you dare float there and put all the blame on me. She needs balance. You should take more time explaining to her why she should heal and less time telling her why she should reject me. Neither of you have yet to fully grasp that we are the three-in-one. No one is right, and no one is wrong. We simply are."

"Your way would fracture her mind; helping during the day and killing at night."

The Dragoness cocks her head to the side and narrows her eyes. "Do you realize what we—no, what *I* did? I saved the Johnsons. The others might have helped get in the way, but it was me who found out where they were, me who got us through the guards, me who saved them, and it was me who razed Thornebriar to the ground."

"And you who wanted to let the man responsible for it all escape. You may have done the heavy lifting, but at the emotional and psychological and possibly the spiritual expense of Bisset. We need her, and we need for her to be stable."

"Detective West arrested Damon in the end. I would've

prevented that, but Bisset wouldn't allow it. We have you to thank for that, but we both got our way." She paused. "So it's all about control for you now?" A smirk slips languidly across her visage.

"No. Bisset isn't ready for the blood that's already on her hands. You've set us ten paces back."

"A child cannot stay a child forever, no matter how badly the parents wish that it could be so. Bisset's already accepted her power, she just hasn't adjusted to the price it demands. But I'll make sure she's ready."

"Ready for what?"

"For herself." She slides her fingers through Bisset's curls, turns, and vanishes mid-spin.

Bisset opens her eyes...

...and finds herself alone on the rooftop with unanswered questions heavy on a mind she hopes is still her own.


Family.

Dishes are passed. Laughter is shared. Stories are told. Life goes on.

All without Giorgio.

He watches his mother, father, and sister as they sit around the table with glasses of wine, full plates, and flushed faces. Every minute or so one of them will glance at the chair where he used to sit. A frown hovers at the edge of their lips before flitting away into a smile.

His mother reaches over and pats her husband on the wrist. He looks over at her with strands of silver shining in his hair and smiles. Giorgio has his father's eyes. His father leans over to kiss his wife lightly on the lips, running his hand through brown curls that remind him of the dead son who is watching them unawares through the dining room window. His father turns to his daughter and his lips move. Giorgio's older sister shakes her head and reaches for her glass of wine, pausing for a sip before she answers.

Giorgio touches a cold hand to the glass and refocuses his eyes and sees his reflection. He steps back. "Why am I always talking to you? You never answer."

The man in the glass stares back.

"What does all of this mean?" His eyes shift and the Quinteros come back into focus. "Being human, being an A-O, being dead or alive, having one power or another. It's just something that's already in you and made manifest by an errant gene. Either that, or it's randomly dispensed by whatever force grinds the wheels of life together."

Eyes shift to himself. His palm presses against the glass and exudes no heat

"I chose this life, it didn't choose me, correct? Tell me it's not all just a book that's already written, only I can't read the words."

He focuses on his family.

"They don't seem to even really miss me." His fingers curl, nails rubbing at the glass. "I wonder if killing all of them would make me feel something." He looks at his hand, searching for the viruses saturating his useless veins and arteries. He wonders which will kill the fastest, which will kill the slowest, which is the most painful, which—

His mother has her hand pressed to his on the other side of the glass. Her mouth gapes, trying to find words that will not twine themselves around her tongue. She wrenches open the door and raises her trembling hand to Giorgio's smooth, very-much-alive face. Her son reaches for her cheek, fingers still and filled with poison. He can feel the heat from her face. She can feel the tingling of unleashed death at his fingertips. He drops his hand and kisses her on the cheek.

Gone.

Her son is gone.

Irina Quintero collapses down to her knees. She doesn't feel her husband shaking her shoulders, she does not hear her daughter's panicked voice. All she sees are chartreuse eyes with nothing inside them.


"I love you, dad."

Miguel Johnson puts the flowers in his prosthetic hand on the grave, kissing the fingers of his other realistic limb and pressing them to his father's marble tombstone. He steps back and Annabelle steps forward, smiling around her tears.

"Hey, dad. Hope you're having a blast up there. Send grandma and grandpa our love." She wipes at her eyes, sniffs. "Sorry you never got to see the Statue of Liberty like you wanted." A choked laugh. "But I guess you can see it from where you are now, huh?"

Anita wraps her arms around her children. "Hi there, handsome. When are you going to stop haunting us? Every time the light's left on in the bathroom I still think it's you. I know that—that you didn't want it to end like this." Deep breath. "Or maybe you did, Charles. You always did fancy yourself as one of those warriors your grandmother told you stories about. Fighting insurmountable odds, dying in glory." She nods her head. "I wish I'd been able to kiss you one last time, look into your eyes and tell you that I love you." She kneels down and kisses his grave. "But you know, Charles, don't you? You always knew what I was going to say before I said it." Another kiss. "But I still want to say it. I love you Charles Johnson, rest well." She rises to her feet. "Come on you two, time we headed back and started supper."

"Whose turn is it to cook?" Miguel nestles his face in his mother's arm.

"Mine." Annabelle holds her mother's hand.

"Guess we should stop by the store for Pepto-Bismol."

Anita's laughter echoes across the graveyard.


Adam stares out the window of the abandoned car dealership, surveying Dominion City submerged beneath a film of light. He presses his hand against the glass. "Then what should I have done?" He turns around.

"You coulda told us you were plannin' on makin' us into a legion of superheroes." Noir taps ash from his cigarette.

"This city needs us."

"No, this city needs you, needs Sovereign. No one else here asked you to unleash The Furies on the world." Leo sits with his back against the wall, knees up. His brow is in a sudden knit. "Where did that name come from, anyway?"

The other man shrugs. "I don't know, it just came to me." He looks out the window and up at the Stratus Building stabbing up from the center of downtown.

"God whisper that in your ear, too?"

"Don't mock him, Noir." Bisset shakes her head at him.

"Do you expect us to be a beacon of hope to these people, Adam?" Giorgio's eyes glow from where he stands in the murk. The shadows sloth off him as he glides forward, wingtips crunching through bits of debris.

"Yes, Giorgio. I don't mean to make you all feel like—like props, like accessories." He extends a hand to the window. "But they're scared and confused. Is there something wrong with offering them a bit of comfort, security?"

"There is when most of the providers of that comfort and security don't give a damn about the lives of those they're supposed to be comforting and securing." Giorgio stands a few feet away. "Dear Damon did nearly the same thing, only he had sense enough to know that what he was doing was an aberration."

Adam glares, eyes flickering platinum. "The two of us aren't anywhere near comparison."

"You're both men, you're both delusional, you both fancy yourselves as leaders. Need I go on?"

"Not gonna stand here and listen to this. Got a loaded bowl waitin' for me back home." Noir starts for the shattered exit.

No one stops him.

"You're not going after him?" Leo presses fingertips to his black eye, wincing.

"I'm not going to force him to do something he doesn't want to."

"And what about us? Are you going to stuff some rousing rah-rah speech into our ears?" Giorgio starts to lean his shoulder against the wall, notices the thick film of dust. He wrinkles his nose and straightens his stance.

"If you'll listen."

No one moves.

"I'm not going to waste your time, and I'm not going to insult you. I could tell you it's your responsibility to protect people, but it's not. I could tell you you should think about your friends and family

**347**

getting hurt because of an A-O incident, but the truth is that you can't protect everyone from everything."

He turns to Leo.

"What I can tell you, Leo, is that even though you're the last person I should ask to do this, you're the first person I want at my side. I see great compassion inside of you stifled under all of your sadness and depression. You're going through enough as it is in your life right now, but you're stronger than you realize. And I think you know it, too."

Bisset.

"Bisset, I've already asked too much of you, more than anyone has a right to. The Dragoness and Seraph tell you you're not insane, that you're simply realizing who you are. The Dragoness has already shown us how powerful she is, how powerful *you* are. I can see Seraph's light inside of you, but I can also see The Dragoness's savage nature in your eyes. I think with more time you can learn to control both of these entities instead of having them control you. It will be you whispering in their ears. You have the strength, take it back."

The undead man.

"I can already tell you and I are going to butt heads if you decide to stay. But I'm going to need you to keep me honest, to second-guess me, even argue with me. I don't know what happened with you and Damon back in Thornebriar, and I'm not going to ask. But I am going to ask that you give me a chance to show you what I'm trying to accomplish here. It's not like your time on this earth is limited." He grins a bit.

Giorgio remains deadpan.

"We shouldn't be afraid of who we are, of who we're becoming." Adam tightens his hand into a fist. "We should grab hold of our power, our blessing, and use it. We shall fear *no* evil." His fist pulses platinum. "Let no man put asunder what the Most High has wrought." He suddenly jumps up and down with a little whoop, his eyes and hands lifting to Heaven. "Yes, Lord I hear you, I hear you. I feel your spirit right here, right now, and I welcome it."

Adam opens his arms and his unbridled joy brightens his face.

"So what's the verdict?"

Later finds Adam and Bisset at the abandoned church.

"So when do The Furies have their first photo shoot?" She turns to laugh as she flicks on the light switch.

"Very funny. I'm just glad you're all on board."

"Except for Noir." She steps over a tipped over pew. "Not that we need him anyway."

"We'll need all the help that we can get."

She scoffs. "Maybe if we offer to pay him he'll join. Are we here for another session?" Bisset looks over her shoulder at him. "Adam. Adam?"

He shakes himself back to the present. "What? Oh, sorry. There's something I want to show you. It's just behind the door there."

Her curls swirl around her head as she glances at the closed door behind the pulpit. She looks back at him with suspicion wreathing her features.

"Go on."

He follows her down the aisle.

She opens the door.

He flicks on the light.

The cell gleams in the emptiness of the room.

"What is—Adam, what is this?"

"It's a containment cell for The Dragoness. In case she ever gets loose again."

Bisset chews on the inside of her cheek. "I don't know if she can be contained."

"It's made of solid titanium. I asked Detective West if it was alright." He studies the cell. "I blessed it myself."

Her eyes become hooded. "The Dragoness isn't a demon, she can't be held back with a prayer and a cross."

"I didn't bless it for her."

"I—" She snaps her mouth shut over her next sentence. She parts her lips and tries again. "Thank you, Adam. Really."

He smiles and nods, a hint of a blush coloring his cheeks. "You're welcome. I'll let you, uh, inspect it. I'll be waiting outside." He leaves her, closing the door behind him.

349

Bisset looks back at the cell and sees The Dragoness inside leaning against the bars. "Did you miss me?" She smirks and runs her fingers over the bars.

"Where have you been?"

She pushes away from the titanium rods, silk emerald pants swishing as she slinks around the perimeter of the cell. "Thought you would appreciate a few nights in your own headspace."

"I spent the entire time wondering when you were going to rip your way out of my body."

Her other half stops, swivels on golden heels, and glares at her hostess. "You make it sound as if you didn't give me permission to take control of our body, to save the Johnsons and burn down that damned community."

"I did, but—"

"No, Bisset, don't mince words. I helped you."

"You—"

"I. Helped. You."

"No, what you did was—"

"I! HELPED! YOU!"

Her words are punctuated by furious drafts of verdant flames, golden-green eyes burning bright.

Bisset stumbles back. She brings her hands to her mouth as the taste of ashes and stale heat dabs at the back of her tongue. She drops her hand, narrows her eyes, and advances quickly on the cell.

The Dragoness watches her and smiles. "You can't touch me, I'm—" Her head snaps back as Bisset's fist flashes through the bars and hammers her in the nose.

The Dragoness blinks, hands hovering just over her face as red liquid drips from her nostrils. She sniffs, runs a hand across her bloody upper lip, looks at the fluid...and licks it. "How did we do that?"

She watches as a familiar smirk graces Bisset's mouth. "You know because I know."

*Somewhere, Roger Miller sings "Little Green Apples"*

Noir lets go of the homeless man's stolen rags and watches as his unconscious body slumps down the brick wall spattered with blood, piss, semen, spit, and a multitude of other fluids.

He lifts the blood-filled syringe to the flickering light cast by the flames in the battered barrel. He rolls up a sleeve, ties off a strip of cloth at his elbow, and slaps at his veins until one pops fat and full. He inserts the needle into the stream of blood, thumb pressed against the plunger.

He looks at the unconscious man.

The woman with frost on her lips flashes on the video screen of his mind.

"Shit."

He takes the needle from his vein and flings it into the flames before walking out the gaping mouth of the alley.


Bisset wakes to sunlight, warmth, and Leo standing on the other side of the blessed bars with a plastic bag in one hand and a Styrofoam cup of coffee in the other. "Breakfast."

"Thank you." She reaches for the coffee and the small sack of cream and sugar.

He examines the cell with the eye that hasn't swollen shut as she opens and pours and stirs. "Wonderful accommodations you have here."

"Makes the Hilton look like a roach-infested dump just off the interstate."

He sits down on a pew. "I was sitting in bed last night thinking about all that's happened since I first looked under that microscope and saw my A-O gene. I thought about how far I've come and how far I've got to go." He glances up at her. "And I realized something about the two of us.

"We both have something inside us we wish wasn't there, that we desperately, so damned desperately, want to change." He lifts a shoulder and scratches at his head, looking up at the shattered stained glass window. "But we can't change who we are, Bisset. All we can do is hope we learn how to make the pieces fit."

She finishes her sip, lowers her cup. "I've come a long way

from sitting in a therapist's chair telling her about the angel and the demon in my head."

"How do you feel about yourself now?"

She looks at the steam unfurling from her coffee. "I've done a lot of learning, about who and what I am. About what I'm not." Her eyebrow quirks upward. "About what I might be." She looks at him. "Just like I'm both angel and demon, I'm both excited and afraid about what's to come." She shrugs. "Balance."

She blinks a few times and notices it in the glory of the morning light. The lambent glow rooted deep in Leo underneath the bruises and cuts has cleansed him of most of the rancid misery and anguish her angel eyes once watched consume and twist his core, his essence. She's never seen anyone smile so wide or shine so brightly. "Leo, you are absolutely radiating. Surely this wasn't brought on by Thornebriar."

He shakes his head, smile widening. "Francie and I are getting married."

Thunder grumbles outside.

Bisset's head jerks back a bit. "Who's Francie?"

"My girlfriend. Well, my fiancée now." He passes the bag of food between the bars of his cage. "Here, before it cools." She accepts the bag with a small tremble in her hand. "I didn't think it was possible for me to love another person as much as I love her." His eyes go distant. "My God, that woman has saved my life. Adam should have asked her to be on the team instead of me." He turns his attention to Bisset. "Well, I just wanted to bring you something to eat. Let me know if I can get you anything else, change of clothes, jacket maybe. Nights are starting to get colder."

A nod. "I will." Laughter still sparkles around her mouth. "Leo?"

He stops and turns, a smile touching the side of his bruised face.

She points at her own face. "I can try to heal that for you, if you'd like."

He seems to remember his battered and bruised features. His smile flops as he raises fingertips to his forehead. "Maybe later. They remind me of something I don't want to forget about just yet." He reaches into his pocket and pulls out a key, holding it up to the light. "Adam wanted me to give this to you. Just make sure you give it back to him before sunset." He tosses the key to her.

The woman in the titanium cell catches it and watches him wave goodbye.

She looks in the bag.

Blueberry pancakes.

Her favorite.


Giorgio stands in the rain, ignoring his drenched clothes. His curls are matted to his forehead and his shirt and jeans stick fast to him. He looks over at the people dressed in black standing under umbrellas. He watches as the coffin speckled in rainwater is lowered into the muddy grave.

Tears intertwine with rain.

Prayers are carried away by the winds.

Faces are buried in shoulders, handkerchiefs, or locked behind rigid masks.

Giorgio looks around the graveyard at all the tombstones. He looks at his home, his birthplace.

He looks down at the grave before him.

It has his name on it.

But he is not in it.

He presses a hand to his tombstone.

Then he walks away into the rain.

Vanishing like a ghost.

Or a distant memory.


Perry is giving Walter a final embrace when there's a knock at the door. The two part and Perry opens the door on a tall woman with kinky black locks flowing free and full around her head like an unbridled galaxy. "Amala." Perry grins. "C'mon in."

"Hey, guys." Amala steps inside the apartment, looks to Walter. "All set?"

"Yeah. Lemme just do a final check before I leave." He hurries down the hall.

"Thanks for takin' 'im. I know you usually reserve using your powers for the older residents."

"Absolutely no problem; you guys are family."

Perry crosses his arms over his chest. "You ever think about working with us? An A-O who can teleport would go a long way in helping us get to crimes-in-progress faster."

She leans a forearm against the doorway. "This coming from someone now working with a guy who can fly." Head tilt. "And I'm sure you wouldn't mind being carried, or anything else, in those beefy, loving arms."

"Yeah, but he doesn't have as much swagger and style as you."


Adam slides into the parking spot under the awning, cuts the engine. "I was going to suggest that I fly you to the airport, but now I'm glad we got caught in traffic." He looks over at Maggie. "Gave us a bit more time together."

She looks out the windshield at the parking deck across from them. "The idea of you flying me to the airport before I fly off in a plane." A soft laugh. "Sounds like a comedy sketch." She turns her blue gaze to him, mirth softening around the corners of her eyes. "So...we agree not to contact each other for a few weeks?"

Adam nods. "As difficult as it might be." Grip tightens on the steering wheel. "But it's probably for the best. We both need some time to get properly adjusted."

Maggie unbuckles her seatbelt, leans over and wraps her arms around his shoulders. "I love you, Adam Kensie. Take care of yourself, and may the Lord watch over you."

"I love you, too, Maggie." He presses his free hand to her back. Then he watches her step out of the car, grab her suitcase and shoulder bag from the backseat, and walk into the Dominion City International Airport. She turns and gives a final wave and smile.

Gone.

Adam's phone vibrates just as his eyes start to burn. Detective West.

"Good evening, detective."

"We got a robbery in progress at a Wholesome Foods in Cade District. One of the perps is a highfalutin A-O who can only eat organic and gluten-free, I guess. Wouldn't be surprised if they're wearin' yoga pants or sportin' a horribly unkempt beard and big-ass glasses without lenses. Can we expect you out on the dancefloor?"

"A choir of angels seems to be playing my song."

"Keep tryin', you've almost got a decent sense of humor."


_____ retreats back to the mental shadows to wait patiently for the next chapter in the story. And to ponder their part in it.

*Dominion City breathes, lives, and pulses around them.*


# E N D

## Acknowledgments

"Furies" (originally titled "Fury Us") was birthed in 2008, back when I was still living in Alabama. Over the years, I met several characters in Dominion City, and in the real world, all of whom helped bring me to where I am today. While you'll eventually meet the many citizens of Dominion City, I'd like to take this opportunity to thank and introduce you to the very real, very kind people who helped me realize my dream of sharing The Furies with the rest of the world.

First, I'd like to thank my parents, Grace and Gregory Gunn, and my Aunt Ann for nurturing my love for the written word. Growing up, I remember sitting in my aunt's lap reading to her at my Grandma Ruby's house, and how my parents took me and my sister to the library every other week. I have a feeling you wouldn't be reading this book if it hadn't been for them.

Jason Heller, I met you at Denver's first comic book convention back in 2012. I was nervous to approach you after your writing panel, but knew it was something I had to do if I wanted to further my writing abilities and career. You have my eternal gratitude for taking a look at the first few pages of this novel and giving me your feedback.

R. Alan Brooks, my writing brotha from anotha mutha, you've been a wellspring of inspiration, encouragement, insight and friendship. Many thanks for helping to guide me on my journey in the short time we've known each other. Maybe I'll have the pleasure of writing a script for *The Burning Metronome* (which everyone should check out...after they finish this book, of course).

Nate Ragolia, a galaxy of thanks for taking a chance on me and the wild imaginings bouncing around in my head! I'm proud to call Spaceboy Books the home of The Furies, and I'm excited to see what the publishing future has in store for both of us.

Finally, I'd like to thank everyone who's encouraged me over the years in my ongoing writing quest. As a perfectionist, there's never a final draft for me, only one that's (please, sweet Jesus) a bit better than the last. Your excitement and requests to read my stories give me the motivation I need to finish my stories and push them out into the world.

No matter what life brings, I know I've been blessed.

*Forever onward and upward*

## About the Author

A world weaver and word wrangler, **O'Brian Gunn** was born and raised in Alabama and now lives in Denver where he writes about geek culture for *Westword*, Pop Culture Classroom and NerdTeam30. His writing sirens often lull him to the expansive shores of the speculative, the supernatural, and the superhuman. While he's had short stories published on Fiction on the Web and The Society of Misfit Stories, *FURIES: Thus Spoke* is his first published novel...and hopefully not his last. You can find him on Twitter at @OBrianGunn.

## About the Publishing Team

**Nate Ragolia** was labeled as "weird" early in elementary school, and it stuck. He's a lifelong lover of science fiction, and a nerd/geek. In 2015 his first book, *There You Feel Free,* was published by 1888's Black Hill Press. He's also the author of *The Retroactivist*, published by Spaceboy Books. He founded and edits BONED, an online literary magazine, has created webcomics, and writes whenever he's not playing video games or petting dogs.

**Scorpio Steele** is an illustrator, graphic designer, and comic-book artist. Among his works he has co-created the educational science-comic series *The Adventures of Mr. Tompkins*, based on the character originated by physicist George Gamow in 1937. To see more of his work please visit scorpiosteele.com

**Shaunn Grulkowski** has been compared to Warren Ellis and Phillip K. Dick and was once described as what a baby conceived by Kurt Vonnegut and Margaret Atwood would turn out to be. He's at least the fifth best Slavic-Latino-American sci-fi writer in the Baltimore metro area. He's the author of *Retcontinuum,* and the editor of *A Stalled Ox* and *The Goldfish,* all for 1888/Black Hill Press.

www.ingramcontent.com/pod-product-compliance
Lightning Source LLC
Chambersburg PA
CBHW051115120726
47905CB00005B/1287